SECOND NATURE

LANDRY BRENNAN

ISBN 979-8-9901538-2-0

To Jon, Jack, and our blanket fort.

PLAYLIST

Playlist

Cowboys Are Frequently Secretly Fond Of Each Other - Orville Peck & Willie Nelson

Till You Get There - Ty Herndon

Where Dirt and Water Collide - The White Buffalo

Come To My Window - Melissa Etheridge

You Should Probably Leave - Chris Stapleton

Because of You - Kelly Clarkson

Ain't No Sunshine - Shawn James

Friends Don't - Maddie & Tae

Billie Jean - The Civil Wars

Love the Lonely Out of You - Brothers Osborne

When I'm Gone - Joey + Rory

Save It For Later - Eddie Vedder

Delicate - Damien Rice

A Bar Song (Tipsy) - Shaboozey

Contents

CHAPTER ONE

DARREN

This gorgeous stranger—Brandon? Braydon? Brendan?—has said plenty all night, but now he can't do much more than hum around my dick while he takes me deep in his mouth. Both of us are fully aware that I'm close. I've told him as much, and even if I hadn't bothered, he doesn't strike me as the kind of guy who couldn't have figured it out on his own.

One of my hands rests against his perfectly styled, jet-black hair, careful not to muss it during the last minute or so we'll be together. I keep my other hand curled around the top of a nearby keg, the grip familiar to me when I've used it dozens of times for this same reason, and I'm struck by the fleeting thought that I should take the next guy somewhere else just for the thrill of a new view.

Mine, not theirs. The keg room at Trailhead is always new to them.

But there are only so many places I can go in the middle of my shift, and the walls of all of them were stained with Beau's handprints years ago, so maybe it doesn't matter. The keg room is good. Convenient. Fine for the purposes it serves.

Supplying draft beer to the bar and getting me off.

"Fuck," I moan. "That's—"

I'm not sure what I was about to say, but once I start to come, I don't care about words anymore. My fingers fall from my acquaintance's head before he's fully swallowed, but he's smiling up at me as I tuck myself back into my briefs and zip my jeans, no shirt to worry about while I'm at work. There's muffled laughter from the bar, the music turned low for now, and I need to get back out there before the next break, when everyone will want another round between rounds.

Brendan—I'm almost positive it's Brendan—cleans his own mess with a towel I've dropped into his hand, and when he stands, he keeps a step between us. Kissing isn't an indulgence meant for whatever we've been up to, and maybe he thinks there will be time for one later.

"How much longer 'til you get out of here?" he asks.

I shrug. "Another couple of hours, probably."

"So, I guess there's no reason for me to stick around," he says. It could sound pathetic, like he's just waiting for me to pull him closer and tell him he's wrong, but his smile hasn't gone anywhere, and he'll leave as gracefully as anyone ever has. "Well, I might stick around for one more cosmo, but that's just because I'm still thirsty."

He licks his lips, and I laugh, and there's nothing more to talk about when I lock the keg room behind us. I return to the bar just as this week's trivia night host—one of a dozen nameless college kids all too happy to keep queer cowboys entertained in exchange for a few free drinks—clears his throat to ask the final question in this set of ten.

"What's the name of the scale used to measure the spiciness of foods?"

I watch as Jake writes his answer on the scoresheet neatly folded next to his nearly empty pint glass, the last sip or two of Guinness bound to be gone in another minute. Noah and Riley are already looking at me, and as soon as Jake's pen lands on the bar, I grin and accept the challenge.

"It's the Scoville scale."

Jake finishes his beer, conveniently hiding his smile, and Riley swipes the empty glass before I can. The quietest of my coworkers is gone after that, off to make a cosmo and anything else the Trailhead trivia night crowd might need. There's a third shirtless bartender working the tables throughout the room—an adorably awkward 20something named Zach who looks kinda cute in his rainbow bandana and tight jeans—but I barely know him. It's not a position we've been able to keep filled for more than a few months at a time, so other than making sure he's not a walking disaster, I focus on my own shit.

I pour another Guinness without asking first, and as soon as I've delivered it, I pop the caps on five beers for a group waving to me from where the mechanical bull sits silently. Someone comes around to collect the trivia scoresheets, and I wipe my hands on a towel just as Noah bumps Jake's shoulder.

"How'd you guys know that?"

"I eat a lot of spicy food," I tell him.

"And I cook a lot of spicy food," Jake adds.

I file that sliver of Jake lore away with the hundreds of others I've collected since he started hanging out at Trailhead—made even easier since we kicked off these trivia nights in the spring—and then I do the quick math on just how long it's been since Jake first walked through our big barn doors.

Eight years, give or take?

Christ, I think only Beau's been around longer, but I was married to him long enough for his presence at the bar to be the one vow we didn't break. I guess Noah has been around about the same amount of time—mostly since he turned 21 and could spend more than an excusable few minutes at the place his mother owns—and for a straight kid, he's probably here more nights than makes sense. But other than Beau and Noah, Jake Callahan is my most regular regular.

I grab good tequila for a couple of women who've been showing up on trivia nights and pour it while I glance at Jake again. "How'd you do that round?"

Noah snorts. "Go ahead, tell him your brilliant ass knew most of them, and I got, like, three."

"Can I also tell him his brilliant ass would've done just as well if he hadn't taken most of the round to change a keg?" Jake asks, air quotes accompanying his last few words.

"Hey, now. I *did* change the keg. Quickly, even," I add. "But then, as long as I was already in there—"

"And not alone," Jake interrupts.

"As long as I was in there *and* not alone, I figured I might as well get to know one of our very happy customers. Or let him get to know me."

Riley slips behind me to grab a bottle of rum, their voice mischievous over my shoulder. "You think you'll know him any better by breakfast?"

"Yeah, now that Beau and Adrian have moved in together, are you inspired to find someone you can play house with?"

Riley's already gone again, and Noah's question is mostly meant to give me shit, but I don't miss the quick hitch of Jake's eyebrow at the mention of Adrian's name. We're all thrilled that Beau's as happy as he is—Jake very much included—but Beau and Adrian had a bumpy start after a tragic end to Adrian's previous relationship, and Jake hasn't quite forgiven Adrian for a mess that probably deserves mutual blame. I've mostly stayed out of it, and I wouldn't be in a position to judge anyway. The times I was a dick to my ex-husband are known to more than the few people I've kept within reach.

Maybe Jake has always been a goddamn saint, but I might need another eight years with him before I can be sure. And right now, everyone is still waiting for some kind of answer from me.

My past transgressions aside, I'm a bartender. I serve drinks and smile at strangers. I fuck around with plenty of them while I flirt with the rest. I'm careful not to promise them more, and it's rare for anyone to expect to see me in the morning, breakfast low on the list of their fantasies. Playing house, even briefly, is unlikely to cross their minds when I can't fathom more than an orgasm or two, so I shrug now. I love that Beau and Adrian have each other, but I also love my life just the way it is.

"Thanks, but I'll stick to shorter games with fewer consequences. I was never all that great at living with someone the first time around," I tell them, clearing my throat before I nudge the conversation back to the subject of our friendly quiz. "And kicking ass at bar trivia isn't about being brilliant. It's about having collected enough random information about enough random shit. I do well because when I'm not here learning from people who talk too much, I'm at home falling down one Wikipedia rabbit hole or another. And Jake does well because he's old as fuck."

"And somehow he still has half the bar eager to find out what his Harley would feel like between their legs," Noah points out.

"I didn't say he wasn't sexy as fuck, too."

And it's true—all of it. Jake is nearly two decades older than I am, but nobody looks at his leather jacket and biker boots and then turns away because he's in his mid-50s. He's the absolute nicest guy who doesn't give a fuck, and his confidence completes the undeniable attractiveness kicked off by laugh lines and a short gray beard. I know he was married once upon a time and has a daughter named Lucy, but I figure he's intent on keeping his love life separate from the nights he's here because he's brought no one to Trailhead.

Nor has he taken anyone from Trailhead home.

I glance at Noah then, his baby face difficult to describe after being lost in Jake's good looks for any amount of time. There's no denying he's sexy in his own way, but he's V's son, and a friend of damn near everyone at the bar, and the guy I've stupidly made out with twice because I don't always leave well enough alone. He's brought a girlfriend here a time or two, but I'm almost positive he's single these days. I'd send him home with Brendan and his cosmo if I thought it would be good for either of them.

A quick look over my shoulder helps me find Riley, but I won't attempt to describe their beauty tonight. More eloquent men have tried and failed at that endeavor, and Riley would stab me with a cocktail pick before I could get far with it. I nearly smile at the thought, but work to keep it to myself, slowly turning my head until I'm back to where I started.

Focused on Jake again, I catch him watching me closely, curious about something I won't have time to explain when tonight's host stops by with the next round's scoresheet. Noah is ready to drink more than he helps, and I hand him a cold bottle just as the host's voice cuts through the soft twang of a song I hear too often. It's no surprise to any of us that Jake isn't announced as one of the current top scores when he never turns in his answers, the wink aimed at me confirming that he's doing this for fun, and not to take a win away from anyone else.

Without having a reason for my certainty, I'd bet all my tips that he doesn't need a credit toward his bar tab.

"Okay, are y'all ready for the first question of this round?" the host asks. He's met with cheers from the rowdy crowd, and when Jake picks up his pen, Noah takes a long drink. I just wait. "The island of Corfu belongs to which European country?"

Noah pulls the beer away from his mouth, his eyes wide when he thinks he has the answer. "Oh, Italy?"

Jake and I take half a breath and dash his hopes in unison. "Greece."

"Of course," Noah says, shaking his head with a smile. "Pretty sure we didn't spend much time studying Corfu in school, so how'd you both know that? Which one of you has been there, and which one is going home to pack a bag tonight?"

"I was there about 15 years ago," I tell him.

"And I've always wanted to go," Jake adds.

The second question of the round cuts us off before we can talk about it more than that, and I move away to clear a couple of empty glasses and close out someone's tab. And for the next several minutes, I answer trivia questions over my shoulder or from a few feet away or while crouching behind the bar to restock everything we've used throughout the night. Jake gets more right than I do, but that's fine—I'm both fiercely competitive and not, and losing to him isn't the worst thing that can happen.

I'm already looking forward to the next time I can beat him and give him shit about it.

The final round features five pictures—anything from landmarks to celebrities to breeds of dogs—for players to identify within two minutes, and I'm still too busy behind the bar to see exactly what's happening on Jake's side of it. Noah shouts about something, the laugh around it giving me a reason to smile, and a quick glance makes me think he must have answered something Jake couldn't.

I'm looking forward to giving Jake shit about that, too.

As trivia night winds down, the final scores tallied and prizes awarded, Riley kicks the side of my shoe in time for me to catch Brendan's wave goodbye. I know it's his subtle offer to stay for one more orgasm if I've changed my mind, but it only takes me a moment to carry that fantasy to its filthy end and back again. Then I let him go, returning my attention to Riley as I grin.

"You know *you* could follow him home," I say. "He was fun, and you deserve that at least as much as I do."

I'm treated to an eye roll and love it, Riley's guard dropped even as I poke at something personal. They know they can walk away and it'll never bother me, but they stay now and it matters.

"Ethan's home this week."

"And that's a good thing?"

"I don't know." Riley reaches for a towel, the extra couple of seconds promising more honesty if I wait them out—and even my impatient ass can manage that. "It's getting harder to tell where I really want him to be."

I nod and move half a step back. "Well, when you're ready to figure it out, you've got a lot of us who will jot down the pros and cons for you."

"Pro: He was the first person to call me Riley. Con: He hasn't said my name in so fucking long, I'm not sure I remember what it sounds like coming from his mouth."

My heartbeat trips over its own rhythm, but grabbing a cardboard coaster only takes a second, and there are enough random pens scattered around that it's easy for me to find one while I catch my breath. I always forget that Riley knew Ethan long before they became a couple, but I'm not interested in their history right now. I flip the coaster over just as Riley begins to protest, my hand up to quiet them as gently as I can.

"You don't want to do this tonight. I know," I sigh, clicking the pen and already scribbling. "And I'll raid V's office for an entire goddamn whiteboard when it's time for the rest, but there's something that can't wait."

Riley. There's someone out there who will understand what a fucking privilege it is to say your name, and he won't stop long enough for you to forget how beautiful it is.

I hand them the coaster, note side down, and meet an icy blue gaze that's anything but cold. "You can finish up here and take off whenever you want, but you know I'm not gonna throw you out if you'd rather stick around for a while."

They kick my shoe again, and I smile in response to their gratitude before we both get back to work. Noah's gone now, cash left on the bar when nobody would care if he drank for free, and I don't bother to comment on it when Jake will leave at least as much behind.

"Didn't feel like taking your new friend home tonight?" Jake asks, looking past me to where Brendan had been sitting. "Seemed like he would've waited if you'd asked him to."

"He would've," I agree. "But neither of us was gonna take it all the way home. Maybe I'll find someone tomorrow night."

"Or the night after that, or the night after that."

My laugh surprises me, maybe even more so when it leaves Jake biting back something similar. "It's almost like you've been watching me for a while."

"Almost."

"And in all that time, you haven't asked anyone to wait for you."

It's too pointed, maybe, when Jake has always kept plenty to himself, but these past several weeks of trivia nights have gifted me with bits of him. Now I'm curious about whether I'm allowed to find out more.

He cooks spicy food.

He wants to go to Greece.

What else do I get to know?

"I won't ask anyone to wait for me," Jake says.

"At Trailhead, or anywhere?"

"What's with the concern? Do I look lonely to you?"

I pull back at that, and Jake picks up his beer, maybe just for something to do while I decide how to answer him. He doesn't look lonely, and we both know that, but I'm not sure that's the point he's trying to make, and I turn another corner.

"What's your type?"

Jake takes a sip, as calm as he's ever been. "Are you looking for an ego boost? Want me to tell you how incredibly attractive you are? Do you need me to compliment your smile? Your body? The intelligence *I* get to witness each week, but most strangers probably miss while their mouths are full?"

I don't answer before I'm interrupted by a guy I once hooked up with at a very, very hot bonfire. He steps up to Noah's empty stool, and I get his tab closed with my usual charm and an invitation to come back again soon. I notice Riley walk by on their way to our tiny closet of an employee area, and by the time I've collected a few more empty glasses and bottles, they're coming back out with the hoodie and earbuds that drown out the chaos I help create. Our trivia night host is long gone, I think, and only about a dozen people remain scattered elsewhere. The two on the dance floor are on vacation from Arizona. The two shooting pool have been shown the keg room before—separately, not together, though I wouldn't be opposed to a group tour. Everyone else is some shade of regular here, a few of them dragging stools closer together while they finish drinks they won't need refilled.

It's familiar, and I love that I already know how the rest of my night will go.

Except for whatever conversation I'm having with Jake.

He's standing now, and I ignore the money he's tucked under his coaster when I lean across the bar. "You're not lonely. I don't need an ego boost. I like your brain, too. And I want to know who you're kissing when you're not here flirting with me."

"You say that like you're not here flirting with me," Jake murmurs, the music just low enough for me to catch it. He eyes my bare chest, and I wonder for the first time whether his leather jacket would fit me if I took it from him, even if I can't imagine why I'd try. "Except I guess I get a pretty good look at most of the people you kiss."

I glance in the general direction of the keg room and nod. "Haven't kissed anyone tonight, just in case you're keeping count."

"There's still time."

"There certainly is."

"Enjoy it then," he says, knocking his fist against the edge of the bar before he steps backward. There's at least one more comment on the tip of his tongue, but he swallows it down. "Goodnight, Darren."

"'Night, Jake."

And whether I would've, I can't watch him leave, Zach swooping by with a goofy smile and a pint glass. "I think everyone's set for the night. Can I get outta here?"

"Wipe down all the empty tables and counter space, double-check for trash and any other glasses, and then make sure the bathrooms are decent."

It's all stuff I'll be doing later, once I've locked the rest of the world out, but he needs to get in the habit now if he's going to last any longer than the rest of the bartenders who have come and gone. Riley and I have worked together long enough to pick up each other's slack—however rare it is that we leave anything undone—but I really want to trust someone else, and I pretend Zach's small scowl doesn't mean he's halfway to quitting already.

I shake off the worry that won't make a difference tonight, and I clean up as much as I can behind the bar while I still have a handful of customers slow about going home. None of us should be on our phones while we're working, but while I'm waiting on everyone, I pull up Trailhead's social media accounts—all set up by Adrian shortly before trivia and karaoke became weekly events here—and browse comments and reviews. V takes the time to respond to most of them when she's here, but I'm nosy and eager to please, so I go through and like the best of them before Zach calls out a goodbye and I don't fight it.

The dancers from Arizona use their arms to wipe sweat from their foreheads when they approach me for one more round, but they're the only two left now. Weeknights can be like this, crowded for a few peak hours and then quiet toward the end, Trailhead located further away from the busier L.A.-area places that keep more people around until closing. I usually get the chance to unwind even before I've made it to my car, and some trashy reality tv is enough to carry me off to sleep once I get home.

Weekends, on the other hand, are expectedly wild from beginning to end, and those nights—or early mornings, really—are when I'm least likely to drive straight home after my shift. I often need a chance to settle down when my mind can't find its own quiet, and it's nearly a routine by now. One I've kept from my friends and exes and regulars and very temporary lovers, but share with one almost accidental friend. A stop I make once or twice a week.

Tonight I shouldn't need it, but something has thrown me, and I'm restless in a way I don't plan to dissect after a blowjob and some trivia.

I leave Trailhead behind me, and by the time I pull into a different dim parking lot, I've come to terms with not knowing why a scalding hot shower wasn't enough to lure me home, and my stomach growls as though it appreciates my surrender. In case I needed any more reassurance, I spot a beat-up Toyota Corolla parked around the side of the building, and another tight thing inside me loosens. Then I slam my car door shut and click my key fob 'til it chirps. The late summer night is perfectly silent as it drags me closer to people who have never demanded to hear all that much from me.

If I remember correctly, something above the front door used to make a noise when anyone came and went, but it's been broken for at least a couple of years. Still, I don't go undetected, and I return a couple of smiles on my way to the same booth I always take, its awkward position next to the kitchen leaving it undesirable to everyone else.

I can't possibly care, though.

When I crash at a 24-hour diner, ambience isn't much of a selling point.

I flop onto the cracked vinyl and drop my phone to the table before I scrub my face with my hands and hide there for a few unnecessary beats. Nothing is wrong—I've been so stupidly fortunate in my life, and that's been true far more often than not—but I need to stop thinking so hard on a night that hasn't called for it. Grabbing my phone again, I pull up a couple of different text threads. I'm tempted to bother any of a few friends who've allowed it for too long, but I doubt any of them are awake to chat, and I don't want to know that for sure. Trailhead's social media accounts aren't active enough for anything to have changed since my last sweep through the comments. Then I thumb through a list of top ten spicy dinner recipes just for the hell of it, close to saving one when the kitchen door swings open and hits the side of my booth.

Trading my phone for the place setting that might've been here for hours, I'm as grateful for the chocolate shake slid across the table as I am for the raspy voice that'll greet me next.

Along with a plate loaded with biscuits and gravy, the heaviness of it bound to soothe me to sleep.

And a side of fries, half of which will be stolen by the young woman handing them over now.

Then several extra napkins, mostly a joke after the night I spilled an entire milkshake in my lap.

"Didn't expect you for another night or two," she says.

I smile up at her and hand over a fry. "Hello to you, too, Sage."

Chapter Two

Jake

I shake hands and smile easily and nod along as all of us promise something about lunch or happy hour. Any excuse to write this kind of thing off is welcome after we've spent all day in a boardroom, and I agree with our younger execs that at least some of this could've been an email. Actually, I believe it wholeheartedly, which is why I'm able to work from home fifteen to twenty hours a week. I've wielded technology wisely after a few decades of learning how often anyone needs to see my face.

Of course, sometimes more important people want us to see *their* faces, and it's why I've been at the hospital since 7:30 this morning, fueled by unusually good coffee, overpriced platters of snacks, and a handful of well-timed texts from my daughter.

It's ten hours later now, and when I've stepped away from the last goodbye, I only stop by my office long enough to grab my bag and make sure nobody is waiting for me there, grateful when

I'm met with a single wave. The familiar rattle of the elevator carries me to the lobby, and I loosen my tie on the way, my shirt untucked and cuffs unbuttoned by the time I've reached the parking garage. I roll my sleeves before I start the car, and I breathe, already so much closer to home.

I love my job and the good I do at the hospital. I love wearing my perfectly tailored clothes while doing it.

I love when I can leave it all behind.

Traffic is expectedly awful at this hour, but I lose myself in a playlist full of the bluesy country that will pull the tension from my shoulders, and the thought I spare for my dinner plans does the same. A moment later, I remember the wine I have waiting for me, and it brings an actual smile to my face. I'll need to call Lucy to thank her—for the bottles she sent and for keeping me company throughout today's meetings—and with nothing else planned for tonight, I've got the time to do it.

After I've wound my way through the hills that lead me home, I pull into my garage and let the automatic door slowly shutter behind me. Leaving my car is the obvious next step, though I'm loath to walk away from the music. I remedy the silence as soon as I can after I've slipped into the house and left my suede messenger bag on the desk in my office, quickly reaching for the sound system we'd had installed years ago. It's gentle when it carries a familiar rhythm through nearly every room of my home, and I'm not interested in being any more disruptive as I climb up the staircase, shedding more professional pieces of myself as I go.

My shirt is fully unbuttoned by the time I get to my bedroom, my tie in hand. Everything else gets discarded neatly, but with little thought, and I throw a tank top and sweatpants on until I can decide what I'll be up to after dinner. Barefoot and comfortable, I jog back down to the kitchen and open a merlot to breathe before I gather everything I'll need for the next hour or so. The music remains perfect, and I hum along with it as I move from one side of the island to the other, a hint of melancholy striking only when there's nobody to steal a cherry tomato or five.

As has been true for a while, everything makes it into the dish just fine.

It's all incredible, though—the effort entirely worth it. This tomato pesto rigatoni has been a favorite for a while, and the fresh basil and mozzarella I add at the very end are guaranteed to make it even better. My stomach growls, and I nearly chuckle, hungry for a while and so close to finally sating it, a promise made out loud. Then I finally pour myself a glass of wine and take my plate to the dining room table. Like so many other things in the house, it's positioned so I can see outside, a wall of windows facing the private backyard that can serve as a playground or sanctuary, depending on the occasion.

Somewhere between my second bite and a third, I pick up my phone, dinner etiquette lax when I'm all alone, and I find a text from Beau waiting for me there.

Darren says you haven't been here in two weeks. Someone better looking than me taking up all your free time?

He's at Trailhead, then. I'd ask if Adrian's with him, but of course he is, and it doesn't matter to me tonight. I hope they have fun.

Nobody is better looking than you. And I've been busy with work, but I'll be there tomorrow night.

Guess I've gotta get smart before I can hang out with you again

I'll answer the questions, you rub my shoulders.

He's a massage therapist, and it feels like a reasonable request. It might've been a reasonable request regardless, Beau never shying away from physical affection.

That damn leather jacket is always in my way

Are you that eager to see the rest of me?

I'd be doing all of trailhead a favor if I help take it off

I smile, the compliment unnecessary but welcome. *If you don't show up tomorrow, maybe next week?*

Or you can drag your ass in here for more than nerd night. we used to see you a lot more

Says the guy who's barely there himself

Darren tell you that?

It's barely related to Beau's question, but I scroll through my texts until I find the last time Darren and I went back and forth anywhere but from across the bar. It's been weeks, and I don't think I'm surprised, shrugging to myself when I return to Beau.

He said you guys are busy with the new place

The "new place" is Adrian's photo gallery, and technically more his responsibility than Beau's, but I don't see a need to make that distinction when I'm sure Beau is plenty involved in getting his significant other set up for a grand opening rumored to be happening soon. Adrian has been an independent photographer for years, but he's only just bought a storefront in West Hollywood, and even I can admit that his pictures will sell incredibly well. He's talented, and because my friend loves him, I'll be there to support them both when it's time.

We are. Still miss your smile

I don't smile that often.

You do for me

Then I'll try to bring my smile around more often. Just for you.

Beau doesn't respond after that, and I don't worry about where he's gone, setting my phone aside while I finish eating, the wine going down as smoothly as I'd expected it to. It's dark outside now, the late sunset getting a little earlier every night, and I think I want to breathe it in. It's unusual for me to leave a mess in my kitchen, but I only pack up the leftover pasta for another couple of nights and leave most of the dishes to soak, eager to move on. Upstairs, I change into swim trunks and grab a towel from the linen closet. Then I'm in my backyard with a second glass of wine, the jets in the spa rumbling to life while I take a sip.

I've got my phone too, and once I'm chest-deep in the hot water, I call Lucy and put her on speaker.

"Hey, dad."

A door slams shut behind her, and I hear the clatter of a couple of other things. "Bad time to talk?"

"Perfect, actually," she says. "Just got home. Now you can listen to me shovel cold Chinese food into my mouth while I look for some old tv show to fall asleep to when I inevitably pass out on my couch in an hour.”

“Luce, at the very least, please start treating yourself to properly heated takeout.”

“Sure. Let me grab a pen. September’s an excellent time to start a list of New Year’s resolutions.”

I sigh. “Should there also be something on there about working longer hours than I do?”

“I knew it was part of the deal when I got hired. New GMs get a hell of a paycheck, but very little time off.”

“Nice paycheck and access to great wine,” I add, glancing at the glass next to me. “I opened the merlot tonight.”

“Mmmm, one of the best we serve here. And the winery’s practically down the street.”

“Ah, the swanky resort life. World-class restaurants, three swimming pools, palm trees as far as the eye can see, and a nearby winery keeping you stocked enough that you can ship a case to your dear old dad.” I get a hum in response and assume she’s busy eating, but I poke for more. “Everything else going okay? Nobody is giving you a hard time?”

Lucy hesitates, and as much as I want to keep blaming the food, she clears her throat to buy herself a few seconds. I tense until she answers with a calm she inherited from her mother.

“Relax, dad. I can practically hear you growling,” she starts. “It’s—my coworkers are awesome. Really. As for anyone else, I think you and I both know there are always gonna be people who—some people don’t like when anything is different. *Any-*

thing. So, there's some of that, but it's nothing new, and I'm fine."

I take her at her word—I couldn't imagine doing anything less after a lifetime of loving her—but I also make a mental note to check my calendar and talk to her about booking a room for a long weekend. Maybe once the weather has cooled.

"Making any friends?" I ask.

"In between bad takeout and an early bedtime?"

"So, probably not a lot of dating either."

There's more noise on her end, and then a perfect little laugh. "For me? Absolutely not. But what about you? Is this the night you tell me there's someone special?"

It's not the first time she's asked me that, but maybe I'm carrying a fresh bruise somewhere, my body made tender by something long intangible. Recent weeks have made me wish I could catch it and pin it down long enough to understand this thing that's made me ache, but I lift the wine glass and take another sip instead. Once I've set it aside, I slip further into the water, the jets at my back as soothing as the music still playing inside.

"Already had someone special, Luce."

"And she died nine years ago, dad."

"Do you think I'm lonely?" I ask, the question almost an echo of the one I'd recently asked Darren with Guinness on my tongue.

"Nope," she answers easily. "But you don't need to wait to feel something objectively uncomfortable before wanting better than that. You can make yourself a snack before you're starving. You can rest before you're exhausted. And you—"

"Can find another someone special before I'm lonely."

"Exactly."

"How did you become so wise?"

"Well, that particular bit was inspired by the time my father told me I didn't have to wait to be miserable before choosing to be happy," Lucy says. "It seemed relatively applicable here."

"It absolutely was."

"So, you'll take my advice?"

"Unlikely," I admit.

"Fine. And you already told me all about work today, so how are things at Trailhead?"

Still mostly submerged, I catch her up on random stories about people she's never actually met, but probably knows too well. I was married to my wife and blissfully in love with her for a very long time, but if Lucy's ever found it strange that I ended up frequenting a gay bar as a widower, she's never said. Maybe she thinks I'm running away from something. Maybe she thinks I'm running toward something.

Maybe she and I will talk about it someday.

Lucy tells me a little more about things at the resort, but I can tell she's winding down, and by the time I lift myself out of the water, I'm getting restless. It's not something that happens to me often—usually I could sit and read all afternoon or stand over the stove for an hour or float in my pool until I've daydreamed the day away—but if pasta, wine, and soaking in the spa haven't been enough to pin me to the ground tonight, I already know I'll have to fly.

After toweling off, I go back inside and silence the music, still uncharacteristically lazy when I pour the rest of my wine back into the bottle and cork it near the sink piled with dishes. I'm too warm. Thrumming with energy. I'm almost positive I have something to smoke upstairs, but I don't even want that when I'm ready to crawl out of my skin. My greatest solace is that I already know the feeling will be gone by morning, this mood reliably fleeting as long as I tend to it, and I hurry to change into jeans, a t-shirt, and one of my favorite leather jackets before I get back downstairs and grab my boots.

When I'm in the garage again, I take a minute to study my bikes, wondering whether my inexplicable need to *go* might be relieved by staying right here. I could take one of them apart and put it back together again. I could do it with all three. I love getting my hands dirty. I love the subtle physical strain of disassembling a motorcycle's engine, and the mental challenge that comes with rebuilding it into something new and still exactly the same.

But another minute tells me this isn't a problem I can solve with my hands, the rest of me too needy.

The garage door slides open.

I pull my helmet from a handlebar, a pair of gloves tucked inside.

Before I realize I can breathe without pain, I'm halfway down the street.

I head west for a while, but Mulholland Drive feels far too familiar tonight, my body leaning into turns before I should know they're there. It's my neighborhood, more or less, the streetlamps ones that have shone upon me for years. I've attended so many parties in so many of these homes—very few in the past nine years, but all of it recent somehow—and I don't think too hard about the trouble Lucy and her friends might've gotten into around here when they were teenagers.

The memories are close, mostly because I am, and while my next exhale still doesn't hurt, I turn around and speed toward Angeles Crest Highway instead.

My thighs are wrapped around the kind of power that I'd like to believe is a bigger blessing than threat, and it's late enough on a weeknight for me to surrender to it more than usual. I'm wearing more than I was at home, but it's been close to an hour since I left, and I'm finally cooler now, the wind offering the chill that will help clear my mind. I haven't ridden up here in a while, and the darkness reminds me to slow when it's time to stop being stupid. And slow is better, maybe, when my heart is pounding and my grip has to remain steady.

Eventually, I need a break, and I take it, pulling off the road where a scenic turnout gives me the room to park my bike and lie down next to it, my helmet still within arm's reach. I'm too old for this kind of nonsense—I can't help but laugh when I try to imagine asking Michelle to relax in the dirt with me when we probably outgrew this sort of thing before she was gone—but it can be tomorrow's problem, everything about *now* forgotten in the minutes I spend staring at the sky.

I'm not sore, and I'm not lonely.

At some point, I close my eyes and rest, and when I'm not

interested in becoming caught up in the future, I tumble backward. Even with the cold ground there to keep me where I am, it feels exactly right. Michelle might not have wanted this specific moment with me, but we'd had a million others together, and the worst part of any ride is not having her weight against my back.

The best part is remembering that I had her pressed close to me until the very, very end.

I'm not sore, and I'm not lonely.

When I'm ready to sit up, I roll with caution brought about by wisdom, and pick up my helmet again. I don't know what time it is, but I also don't check, and it only surprises me that I wonder whether Beau and Adrian are still at Trailhead with Darren when I've never felt like I was missing out before. I smile again when I think about what it might've been like to bring Michelle there, an impossibility when I hadn't even known the bar existed back then, but she would've had a great time flirting with shirtless bartenders and riding the mechanical bull and dragging me onto the dance floor.

In an even more impossible world, she would've loved Beau and Darren for a hundred obvious reasons, and probably a few less so. She and Riley would've been a special kind of trouble together, because I know little about them, but I think Michelle would've known it all. She would've damn near adopted Noah, even if he already has a kickass mom of his own. And as much as Michelle could be an outright bitch when she wanted to be, I think it would've pulled her closer to Adrian before it pushed him away, and it's so easy to see her laughing and flipping me off about my disinterest in him.

Lord, help me.

I'm not sore, and I'm not lonely.

Yet.

I blame my daydreaming on my mood, and my mood on whatever got into me after sitting at a boardroom table for too long. Then I stand and return to the motorcycle that's been patient long enough.

Winding back the way I came, I think I'm in a hurry and very much not. I'm done with the need to be far from home, but also okay with existing out here, everything a little colder and a little darker, but somehow still a comfort as I move through it. Minutes pass quickly and seconds are long, and as I ride along the north side of Griffith Park, I'm only sorry that it's not early enough for me to cut through to the observatory. I spare a thought for James Dean, Natalie Wood, and Sal Mineo, and race along until I'm passing Forest Lawn, sparing a thought for countless others, too.

It brings me back to Michelle, and then to Lucy. Another moment has me distracted by the hospital and Trailhead. I think about the mountains and the desert and my backyard, and I want to be everywhere at once. I'm almost forced into a slight detour as it is, close to missing my exit when the late-night lack of traffic makes it easy to stop paying attention, but I shake my head and try to refocus.

That doesn't help. Or it's too late for it to help. It's about to end badly either way.

Something scurries across the road—a possum or a raccoon or a skunk, I suppose—and any other time I might have slowed the bike and swerved smoothly and suffered nothing but the subtle shift of adrenaline that would've left me shaking. Tonight, though. Tonight, I've been anywhere but here, and it costs me because I don't want to hurt anything else. I swerve too hard and overcorrect from there, leaning right before I jerk to the left.

I feel none of the impact when I skid out of control and crash into the dirt embankment just off the highway. I hear nothing either, but I taste blood and can't decide how I feel about that being the only thing my brain cares to register. My motorcycle is on top of me and my awkward landing has me taking inventory of everything now, but I can breathe and clench my fist and scrape the heel of my boot against the ground, so if I'm dying, I'm not there yet.

A car drives by, or maybe a few of them do, but depending on how far away I landed, I don't think I'm all that visible to anyone looking straight ahead. Shouting for help doesn't occur to me—hell, finding my phone and literally calling for help never crosses my mind—and I lie there long enough to start shivering, the moon close to questioning my sanity.

When I'm frustrated enough to fight my bike, I scoot out from under it and get unbearably loud and angry when I feel part of it tear against my thigh. Something is wet there—I don't think I could've known that until now, or maybe it's only just happened—and I have to ignore it if I'm going to make it home tonight. Moving again takes more effort, but however clumsy

I am, I get clear of the motorcycle and throw my gloves to the ground.

Another car passes, and I stay low to avoid being found now, my pride unforgiveable, but persistent all the same.

Whatever didn't hurt before hurts terribly when I fight my way to my feet, but after I've removed my helmet, it's the first good look at my wrecked Harley that comes close to breaking me. My phone is badly cracked and won't turn on—a predictable consequence I could've done without—and that stings, too. I don't want to be here anymore, but I'm stuck, suddenly sharply aware that I'm too far north to even consider walking home.

What if I turn in the other direction?

Will it do me any good?

What time is it?

Asking questions without answers is a lost cause, and unless I want to make enough of a scene to force a car to stop for an old and bloody biker, I have to take a chance and walk somewhere else. A couple of steps suggest I'll succeed just long enough, even with a limp I don't want, so I leave my bike behind and keep going. The sidewalk is right there. Then an intersection I cross with the light. I don't know how many blocks I have to go—I can't put that much effort into counting right now—but I don't slow down when I don't know whether I ran out of time a while ago.

I want to go home, and I need help to get there.

But what if my help is already gone?

Chapter Three

Darren

It's our most reliably quiet night of the week, maybe because it falls between karaoke and trivia night, and isn't close enough to benefit from any weekend excitement. The last customer left about fifteen minutes ago, and I've been prepared to lock up for the past ten. V hadn't worked tonight, and I'd encouraged Zach to leave exactly as early as he'd hoped, and while there'd been enough business to leave me satisfied with the tips I'll be taking home, there'd also been time to get most of the bar restocked and cleaned in between.

I glance at my phone, open to an article about the best wineries in Texas, and I swipe that away when I see that there are only five minutes left until we close.

Five minutes left.

Until we close.

Which is why I groan when one of the barn doors begins to

open.

I have a decent amount of leeway here, V trusting me to make decisions for Trailhead all the time. It wouldn't be terrible for me to greet the new customers at the door, explain that we're already shut down for the night, and politely send them on their way. I know I've been less professional about more important things, and as long as I don't earn us a dozen scathing reviews, turning away last-minute business shouldn't be a big deal.

Leaving my phone behind, I make my way across the sawdust-covered floor, frowning when the heavy door is being pulled open more slowly than usual. For a moment, I wonder whether it's someone getting up the nerve to walk into a gay bar for the first time, nervous curiosity bringing them closer to something they've sought, but haven't quite found. If that's the case, I may invite them in after all, just so they can talk. Maybe they'll breathe a little easier by the time they go home again.

I'm an arrogant bartender with no shirt and abs for days, but that can only help, right?

Or not.

I think I freeze between one table and another when I finally see him. It's the torn sleeve of his leather jacket that catches my eye first. Or it could be the grotesque gash in his leg. There's also blood in the gray of his beard, so that's probably what makes my heart skip its next beat. He's staring at me—some god-awful mix of exhaustion and pain and frustration—but he's *there*, and I close the distance between us faster than I would've thought possible a minute ago.

"Holy *shit*, what happened to you?" I ask. It's a stupid first question though, and I shake my head before I clock the dirty helmet in his hand and try again. "Did you crash in the parking lot?"

Jake takes a step forward, and I steady him there whether he needs it or not. "On the off-ramp."

With one hand hovering near his injured body, I reach past him to lock the barn doors and keep any other surprises at bay, and my brain attempts to pull up a map of the entire L.A. area so I can figure out what the fuck Jake's talking about. I narrow the nearby freeways to two, and then turn back to him.

"At best, that's what—a mile and a half? Two miles? Is your bike still there? Did you walk all the way here? Is anyone else hurt?"

"You talk a lot."

"Yeah," I agree. "Do you need me to start all over again?"

"There was nobody else," he sighs. "I walked. The bike is wrecked. And I need a ride home."

I laugh at him. Actually laugh. It's probably to convince myself that everything's fine as much as anything, but I also can't believe he thinks I'll just put him in my car and drop him off like he's not actively bleeding into his jeans. Even if I hadn't been raised by a nurse, I don't think there's any way I'd be hurrying us out the door.

"You need a lot more than a ride, old man. We're gonna get you cleaned up. Make sure you don't need legitimate medical attention after fleeing the scene of an accident."

Careful to stay at his side without crowding him, I move us toward the small hallway that leads to the bathrooms, keg room, employee room, and V's office, and if he's surprised by where we end up, he doesn't say. I've got keys hooked to my belt loop and I use them to let us into the office, leaving the door open so Jake doesn't feel the need to walk another couple of miles just to get away from me. He's limping, probably only because he's physically incapable of pretending otherwise, and I do him the favor of not calling it out.

V has a couple of chairs, but I ignore them and clear half the desk instead, nodding for Jake to sit there. He's still clinging to his helmet, and when I tug it from his grip, he startles just enough to make me think he'd forgotten it was there, our eyes meeting when I study him for an extra second or two. Eventually, I move away to set the helmet on top of the filing cabinet and open the top drawer, a first aid kit kept there for occasions far less serious than this.

Jake raises an eyebrow. "Are we really about to play doctor?"

"Is that a thing for you?" I ask, winking just because I can. "I wasn't planning to take it quite that far, but I learn something new about you every week, and I'm willing to run with this one."

That gets a smile out of him, and I'm proud of myself for it, even if it only lasts about as long as I expect it to, slipping when I frown at the streaks of blood on his face. I don't think he has any actual injuries there, especially since he'd been wearing his helmet, so I leave them alone for now. My next concern is whether he has any obvious damage to his torso, and I'm as gentle as I can be when I reach for his jacket. Jake tenses anyway, and I back up so he can remove it himself.

"Even the medical professionals usually let me do this much on my own," he mutters.

"That's fine, too. I'm okay with watching."

I say it too softly and forget to wink, and there's no smile this time. The jacket is gone though, so I ask him to lift his shirt for me, and I press a palm to his skin as soon as I can. My other hand stays curved around his shoulder as I check for tenderness or swelling or severe bruising that won't wait for later, and I say nothing about the rosary Jake has tattooed over his heart. At a glance, I can tell I'll need to clean a scrape on his arm and get past the blood on his hands, but I'm in a hurry to look at his leg, and other than running the tips of my fingers over the wounds, I let him go.

He glares as well as he can when he's this tired. "I suppose you want my jeans off, too."

I really don't, and that's what sucks. I don't want any of what's happening right now—not the *way* it's happening—because I know Jake is in pain no matter how much he'll keep trying to hide it from me. Holding out my hand to help him stand again is the best I can do until he stops with his jeans somewhere around mid-thigh, and I realize the denim is too sticky from the ugly gash there for him to do anything else.

"Sit."

The sharp edges of my command do their job, or Jake's become resigned to his fate, and he's back on the desk when I carefully slide one hand under his jeans and pull them down with the other, keeping everything from dragging against him on the way. Neither of us says a word when I leave the jeans bunched around his ankles, an alcohol wipe unwrapped before I start to clean up the blood that seems to be everywhere, but on its way to drying. Even while I'm grateful for that much, I need a new wipe almost immediately, and once I've thrown the old one away, I give myself a minute to think. Then I spot a half-empty water bottle V must have left behind, and I nod to myself, taking the rainbow bandana from around my neck and wetting it before Jake's fingers close around my wrist.

"Darren."

"Jake," I start, leveling him with a cautious stare. "Let me do this. Please. I need to know how bad it is."

I linger on the blue-gray eyes I think must match my own, and when he lets me go, my gaze falls to his lap and the thighs made strong by years of riding his Harley. There are easy jokes to make about it all—the innuendo tempting on the tip of my tongue—but while I'm not against the break they might provide, my timing matters more than ever. I kneel between his legs and bring the wet cloth to the wound, too quiet again when I check in with him.

"Any nausea? Blurred vision?"

"I can see you just fine."

"I'm serious," I tell him. "Do you think you might have a concussion?"

"I forgot your mom's a nurse. Guess you get this from her."

"How to give a shit about someone who's hurt?" I snort. "Yeah, I guess so."

The bandana has done its job well, Jake's leg mostly clean, and I push my hand toward the hem of his boxers, nudging them out of the way so I can get a good look at the jagged cut. He hisses, and as much as I'm sorry for however that might've stung, I forget to apologize when I swear under my breath instead.

"Am I bleeding out?" he asks, his voice still strained.

"No, but it's not great. You need stitches."

"I'm not going to urgent care to get them, so put a bandage on my leg and take me home."

I roll my eyes and toss the bloody bandana into the nearby trash, then open another alcohol wipe for one more sweep of his thigh before I do as he's asked. One of my hands is splayed up high, holding him still while I finish cleaning, but for the second time tonight, his fingers wrap around my wrist, and it surprises me enough that I stop to glance up at him.

Head injury or no, his eyes are blazing when they lock with mine, and then I blink and take in everything else at once—the exaggerated rise and fall of his chest, the way his hand has moved over mine, and the boxers that hide less than they did a minute ago—and I ease away from Jake just so I can smile again.

"Been a long time since you've had a man on his knees for you, huh?"

Unconcerned about his actual answer, and unsure I'd get one anyway, I grab the first aid kit and fumble through it for every-thing I'll need next. I take longer than necessary, for his good or mine, and just for the chance to distract myself from thoughts I didn't expect to have, I go on.

"Tell me what happened tonight."

"I was feeling restless after dinner, so I went for a ride. Angeles Crest." He clears his throat, and I keep my head down as I prep the butterfly bandages. "Just relaxed there for a while, then headed home. Got off at Vineland and—I don't know. A possum or something ran across the road, and I swerved too hard. I slid. The bike ended up on top of me."

With my pulse settled, I focus on the wound and how to close it as neatly as possible. "Since you didn't call, I'm guessing your phone didn't survive the landing?"

"Maybe I just wanted to surprise you."

"Congrats on doing exactly that." I chuckle and place one strip across the cut, then another, before something else occurs to me. "You think you were limping because your thigh got ripped open, or did you fuck something else up?"

"Just this. I'll be fine."

"Your body's gonna hate you tomorrow."

"Pretty sure that still counts as 'fine.'"

I stand once I've got his leg looking like it's something that might heal, and I spend time cleaning the smaller scrapes on his arm and the residual mess on his hands. There are goosebumps covering his skin, but I let us assume he's cold, even if I'm the one without a shirt. Then after another minute or so, I reach for his beard and the blood dried there. Jake's jeans are still around his ankles—I don't want him to have to feel bloody denim pressed against his skin until absolutely necessary—so I'm careful to stay closer to his side when I wipe his jaw with a damp piece of gauze.

As I'd suspected, Jake isn't cut anywhere on his face, and when I move to his neck, I think he's fine there, too. By the time he'd removed his helmet after the crash, he'd probably had blood on his hands from everything else, so I take my time finding all the traces left behind now, and we're both quiet when he lets me guide his head from side to side. There's something about the way he's baring his throat to me when I want a better look, each moment drawing me nearer to him, and I fall into the ease of it all, forgetting to think when my mouth lands next to his ear.

Then it becomes too easy to speak. "You smell like wine and chlorine."

Jake remains remarkably still until he manages the slightest nod. "Ah, so now you're a nurse *and* a detective."

I know it's a joke, but it's the first time I wonder whether I've jumped to lazy conclusions instead of listening to what he's really said. He told me he'd been restless after dinner and went for a ride, but there was no reason for me to assume he was alone—or even at his own home—and maybe the way he'd stopped my hand from moving against his thigh had nothing to do with me.

And everything to do with someone else.

I'm certainly not jealous, but my curiosity is piqued. I don't know Jake well enough after the eight years we've spent across the bar from each other, even if recent weeks have made me want to ask, and suddenly I'm trying to imagine the man he might've been with tonight, before he ended up here with me. My questions wait, only so I can take a step back and attempt something predictable first.

"I've been told I'm a damn good bartender, too."

"Damn good," Jake echoes. "And you're sure enough about it that you don't need me to agree with anyone who's said it before."

"Where were you drinking tonight?"

"At home."

"Alone?"

"Are these questions coming from the detective or the bartender?"

I shrug. "Maybe they're from your friend."

"Maybe they are," Jake says.

He studies me for a few more seconds, then scoots off the desk with a wince. I catch him there without thinking, my hands at his waist, and when we both realize he needs help to get dressed again, I feel like the moment should be so much more awkward than it is. I mumble an apology, mostly because it seems like the next line in a script I don't know all that well, and crouch to get a grip on his jeans. Then I make the mistake of looking up at Jake again, too close to kneeling for the second time tonight.

I don't hurry to stand. He doesn't turn away.

"It's never happened. A man on his knees for me."

Questions I'd had before become tasteless on my tongue, and I swallow hard before I begin to cover his legs with jeans that fit him too well. I rise slowly, conscious of the bandages as I move past them, and I think maybe I hold my breath until I'm forced to let it go.

"Because you'd rather give than receive?"

"Haven't been on my knees for a man either."

"I don't understand," I say, face to face again and blinking up at him. Without warning, his hands cover mine, and he doesn't speak when he loosens my hold on his jeans, able to tuck himself in just fine, even if I think I would've helped with that, too. I tell myself to tease him about something, but I don't have it in me when he's caught up in sleepy honesty, and I keep my voice low when I trip and fall into the same. "When I was touching your thigh, you—*reacted*. You didn't hate it."

Jake chuckles, though it's too serious. "It's a good touch. Just not one I'm used to."

"From me?"

"From anyone. My wife died a long time ago, and there hasn't been anyone since."

It's a heavy sentence that carries no extra weight. Jake doesn't want my sympathy, nor is he grieving in this moment, his words a simple statement meant to explain a complicated thing. I don't offer any of what he'd brush off anyway, still so close to him when I go on.

"There were no men before her?"

"We met as teenagers. Got married just before we turned 20," he says. "It's never been more than a hypothetical to me."

"But you've thought about it?" I ask.

Jake's eyes drop to my bare chest and back up again, his smirk a lot like most of mine. "I could get a Guinness anywhere."

That startles a laugh out of me, and I finally give us both some breathing room while I put the first aid kit back together and stash it in V's drawer. Jake fastens the button on his jeans and pulls his belt tight, and if it draws any of my attention to his body again, I think I have to ignore it. I have to do a few other things too, and I nod toward the open office door.

"I need to finish closing up, but it shouldn't take long," I tell him. "Sit down. Relax if you can get comfortable enough in one of these chairs."

Jake waves me away, and my only stop on the way back to the bar is to grab my t-shirt, wallet, and car keys from the employee room. I'm grateful again for the slow night that allowed me to knock out most of my closing routine before Jake stumbled through our barn doors, and as I move to lock the door to the beer garden I'd finished clearing an hour ago, I make a phone call and ask for a favor.

It'll cost me a couple of them in return, but I'll do a dozen if I'm asked.

My quiet goodbye comes a minute later, and it echoes long enough for my chest to tighten around my next several breaths. While I turn off the bar's decorative lights and the music I barely hear anymore, I let logic war with whatever happened between Jake and me in V's office, mostly because I don't want to say goodbye to *him*, and I don't think I should. Busying myself with my register and the night's sales reports distracts me for a bit, but then I've got a stack of cash and receipts in my hands and my phone in my back pocket. I move away from the bar and leave any unsteady pleas behind, knowing I need to go back to Jake with something more certain than the soft suggestion my heart has made.

When I return to the office, my sigh is all relief, the sight of Jake enough to make up my mind, as though that wasn't done in the shadow of my denial a while ago. He's wearing his battered leather jacket again, and the physical damage to it does nothing to make him appear less vulnerable where he's fallen asleep in one of V's chairs, his head tipped backward to rest against the wall behind it. My eyes fall to his throat again, then down to his bloody lap, and I turn away to give him one more minute of peace while I put the money into the safe and leave a note for V.

He doesn't stir until my hand is on his shoulder, and the look he gives me is both what I want, and what I don't want at all.

"Hey," I murmur. "I'm all done here, and we can go, but listen—I don't think you should be alone tonight. Not with a possible concussion."

"Told you I'm fine," Jake grumbles.

"And I'd rather know that for sure, so you can come back to my place, or I'll stay at yours."

Jake pushes himself up from the chair and gets as close to me as either of us would dare—or his injuries will allow—licking his lips and glaring at me in a way that does nothing to scare me. I'm ready for the challenge, rising to it with a smile when he shakes his head.

"I admitted I liked the way you touched me, and you think that's enough reason for us to spend the night together?"

"Wiping out on your motorcycle is enough reason for us to spend the night together," I argue. "The touching was nice, but I don't actually have plans for more of that."

"And if I say no?"

"Then you can sit back down, and I'll get the entire group chat over here to poke at you until morning."

Even as I threaten to summon everyone to Trailhead, I try not to think too hard about the afternoon all of us—V, Noah, Beau, Adrian, Riley, Jake, and I—had spent in WeHo together this past March. We'd been handing out promo for the bar, but when everyone else had headed home, I'd kept Jake with me before and after I fucked a hot lawyer in a nightclub bathroom. The whole point was for the two of us to go out and get laid, but I feel a little stupid now, and more selfish than usual. I wonder how Jake had felt that night, surrounded by eager hands and hot tongues and filthy promises he wouldn't have fulfilled.

There are so many things I want to ask him now, but he needs to sleep, and I need to get out of my head.

And I'm not sure anything is made better when Jake takes a half step back and scrubs a scraped hand over his face.

"My bike is just lying there, and I didn't even—I need to call a tow truck or—can I use your phone to—"

"No, hey, it's okay," I interrupt, closing the distance between us again, my hand flat against his chest because the touching *was* nice, and maybe I'm a liar. "It's done. It's taken care of. I called Beau, and he and Adrian are on their way to get it. They'll bring it here, and we'll figure out the rest tomorrow."

"They *what?* They can't—"

"They can. Beau has a ramp for the truck, and it's not like there's a bunch of traffic out there right now."

"It's the middle of the damn night. Please tell me you didn't wake them up."

"Of course I did," I say. "But it's one less thing for you to worry about, and I'll keep their apartment stocked with good whiskey and wine 'til we're even."

"You know Adrian doesn't like me."

I drop my hand but don't step back, my voice low. "And you know the only reason he doesn't like *you* is because you don't like *him.*"

Jake takes a deep breath I can feel a second later, and then he looks over my shoulder, his jaw working to fight off the feelings that have caught up to him, in part because I pushed them in that direction. I watch the battle closely, and I don't give him space, but I wait him out because it's the least I can do when he stops thinking about Adrian and remembers to be frustrated with me.

"I haven't had anyone over to my house in a long time," he says after another careful breath. "And nobody has spent the night."

There's plenty left unsaid, but neither of us needs to hear it. "Then come home with me."

"M'not spending the night at your place."

"Jake—"

"You can stay with me," he sighs. "You can be the first."

Chapter Four

Jake

My helmet is in my lap, and I hate that I don't remember bringing it to Trailhead with me, but then Darren starts the car, and I get distracted by a few seconds of whatever generic pop song catches me off guard. He silences it and doesn't explain his poor taste, nor do either of us attempt a conversation, the drive to my house not long enough to require one. I give him the directions he needs and ignore the ache I feel from head to toe, eager to crawl into my bed and start over again tomorrow.

But Darren will be there, too. Tomorrow. Or later today, I suppose. And the quiet roads make something about that loud.

He knows things about me now, and while I don't think I'd ever meant to keep any of it a secret, I'd held on to those confessions for years, and I'd be lying if I said the words hadn't fractured something in me on their way out. Now I need to figure out whether I want to tuck the honesty back inside before I heal, but part of me thinks that choice was made before we left the bar.

Darren will be there tomorrow. Or today. And I'm okay with that.

"Nice neighborhood," Darren says, a glance thrown my way as we turn onto my street. "Don't think I imagined you coming home to a place like this."

"Is this where I ask why you were imagining me at all?"

Another glance is followed by a quick half-laugh and the shake of his head. "Which one is yours?"

I point toward my spacious Spanish-style house, partially hidden by the surrounding greenery, and the long driveway leading to the garage. Darren parks and gets out, and while I expect some exaggerated praise or a long, low whistle, he's quiet when he stands next to his open car door and studies as much as he can see from there. I stop studying *him* and fight my own body until it unfolds from the passenger seat, then I slam my door and take tentative steps forward without worrying about whether he'll follow. My front door is up a small series of steps I don't want to climb, and I'm preemptively pissed off about having to make it upstairs just to sleep in my bed. Fortunately, I'm only a little breathless when I let us in—surprised and grateful that my keys made it this far—and hear Darren flip the lock behind me.

Maybe I should've done that myself, but I don't feel like turning around.

When he takes the helmet from my hands for the second time tonight, he doesn't ask me to.

Putting distance between us again, I prop myself against the wall to struggle with my boots, and Darren's kind enough to ignore me while he kicks off his own shoes. When I finally chance a look over my shoulder, I gesture aimlessly at everything that lies ahead before we walk again.

"Sorry, I'm not up for giving you a tour of the place."

"I didn't come here for one," he says. "I can see the couch and blankets from here. Once we get you settled, I'll be fine."

I stop abruptly at the bottom of the staircase, frowning at the idea of him spending the night down here, but when Darren's hand is firm against my lower back, I move again and do my best to respond.

"I've got a guest room upstairs," I tell him, and if he wants to say something about my admitted lack of guests, I never get to hear it. "There's a nice bed and plenty of blankets in there, and you can borrow something to sleep in."

Even as I make the offer, I try not to wonder too much about what it means—Darren wearing my clothes while sleeping in a bedroom down the hall—and I'm strangely glad that each slow step hurts as much as the one before. He probably can't see my scowl, but I know he hears all the small sounds I don't bite back, and he moves impossibly closer with each one while I remind myself to be frustrated by his proximity. There's no real risk of me falling, but my pride is a hell of a thing, and I think having his body pressed to mine will put me in danger of some other deadly sin if I don't tell myself to stay mad about his reaction to my injuries instead.

We reach the top of the stairs, and I lead him to my bedroom, his touch gone even if I know he hasn't fallen far behind. I get rid of my leather jacket without Darren's help and toss it over the back of a chair, and then I pause in front of my dresser, and he wanders across the room.

"Hell of a view," he says.

"It is," I agree. I've got a balcony, and it overlooks the pool and gardens and firepit and dining area below, and if this were any other night—or if I were any other man—I think I'd encourage him to step outside and enjoy it as long as he'd like. Of course, it's not and I'm not, so I focus on my open drawer. "Will a pair of shorts be okay? Or I have pajama pants if you'd prefer those?"

"Anything is fine. Or nothing. I can—I mean, I've got my underwear, so—"

I don't have time for an entire back and forth with someone trying to be gentle, so I grab whatever's on top for him and something beneath it for me, and I don't bother with a shirt for either of us. When I turn around, I find him standing near my bed, and I want to laugh at how ridiculous it is to have this man in a space nobody has occupied in nearly a decade. Darren Wheeler—bartender extraordinaire—is unapologetically promiscuous and too willing to share experience that extends far beyond the ability to pour perfect shots without looking. He could've been in anybody's bedroom tonight, and waiting in mine makes no sense at all.

I'd give him a way out if I thought he'd take it, but then he walks up to me with a curious grin and pulls a pair of sleep shorts from my hand.

"Sorry," I mumble.

"For?"

"I zoned out for a minute. It doesn't usually take me this long to pick out something to wear."

"Maybe not, but I already told you it's a hell of a view," he says.

"That was about the balcony."

"And it's true all over again."

My eyes fall closed and maybe I sway a bit, but when he steadies me there, he's too much without trying to be anything, and I have to look at him again.

"Let me show you where the guest room is."

Darren frowns at the shorts I'm still holding. "Let me help—"

"I've got it. I was fine before, and I'm fine now."

"I took care of your jeans the last time."

"Ah, yes, part of the touching," I say dryly. "I remember it well."

"But you don't want me to touch you again?"

"A cut on my thigh was never meant to be bait."

The low sound Darren makes is somewhere between a laugh and a growl, and despite a thousand reasons not to, I'm watching his mouth too closely when he speaks.

"I'm not that hungry, Jake. I don't bite unless I want to."

He backs away from me then, and moves toward my bedroom door, unnaturally patient in a way that makes me want to scream. I throw my sleep shorts onto my bed and pretend the movement doesn't strain a body that's been through too much, swallowing anything that might give me away. Then I'm stepping past Darren, my limp less pronounced if I'm stubborn enough, and he follows me down the hall.

The guest room is probably more ready than it's ever been, everything refreshed when Lucy moved to the desert, just in case she ever needs to come home for a night. I turn on the light before giving Darren a moment to look around, and I hate that I shiver when I feel him at my back.

I'm wearing a basic t-shirt and bloody jeans, but I shouldn't be cold.

"Like I said, there are plenty of blankets and some extra pillows, and the bed is very comfortable. The bathroom has clean towels, a new toothbrush and toothpaste, plus shampoo and everything else for a shower. You're welcome to anything you want from the kitchen, too. Make yourself at home."

Darren finally delivers the low whistle I'd expected all along. "I had no idea. And I feel so stupid."

"You? Stupid?" I huff, incredulous and too exhausted to hide it.

Turning toward him helps nothing while he's as close as he is, and when my balance is thrown again, he catches me easily. His hands stay at my waist as he shrugs.

"You live *here,* and you have a guest room with a new toothbrush, and you sleep in actual pajama pants after spending a quiet night with wine in a backyard that looks like *that,* and I—I just didn't know."

"Ah, we're back to your imagination again," I murmur. "Is this a problem you have with all the men you drive home?"

His grip on me tightens. "I don't imagine them doing much beyond writhing beneath me."

"Beneath you?"

"Or they can pin me to their mattress. Or we could find the nearest wall." Darren pauses and tilts his head. "Did *you* imagine I'd be particularly picky about that?"

I'd love to tell him I've never thought about it at all, but I've been celibate, not dead, and I ignore the question entirely while probably making things worse.

"Is there anything else you need from me tonight?" I ask.

Making eye contact is dangerous when I'm this tired and Darren's fingers slip under the hem of my shirt just so he can feel my skin again. Maybe touching me is about the crash, and maybe it's not, but suddenly I don't know how I want him to answer my question. I *do* know that my jeans are too tight, and it's been so long since I've had someone in a position to relieve that ache for me, and maybe something in my expression gives all of that away.

He smiles. "Is there anything else you need from *me*?"

"I wouldn't know where to begin."

It's probably too much to confess this far away from a church, but it's the truth and I can't be ashamed of it now. Something about my tone, stripped down to nothing, gets to Darren though, and I watch him exchange his charm for something terribly honest. I don't know whether what he says next will heal me or tear open the wounds he's only just wiped clean, and maybe he doesn't either, everything silent between us except for each ragged breath I take while I wait.

"You need to sleep—and *soon*," he finally starts, his hands threatening nothing when they inch higher and hold me still. "I'll check on you a few times, but other than that, I'm going to leave you alone. It's been a really long night."

"That's not what you wanted to say." I narrow my eyes, frustration close to pooling there. "It's not what you were going to offer. Are you really that worried you'll break me with a few words? A suggestion or two?"

"I'm not worried that you'll break. Not even close."

"Then why are you biting your damn tongue?"

I'm quiet when I ask, and quieter when I wrap my calloused hands around his wrists. A second later, Darren pulls back or I push him away, and while nothing is wrong, neither of us is more comfortable with the distance between us. I still ache and know without a doubt that I'll fall asleep ignoring it, and I think I'm close to taunting him with as much when he shakes his head.

"Go to bed, Jake."

I leave him there because I don't have a reason to stay, nor the energy to fight. Each step toward my bedroom has my filthy jeans rubbing me in a few wrong ways, and I fall back against my door as soon as I've closed it behind me. There's no reason for it to happen tonight—I know it *won't* happen—but I can't remember the last time I cried, and I wonder whether I'll be alone the next time I do.

The odds are overwhelmingly in favor of it, but my sudden doubt is sharp enough to make me yearn for something indescribable.

Reaching for my belt gives me something better to do, but

once it's unbuckled, I don't bother with it more than that. I take care of the button and zipper next, but when I start to push my jeans down, I wince at the reminder that my body was under a motorcycle tonight. I've still got the door behind me for support, and I rely on it to get me through my next few breaths. None of what I'm feeling is all that bad, but everything is awful as soon as I try to bend forward again. I push at my jeans one more time, but my head hurts and my torso is tender and my leg is screaming until I realize I didn't take anything for the pain. I don't want to move, but I think I have to.

And then there's a knock at my door.

I roll out of the way as much as I do anything, landing clear of the door so I can invite Darren into my bedroom for the second time tonight. His eyes drop to where my jeans are bunched around the wound on my thigh, my boxers visible just above that. My focus is drawn to the shorts he's wearing and the shirt he isn't.

"Tylenol," he whispers.

It's just a coincidence that he remembered at the same time I did, but it feels a little divine, and I slump against the doorframe. "Kitchen. Upper cabinet by the sink. A glass, too. Water in the refrigerator door."

Darren leaves without a word, and I shuffle to the chair already holding my torn jacket and drop into it too carelessly, shifting until ripples of pain settle. I roll my eyes when I see my sleep shorts in the middle of my bed, far out of my reach. I'll have to get these horrible jeans off me before I can care about changing into them anyway, so I fumble for a good grip while also keeping the material away from my bandaged thigh. My coordination is shot—a victim of the ridiculous hour more than anything that would concern me—and it's only my stubborn ass that keeps trying until a cool glass of water is pressed to the side of my arm.

I take it with one hand, the other open for the capsules Darren drops into my palm. He turns away as I swallow them and returns with my shorts, and before I can thank him for that, he kneels between my legs.

Again.

He's careful when he eases the ruined denim over my thighs, but he stops being careful with *me*, and it leaves me unable to speak. His touch extends further than necessary as he pulls my jeans the rest of the way down my legs, Darren's fingertips trailing against my skin from my knees to my ankles, and I don't think I'm surprised when he removes my socks, too. Once he's set everything aside, folded almost too neatly on my floor, he only needs to help me with my shorts, but he never looks in their direction.

Instead, he wraps his hands around my bare calves, and he looks up at me. "I like being here."

I have no idea whether *here* is about my house or my bedroom or the position that would allow him to take me apart if he were so inclined, but I'm not sure it matters. I like him being here, too.

Darren moves, my continued silence taken for the acquiescence it is, his grip sure when he uses it to widen the space I hadn't known he'd claim as his own. His fingers are light against me after that, teasing except for the way they'd do as I'd ask if I had the voice for that sort of thing, and neither of us seems to blink.

Neither of us is a coward.

"If you don't want me to bite my tongue, I won't," he says. "I'll tell you everything."

"Okay."

A raised eyebrow suggests he wasn't expecting that, and he studies me all over again. "Is it?"

"I have a really good life. I'm happy."

"And you're not lonely," Darren adds. "We covered that a couple of weeks ago."

"Mmmm, yeah," I rasp, my voice as worn as the rest of me. "But it feels like I've been repeating it a lot lately."

"Is it becoming any less true?"

"No. I haven't gone nine years without this because I have some perverse need to become a martyr."

He nods and makes a sound I barely hear before one of his hands slides higher, toward the wound he bandaged. He doesn't even pretend to care about it now, bending forward to drag the tip of his nose against my other leg, his breath warm along the inside of my thigh when he goes on.

"Tell me more about your perverse needs."

"Pretty sure you were going to tell me."

"And then what?" he asks.

"And then I'll agree with you."

Darren raises his head, curious and undoubtedly aroused. I

can't see his shorts from where I sit, but he's got his eyes on the front of my boxers, and I let him look. This isn't the time for that though, and we both know it, so he does what he can to clear his throat.

"You've got a really good life and you're happy," Darren says, his fingers toying with goosebumps I thought I'd left at Trailhead. "After all this time, you don't need this."

"I do not."

"But you *want* this. You're still letting me touch you."

"And you're still biting your tongue."

I offer him a tired grin as I call him out, and I think I'd stay here and listen to him tiptoe around his point all night if I weren't ready to fall asleep where I sit. Darren must understand, and he stops touching me long enough to pick up my shorts and hold them close to his chest.

"Do you really want to wear these to bed, or are you okay sleeping in your boxers?"

"The boxers are fine."

He could let the shorts go again, but he doesn't, his gaze steady when it finds mine. "I really like touching you, and I want to touch you everywhere. *Everywhere.* Maybe I've known that for a while, or maybe I just figured it out tonight, but I want it to be me. If you're ever gonna fuck a man, I want it to be me."

"You know I'm not looking for the love of my life."

"None of the men who fuck me are."

I pause at that. The reminder that casual sex is a habit of his. It doesn't bother me, and I'm not sure it was ever all that far from my mind. In fact, this is safe precisely *because* it's a habit of his. I genuinely like him, and he's exactly as attractive as he thinks he is, and I trust the hands that have taken such good care of me since I tumbled into Trailhead. I also trust that he'll want nothing beyond whatever we're starting tonight.

It *is* more than that though, and maybe I understand that already. I'm one of many, and very much not, and it has me reaching for him now.

My fingers comb through his thick blond hair and hold him there. "What are we about to do?"

"Anything we want," Darren says, almost sweet when he covers my hand with his own and pulls it from his head.

He helps me stand then, the moment hushed because it might deserve that, and I mostly fall into his arms, my body done with me a while ago. Both of us exhale, and I don't think it matters that I'm bigger than he is when I become small and bury my face in the crook of his neck. He's keeping me upright, but when I feel him shake, I wish he could spend the rest of the night telling me why. Instead, I'm the one to open my mouth against the warmth of his skin.

"I haven't touched you yet. I want to touch you everywhere, too," I mumble.

"You can. This isn't—" Darren cuts himself off and shifts his grip on me, one arm fully around my back and the other low enough for his hand to slip just under the waistband of my boxers. The pressure at my lower back is there to keep me still while he very, very slowly rocks against me. "You wanted me to tell you everything, and maybe I only sort of did that, so I'm going to be perfectly clear. I want to touch you, and I want you to touch me, and I want us to fuck. But I don't want all of it to be over in a single night. I want to hear the sounds you make when I suck your cock, and I want to know what you look like when you suck mine. I want to know how many ways I can make you come and what you taste like when you do. I want to learn every filthy fantasy you've ever had and then share some of mine. You're so fucking smart and funny and *good*, and I don't know why we aren't better friends after all these years, but I want to get to know you. We're not looking for love, and I wouldn't know how to find it anyway, but I want this. I want to be your friend. I want us to fuck. And while nothing more than this can happen tonight, some other time, if neither of us wants to stop, we don't have to."

I moan pathetically—I know I do—but I can't remember how to feel embarrassed by anything when I'm pressed to Darren like this. He steers us toward my bed, and I finally look at him again.

"Just friends?"

With his forehead against mine, he hums. "Yeah, and I want that either way. Tonight's been wild, and if we change our minds about everything else—even if I never hold you again—I still want that."

"I won't change my mind," I argue.

"Neither will I," he smiles. "But tell me again in the morning."

CHAPTER FIVE

DARREN

I do as I'd promised, shuffling down the hall a few times to check on Jake, careful not to stare too long once I'm sure he's breathing and reasonably comfortable in a bed that must be at least as stupidly luxurious as the one he's allowed me to use for the night. His sheets and duvet are two shades of dark blue, and Jake and his boxers are mostly buried beneath them and the darkness. Still, moonlight has been invited in by curtains left open, and it kisses his gray hair until the sun starts to rise.

But again, I'm not staring, quick enough about each visit to fall back asleep more easily than I think I should.

And a little more deeply each time.

Eventually, when I open my eyes again, I can tell it's late morning, everything about it familiar to me even in an unfamiliar place. I'm hard, but I only bother with a few lazy strokes over Jake's shorts before I realize it's been too long since my last visit to his bedroom. Willing my body to relax, I sit up and rub a hand over my face and force myself out of a sleepy daze I usually enjoy for a while. Then I stand, the carpet thick beneath my bare feet. I should probably take a minute to pee first, but my first steps carry me toward Jake instead, and I don't feel like going anywhere else.

His door remains cracked open, just as I'd left it a few hours ago, but nothing else is the same after that. His bed is perfectly made, and the silence is too loud.

I'm not sure why I expected him to be asleep when most people aren't on my strange schedule, except that Jake was up as late as I was, and his body must have screamed at him to rest. And really, I think I just wanted him to be right here, within reach.

The next moment has me turning toward his bathroom, my stomach upside down before I've even fully imagined how he might've passed out there, but it's empty, too. I take another couple of seconds to clock the subtle scent of coffee from downstairs, and then I imagine him under a pile of expensive blankets while he sips from a favorite mug. That would be fine, of course, but when I see a piece of paper tucked beneath the corner of a decorative pillow, I know he's not home at all.

Had to take care of a few things at work. Yes, I can see just fine. No, I'm not bleeding out. Help yourself to whatever you want and don't rush to leave. And maybe you don't need the ego boost, but thank you for being a damn good bartender.

I read the note again, and I can't tell whether I'm worried, angry, hurt, or disappointed that he left with no other goodbye and is too far away for me to give him shit about it. I read it a third time and smile at a compliment that sounds grouchy somehow. Jake really shouldn't be moving around as much as he is, but he knows that as well as I do. And he's got some kind of businessy hospital administration job, so I assume he can find help from a doctor if he figures out how to ask for it.

As soon as the note and I are back in the guest room, I pick up my phone to say so.

"I wondered whether I'd get this call," Jake grumbles.

"Good morning to you, too. Or should I drop the *good* part of that because your body's busy reminding you of how stupid it was to leave the house today?"

"Maybe you should drop the *morning* part because it's barely that anymore."

I chuckle. "Well, it's a relief to know nothing has changed after last night."

"Nothing?"

"Not this. Not us," I say. "And yes, of course you got this call. Please tell me you've sought some kind of professional medical attention."

There's an audible breath or two and then the slam of a car door before Jake answers. Sort of. "I'm leaving here now. Be home soon."

I don't know which hospital Jake works at, so I'm not sure what *soon* means, but he's gone before I can ask, and I wasn't planning to stay on the phone all day anyway. With at least some time to myself, and Jake's word that I don't need to leave right away, I finally make it into the bathroom to pee and brush my teeth, following that up with a hot shower. It feels exactly as good as I expect it to, but I end it before I can wonder what would happen if Jake walked in on me. Apart from any idle curiosity, I've never actually fantasized about him, and even after last night, I'm not sure it's the best time to start.

I'm perfectly reckless about the sex I have, and unapologetic about it as long as I'm not stupid, but even *thinking* about fucking Jake might require caution I rarely exercise. He doesn't want me biting my tongue, but I should at least keep my hand off my dick for another minute or two.

I grab a neatly folded towel from the rack and dry myself quickly, and then I dig around under the sink until I find a plastic bag I can use to carry my briefs and socks home. With that in hand, I return to the bedroom and opt to pull my jeans over my bare ass before leaving Jake's shorts on a bed I make because it feels like the right thing to do. I've barely worn my t-shirt, so it's fine to throw on now, and I do that before I comb my fingers through my hair and leave the rest behind. Mostly awake but in need of coffee, I make my way downstairs, and sort of stumble at the sight of things I'd missed last night, too focused on my need to take care of Jake.

His house is stunning, obviously. I'd known that much from the moment he steered me toward this neighborhood, and confirmed it easily before coming to a complete stop in his driveway. Even with my attention on Jake, we moved just slowly enough for me to appreciate the balance of stucco, wrought iron, greenery, and the gorgeous terracotta steps that led us to his front door.

But inside, I'd noticed little until now.

Barefoot and gentle, I duck in and out of what must be his home office because, even at my nosiest, I'm uninterested in creeping into every space he's kept private for years. I know I'll end up in the kitchen, so I pass that for now, and find myself in the dining room instead. My house doesn't have more than a small area with a table and chairs, but I'm unsurprised that Jake eats at a gorgeous dark wood table, probably walnut and probably custom-made. It's surrounded by artwork I'd like to study, and a buffet topped with bottles of liquor I'd like to drink. More impressive than any of that is the view, floor to ceiling windows allowing me to take in the backyard I'd admired from above last night.

I think back to Jake's admission that he hasn't had anyone here in a long time, and I ache again with the implications of that. It's not that I don't believe him when he says he's not lonely, but I wonder whether he's carefully carved out some pocket of loneliness here, close enough to reach out and touch before he busies himself with hospitals and Harleys and a few rounds of trivia and a couple of rounds of Guinness. His backyard is designed for more than his solitude, though, no matter how much I'm sure he enjoys the quiet, and I blink hard the moment I imagine myself sharing croissants and coffee with him on side-by-side lounge chairs.

Blinking one more time brings me to the idea of poolside blowjobs and the chance to ride him while the firepit blazes at my back, and I have to press my hand to the front of my jeans for some quick relief before I step away from the window.

The living room is full of the comfort that seems to be forgotten in many of these multimillion-dollar homes, coziness too often lost to the desire to show off to a bunch of people who have all the same things. I can't imagine Jake has ever cared enough about bullshit like that, and while I know nothing about his wife, I doubt she was ruled by ego either. There's an overstuffed couch, loveseat, and recliner surrounding a coffee table stacked with food and home magazines, and the number of throw blankets and pillows reminds me of Beau. I'm drawn past them, though, appreciating the tv mounted above a stunning Spanish-tiled fireplace before I wander close to one of the wide bookcases on either side.

I don't have time to take note of more than the several architectural design books gathered on one shelf before I hear the garage door and bite back any of the new questions forming on my tongue. I'm not all that concerned with being caught snooping, but I move toward the kitchen, and my first closer look at it since I'd grabbed the Tylenol last night. It's a little messier than I would've expected, except that another glance makes me think it's a chore Jake must have abandoned for his bike ride, and I smile at an impulsiveness that feels new to me. I think my smile falters when the door from the garage opens to a small hallway just off the kitchen, and I see him for the first time since he'd slept soundly enough for me to do the same. The wall behind him does a good job of holding him up, and it's probably the nicest possible observation I could offer when pain complicates each new breath he takes.

"Morning," I say.

"Afternoon," he argues back.

I roll my eyes and take a step forward. "Was work that important?"

"Yes," Jake sighs, holding up a hand when I move even closer. "I don't want you to play nurse, and I don't want you to help me out of my clothes again."

He's wearing nice pants, loose enough to be mildly kind to the worst of his wounds, and a button-up too warm for the day, but convenient for covering scrapes that might capture someone's attention. I have no idea whether he usually wears a tie, but he didn't bother with one today, maybe worn out by the time he buckled his belt or pulled on his socks, and his shoes slip right off, kicked toward me like a gauntlet thrown.

I lick my lips and stare him down—this battered and beautiful version of a man I've supplied with more pints than I could count.

"You *never* want me to help you out of your clothes again? Or just not while you're too pissed off and stubborn to thank me properly?"

"Have you always been this cocky?"

"Of course," I smirk. "I'm a spoiled rotten only child."

Jake raises an eyebrow, and the tension he brought home relaxes just a touch. "You were raised by a hardworking single mom, and Beau swears she's a saint."

"Amen."

"Makes it harder to believe that she spoiled you rotten."

"Ah, in that case, maybe I'm not so cocky either," I say, taking another step so I can get a better look at the clothes within my reach. They're not the leather and denim I know well, and I'm spellbound. "Maybe I'm just confident. Like you."

"Mmmm. And is this part of becoming better friends?" Jake asks. "Realizing how alike we are?"

"The very beginning, I think."

"And what happens next?"

Undoing my minor efforts to get closer to him, I move back and grin. "You're gonna go upstairs and get changed into something better suited for your couch. And I still haven't had coffee, so I'm gonna help myself to whatever sinfully good shit you brew here."

"It's just from the farmers market," Jake says, slowly pushing off the wall.

I chuckle and watch him walk away, his limp likely frustrating us both. "Is now a bad time to point out how alike you and *Adrian* are?"

He does his best to throw a glare over his shoulder, but there's no chance it'll bother me, and my only concern is whether he'll get up and down the stairs without his stubbornness giving him too much trouble. I don't check on him, though. I don't follow. I'm nobody's father, and I'm definitely not Jake's.

The aroma of the coffee beans has a hold on me within seconds, and when Jake still hasn't returned by the time I've got a full mug in my hand, I decide to busy myself with the dishes he left soaking in the sink. My own chores tend to be an all-or-nothing thing, but I don't mind setting the coffee aside to take care of one of his. It's easy work, and I'm a few minutes into it when I hear him half-growl behind me.

"Didn't know I needed to add housekeeping to the list of things I don't want from you."

I don't turn right away, at least a little surprised when he steps around the island to come closer instead. My hands are still covered in soapy water, so I continue scrubbing the pot I've already started, and finish rinsing it just in time for Jake to reach over my shoulder for a dish towel hanging on the wall.

"Does it make it okay as long as we do it together?" I ask.

"We're not doing it together," Jake says. "I'm taking over because you're stepping aside."

After he pulls the pot from my hands, I finally turn off the water and face him again, curious and pushy about it. "Is this an I-don't-care-that-I'm-hurt pride thing or an I'm-not-used-to-having-people-in-my-kitchen territorial thing?"

"Will one answer satisfy you more than the other?"

"Nope. I'll leave either way, but I *am* glad you want to know how to satisfy me."

I'm going for sexy levity, but Jake studies me in response and lets the innuendo slide. "Would it really be that easy for you to give up on the idea of helping me?"

Something flares in my chest as he moves away, indignation burning as I consider a question that carries no self-deprecation. Jake's tone suggests no resignation and no fear. He's not accusing me of a damn thing.

And I'm going to defend myself anyway.

I wait while he puts the pot away, careful not to say a word when the motion is enough to make him wince. When he's silently pulled himself together and meets my eyes again, I'm right there, and I let my hands fall to his waist, just to keep him still. The soft cotton of his t-shirt and sweatpants offers one hell of a contrast to the firm body just beneath it, but it's not what I want to talk about.

"I'd like to be really fucking clear about what's happening here," I start, my voice steady because I'm not afraid either. "Cleaning up some blood and bandaging your leg was me helping you. Giving you a ride home was me helping you. Fetching Tylenol and getting you out of your clothes was me helping you. Washing a couple of dishes was me helping you. If you don't want any more help from me, I'll do my best to back off, *especially* if it's something you've done alone for the past eight years, but—"

"Nine."

"What?"

"Michelle died nine years ago," Jake says. "I just figured that was something you should know, even if it's not another way we're alike."

"Michelle," I echo. "Don't think I've heard you say her name before."

"I guess I figured that was something you should know, too."

"Guess so."

He smiles. Barely, maybe, but it's enough. "What else were you going to say before I interrupted? You had a nice little speech going."

I still have a point to make, but Jake doesn't need to keep standing in his kitchen to hear it, and I let go of him to comb my fingers through my wet hair instead. I've got coffee waiting for me on the counter, and we might as well sit down somewhere so I can enjoy it.

"How about I finish my nice little speech on your couch, so you can give your leg a break, and I can drool over your backyard one more time?"

Jake steps to the side and waves me toward the living room, and I don't worry when he doesn't escort me from one place to another. There's a second or two I consider running upstairs to change back into his shorts—the tight jeans that earn me tips at work aren't the best for relaxing at anyone's home—but I really don't think I'll be here much longer, and maybe something should be uncomfortable enough to remind me of that. Jake joins me after I've settled at one end of the couch, grabbing a pillow and lying down with his head at the opposite end and his bare feet in my lap.

The moment is domestic as fuck, but he doesn't mean it that way, and I ignore it entirely. "You asked if it would be that easy for me to stop wanting to help you, and then I listed a bunch of ways I've helped you since last night. But I need you to understand that everything I said in your bedroom—wanting to be the first man who is *really* on his knees for you and wanting whatever comes after that—none of that is about helping you. I'm not doing you a favor, and it sure as hell isn't charity."

"What is it then?" Jake asks.

He's no more prone to bullshit than I am, and he's asking because he genuinely wants an answer, but for as much as I've already told him, I think I need some time before I respond. I take a long sip of coffee and find a loose thread hanging from the bottom hem of his sweatpants. Then I roll it between my finger and thumb for a while before I look up at him again.

"Tell me about your job."

If Jake minds the change of subjects, he doesn't say. "I work in palliative care."

"But not as a doctor."

"No, I'm on the administrative side of things, and I have a team of doctors, social workers, nurses, etc. I'm proud of my work, but they do the best of it."

"And you chose palliative care instead of hospice?"

He shrugs. "I've done plenty of that, too."

I'm close to asking about Michelle—how she died and whether his experience with palliative or hospice care became important nine years ago—but maybe he knows that, and maybe it's why he keeps talking.

"When I was at the hospital this morning, I had a friend look at everything," Jake says, rolling his eyes as he gestures up and down his battered body. "Got some antibiotics and a pleasant lecture about the danger of internal injuries and the importance of stitches—and yes, proper concussion protocol—but he expects me to recover just fine."

I nod slowly and don't hide my smile behind my mug. "A friend, huh? Guess you've got more of those than I thought."

"Relax. It's nobody I'd want giving me a ride and taking me to bed."

"Mmmm, just wait 'til we do those the other way around," I tease, my hand wrapped around his ankle now. "Unless you've changed your mind about that."

"I haven't."

Jake yawns then, and I admire how vulnerable he is, something more obvious about it in the daylight, even if I'd had my hands all over him in the middle of the night. He needs to rest, and I need to go home, but I tip my head toward the kitchen first.

"Do you want me to grab more Tylenol for you?"

"No," he chuckles. "Theo gave me something much stronger. I took that before lying down here."

"Oh, you're about to be a lot of fun. Bet I could beat you in a round of trivia, too."

"You've beaten me before."

I snort. "Barely."

"Maybe my suffering will be enough to give you an advantage tonight."

"Oh, no way," I argue. "I love that you love trivia night as much as I do, but please do not drag your broken ass up to Trailhead tonight."

"I have to deal with my bike, and I told Beau I'd be there."

"You know Beau will help with your bike if you call him. And that'll make him a lot happier than if you show up at the bar just to see his sorry face. So stay here. Nap when I leave. Order food. Ignore the rest of your dishes. Take a book out back. Finish the bottle of wine on the counter."

Jake closes his eyes for a few seconds, already groggier by the time he opens them again. "I have to work, too."

"I highly recommend doing that after the nap, but before the wine," I say. Then I carefully slide out from beneath his feet and keep my coffee close as I stand. "Seriously, I'm not gonna threaten you with the group chat again, but I'd *really* like you to heal sooner rather than later, so please take a break from us for a while."

"If you're not too busy in the keg room, do you think you could text me a few of the really good questions?"

I'm so glad I'm not halfway through another sip, my laugh quick and sharp. "Gonna be free to text you questions all night long, old man."

"Are you gonna keep calling me that when we're—" Jake shakes his head and sighs, but I swear he blushes, too. "When we're better friends?"

"It's not usually my thing, but I guess we'll find out."

"Hey now, I've been around you long enough to know I won't be your first old man. What about the attorney in WeHo?"

Jesus. I'd wanted to ask him about that night, and now that he's brought it up, I have a different point to make. I smile down at him, fully aware that I'd rather drop to the couch again.

"I didn't mean that older men aren't my thing—just that I rarely get off on calling them something sweet mid-fuck," I explain. "Might complicate things more than I'd like."

"Ah, of course. Gotta keep that emotional distance when there's nothing else between you."

I wink before I turn and take my coffee back to the kitchen, doubling back afterward so I can jog upstairs and grab the few things I'd left in the guest room. By the time I return, Jake's pulled a light throw blanket over himself, probably the perfect counter for the air conditioning humming from everywhere else, and his eyes only flutter open when he hears me step close enough to catch him on his way to a nap.

Years at Trailhead have given me plenty of chances to see Jake when he's tired. Hell, last night—or early this morning—I'd watched him sleep in his own damn bed. But something about this is different, and I'd be a fool to compare it to any of the other times I've walked away from someone too worn out to bother with a more enthusiastic goodbye. Jake's a friend, and I'm going to see him again soon enough, and this is barely a goodbye at all.

It still feels like the end of something important.

I pause and think maybe I need a nap of my own, especially when I don't just thank him for the coffee and run.

"Hey, Jake?"

"Hmmm?"

"You asked me what this is," I start, pausing almost immediately to clear my throat. "If it's not help or a favor or charity—you want to know what this is."

"I do."

I press a fist to the back of the couch, careful not to reach any further before I nod once, confident all over again.

"It's a fucking privilege."

CHAPTER SIX

JAKE

I'm relieved, actually, that I'm not expected to be at Trailhead for trivia night. I was knocked out for most of the afternoon, and by the time I forced myself awake again, my body made it known that even the backyard would be off limits, too far for me to travel. When I saw Theo at the hospital earlier, he'd reassured me I'd escaped the kind of major damage that could've ruined me—if it hadn't killed me outright—but now that I've been sitting up for a minute or two, I'm vaguely interested in a second opinion.

I ache from head to toe, and I haven't dared to face a mirror for the worst of it all. Unfortunately, I need food before I even get that far, my second pain pill on hold until I've had something to eat and wasted some time. I don't think I can stand long enough to make dinner yet, but my phone is next to me, and I need to call a towing company about bringing my Harley home.

Once I've made those arrangements, I owe someone an apology and my appreciation.

Sorry I dragged you out of bed to deal with my bike last night but thank you.

Beau responds frighteningly fast, and I wonder whether Darren is watching him. I don't worry about whether Adrian is.

Hey you're awake. I was under strict orders to leave you alone. And you know you can drag me anywhere

Sorry I'm not there tonight. Say hello to Darren and Riley for me.

Stop apologizing. We're not there either. Darren told us you'd be resting. How are you feeling

My thumb hovers over the screen for a minute because if they're not at the bar, then Darren went out of his way to tell Beau to let me sleep, and I don't know what to do with that. My head isn't all that clear anyway, but it's heavy now, and I ache in an entirely different way. It's a friendly thing to do, sure, and giving me time to recover has nothing to do with any future plans we've made, but it feels quintessentially Darren in a way I barely know and somehow know very well.

Tired and sore but it's nothing that won't heal. I'll eat and then sleep it off.

Glad to hear it. And tell me when you want me to pick up the Harley from trailhead. I can drop it off at your place any night after work

My hand hovers over my phone again, curious about how much Darren said—whether Beau knows where I live, and that I didn't spend the night alone—but I keep my response brief.

You've done plenty. A tow truck can handle the rest.

You're hot but you're stubborn. Fine. Just don't crash and burn on us next month

Next month?

Now it takes some time for Beau to answer, so I struggle to my feet and make my way to the kitchen to pull leftover pasta from the fridge. I'm tempted to eat it cold, which is enough to remind me of Lucy, and I wonder whether I should call her to let her know about the accident. I decide against it only because I'm fine, and she doesn't need to worry about me. My dinner gets reheated, I take several deep breaths, and by the time I'm settled at my table to eat—with water instead of wine—my phone chirps with a new text.

I want it to be a trivia question, I think. I don't hate that it's Beau again.

Sorry Adrian was telling me to stop bothering you

You haven't bothered me yet.

Next month is his grand opening. We thought it might be sooner but Mason has a bunch of new paintings he wants to debut the same week Adrian's gallery opens so we're waiting

Mason Burnett is an artist with a gallery in West Hollywood, his work loudly erotic and something I'd probably buy for a couple of my walls if I weren't busy reminding myself that I really want to own several of Adrian's photographs first. Mason's been to Trailhead a few times, and we met briefly once. He'd noted Adrian's talent there in the spring, and from what I understand, he's the reason Adrian is making this huge career leap. Beau's comment leaves me a little confused, though.

Why is Mason calling the shots for Adrian's big night?

Careful. You almost sound concerned

I snort and assume Beau can imagine it just fine. *Hardly.*

It's not a problem. Mason's ego helps Adrian more than it hurts

Okay. Do you need anything from me?

Just put yourself back together so weho can lust after your face and Adrian's pics side by side.

I roll my eyes and pretend I'm not smiling as I type some kind of promise for Beau. I eat my dinner in silence, mostly because I haven't bothered with music all day and don't have the energy to do anything about it now, and I catch up on a handful of texts from colleagues checking in on me. This morning, I'd rearranged a couple of things in my schedule and let everyone know I wouldn't be back at the hospital until after the weekend, so some of them are expectedly curious, and I give everyone the shortest possible story for my sake.

Last night was a strange one, and I think I can barely explain it to myself.

Another glance at my phone shows that the one person who might understand it best is too busy with work to be talking to me if I'm not on the other side of a pint glass.

I clean up when I'm done eating, and I shuffle through a check of locked doors and turned-off lights before I make sure I have a glass of water to bring upstairs. Having to be cautious with each step is a frustrating contrast to the ride I'd taken through Angeles

Crest, but it's one more chance to remind myself that I'm not dead, and that's a habit I've been familiar with for years.

When I step into my bedroom, it's the first I realize that as much as I *hurt*, I'm not tired after sleeping all afternoon. I'd forced myself through a brief shower before going to work, but now I set the water, pain pill, and phone on my nightstand, then turn for the bathroom and the opportunity for a longer, more helpful shower tonight. I'd love to soak in my oversized tub, actually, but the gash on my thigh won't allow for that, and I sigh when I put an extra bandage over Darren's butterfly stitches for the second time today.

A closed door helps steam fill the bathroom quickly, and I step into the stall to let the hot water relieve some of the discomfort I expect to carry for days. Crashing like I did would've hurt anybody, but I'm on a slow slide toward 60 now, and on a night like this, it's hard to forget. I'm strong, and I've never damned my body for anything, but when I look down at myself—wet chest hair gone gray, muscled leg torn open, skin marred by the evidence of a life well lived—I imagine what it will be like to be naked with a man who probably has so few scars and far less physical proof of his age.

I wonder if I should be more nervous than I am.

I've been wholly aware of my attraction to men since my early 20s, but I was married by then, with a baby on the way, and any fantasies remained vague, distant things. Throughout the past several years, hours with a drink in my hand have given me reason to daydream in more detail, but I'm not sure I ever thought something would come of it, my needs met for so long that I've mostly ignored the idea of them since.

I'm not lonely.

But I'm so incredibly sore.

And maybe neither matters once I've scrubbed my body clean, and I stare as the last of the soapy rivulets covering my skin run clear. A second later, I picture Darren's fingertips tracing those same crooked lines, his beautifully arrogant smile calling me to relax under his touch. I'm calm now and breathing easily, but I reach down to where I'm so obviously aroused by the thought of his hands on me, and I begin to stroke myself like he might. For a guy who must have perfected the quickie years ago, he'll take his time with me—I'm certain of that even when I can predict little of anything else—and I keep myself from hurrying through anything tonight.

I have no idea whether showers are something friends share, but I feel sexier in the water than I do almost anywhere else, straddling one of my Harleys probably the only place I feel more powerful. If Darren won't join me here one day, maybe I can at least give him a ride.

That makes me choke, and my perfect rhythm stutters. I want it all.

My shower is huge, and the small bench seat gives me every excuse to sit down, so I pause long enough to adjust the angle of the spray and make myself comfortable all over again. I'm leaning back against the cool tile wall, my legs spread, and it's all so much like V's office and my bedroom, when Darren knelt there and claimed the space as his own. The memory has me wrapping my hand around my shaft again, eager to prove that I didn't want him to bite his tongue last night, nor do I want him to stop talking anytime soon, and if any of my body protests the beautiful tension building now, there's enough in me to soothe it, too.

Touching myself like this hasn't always been about drawing out my pleasure. It certainly hasn't been a chore either—it feels great, and I won't offer a confession for any sin like it. But I've spent so many years indulging in food and drink and music and travel, that sex has become an afterthought more than anything. It's easy to want this though, and it won't take much longer, especially when I can see Darren so easily. Hear him, too.

If you're ever gonna fuck a man, I want it to be me.

My grip tightens, whether it's a conscious choice or not, and I make no effort to loosen it again. I've gone a while without this and I'm on edge now, desire taking shape in a way it hasn't for years. My mind jumps from one filthy thing to the next, and it's over so soon after that, my release there and gone when the water rinses it away. I take longer to catch my breath, and I stand only because I'm eager for my bed and pillows and the chance to sleep deeply until morning. My foggy bathroom blankets me when I step out of the shower, and after I've grabbed a towel, I look toward a mirror I can barely see. Bare but hidden, I decide to forgo any self-care routine that takes longer than the time I need to brush my teeth and tear the extra bandage from my thigh.

Returning to my bedroom on legs that still feel weaker than

I'm used to, I find the shorts Darren set aside last night, and I grab those and a t-shirt once I've pulled a pair of boxers on. My phone shows notifications for several emails I swipe away and one more text from someone at work, but there's nothing from Darren and no reason for me to bother him. I sigh and prop a couple of pillows against the headboard, then crawl into bed with a book I haven't touched in a week, the thriller not quite thrilling me yet.

I don't pay attention to how long I've been reading—only happy the story has become significantly more interesting—but the sound from my phone is enough to startle me in the silence of my room. Blinking, I realize it's late, and that trivia night ended a while ago, but of course the message is from Darren, and I tap it open.

You still up?

My smile probably doesn't matter when he can't see it, but it feels good after the past 24 hours. Before I settle back against the pillows, I take the painkiller and drink half the glass of water, then I answer Darren.

Usually asleep by now but awake tonight.

Waiting up for someone?

Depends. Is someone about to tell me he changed his mind about spending his shift in the keg room?

Haven't changed my mind about anything. Zach called out. V stayed. No phone time for me

And no trivia for me.

There's an extra beat or two before the next text, and I use the time to set my book aside and scoot further down the bed. Then a picture appears on my phone, a dim snapshot of the back of a bar receipt with a scribbled question: What's the collective term for a group of flamingos?

Oh. He wrote one down. I hurry to respond. *A flamboyance. That had to be a hit at the gay bar, huh?*

Lol it really was. But I think I'm a bigger fan of a murder of crows

I'm partial to an exaltation of larks.

Didn't know that one. but happy as a lark? Makes sense

I'm not surprised that Darren made the connection that quickly, but I shake my head, amused by it all the same.

Another picture arrives: Who are the only siblings to have won Oscars for lead acting?

It takes me a moment, and I'm disappointed in myself for that, but before Darren can accuse me of looking it up, I answer him.

Joan Fontaine and Olivia de Havilland

Of course. You a fan of old movies?

Not necessarily a huge fan, but I have some favorites. You?

Nah, that's a Beau thing. I watch a bunch of shitty tv.

Guilty pleasures?

Except without the guilt

I have nothing to say to that, but it doesn't matter when he sends me another question, and another after that, my eyes getting heavier after he and I have gone back and forth about a handful more. When I get a couple of them wrong, Darren gives me shit as well as he would've at the bar, but there are chances for me to tease him too, and I don't miss. I yawn though, and at some point I need to admit it before I fall asleep and disappear on him entirely.

It's way past my bedtime and you need to close up.

Darren doesn't respond right away, and I figure he's either busy serving the last customers of the night or getting a head start on the closing I just mentioned. It's only then that I wonder whether he'd thought about coming over tonight—to check on me or for anything else he's just started to want—and while I don't think he'd be bothered by my need to sleep, I'm close to making sure I haven't let him down.

And I can't figure out whether telling him about my shower would make anything better or worse.

Before I can worry about it, Darren's back.

You're working from home tomorrow?

I am.

And not coming to the bar right?

I don't have the energy to chuckle, but I think I try. *Have I been banned from trailhead? Do you plan to send Beau over to guard my door?*

Maybe I'll send Adrian instead

You really would

Lol

My eyes fall closed, and I tell myself to open them again, at least to be polite and say goodnight, but I'm so tired now. The shower and orgasm and painkiller, combined with being comfortable in bed and chatting with Darren, have relaxed me in a way that I needed, and I'm not sure I have the strength to fight back against something that feels so good. I leave my phone somewhere in the space next to me—one I haven't rolled into in the past nine years, and won't move any closer to tonight—and a few seconds or several minutes pass before I hear the sound of one more notification.

A text I don't read until morning.

Missed having you here tonight

As the next several days pass, I'm feeling better. At my age, it'll take me a while to get back to the shape I was in before the accident, but I'm not limping, my bruises are on the other side of their worst, and I can sleep without meds, over-the-counter or otherwise. My broken bike is back in my garage, and I haven't decided what to do with it yet, the damage done there separate from any other wound still healing. It's fine, though. I'm fine.

My return to trivia night is fine, too.

Noah greets me with the relief of someone who'd believed I survived my accident, but needed to see it for himself. Adrian sits back with a predictably neutral smile while Beau hurries to smack an obnoxious kiss to my cheek. A moment later, Riley takes all of us by surprise when they slip out from behind the bar and wrap their arms around me. The words whispered in my ear aren't anyone else's to know.

It's all more than fine, actually, except that there's a huge bachelor party taking up a third of the room and probably all of the beer garden. Beau, Adrian, Noah, and I all tip well, but we're no match for the rowdy groom-to-be and his friends, so Darren rarely has time for more than a smile in our direction. With Riley around, I'm not sure I'm the quietest among us, but I sip my Guinness and answer every quiz question and say very little.

I watch Darren's back-and-forth more closely than usual, but my friends are easily distracted by noise and laughter, and Riley is the only one to raise an eyebrow in my direction. They could be curious about my recovery. I doubt it's that simple.

My second beer is long gone by the time I unofficially win, and Noah has already ducked out. I need to go home too, but Darren catches my eye right after I've said a polite goodnight to Adrian and just before Beau wraps me in a hug. Meeting Darren at the other end of the bar requires effort I've never made at Trailhead—pushing past a crowd to get to a gorgeous, half-dressed man isn't usually my thing—but he's grinning when I get there, and I think it's worth it.

"Sorry I didn't get to talk to you tonight," he says.

"You've been a little busy," I shrug. "And you're talking to me now."

"Did they tell you about Adrian's grand opening?"

I nod. "Beau gave me the heads up last week, and then I got more of the details tonight."

"Great, so—" The bachelor calls for Darren then, happily drunk and about as loud as I'd expect at this point in the night.

Darren turns to him, then back to me, his hand wrapped around my elbow. "Do you want to go out for tapas with me?"

The jump from a WeHo photo gallery to a tapas date doesn't feel like a logical one, but Darren is already backing away with the promise to explain more later. It probably doesn't matter when my answer would be the same either way, and I relax like it's the type of invitation I get from friends all the time.

It used to be, before most of them stopped trying, but I'm grateful for another chance. "Yeah, that sounds great. Just text me a time and place."

I leave then. He sends me the name of the restaurant the next day, and we make our plans. On Saturday, I'm restless enough to rely on weed and motorcycle repairs to keep me busy, and smart enough to make sure one doesn't overlap with the other.

Tonight, I don't need either of them. Tonight, I'm driving my car, and I'm on my way to meet Darren.

As usual, my music is loud, and the perfect company to keep when nobody else is around, and I only turn it down when I'm close enough to look for a place to park on the street. When I've found something a block away, I step out of the car and stretch between one deep breath and another. The early October night is warmer than usual, and without a Harley as an excuse to wear it, I've left my leather jacket at home. My dark green t-shirt fits tightly and suits me just fine, my jeans and boots are a way of life, and all of it makes me feel good. But even with that confidence, seeing Darren fully dressed makes me stumble a little every time it happens, the hundreds of nights I've seen him shirtless at

Trailhead far outweighing the hours I've spent seeing his torso covered.

I smile at him as I approach the restaurant, surprised that he's early.

But I need to stop being surprised by him entirely.

He pushes off the wall he's been leaning against, and when I dodge the mischief in his eyes, I find myself close to reaching for the buttons of his linen shirt, simply because they're new to me.

Most of this is new, and the reminder hits hard, but then I nod toward the front door. "Let's get inside so you can explain what we're doing here."

The restaurant isn't particularly big, and we're guided to a small rounded booth against a wall whose cracks and peeling paint add to the ambience more than they detract. That there's ambience at all is a strange thing to note when we're a couple of hungry friends prepared to eat our weight in tapas, but I love good food, and I'll enjoy it no matter how dim the lighting might be, and no matter how softly the music plays. With our menus in hand and the hostess gone with a silent nod, we decide to share a pitcher of sangria and browse the long list of tapas.

"Wait," Darren says, his hand pushing my menu toward the table. "Obviously we can order anything tonight, but the explanation first—I was tasked with finding a place that can cater Adrian's gallery opening. And there are a hundred places to choose from, but I figured this might work well. Classier than traditional bar appetizers. Still small enough that nobody has to spend a long time eating at once. I know Adrian's serving beer and wine, so these should pair well. What do you think?"

My eyebrow rises and falls when Darren mentions Adrian, but we both know I want to help, so I lift my menu again. "Yeah, there are things here that won't work—messier options better for a night like this—but plenty that people can pile onto small plates and go. Have you been inside the gallery to see what the space is like?"

Our server stops by long enough for us to ask for the sangria, and then Darren tracks the guy's ass all the way back to the kitchen. It's a nice ass, but I'm not sure I've ever been as bold about wanting to follow one across a room. I'd make some kind of joke about it, but then Darren's eyes are back on mine, and I remember I asked him a question.

"No, I haven't seen it in person, but Beau sent me some pictures. There isn't much room, so we'll either need to plan for servers to walk around with trays or set up a few separate stations around the gallery."

I nod. "Not ideal, but not unexpected either. Is there a budget?"

"We can't go completely off the rails, but there's enough money to feed everyone more than bread and cheese."

I nod again, and both of us make room for the pitcher and glasses the server brings. We haven't done more than glance at the tapas list, but Darren and I are easy to please, and it's not difficult for us to pick out some mushrooms, shrimp, chorizo, eggplant, squid, and Manchego before the nice ass is gone again. We tap our glasses together in a wordless toast, and then I sit back to study the restaurant, moderately busy for a Sunday night.

"Have you been here before?" I ask.

"Nah, I just looked it up online and thought it seemed like a decent idea." Darren stops and tilts his head without bothering to hide his grin. "Why? Did you expect me to have connections here?"

"I expect you to have connections everywhere."

He laughs, and the dimples I've known for years take a long time to fade. "Oh, come on. You've been out with me before. I don't know everyone."

"No, but you get to know them very quickly," I point out. "And it's been months since I watched you charm half of WeHo, so a Spanish chef or two didn't seem out of the realm of possibilities."

"*We* charmed half of WeHo. Don't even fucking pretend you don't know what you're like."

"No, no, no. Please tell me what I'm *like*."

Darren seems to think about it for a minute, stalling with a long sip of sangria until I finally give in and do the same. Even in a small booth, there's some space between us, but he leans into it now, the glass still in his hand while he looks at me with a challenge in his eyes.

It's probably a reflection of my own.

"Fine. Obviously, there's the whole 'daddy' thing, but that speaks for itself, and you might as well own it. It's hot. But other than that? You're the strong, silent type. Out of reach somehow. Unapproachable, even if you're one of the nicest guys I've ever known. But men are suckers, and they dare to try anyway, and then you flirt with them more smoothly than anyone on that side of the bar."

"Nice caveat. Riley *is* quite good at making everyone fall in love with them," I tease. "Barely has to try."

Darren starts to shove me, but I think he remembers my accident somewhere halfway through, and he does what he can to pull back at the last second. It leaves him closer to me than he'd intended, and he doesn't have time to do much about it before our server returns with a tray full of food. We get easily distracted then, and I doubt either of us is sorry. Everything on the table is incredible, and our best attempts at conversation are mumbled compliments about one flavor or another. Everyone at Adrian's grand opening will be incredibly well fed.

Our shoulders remain pressed together, easy only because Darren's left-handed and has no reason to give me space. The sangria goes down smoothly, and we keep offering each other bites of things we've already tried. Neither of us is tipsy, but I think we're both close to sated, and small talk feels new when we haven't wasted time on it before. I'm not sure how much longer passes before we push the last of the plates away, but then we're still touching and too lazy to put distance between us.

I think it's only when I can't suppress a yawn that anything changes.

"You should probably get back home," Darren says. "You're looking a lot better since the night I tucked you into bed, but I'm not gonna be responsible for keeping you up too late."

"No?" I ask.

"No."

He gets our server's attention then and pays shortly after, my fight to take care of half of it—at the very least—lost before it's really begun. I surrender and thank him, and we're outside before I think I want to be, but I sort of wave over my shoulder in the direction of my car and try to remember how a night like this is supposed to end. It's not a date, but it's not Trailhead either, and I'm grateful for the confidence that keeps my head up while my heart pounds.

"Thank you for dinner."

"You're welcome for dinner. Mind if I walk you to your car? I parked over there, too."

"No," I say. "I don't mind at all."

It doesn't take long to get there, but something about rounding the corner and ending up in the dark—the dim of the restaurant only partially preparing us for this—makes me wonder just how far we've gone. Darren has never seen my car before, but he's following closely enough to slow when I do, and instead of moving toward my door, I back myself against the passenger side and don't blink when he crowds me there.

"Are you planning to stay out a little later?" I ask. "You're a night owl. You probably have plenty of time to grab another drink or two."

"Is that your way of asking if I'm gonna get laid tonight?"

"It's been known to happen."

Darren grins. "Happens all the time."

"Then yeah, I guess that's what I'm asking."

I don't know why I'm so curious about his sex life when I've had a decent view of it for years, but I don't run from my question, even when I think he'd let me. And Darren's smile hasn't gone anywhere, but he takes another several seconds to respond, like maybe he's giving me time to change my mind.

"Not sure I'll go straight home from here," he says. "But I won't be fucking anyone, and nobody will be fucking me."

It's on the tip of my tongue to ask where he'll be, but something about it seems off limits, and I nod instead. "Have fun and be safe then. And I'll see you back at Trailhead this week."

"Hmmm."

"Hmmm, what?"

"You *don't* know, do you?" Darren murmurs. "I mean, you know you're attractive and you know you're smart and you know you've got a good job and a great house and plenty to offer someone if that were a thing you were looking to do, but you—that night in WeHo."

I raise an eyebrow. "What about it?"

"You could've had anyone you wanted."

"As long as I didn't want you, right?" I chuckle. "I'm pretty sure you were halfway to the bathroom with that guy before you even remembered I was there."

"I remembered you were there, Jake."

"Okay."

He shakes his head and reaches for the hem of my shirt, but it's nothing like the times he's touched my clothes before, and I don't know what comes next. I trust that he does, and I keep my eyes locked with his, even when he moves to tuck his fingers into the front pockets of my jeans. The placement of his hands helps keep a careful distance between us when Darren finally leans forward to drag the tip of his nose over my beard, his mouth open just below my jaw.

"I'm not going straight home, but I'll get there eventually. And because I have no plans to hook up with anyone before that, there's a damn good chance I'll be horny and eager to come. You'll already be sound asleep, so I can't come *with* you, but that might not stop me from coming while I'm thinking about you." He pauses when I shiver, and then I feel him exhale against my skin. "Is that okay?"

"Yes," I say just before I clear my throat, sharply aware he must be able to feel it. "I did it the other night."

His breath catches and he pulls back to look at me again, his eyes wide. "You did what?"

"In the shower. I thought about you."

"Tell me."

"Darren—"

"You don't get to bite your tongue either," he argues. "This has the potential to be a lot of fun, but it only works if we talk. I don't want to hold anything back. Not if it's about us."

When he says *us*, I know he's referring to our little agreement, but something about it makes me shiver a second time—that single-syllable commitment from a man who must've told himself not to make them anymore. I don't have that kind of vow left in me, but I can do as he's asked and thank the wind for sweeping it away.

"The night after the accident."

I stop and take a deep breath, and when our foreheads are pressed together, I'm not all that sure how it happened. It doesn't matter, except for how much I swear I can feel him against my lips while we're still too far apart for that to be true.

"Tell me," Darren says again.

"I wanted to take a hot shower. I wanted to relax. My whole body ached, but when I looked at the water running down my body, I thought about you touching me like that."

"Good. I'm glad you thought about me."

"Are you?" I ask.

"Of course," he says. "Did thinking about me make you hard?"

"Your fingertips tracing the path of the water. You telling me to relax. Yeah, I—it did."

"Say it."

"It made me hard," I sigh.

"And then what?"

I nudge the tip of his nose with mine. "I don't know what to say about it."

"Had you ever gotten yourself off while thinking about a man?"

"No."

"Have you ever told someone you got off while thinking about them? Said those actual words? 'I made myself come while I was thinking about you?'"

"No."

"Will you do it now?"

My hands have been at my side, curled into loose fists when I wasn't paying attention, but now I lift them to Darren's forearms and hold on. He wants this, and I want to give it to him, but I take a moment to wait for the shame several priests once promised I would feel for a few different sins.

It doesn't come, and I'd never really expected it to.

Maybe Darren wants to reassure me of something, though. He finally lets go of my pockets and rids us of the last couple of inches between our bodies, and just as I notice his arousal, his mouth skips past mine and stays closed when he presses it to my neck.

I lick my lips and remember sangria and showers. "I made myself come while I was thinking about you."

CHAPTER SEVEN

DARREN

The french fry being unceremoniously dunked in my chocolate shake is gone a second later, but I finished all I wanted
to eat a while ago. Sangria and tapas left very little room, and I've
never minded sharing. Besides, there's too much going on in my
head for me to crack a joke about my favorite food thief, and I
plant both elbows on the table and rest my chin in my hands.

"I almost kissed a man tonight."

Sage snorts as she grabs another fry. "Oh, breaking news. Local
gay stud nearly engages in an act favored by middle schoolers
who spin bottles."

"Hey now."

"What? Why do you sound so surprised? And why did you only
almost kiss him? He's not straight, is he?"

It's my turn to snort, just as I fall back against the booth. "No,
not straight. But also—he's not someone I'm supposed to kiss

just because I enjoyed sharing dinner with him. I'll kiss him some other night, when we're—"

I trail off and sip from a shake I don't want anymore because it's probably kinder than treating a 20-year-old to the story of another escapade—past, present, or future—even if she's calmed my busy head a hundred times before. I'd met Sage her second night of working here as a teenager, and my habit of making people comfortable around me had meant she'd stopped shaking by the time she brought me carbs and ice cream that very first time. Then she'd turned around and mastered that same habit, and while I've never been as unsteady around her, Sage figured out how to keep me still better than when I was on my own, and quieter than I knew how to be anywhere else. Within weeks, our middle of the night conversations had turned to friendship, but it means we know each other well. She smiles now, too curious for her own good.

"So, you're planning to fuck him."

"I am."

"But you went out to dinner with this guy tonight, had a great time, and couldn't kiss him goodbye because you haven't fucked him *yet*?"

"Come on, what's with the filthy mouth?"

"Don't baby me, Darren."

"Wouldn't dream of it, kid," I say with a wink. "And yeah, he and I—we weren't on a date. I've known him for years, and recently we talked about fucking around together, but that's it. I shouldn't want to kiss him goodnight. Not like that."

Sage slides out of the booth, other tables deserving of attention, too. "God forbid. It's gotta be all or nothing, or else you'll accidentally fall in love."

I ball up one of my dozen napkins and throw it at her before she can walk away, knowing full well that she's sassing me and ignoring the way my heart pounds in spite of it. For our own messy reasons, Jake and I don't do love anymore, but Sage hasn't experienced that kind of heartbreak, and I'd rather keep her belief in fairy tales intact.

Her belief in that one, at least.

For everything she knows about me, I've learned plenty about this young woman and her own story, and her faith in a happily ever after is one of the few things that motivates her day after day. Her parents have been married since about five months before she was born, and they've stayed together through another six babies after, and when Sage can forget how difficult her life has been, she wants little more than what her parents have. They're all stretched too thin though, and she's been working to help support the family for a long time. From what I understand, that's also true of her closest sibling, River, though I've only met him once.

I hope he believes in love, too.

But I've been done with it since my divorce, and Jake's been done with it since his wife died, and while kissing someone without being halfway to an orgasm is certainly a thing people do, I think tonight I would've been reaching for something that isn't there, and I like to keep my hands free anyway.

For a moment, I consider waiting for Sage to return so I can make an argument on my behalf without hurting either of us. Instead, I leave too much cash on the table and give her a grateful wave on my way out the door. Even an incomplete conversation with her has relaxed me, and the short drive to my house is one I make without the restlessness I'd brought to the diner. Once I'm home, I'm comfortably sprawled on my bed within minutes. I do exactly what I told Jake I would, each familiar stroke of my cock made more interesting when I remember he got off thinking about me. His confession wasn't one I expected, but I replay it over and over now. When I come, as unabashed about it as ever, I only wonder how much longer it will be before he can hear me.

The next day, we all receive texts with an official invite to Adrian's gallery grand opening later in the month, and when V quickly agrees to cover Trailhead with Zach, it means Noah, Riley, and I can RSVP immediately. It takes Jake longer, probably because he's in his office buried under work, or maybe on the phone with his daughter, but after another hour or so, the group text receives his yes, too.

I don't actually talk to him until he's back for trivia night again. He walks in wearing a leather jacket so similar to the one torn in the crash that I might not have known it was any different if I hadn't seen the damage myself, and his jeans fit him as well as any pair I've admired before.

I'm shirtless, of course, and I hope he's admiring me, too.

It's difficult to keep from going straight to him, but a line of bottles and drafts in front of me keeps me busy, and I nod a casual hello before I hand out the beer and move on to another couple of drinks. There's always a rush of orders right before the host rouses the crowd, and I'm grateful for the chance to move with it tonight. Last week's bachelor party meant I didn't have to consider how Jake and I might have changed after his wreck, but our dinner only muddied friendly waters, and I think I'd underestimated the reaction I'd have to hanging out with him here. We'll spend the next few hours in a space shared by people who know both of us well, and there's a chance that a conversation with him could give too much away.

My friends can know about everyone else I fuck around with, but I don't think I want them to know about Jake.

And really, I can't imagine Jake would want everyone at Trailhead involved in his personal life. He's always mostly kept to himself, and whatever his motorcycle crash knocked loose between the two of us, I'm guessing he'd prefer that it stay there. As much as I love everyone here, they'd have so many opinions, loud and uncensored, and I don't—

I don't want anyone to point out just how stupid it is to expect me to be good for anyone.

So, while I only sort of kinda meant to, I've somehow switched ends of the bar with Riley, giving them more time to talk to our friends for the second week in a row. I refill a few drinks for our liquor vendor and the friends he's brought with him, and I monitor Zach's work around the room. Our spare bartender is still cute, and I'm still unsure he'll last through the end of the year, but neither requires an intervention on my part, so I take inventory of the rest of the crowd. Most of the stools at the bar are full, as are the high-top tables scattered throughout Trailhead, so many people waiting with a pencil in one hand and alcohol in the other. I wink at one I followed home a year ago. I wink at another I think I'd follow home now. I spot two couples shooting pool, and both will tip incredibly well as long as Zach doesn't fuck it up. Nobody is riding the bull, and that's been true more often than not lately. I make a mental note to ask V about it, but then the host taps the mic, and I let my heart beat a little louder while I listen for question one.

I throw a look over my shoulder, in time for Jake to level me with a curious stare, and then trivia night officially begins, and I pour someone a gin and tonic before mouthing the answer to him the second he's done scribbling his own. It continues like that for a while—hear a question, serve a drink, match Jake's answer with mine while nobody's the wiser—but when the first round is over, my seven correct to his eight, I still don't move any closer.

Riley, as usual, kicks my shoe. "You're not mad at him."

They're not asking, but I shake my head anyway. "No, not at all."

"Are you scared?"

"Of?" I ask, clearing a few empty bottles from the bar and smoothly popping the caps of their replacements.

"Jake riding a motorcycle again. Or crashing a motorcycle again, I guess. Beau and Adrian told me what it looked like the night he got hurt, and—"

"He was here last week," I interrupt, my voice firmer than it needs to be. It wasn't until the afternoon I brought Beau and Adrian a case of wine and two bottles of whiskey that I'd heard the details of what they'd seen on the off-ramp. How far Jake must've skidded. How ridiculously heavy the bike was. The blood that seemed to be everywhere, an image my big bear of an ex couldn't shake for a couple of days. I swallow around the reminder of it now. "If I were scared, don't you think it would've bothered me then?"

Riley smiles. "You were busy with the party, and he drove his car last week."

"Of course he did. I don't know how you know that, but it feels right that you know that."

"You haven't answered my question," they say, steady as they stare and their eyebrow piercing shifts higher.

"Nah, I'm not scared. I was concerned the night it happened, and wouldn't have wanted him to get back on a bike too soon, but that old man knows what he's doing, and it wouldn't do me any good to be afraid of it."

Riley nods, and it feels like I got away with something. I gesture toward the beer garden, willing to miss the start of round two while I check on anyone drinking outside tonight. I love it out there, and I give myself a few seconds after I first push through the door to take it all in. The string lights hanging overhead are probably more trendy Pinterest wife than gay shitkicking beer lover, but maybe it's good to take people by surprise once in a while. We have large picnic tables lined up in two rows of three, a bathroom tucked into the corner, and a muted version of the music people dance to when they're not taking a test for fun. I'm not sure whether any of the details are the draw for me, or whether it's simply the relaxation that comes with drinking outdoors. The freedom that comes with a deep breath and quiet conversation.

I'm romanticizing it, probably, but I might as well get starry-eyed over a beautiful night if I'm not looking for someone to fuck me in a dark corner of it.

There are seven people out here now, the most interesting among them a tall, gorgeous nerd curled over the book he's reading. The other six are coupled up at a single table, and I push away from the building to check on everyone. None of it takes me long, but by the time I'm sliding behind the bar again, I only catch the very end of question ten and the careful tilt of Jake's head.

I really need to go over there.

But because I've already started working this end of the bar, and because Zach is distracted by two of the men bent rather beautifully over the pool table—his good tip is probably a sure thing now—I get waved down for half a dozen tequila shots. Once I've poured those and handed over the requisite salt and limes, I hear the host announce the next round, and I'm ready to duel with Jake. Two underage kids with terrible fake IDs derail me, and I sigh.

Sending them on their way doesn't take long when they don't put up a fight, but then I'm grabbing three more beers and a shot of whiskey, and I can't do much more than turn to give my friends a thumbs up or down for each question as the host rolls through them. I make it to them, finally, for the last one, standing just behind where Riley has leaned across the bar to brush a finger over a cut on one of Beau's knuckles.

"Here's the last of round three," the host says. "What do you get if you multiply all the numbers on a roulette wheel?"

"A fucking headache," Noah snorts.

Adrian half chokes on his Jack and ginger, and I'm not sure I've ever heard Riley legitimately giggle before, but Beau is enamored by both of them while I look at Jake. His pencil is already down.

"You knew it immediately," I say.

"So did you," he fires back.

"Oh, great," Noah starts. "Is this where we find out that Darren used to be a flair bartender in Las Vegas, and Jake is a high roller who regularly stays in a penthouse on the Strip?"

"Hey, why can't I stay in a penthouse?" I ask.

Beau smiles. "I'm sure you've been invited to plenty of penthouses, you pretty, pretty woman."

I roll my eyes and meet Jake's again, suddenly curious about his gambling habits and whether he'd look better all dressed up for dinner and a Vegas show, or in nothing but some wet swim trunks while sipping a cocktail from a poolside cabana.

I wonder how hard it would be for me to find out.

The trivia host rolls past us, ignoring Jake's paper as he goes, and then Noah looks back and forth between Jake and me.

"Okay, what was the answer?"

"Zero," Jake says.

"There's a zero on the wheel," I add, maybe just to play along for another moment or two. "So, it doesn't matter how many other numbers there are—multiplying anything by zero will always equal zero."

Noah takes that in, and a wink from Jake goes unacknowledged by me when I disappear again. I make a sweep of the room being largely ignored by Zach, grateful for the way most of the crowd has been too engaged with fun facts to notice, and I breeze through drink refills with no need to think all that hard. Everyone is gearing up for the last regular round before the fifth and final one, but I find myself in the beer garden again. The group of six has left, either helping themselves to the darkness on either side of the building or cutting through the bar while I was busy fantasizing about Las Vegas, but the reader is still buried in his book, and I leave him to it.

And maybe I don't have a choice about that when Beau backs me against the wall, his deep brown eyes close to a suspicious glare.

"Hmmm. You're not mad at me," he says.

"Why does everyone think I'm mad tonight?"

"Because it's your favorite night of the week, but you're not spendin' it with any of your favorite people. You could pop a hundred bottle caps, chug a beer of your own, and still beat everyone but Jake at this shit. I've never seen you focus so hard on a liquor pour in the decade I've known you, nor do you usually hand over that side of the bar to Riley, so yeah, my first guess was that you're mad."

"Oh, please," I scoff. "You love Riley."

"I do, and that was definitely not my point."

"Right. Because your point was that I'm not mad."

Beau growls, and it's strange that I still remember what the sound tastes like. "Adrian wanted me to thank you again for giving us the lead on that tapas place."

"Yeah? Did you guys get that worked out? Will they cater the opening?"

"We did, and they will. Do I even want to ask how many restaurants let you 'sample' something before you picked a favorite?"

"Wasn't like that," I tell him. "I only made one stop."

He chuckles a little at that. "He was that good, huh?"

"He—who was good?" I ask, my cheeks warm in a way that's always been more Beau's thing than mine. I don't think Jake told him we were out together, but they've been sitting next to each other at the bar tonight, and I've been anywhere else, and maybe—

"Whichever tapas chef gave you a taste test."

I laugh. From anyone else—or spoken to anyone else—Beau's words might angle close to cruel, but the past year or so notwithstanding, he's been with nearly as many people as I have, and I know he doesn't care whether I'm fucking my way through a couple of restaurants a night. And I might argue that if I'd really hooked up with someone at the Spanish restaurant, then he and Adrian would've gotten a hell of a deal on the catering, except that his assumption saves me from having to explain that I took a friend out for a nice dinner and never made him come.

"The food was good, and the gallery opening is gonna be incredible. And Adrian is very welcome," I say. "Are you gonna fuck off now?"

"Mmmm, are you still takin' me out for my birthday next week?"

"I always do."

"And I can give you more shit then?"

"You always do," I chuckle.

Beau gives me a kiss on the cheek before he flips me off with a smile, and I knock his cowboy hat sideways just because I can. A second later, I follow him inside and can't help but look down the bar at the way Jake is laughing at something Noah must've said, and Riley delivers another Guinness, and Beau stands just behind Adrian to rub his shoulders until he moans.

The trivia host moves on to the next question—I don't even know what number they're on—and I restock a couple of things and clean a few others. Zach is actively working again, so he ducks behind the bar for anything he needs, and I drift closer to Riley when I need to make room, staying there long enough to be stumped by a question Jake doesn't know either. I'm busy closing out a tab and handing out another draft beer when I hear the host wrap things up, and when I turn around again, Adrian is sliding off his stool and into Beau's arms. They haven't been playing anyway, so they don't need to stick around for the final round, and the goodbyes are predictable when there are hugs and kisses and some version of a polite nod between Adrian and Jake. Riley blows a kiss, and I do the same from further away.

With a bit of a break for scores to be totaled, I have time to handle a quick wave of requests from our liquor guy, four 50somethings who have nothing on Jake, and a slick regular I'm convinced will run for office someday. We all trade smiles before I turn toward the register and Riley lands next to me, their hands wrapped around a towel. It's a tell, and I'm ready to give them my attention for whatever they need.

"Do you think this grand opening party is a plus-one kind of thing?" they ask.

Oh. Well. The compassionate and selfish parts of me collide, and I swallow hard just to censor a response or two. "Did you not want to ask Beau, or did you just not get a chance tonight?"

"Didn't get a chance. Not with everyone—"

"Yeah, no. Totally get it," I say when Riley trails off and looks somewhere over my shoulder. "And I think you're absolutely welcome to bring a plus-one. I can't imagine Adrian would have the slightest problem with it, but I—do you *want* to bring some-one?"

They frown, and the host announces the final round, and I run someone's credit card and twist the cap off a bottle for someone else. The night is winding down now, and my focus on Riley has barely wavered, but it hasn't helped me get an answer any sooner, so I try a slightly different approach.

"Would it help if we do the pros and cons again?"

"Pro: Ethan has been in town more often, and I think maybe he's trying. He's taken me out a couple of times, and he might say yes if I invite him. Con: Even when we go out, I don't feel the way I do when I'm with all of you."

"How do you feel with us?"

Riley's pale blue eyes meet mine for an important second and then shift away again. "Like I can breathe without it hurting."

I nod and move to grab another coaster, clicking my pen too many times before I start writing.

Riley, you deserve to breathe without pain every single day, whether we're with you or not. And no matter what anyone tries to do for you, if it still hurts, it's okay to want better.

When I press the coaster into their palm, I hold it there, testing limits in a way that would have Beau thumping the back of my head. But Riley doesn't flinch, and I'm not all that surprised when they make eye contact again as I speak.

"I'm not gonna have a date, and Jake won't have a date, and maybe Noah will bring some pretty girl to a queer photo gallery, but that barely counts. Mason will have a date or several, but I'm not sure that counts either. You get to do what's right for *you*, and I swear I'll try not to say shit if you bring Ethan. And if you come alone, I hope each breath you take feels fucking perfect."

I walk away then, and at some point during my conversation with Riley, Jake and Noah had huddled over the final round's pictures in time for Jake to be the unofficial winner. Probably. God knows I've been all over the place tonight. But they're just finishing up as the host counts down, and I let Riley clear their drinks, surprised only when Jake asks for one more.

He's sticking around then. I'm not used to that.

Kinda wish I could sit down and drink with him. I'm not used to that either.

But at least a few more people need me, and I know Zach is already angling for his escape, so I stay where I'm at and take care of business. Trivia night gets wrapped up with a flourish, and I greet the winner with a congratulatory grin when I credit their prize toward their bar tab. Then I wave Zach off before I duck outside again, the reader gone now, and no sign of a mess left in his wake. Mess or not, I need to wipe down the tables, so I turn for the small server station we keep stocked for our busier nights, and I run right into Jake.

He catches me at my hips, his thumbs brushing over my bare skin. "Hey there."

"I'm not mad at you."

"For needing to use the restroom?" He smirks, and whether it's a response to my comment or the choice to touch him back, I'm not sure. "I'd hope not."

"No, I—wait. There's a bathroom inside."

"There sure is, but it's totally full, and I got impatient."

"Did you?"

Jake cocks his head. "I did."

"You're having another beer."

"Are you concerned about my bladder or the bar inventory?"

I laugh. "Neither, really. But you usually leave once you've sufficiently kicked my ass at trivia."

"Impossible to know whether I kicked anything tonight. You were awfully busy."

It's a blatant callout regardless of how gently Jake delivered it, and we both know it. We're probably stupid for standing so close to each other—our hands on each other wholly unnecessary—but the Trailhead cameras are aimed over our heads to catch the picnic tables, and nobody will spot us here unless we end up sprawled across one of them.

Or unless they open the back door, but that threat isn't enough to make me let go.

"So, is that why you're having another? In case I slow down?"

Jake studies me for several seconds and I get half hard under his stare, but then he tips his head to the side. "I really do need to use the restroom."

I take an exaggerated step backward, and once he's out of sight, I return to my quest for a wet towel. I'm somewhere between one table and another when I hear the bathroom door open and close, but I don't turn around, proving a point to myself more than anyone else. I double-check for any trash on the ground as I clean, leaving the string lights on just in case anyone wanders out here before I close.

Back inside, I glance at the fifteen or so still drinking, and then I pull my phone from where I'd tucked it behind the bar hours ago and make my way over to Riley and Jake.

"Noah took off?" I ask.

"Yeah," Riley confirms. "And he said he probably won't be here next week, so we'll see him at Adrian's."

"I might skip next week, too," Jake says. I raise an eyebrow, and he goes on. "There's a bunch of stuff going on at work—regional meetings and assorted bureaucratic fun—but a night in WeHo sounds like the perfect way to recover from that."

"Weird. I usually have to recover from the night in WeHo," I say.

"Gotta start choosing a bed over a bathroom stall," Jake teases.

Riley works on restocking the half of the bar I abandoned for the night. Once I've closed another couple out, I pull up the Trailhead socials again and scroll through anything new since the last time I liked and commented my way through it all. A few minutes in, I find something that gets my brain rolling.

"Hey, do either of you ever read the things people say about this place online?"

"Like reviews and stuff?" Riley asks, a rack of glasses in their hands.

"Nah, more like questions and comments on all the social media accounts Adrian set up for us."

Jake takes too long to swallow a sip of his beer and then shrugs. "I haven't been on any of my accounts for months."

"Yeah, I deleted most of my stuff a while ago," Riley says, dropping the rack onto one of the coolers to unload the glasses.

I lower my phone and put my hand on my hip. "Most?"

"I'm not on anything where I'll find an official Trailhead account. And why are you asking? Is something wrong?"

"Not at all, but I—someone asked if we have live music here, and someone else said no, and then someone else said, 'Oh, it would be sooooooo cool if they had a band come in like once a week,' and a bunch of people liked that."

Jake nods. "And now you're wondering whether that's the next big thing V should consider."

He's right, of course, and I look around the bar from where I stand. We host trivia and karaoke from the dance floor, but that's probably not a great option for a band when people will want to dance to any live music being played. Rearranging the high-top tables and stools on the other side of the dance floor would make some room, but I don't think cramming the band and dancers next to each other is much better. The pool tables are too much of a draw to go anywhere, but there's the—

I almost smack myself in the forehead, because I could've saved myself some trouble by starting with the one area that's been ignored more often than not lately.

"Nobody really rides the bull anymore," I say. "I think we could probably do a small stage setup over there if V would go for it."

"Might be worth looking into," Jake agrees. "But she'd have a lot of numbers to run before you go telling everyone it's a sure thing, so you're gonna have to bite your tongue for a minute."

"Or you could bite it for me."

It's out of my mouth before I can stop it, certainly no worse than a thousand other things I've said to anyone I've served in my years here, but still weirdly dangerous when Jake's looking at me the way he is. Riley doesn't take me nearly as seriously and shakes their head instead.

"Talk to V, let her decide, and then you can go wild with all the little people in your phone if she says yes. Of course, then she'd also have to find an actual band, so maybe you can ask those same people for help."

"You mean you can't find us a band from your super-secret site?"

Riley treats me to a very pretty eye roll and wanders off to finish anything they need to do before they go home. Jake taps his glass against his coaster a couple of times, and I don't miss that he's got less than half his beer left to drink. It has me shoving my phone into my back pocket so I can lean across the bar and give him my full attention.

He grins. "You slowed down."

"That I did. But you're not gonna be here much longer."

"No, I have to be at work early tomorrow morning."

"And a lot next week," I add. "So, I probably won't see you then."

"You probably won't. But you could come home with me after the gallery opening."

It's bold, maybe. Or would be in a hundred other scenarios, but I already crossed more deeply drawn lines when I told Jake I want him to fuck me, and an invitation like this is nothing at all.

It's everything, too. I'm far too smart to pretend otherwise.

"And just as I was about to drag you to the keg room," I murmur.

"You were not."

"No," I say. "I would never."

I straighten just as Riley reappears, layers of their personal armor in place before they wave and head for the barn doors. Jake continues to drink, Guinness becoming the sand in an hourglass, and I feel like there are things to say or do, but I have no idea what any of them are. He'll leave soon, and both of us will be busy, our work and sleep schedules offset enough to require effort for us to meet in the middle. And while we could do that this weekend, maybe Adrian's celebration will be the smoothest way for Jake and me to end up sweaty and breathless without calendaring a separate occasion entirely.

A group of four stops by to drop off their empty glasses and close their tab, and others who've been done for a while leave without a word. Usually I'd go wipe down their tables, but I don't feel like moving all that far away yet, and I wouldn't have had the chance when Jake clears his throat.

"Did the rest of your Sunday night go as planned?"

I turn to meet the mischief in his eyes. "You mean, did I really stop somewhere to *not* fuck before going home to take care of that all by myself?"

"Yes."

"I really did."

"Glad to hear it." Jake grins and chases it away with the last of his beer, the glass soundless when it hits the coaster. "And with that, I'm gonna say goodnight."

He slides off his stool, and turns for the bathroom first, and I use the time to make sure the three guys left in the bar—all of them older than Jake, bigger than Beau, and as comfortable in mesh as Mason—need nothing from me. As long as there are no surprises, it'll be an easy rest of the night for me, and Sage probably won't see me again until my weekend restlessness hits too hard.

I've never told anyone about my trips to the diner, and when Jake returns, I'm strangely curious about whether he has any habits like mine.

Maybe I could ask him over biscuits and gravy, french fries, and a chocolate shake.

"See you in WeHo," I say.

"And then we'll go back to my little home in the hills?"

My head tips back when I laugh. "Yes, we'll go back to that very little home of yours."

He's through the doors seconds later, and it feels all wrong, saying goodbye to him from so far away when I'd been able to press my body against his less than a week ago. I rub my hands against the front of my jeans and glance at the well-dressed bears before I escape from behind the bar and mumble a quick promise to be back in a minute.

Jake is parked where he probably always is, but when I see him climbing onto his bike, I think maybe Riley wasn't all that far off when they'd asked me whether I was scared. My heart kicks at my chest, and I almost forget to move from where I stand just outside the barn doors, finally remembering to speak up just as Jake reaches for his helmet.

"Hey."

He throws me a look over his shoulder, somehow unsurprised

to see me hurrying toward him. "Did I forget something?"

"No, not really," I say when I catch up. "I just thought we should—"

I trail off because I'm about to make my point just fine. The fingers of one hand find his leather jacket and hold on tight, and I use my other hand to cradle the side of his face just before I bring my mouth to his, open for him already because I'm not great at doing anything halfway. For someone who hasn't kissed in nearly a decade, Jake figures me out easily, and his tongue is warm against mine like he'd been ready for it all along. I moan, and then he does too, and it takes a stupidly long time before we want to be anywhere but deep inside each other's mouths.

When I manage to pull away, he licks his lips, and I barely stop myself from going back in.

"Darren."

"Yeah. Hi. Or bye, I guess." I rub the back of my neck and remind myself that none of this is a big deal. "Not that we couldn't have waited to do that after the party, but it seemed like it might be helpful to take one small step before then."

"Just a teeny tiny step," he says. "Hardly significant on its own."

"And now it's time to find out where we go from here."

CHAPTER EIGHT

JAKE

My black pants are tailored to fit me perfectly, and I know my dark purple shirt will look even better if I leave the top few buttons undone, my gray chest hair on display for anyone daring to look. Of course, at the grand opening of a photo gallery in West Hollywood, I assume damn near everyone will dare, and I don't think too hard about the one person who will take it further than that. Instead, I add my nicest leather jacket—more than I need tonight, but exactly what I want—and as I run a hand over my short beard, I admire how well I've combined decades of confidence with a couple of weeks of recklessness.

I want to be wanted, and I know I am.

There's a part of me that needs to be more precise about it than that, because it feels important to acknowledge that Darren wants me *physically*, his bedroom monologue and our incredible first kiss proving that much. But no matter how long I stare at myself in the mirror, I can't pretend that's where it ends for either of us. He sees me as far more nuanced than anyone described in terms of a single superficial desire, and for as much as he's correct about me, he must know it's true of him, too. He'd called me smart and funny and good, but we're evenly matched on every level.

Maybe the better point to make is that neither of us wants each other *romantically,* and I nod at the relief that comes with leaving my heart undisturbed.

Downstairs, I put my shoes on and grab my keys and wallet, my phone already in my jacket pocket. The drive to the grand opening is as chaotic as I expect it to be on a Friday night, but any tension I feel is the good kind, and I lean into it now. I won't deny that I'm nervous too, but I know honesty will get me everywhere, and I only get goosebumps when I think about how well Darren will reward me for it later. Seconds of daydreaming leave me with the need to attempt advanced calculus until I can keep my arousal at bay, but then I'm parking on the street and the tension returns to drag me out of the car.

While I'm certainly here to support Adrian, I had no interest in arriving early enough to get caught up talking to him without something of a crowd, so there's a notable buzz from the gallery when I'm still a couple of stores away. I'm more focused on that than anything else around me, so I'm almost at the door before I notice the familiar smile—more timid tonight than at Trail-head—approaching from the opposite direction.

"Hi, Riley," I say with a smile of my own. "It's good to see you here."

I think I mean that it's good to see them here without their significant other, whom I've never met and don't like, but I don't dwell on it either way. Nights at Trailhead are always a little better when Riley's around, and I'm sure it'll be just as nice to have them around tonight.

"Good to see you, too. I don't really do this sort of thing, so I'm glad I don't have to walk in there alone."

It's not a sentiment I share when I've been mostly alone for a very long time, but I nod as we step inside. "Serving a crowd from behind the bar is entirely different from mingling among those same strangers."

Riley doesn't have time to respond before we're met by Beau, his cheeks pink and his brown eyes shining with pride, as handsome as ever when none of his face is hidden by a cowboy hat. He ushers us forward to where a small table has been set up with the beer and wine Darren had mentioned over dinner, and Riley claims a bottle of water before I accept a small cup of red. We're barely a sip in when Beau is gesturing around the room.

"There are three small spots set up with food, so you can stop by any or all of those. Adrian and Mason are makin' the rounds, and both of them can answer any professional questions you have, but we didn't really invite you here for that. I mean, you *can* buy stuff. I think he's so fuckin' talented. But you're here because we love you and just wanted you to celebrate with us. Neither of us expects you to do anything but relax and enjoy yourselves."

"Fucking hell, Beau, they're not gonna enjoy themselves if you don't let them swallow. Trust me, I'm an expert on that topic."

All three of us turn to find Darren's shit-eating grin, and Beau plants a kiss right on it before responding. "We all know, and we're so, so proud."

Darren's got a beer in his hand, and he raises it for a toast. "To Adrian, who I assume has better things to do tonight than hang out with us."

We all drink to that, and there are probably a few more jokes Darren would love to crack, but Beau has more to say, and I think it would be difficult to find anyone who doesn't want to listen to him.

"If you do walk around to look at his pictures, you'll see a handwritten note from Adrian near the bottom of each one," Beau starts, his focus mostly on Riley, though Darren and I get a quick grin aimed our way. "For a lot of people, the emotions Adrian tried to invoke will come easily, and he loves that a moment he's captured can have a powerful effect on anyone. But he also thought others might be interested in knowing how *he* feels about his pictures, before or after anyone's taken the time to figure out their own feelings about what they see. He wrote a little about them, and he hopes they help."

Beau's explanation carries an air of formality that makes me wonder whether Adrian made him rehearse it in the car on the way here, but I stop myself from being bitter about it when Riley moves a little closer to Beau. They aren't looking at him, their gaze locked on the nearest wall as they take a deep breath, and I hold mine.

"Yeah, I think that could mean a lot to people. The effort—" They reach for Beau's hand and hold it for a second that doesn't last long enough. "It matters, and I hope he knows that."

I wasn't privy to whatever conversation between Beau and Riley, or Riley and Adrian, or Adrian and Beau might've precipitated this one, but I understand the gist of it and appreciate what Adrian's done for at least one of his guests. And while I don't know where to go from here, Darren does.

"Where's the erotic section? I want to start with those."

"And if Adrian's notes are good enough, maybe you'll finish there, too," Riley says.

The unexpectedness of the quip sends Beau into a coughing fit, Darren patting his back until Adrian arrives to investigate the commotion. The gallery is starting to fill, but there's still room for all of us to greet him without acrobatics. Darren goes for the immediate hug, Riley leans in to give Adrian a gentle kiss on the cheek, and I smile in a way that doesn't feel forced.

"Congratulations on your big night," I tell him after a sip of wine. "I'm looking forward to seeing everything you've got here."

"Thanks, Jake."

There's a high-pitched whistle from several feet away, and we all turn to watch Mason—made taller by the crate he's standing on and the platform shoes he's chosen to wear—wave his arms in the air as though the sound itself wasn't enough to get our attention. To call him flamboyant would be reductive on a few levels, I think, but his shirt has the word spelled out in sequins, so perhaps I can be forgiven the slight.

"Welcome, everybody, and thank you so much for being here to celebrate Adrian Ortega and his absolutely stunning photography. My name is Mason Burnett. I have a little art gallery two blocks away, and I'm incredibly excited to have another talented fucker so close to me. Everything displayed on the walls tonight is available for immediate purchase, or you can place custom orders for other sizes—and don't we all wish we could get custom sizes sometimes?" He pauses for the laughter we all deliver, and I chance a look at Darren just because. "Please help yourselves to the delightful little food and drinks and keep your filthy hands off everything but me. Adrian and I are both here to answer any questions you may have, and all complaints can be directed to the dumpster out back. Thank you again for spending your evening with us. Adrian loves you dearly, and I'm here for a really good time."

Adrian waves at the crowd but bites his lip when he looks at us a moment later, his comfort level in a crowd like this much closer to Riley's than Darren's. He's just about to reach for the hair that's fallen over his forehead, but Beau pushes it back for him, and while it's not the first time I've watched him do it, the gesture hits me differently tonight. It's been a long time since I've had permission to touch someone so easily, and I blame those years for why my fingers brush against the small of Darren's back, just to bring him closer to the group of us and nothing more.

It helps my case when Noah arrives then, and we're all pressed more tightly together in the increasingly busy gallery. Everyone shifts to make room for him, and Darren's hand ends up on my thigh while we're distracted by hugs and hellos, gone again when Noah gives Adrian a sheepish grin.

"Sorry I'm late. Bullshit at work and far too much traffic and all those dumb excuses nobody cares about once they've got a drink in their hand. Super impressed by you, though. Congrats on the big day."

"Thank you. And everyone is kinda coming and going tonight," Adrian tells him, stealing a quick hug as much as the space allows. "I'm grateful that all of you made it. And your mom sent a ridiculously beautiful flower arrangement that I'll put on display as soon as this place clears out again."

"Wonder what it would take to get her to bail on Trailhead for a night—when Darren and Riley aren't covering for her—so she can party with us properly," Beau says.

Darren is careful to avoid choking on his beer when he fights back a laugh. "We were all out together to do the bar promo in the spring, and she couldn't handle being away even once she was already with us. Remember, she and Noah went back to check on everything."

"Yeah, and she was ready to leave WeHo long before we actually did—and then she ended up working behind the bar 'til close," Noah adds. "To get her to take a legit night off, with neither of these two working? One of you would probably have to get married."

Suddenly everyone is looking at everyone else, eyes wide.

Adrian smiles easily. "Nope. Beau and I have already had that conversation, and there will be no wedding."

"Been there, done that," Darren says.

"Been there, done that," I echo.

Riley seems surprised that we've paused long enough to want an answer from them, but then they shrug. "I left my plus-one alone tonight."

Both Beau and Darren look exceedingly proud, and then Darren turns back to Noah. "Why can't you be the one to get married? Then V would have to party all night."

"Funny. I can't manage to date a woman long enough for my mom to *meet* her, much less attend a wedding for her."

"You know," Darren starts, a thoughtful finger raised in the air. "If you're still having woman troubles, might I suggest you try—"

"You *have* suggested," Beau interrupts.

"And I *tried*," Noah laughs.

I watch them all tease each other for another several seconds and can't quite decide whether I want to hear more of that story later. My eyes meet Adrian's for a moment, and I think he might already know what this is about, but before I could even think to ask, he takes a deep breath.

"Not to run from this cute trip down memory lane, but I should probably make the rounds and woo as much of WeHo as I can," Adrian says. "Enjoy the pictures, but don't feel obligated to buy anything, no matter how mean Beau looks when he threatens you. We all know Riley can take him."

There's probably something to learn there too, but I mumble my goodbye alongside everyone else's cheerful ones. With Adrian lost to the crowd, Beau is excited to show Noah and Riley around the gallery, and I assume he leaves Darren and me behind because he's all too familiar with Darren's mouth and won't force me to manufacture a string of compliments for a man who's less than a friend. Of course, that means Darren and I are free to explore together, and with the room pushing the limits of the fire code, it's easy to explain why we're touching in at least a few different places.

I'd say I'm too warm in my jacket, but the gallery has been kept notably cool, and I don't think the temperature has anything to do with what I'm feeling.

It's the worst possible attempt to distract myself from anything, but I take the time to study Darren's outfit more closely now that the rest of the Trailhead crew isn't around to care where I look. He's wearing black ankle boots with studded accents that might reflect the gallery lights if the crowd weren't blocking every path. Of course, I care little about shoes when I move on to his burgundy pants, tighter than the jeans I know well, and I admire their success at showing off everything without shame.

Everything.

We're both aware that I'm staring, but Darren doesn't make a sound, nor does he attempt to draw my attention somewhere else. It's sexy—both his confidence and his patience, actually—and it loosens some of what's been pulled tight in my chest. He's been cocky since the day we met, but tonight he's already giving me every chance to take what I need, including this bold appraisal of his body, and he hasn't met it with the smirk I've seen him offer a hundred other men. I'm sure that time will come, but there's no hurry, and my eyes meet his briefly before I look down again.

His thin gray sweater looks impossibly soft and almost certainly expensive, and I'm unsurprised that Darren knows when and where to spend his money. After years of sitting across the bar from him, the past several months have shown me how much we have in common, and I think I might own a couple of things just like this. When I lift my hand and bring it close enough to touch, he only covers it with his own and guides my fingers over the material lying flat against his stomach.

Darren holds me there and takes a sip of beer as if the moment isn't important, but neither of us is going to lie like that out loud, and I drink my wine to keep my mouth full, too.

I don't know which one of us moves first, but there's been an unspoken agreement to let go and ease our way past the other guests so we can see what Adrian's chosen to display for his grand opening. V had a handful of his photos printed onto large canvases for Trailhead, so I'm aware of Adrian's tendency to capture the fleeting details missed by anyone waiting for their subjects to pose. His gift is undeniable, even by someone as difficult as I am, and I'm already fairly certain I'll order at least a few framed pictures before I go.

We pause in front of a black-and-white photo of a man's hand, his paper-thin skin covered in liver spots and wrinkles and wrapped around a waffle cone. There's something about those details alone—the visible contrast of age and innocence—but everything is complicated by the melted ice cream dripping over the back of his hand and the inability to see his reaction to it. Is the sun shining on his smile? Does the mess frustrate him? Does he lick it off or find a napkin or ignore it in lieu of finishing his treat? And the thing is, Adrian would know. He took the picture and saw everything and then chose to give us no more than this perfect peek.

Or maybe there's something in his handwritten note, but I decide not to look. What's right in front of me is enough.

"Have you bought any of his stuff?" I ask.

"For my place? Nah, I haven't really—" Darren cuts himself off and shrugs close enough for me to feel it against my shoulder. "But I think my mom might really like some of these. Maybe I'll pick something out for her."

I swallow the last of my wine and turn toward him. "What were you going to say about your place?"

He doesn't answer right away, finishing his beer before he takes my empty cup and leaves to discard both. Unbothered, I slip behind another few guests until I'm positioned in front of a second picture, this one in color. Freshly mowed grass. A brand-new gravestone, made for someone who didn't live to see their 27th birthday. And a muddy boot, its shoelace coming untied, angled to suggest an intentional stop and the chance to mourn this loss. Lovers? Siblings? Friends? A stranger who caught the eye of this passerby and gave them a chance to say goodbye to a dozen people they'd forgotten?

Adrian probably knows a lot less about this one, and it doesn't matter when I ache either way.

Then Darren returns, his hand just under the back of my jacket when he steps closer than necessary, even in a crowded room. "I haven't really done anything to the house since Beau moved out. It's a nice little place. Nothing *needs* to be done, so I just—haven't."

It makes little sense that a man who doesn't stop moving hasn't redecorated several times over, but I let that go and approach from an angle that feels less like a diagnosis I'm not qualified to make.

"And it's never strange—bringing guys back to a house that's very much the one you shared with your husband, and not one that you've made your own?"

He licks his lips and watches me carefully. "How much have you changed about your house in the past nine years?"

"I don't bring anyone home."

"Neither do I."

It's immediate, my recollection of Darren's invitation to stay at his house the night of my accident. At the time, I'd been so far gone to my vulnerability, and I hadn't considered the possibility that there was anything that could've turned Darren upside down. I know he's prone to the kind of sex that wouldn't often follow him home, but I'm shaken by the knowledge that there's been nobody at all. I'm suddenly curious whether our same filthy conversation would've taken place in his bedroom too, or whether he was only willing to drop to his knees on my floor. Then my voice fails me for reasons I can't explain, but he's patient with me all over again, and I don't fight hard enough to thank him. Not yet.

Eventually, I clear my throat. "So, is there really an erotic section here, or were you just giving Beau a hard time?"

He smiles slowly, a beautifully crooked little thing. "I have given Beau many, many hard times, but there is also an erotic section here, and I'd be happy to spend some time there with you."

"There are probably a lot of people over there already."

"Is that your way of saying you'd rather stay where we are?"

"No," I answer. "It's my way of saying we're going to end up pressed even closer together as soon as we get there."

His hand falls away from me, but I catch him easily, my pinky linked with his so I don't lose him when he leads me toward the back of the gallery. The layout of the primary space is simple—four rectangular pillars in an otherwise open room—but beyond that, there's an area separated by a pony wall on the left and a more closed-off section to the right. I assume the latter is for the restrooms, and probably a small office, but we end up surrounded by at least a dozen people murmuring about the display here. I think hanging these in the furthest corner of the gallery was probably for Adrian's comfort, but he should be ridiculously proud, and I guess I'll have to tell him that later.

For now, I'm caught up in quiet lust.

Two fingers pushed between barely parted lips. A hand splayed over a deeply arched bare back. Fingertips nearly lost in the dark curly hair at the end of a happy trail. The tip of a tongue tracing a vein that must be exactly where I think it is, except that the picture is cut off so precisely that nothing more is given away. A zipper being tugged downward, over a bulge prominent enough to suggest something weeping with need, and from where I'm standing just behind Darren, I don't deny that it's a sensation I know well.

Darren reaches back for me, his hand slipping between us to stroke me once, then twice. "Are you getting hard while looking at my ex-husband's dick?"

"Pretty sure I'm getting hard thinking about yours."

"Jake."

"What? Did you think I wouldn't answer your question?" I ask, the tip of my nose brushing against the shell of his ear before I leave room for plausible deniability. "In all the time you've known me, have I ever been shy?"

"Not at all, but you've always been private. And you've never had a man touch you like this in the middle of a fancy gay party. Wasn't sure you'd let me get away with it."

My eyes fall to a picture of a man's chest, covered in dark hair just starting to gray, and wet streaks of milky white. It must be Beau again, unless Adrian has other models willing to bare themselves like this, but I don't care who it is when I envy the state he's in. I twitch, and Darren adds more pressure just before he takes his hand away, but I focus and keep my voice steady.

"I'm plenty private, and I've never had *anyone* touch me like this in the middle of a fancy gay party," I clarify. "And I think you have a good idea of what you can get away with."

"Do I?"

"We can't cause a scene. I won't do that to Beau or Adrian."

Darren nods, his back still turned. "And we can't leave yet. We haven't been here that long, even if I think we'll both spend enough on these pictures to cover the cost of an apology."

"You planning to hang nudes of your ex in your bedroom?"

"No, but if you want to hang them in yours, don't let me stop you."

I smile, even if he can't see it. "I'll have enough to look at in my bedroom, won't I?"

"Anything you want to see," he agrees.

We're quiet for a minute or two, moving toward the last few pictures, though I don't know how much either of us takes in when our minds are elsewhere now. Or I suppose we're thinking about a lot of the same things Adrian has captured, matted, and framed, but no matter how many jokes we make, none of it involves our friends this time.

"I'm not shy, but I am nervous," I say.

"I'm glad."

"Why?"

When he remains quiet again, it's just like when I asked him about his home, except that he doesn't walk away from me this time. Instead, he glances over his shoulder—the side where I'm not blocking his view—and decides something. I trust him. I wouldn't be here if I didn't. And it's why I don't hesitate when he murmurs a command.

"Follow me."

We escape the crowd without the crowd caring that we're gone, and Darren leads me down a small hallway behind the walled-off section. As I'd guessed, one door is marked for staff only, even if I've heard Adrian is working alone for now, and then there are two restrooms, one unlocked when Darren reaches for the handle. Practiced at this, he shuts the door, flips the lock, and pins me against the wall next to it, his hands at my waist.

I barely have time to moan before his tongue is in my mouth, welcome and warm, and just as I'd had to remind myself when he kissed me outside of Trailhead, any comparison I could make will cut me deep. This is Darren, and he feels and smells and tastes like someone new, and I let myself have this for the few seconds it lasts. Then, when he stops to look at me and the world slows down, I stifle a laugh and shake my head.

"You said you'd never drag me to the keg room, but you thought this would be okay?"

"It's practically new," Darren says.

"Oh, well, as long as we can be the first."

"We're not fucking, though."

"No?"

"No. You asked why I'm glad you're nervous, and it's because it's a reminder that even after I had my hand on your dick out there, we can't fuck in a bathroom, practically new or not. We're not gonna fuck behind the building or in your car either. Hell, tonight, we don't have to fuck at all. This is new for you, and I'm not gonna treat you like someone who can't handle it, because I'm not that fucking stupid. But I *am* gonna make sure this is fun for both of us, and that specific fun is happening much further away from a bunch of photography-loving partygoers."

I do what I can to ignore the ache he's alleviating with each roll of his hips, the movement nearly unnoticeable except for the way I'm desperate for it. "So, you just brought me here to kiss me and promise me my own comfortable bed?"

"No, I brought you here to suck your dick and make you come."

His hands have already moved to my belt, and he's deft about unfastening that and anything else in his way. He doesn't stop to ask whether I want this, but I don't expect him to when we both know the question would frustrate me. We're friends who have agreed to play this game, and even without having discussed the rules, I know the only one in place is that we'll set our own limits. Darren will do anything he wants—and he'll do it well—unless I speak up to say no.

And I don't.

Won't.

Because we lack the luxury of time, Darren drops to his knees without fanfare, and I already know he can show off a hundred other skills on a hundred other nights. He only pushes my pants and boxers out of the way as much as he needs to, and he doesn't pause to study how turned on I am, nor do I pause to worry about how wet my tip must be by now. Instead, I gasp as he slides his mouth over me quickly and then pulls back with his tongue pressed to the underside of my shaft. One of his hands holds my shirt out of his way while the other fondles my sac, his mouth leaving me slick and sloppy when his head bobs forward and back again.

And again. And again.

I'm sure Darren has done this far too many times to count, and it's probably rare for him to be anything less than enthusiastic about it, but I'm still stunned when he slows to look up at me with such unabashed satisfaction. I think I'd tell him that, but he's gone again, too busy memorizing every ridge and vein and the slight curve that only one other person has ever loved. It's another comparison I can't allow myself to make, so I bite my tongue and let his take me apart.

The blood rushing through my body chases memories that chase back, but when he relaxes enough for me to hit the back of his throat, the side of my fist knocks against the bathroom wall and my other hand clasps his shoulder. Darren hums around me in response, and then with his mouth still full and saliva visible everywhere, he looks up again to find me staring. My face is warm, and my lips are parted until I have to trap the whimper threatening to give so much away, but I think my restraint is admirable. It's been so damn long since I've been here, but he wants more from me, and he isn't anything less than blunt when he makes his plea.

Darren backs up and teases my slit without breaking eye contact, and then he smiles. "You taste so good already, but I want it all. Let go of my shoulder, hold the back of my head, and make me swallow every drop."

I make a helpless noise—the same one I'd barely contained before, I think—but Darren sounds nothing like her, and I need to *stop*, and I need him to keep going. The years have let me forget the intensity of this, and I want badly to remember his talented mouth simply because it's his and nobody else's. His hand falls to his lap just long enough to press the heel to the front of his pants, and his growl makes me shiver.

Eventually, I do as he's asked though, my fingers curling into his hair and making him growl a second time. He takes me deep again, sucking and stroking while my breathing becomes more ragged, and for a few moments I regret letting him start something that has to end so soon. The feeling doesn't last when I realize it would be over quickly either way, and my grip on his head tightens as I mumble a string of things both carnal and contrite.

Holding my shirt against my stomach means he can feel when my muscles start to flutter, and it's sexy as hell to know he won't let me finish anyplace but where he can swallow. And then I spill into his mouth, and I close my eyes for every familiar, brand-new second of it, the sight of him something I'll imagine later. We'd never been loud during our discreet indiscretion, but there's an abrupt shift to silence that has me close to begging for his voice as I ride the last waves of my orgasm. He must know, because he speaks softly while my body trembles under his touch, and I have a few more seconds before he eases away from me and gets back to his feet.

He looks like he wants to kiss me again, but maybe he doesn't know how I'd feel about that, and there's no time for a conversation about it now. I begin to put myself back together, and he turns toward the sink to splash some water on his face until he looks like someone who wasn't just on his knees for a friend.

"What about you?" I ask, more hushed than I need to be.

"Later," he says, throwing the paper towel away and adjusting himself about as well as he can. "We've been in here for too long already, and if Beau notices, he's gonna do that math impressively quickly."

I narrow my eyes for a split second, but then I nod and reach for the lock. "I'll duck out first and go for more wine before I get lost in the crowd."

"And I'll find you there."

CHAPTER NINE

DARREN

By the time I rejoin the party, Beau and Adrian are talking to someone holding a couple of large frames, and I'm nosy enough to want to know what they bought. I let my curiosity go when I spot Mason talking to a man I recognize and can't quite place, but then the guy ducks his head and I realize it's the beautiful nerd from the beer garden, his book nowhere to be seen tonight.

Small, gay world.

Since first arriving at the gallery, I've seen a handful of others from Trailhead, regulars Beau and Adrian know well enough to have extended an invitation. I smile at a few more of them now and encourage them to visit the erotic section before they leave. On the other side of one of the room's large pillars, Noah upholds his reputation for being able to snag the attention of the many hot men he swears he doesn't want to fuck. He's drawn two of them close, and the smile on his face suggests he doesn't mind at all. Of course, he probably has no idea they're flirting with him, but he'll figure it out eventually. He always does.

I don't see Riley anywhere, but with everyone else scattered, I'm guessing they're long gone. Really, it's a testament to their love for Beau and Adrian that they were here at all. They're paid to deal with the chaos at Trailhead, but they tend to avoid it everywhere else, turning down almost every invitation we extend on the nights we want to become some other bar's problem.

Come to think of it, Jake turns those invitations down too, except for the night I enjoyed a different dick in a different bathroom, and he waited with a thirst for good bourbon and a hunger for nobody. But I was on my knees for him tonight, and I'll be in his bed later, and I think those hours together will change things in a way five minutes never could.

I think I should admit that I'm a little nervous, too.

And then I think it might be better to let him believe in my arrogance instead.

I find him with the wine he'd mentioned and a plate of tapas that's a pleasant surprise. Jake's standing in front of another wall of pictures, and I steal a piece of artichoke from him, mostly because it's the kind of thing most of my friends would expect me to do. When I look past the gray in his beard, I catch a small grin, but he doesn't turn to me, still focused on the picture hanging just above eye level. It's a man with one arm positioned behind a little girl, not quite touching her, but ready to catch her even though she's safely secured on the carousel horse she rides. Adrian took the picture from at least a few feet back, so neither of their faces are visible, but the girl's head is thrown back in laughter—ribboned pigtails flying wild—and she has no idea that the man wants to protect her so badly. Maybe it's a father and daughter, and maybe it's not, but it's enough to make me break the silence either way.

"Do you have a lot of pictures like this from when Lucy was little?"

Jake opens his mouth, closes it, and then opens it again, and I could swear there was a frown somewhere in between it all. It leaves me curious about what I thought would be a simple answer, but before I can push like the asshole I am, he shrugs.

"Yes and no. Most of that stuff has been packed up for a long time," he explains quietly. "We had fun on carousels and took lots of pictures. I just haven't looked at them in years."

I think back to when I'd been in Jake's living room, and I'm frustrated I didn't have more time to look at the picture frames arranged like perfectly placed memories. They were there, which means Michelle's death probably didn't lead him to keep their decades together out of sight, but I know I don't understand those kinds of wounds. I guess it's possible that some scars fade better than others, and I'd rather see him smile again.

I watch as he takes a deep breath, and then I nudge him gently with my shoulder.

"Maybe the two of you are due for another trip to the fair. You think she'd be up for it?"

"I'll be sure to ask the next time we talk," Jake chuckles, relief in his eyes when he finally glances my way. "How about you? Did your mom take you to those kinds of places when you were a kid? Go on all the rides with you?"

"She did, yeah. She worked some long hours, and I didn't always get it—I was a selfish little kid—but she made the most of her time off with me. The county fair, the zoo, the beach. All that stuff."

Jake takes a sip of wine, and then it's his turn to nudge me back. "A kid wanting to spend more time with his mom isn't exactly selfish. It's special, and I'm glad you're still close to her. I know Beau loves her, too."

"And the feeling is mutual," I say.

We move over and spend a minute looking at a few new pictures. I steal more food and consider grabbing another beer. Jake drinks his wine and tilts his head, and I'm ready for whatever he has to say by the time he says it, something very obviously on his mind.

"This is none of my business, and you don't have to answer, but—"

"I'll answer anything, Jake," I interrupt. "Anything."

He gives me a little huff of a smile and a nod. "Was your father ever a part of your life? I've only heard you talk about your mom, so has he been around at all? When you were a kid or, I don't know—even as an adult?"

"Ah. No. They weren't married, and he bailed while she was pregnant. Apparently we ran into him once when I was a baby, but that was it. My mom said he moved around a lot, so hanging out with him wasn't an option, and then there was nothing until I got a random card about two weeks after my 14th birthday, probably because he didn't know when my actual birthday was. I found it in the mail before my mom did, and I burned it before it could hurt her."

"What about you? Did it hurt you?"

I freeze at that and suck olive oil from my finger and thumb. A minute ago, I told Jake I'd answer anything, but I'm not sure I have a good one for him now. It's not a question I've been asked before, everything about my father as simple as "he left before I was born" and "I don't know where he is now." The man is a fact of life, and little more than that, except that another glance at the carousel picture has me borrowing Jake's frown, the pull in my chest weirdly reminiscent of what I'd felt when I'd taken a Zippo to a Hallmark card a lifetime ago.

"Yeah, maybe it did," I say. "Maybe—"

"Hello, once again, to my two friends with the deepest pockets," Beau calls out, his voice low as he throws an arm around each of us. "Would you like to finish that sentence for us, Darren? 'Maybe I will buy half a dozen giant pictures to hang in the house you left me.' Did you check out the naughty section? There are some good ones over there."

"What makes you think I need to buy giant pictures of your dick, babe?"

Beau drops his arms and shrugs. "They're much better quality than the ones you have on your phone."

Jake nearly chokes on the last of his wine, and it's probably his own fault for trying to drink while Beau and I are in banter range, but I mumble an apology anyway, and Jake shakes his head as he claps Beau on the shoulder.

"I will absolutely buy a few things," he says. "But I'm probably going to wait until I can stop by after work next week. This opening is great, but I'd love to browse without a crowd."

Beau raises a familiar eyebrow. "Really? You'll come here to see Adrian?"

"Relax," Jake smiles. "It makes me a customer, not his best friend."

"I'll take the fingers in the mouth and the zipper over the bulge," I tell Beau. "And pick out something nice for my mom. She'll be thrilled to get a gift from you."

Beau kisses me on the cheek and hurries off like he's afraid I'll change my mind, and Jake reaches over to smooth the sleeve of my sweater when it's already fine.

"Did you just buy our way out of here?" he asks.

"Something like that. I mean, I would've bought them either way, but there's no reason to stick around all night. I assume you have snacks and drinks at home."

"I do."

I flash the grin that pulls in so many tips and keeps the keg room occupied. "Then let me pay Beau for the pictures while you say your goodbyes. I'll probably be a few minutes behind you, but I'll meet you there?"

"I'll be waiting."

The garage door is open when I pull into his driveway, though there's no actual space to park in there, and I'm not sure what I would've done if he'd given me room. I leave my car where it is and make my way past his car, three motorcycles—one unsalvageable except for how Jake will probably salvage it—and too many storage boxes to count. Bold enough to keep going, I press a button I find on the wall just as I reach for the handle to the door that will let me into the house, the garage quickly closing behind me. My next couple of steps carry me into the same small hallway where I'd found Jake after his ill-advised workday, and I pause there to take off my boots and wonder whether I should call out for him from where I stand.

In the end, I stay silent because something about the moment demands it, and I have no doubt he knows I'm here.

I comb my hand through my hair and can't help but smile when I think about how he'd held the back of my head earlier, my dick already half hard when I stop just shy of his kitchen island and he appears from the opposite direction. His leather jacket is gone and he's barefoot now, looking exactly as sexy as he knows he is and somehow humble about it, too. Or maybe it's the nervousness, again or still, because I feel the same kick in my chest when he leans against a countertop and doesn't come any closer.

"Sorry I'm a little late," I say. "Beau and I were talking, and then

Adrian came in to thank me for—"

Jake holds up his hand. "You're here and I'm here. You don't owe me an explanation."

I believe him, but neither of us moves, still more than a few feet away from each other. There are a lot of things I could say or do, but it all takes a minute to settle in my head, and I think I'm unexpectedly quiet when I speak.

"You're not really the jealous type, are you?"

"For about a dozen different reasons, no. And especially not about you and Beau, regardless of anything you might've wanted to buy tonight."

"Even if I also have pics of him on my phone?"

"Even if," Jake says. "And I'm a little surprised you're asking. This isn't an exclusive arrangement, is it? What good would it do me to be jealous?"

That's entirely fair and something about it stings all the same, so I don't answer, finally taking a couple of steps toward him instead. "You look really good right now."

"I look the same as I did thirty minutes ago."

"No, you don't." I take another two steps and run my fingertip over the buttons of his shirt. "There's no jacket."

"You don't like my jacket?"

"I love your jacket, but that's not my point. You look really good because you're a little undone."

"Imagine how I'll look when I'm a lot undone," he murmurs.

"Oh, I have."

I'm still touching him, my hand curved around his ribcage

now, and it's as easy to feel the deep breath he takes as it is to see it. This is different from when I'd dragged him into the gallery bathroom, the spontaneity of that forgiving him the sin of premeditation. The same could be said about the night I'd kissed him outside of Trailhead, I suppose. But he invited me into his home tonight, and while I don't think either of us has specific plans for what happens next, I also don't think either of us has arrived here with a bunch of limits.

It's beautifully damning, really, and Jake clings to my forearm before looking over my shoulder. "Should I make us something to eat? Or are you thirsty?"

There are jokes to make, but I behave. "I was kidding about the snacks and drinks, but if you want something, I don't mind."

"There's wine. Or I've got plenty of liquor, too. Or there might be—" He stops and sighs. "I'm not actually sure what you like other than the beer I've seen you drink and the pitcher of sangria you shared with me."

"I like everything."

The exaggerated wink I give him is enough to crack something that we needed to break, and he chuckles as he slips away from me. "Of course you do."

I watch him pull a bottle from a rack built into the island, a corkscrew from a drawer, and two glasses from where they've been recently washed, and he looks as good opening and pouring wine as he does anywhere else. I'd told him that the chance to be so many of his firsts is a fucking privilege, and it certainly is, but *this* is a privilege, too. This chance to watch an ornery biker—one who's been all Guinness and leather for years—skillfully open a bottle of pinot noir and hand me a glass while he's barefoot in his picture-perfect kitchen.

The black bleeding into his light eyes suggests something far less refined, and I'm all too happy to accept that too, grateful for the toast he offers me now.

"To friendship?"

"To friendship."

We sip and stay apart all over again, and there's probably some risk of me leaving him right here if we don't figure out where else to go. With anyone else I'm fucking, I'd already be bent over the island, or maybe the couch or a desk or the dining room table. With any friend I want to get to know better, I'd be sitting next to him by the firepit and asking questions until sunrise. Jake is everything at once, and I don't think I've ever known the friends and benefits to be so evenly matched.

My next sip becomes a gulp.

"I don't know what I'm doing," Jake sighs. "And at this point in my life, it's not a feeling I'm used to. The uncertainty."

"You're not uncertain about *what* we're doing, though. You're not having doubts about whether you want to do it."

"Not at all. But now we're in my kitchen, and there's nothing in our way. No bruises and bleeding. No trivia night or hospital meeting. No gallery crowd. And with nothing to stop me, I'm not sure how to get to the other side of this."

"This?" I ask.

"Wanting you to touch me again and not knowing how to ask

for it."

I close my eyes and force them open again because he needs me to know what *I'm* doing, and while everything he just explained seems backward—having nothing in the way should make it easy to get anywhere we want to be—it's exactly why I was hesitating, too. We're going into this both greedy and careful, and however contradictory that feels, it's arousing as fuck.

And more than a little terrifying.

There's a second I consider setting our glasses aside just to touch him right here. He wants it. He asked for it, if only by admitting that he doesn't know how to. If I took his wine away and opened his mouth with mine, we'd be ready for everything else within seconds. I could be back in my car in half an hour, and home another thirty minutes after that.

Could be and won't be, because I wrap my hand around the bottle of wine instead and nod toward the stairs. "Do you mind if I bring this to your room?"

"No."

"Then lead the way."

Jake takes another sip first, then he pads across the kitchen, and I follow him wordlessly. As soon as we're in his bedroom, I set the bottle and my glass on his dresser, and he turns to watch me leave my phone, keys, and cards there, too. He drinks while I pull my socks off, eager to feel his ridiculously soft carpet beneath my feet. I stop without undressing any further, grabbing the bottle to top both of us off before I move across the room and help myself to the balcony door. It's mid-October and the night is cool, but the goosebumps on my skin have little to do with the temperature outside.

I want to check Jake's body for goosebumps too, but I'm still when he stands next to me, and we drink with no need to talk right away, the comfort of it not something I'm used to.

"You like the wine?" he asks eventually.

"Mmmm, it's very nice. Smooth. Rich. Fruity."

"Did you pull that assessment straight from your Grindr profile?"

"Rich? No," I huff, my pointed look between his bedroom and his backyard impossible to miss. "And I'm definitely not pulling anything straight."

He smiles, then lifts his glass. "Lucy gets a bunch of wine from the resort and sends it to me. I'll let her know this one's a keeper."

"It is," I agree. "Just holler when you need my opinion on another bottle."

"Careful. She sent an entire case."

"No warning necessary. I'm in." After another taste, I gesture toward the pool. "Do you swim a lot?"

"Yes."

"Do you swim naked?"

"It's happened."

"And you've enjoyed that?"

"I have."

I don't think he's being intentionally coy, but the short and sweet responses make me wonder whether skinny dipping was something that he did with Michelle, and maybe never since.

And *that* makes me wonder whether she lingers anywhere I won't be welcome.

"I've got no plans to tiptoe my way through anything with you," I say. "I'm almost always horny and very often loud about it, and that won't change. Even when I'm not horny, I tend to be loud about the things I want, and I don't always ask permission when I should."

"Is this your way of saying you want to swim naked with me?"

He's already lifted his wine glass to his mouth again, and I can't quite read his expression, so I match him with a sip of my own before I answer.

"It's my way of saying there's a lot I want to do with you, here in your bed and in about a thousand other places," I smile. "But if there's anything—a meal or a movie or a lounge chair or a freaky sex position that isn't mine to have, even for a minute—I need you to tell me that."

"A minute, huh? I have to admit, my expectations were far higher for you."

I snort, grateful I'm not trying to swallow. "Come on, Jake. You know—"

"I do know, yes," he interrupts. "And I understand. You're about to upend my life, and because I don't want to be coddled, and because you wouldn't dare coddle me, it'll be up to me to stop you from touching sacred things."

"I really wouldn't dare."

Jake looks down at his backyard, then his eyes meet mine again. "I'm not a sacred thing."

It's the second time he's asked me to touch him without demanding it outright, and I'm done holding on to my wine when I could hold on to him. I take his glass, and I'm gentle when I set both of them on the small table in the corner of the balcony—and even more so when I turn back to him and reach for the top button of his shirt. It's unnecessary, but I've had just enough wine to make me want to do something nice, and undressing him feels perfectly kind. Maybe it's important too, being able to do this without fresh wounds in my way, and once I've tossed his shirt just inside the bedroom, I take the time to trace his tattooed rosary with my fingertip. His heartbeat is right there, but I leave it behind to tease his nipples, my eyes meeting his so I can study his reaction before I scrape my nails down his body, stopping only when I hit the top of his pants. I unfasten his belt and button, and I tug on the zipper, but then I drop it for another chance to flatten my pretty hands against his gray chest hair, Jake watching my every move when I slide up to his shoulders and down his bare arms.

Then it's not enough to have him watch me, and I lift one hand to his mouth and slip two fingers past his lips, a recreation of the picture I bought from Adrian. Jake accepts them easily, sucking like a goddamn natural while I grow impossibly hard and barely stop myself from rutting against his thigh to come just like this. Pulling back a little, I use enough pressure to get him to open for me, and then I lick into mouth, filthy about it because I'm done with nice. He moans beautifully, and the kiss stays sloppy even after my hand finally falls away, wet fingers scrambling to finish what I'd started with his zipper. I'm interrupted when he makes a more frustrated sound and grabs my sweater, and I don't fight back when he pulls it over my head and drops it anywhere.

Jake has seen me shirtless too many times to count, and he doesn't stop to look at my body now, his tongue warm and eager against mine when we begin to claw at each other. If he's been tentative before—or could be again—there's no sign of it now, and I get swept away by this man who's so new at this and not new at all. This man who was far more bothered by my need to bandage his wounds than by my desire to be on my knees over and over again. This man who barely swears, but told me about the night he made himself come.

"You are so fucking sexy," I mumble, sucking at his ear and his neck and his shoulder before I find his hand with my own and use it to raise his arm. I run my tongue along the inside of his bicep, then I trace the same path with the tip of my nose while he trembles in my grasp, my breath teasing him from armpit to elbow and back again. He's pliant and panting, but I've hardly done anything, and I need him to know how feral I can be when my dick aches like it does now. With my face buried in the patch of perfect hair under his arm, I let the smell of him overwhelm me until I give in to the temptation to lick and bite and growl, and the sharp and sudden grip he has on the back of my head is even more forceful than when I'd been ready to choke on his cock. My mouth is open, and I'm hungry, and I can't help but appreciate him. "You taste so good."

The hand in my hair drags me back for a messy kiss. "What do you taste like?"

There are so many ways to answer him, but I like when his tongue is in my mouth and I encourage as much of that as I can get while we grind against each other on his balcony. In a minute, I know I'm going to walk him back inside and get him naked and sprawl across his bed and give and take until we can hardly move. First though, I force a hand between us and work past everything keeping me from getting my dick free, my mouth still open for Jake while we pass a dozen needy sounds back and forth. Then I slowly drag my thumb over the head of my cock to get it nice and wet, reluctant to back away from the kiss, and all too happy to make it worth it.

"Here," I say, brushing my precum over his lips. "Taste me and tell me you want more."

He licks it slowly and never looks away from me. "I want more."

It's the final push I need to take his hand and bring him back inside, fine with leaving the balcony door open because the entire world might as well hear us when we come. I nod for him to take off his pants while I do the same because not everything requires that tender kind of help, and I hang back while he drags the duvet and sheets out of our way. For all my bar and bathroom liaisons, a bed isn't new to me, and I easily kiss Jake again on my way to lie down, pulling him with me. We tangle together almost too well, our bodies knowing just how to fit without either of needing to focus on more than another kiss, slow and deep about it until he smiles against my mouth.

"I probably should've checked with you first, but I bought condoms and lube. They're in the nightstand drawer."

"Why would you need to check with me?"

"I don't know. Maybe you've got endorsement deals or frequent flyer miles."

I laugh so hard I move his entire body with mine, and it feels stupidly good. "I'm sure whatever you have is perfect, but we don't need anything yet."

"No?"

"Unless you're in a hurry."

"I'm not," he says.

"I'm glad," I whisper.

I wrap my arms around him and keep him close, and he knows exactly how to move against me without ever having done it before. It should scare me, probably—how much I don't have the upper hand in a situation that might've guaranteed it—but I trust Jake implicitly, and I'm too fucking hard to care about anything else.

He's hard too, his cock sliding against mine while we kiss and moan into each other's mouths. My hands coast over his strong back and to the curve of his ass, and I use my leverage there to keep us rocking almost lazily, one of my legs hooked around his because I want him to stay.

"I didn't—this wasn't something I'd thought about," Jake says, the scrape of his beard welcome when he kisses my neck. "It feels so good, but it's been a long time, and I think I skipped ahead to the rest of what might happen."

"This feels fucking incredible, and whenever you want, we can both come like this. But I want to know about whatever else you've been thinking about."

He props himself up on one elbow, his grin both confident and full of doubt. "I'm not sure what to say. Dirty talk has never been a habit of mine."

"It doesn't have to be a habit, but a couple of filthy words from you could fuel my dreams for weeks."

"The gallery restroom wasn't helpful enough?"

Well, he's got me there, actually. Jake's perfect, and the weight of his dick on my tongue and his balls in my hand are what I'll remember the next time I'm bored or lonely. I'd suck him off again now, but tonight's only sort of about me, and I distract myself by touching my fingers to his lips and pushing him to talk again.

"Did you think about getting your mouth around my cock? How slow you'll go at first? Feeling that stretch in your jaw?" I ask. "None of that's too dirty. You can tell me that much."

He disappears on me—or slips away, I guess—moving down my body until he's close enough that he could swallow me whole. I hold my breath, fully aware that there's a fine line between encouraging this and scaring him off entirely, but my cock is still resting against my stomach, heavy and waiting. Jake runs his finger along the entire length of it, base to sticky tip, and watches it jerk in response when he plays with my foreskin.

"So far, everything has been familiar to me," he says. "Familiar enough, anyway. Kissing, grinding—yeah, obviously you feel different, but it's not totally foreign. Same with when you made me come earlier. And this—touching you like this. I've touched myself, and even if it's not the same thing, I'm not afraid of it." Jake takes my dick in his hand then, stroking it slowly and proving a point that didn't need proving. "I've been attracted to you for years, and I would've been okay with never doing anything about that. But now that we're here? Yeah, I'm vibrating out of my skin, but there's really only one thing that feels completely new. Only one thing I really don't know how to do. And it's everything you just said."

"*You* say it. Please."

Jake's hand stills when he lowers his head, his exhale warm against my dick when his lips just barely land there. "I've thought about getting my mouth around your cock."

It's the last thing he says before he moves to do exactly that, and I struggle to keep my eyes open so I don't miss a second of it. He doesn't go much further than the tip, and when I curve my hand around the back of his head, I need him to know it's not because I'm demanding more.

"Take your time. Try anything you think would feel good to you," I say, and between the encouragement and instruction directed at him, I slow down to feel the pressure from Jake's mouth. He's teasing me, even if that's not his intention. He's different from Brendan and a hundred men like him, even if it's all the same. It leaves me close to dizzy over sensations I know well, and I squeeze my eyes shut while I regain control. "You're so fucking hot, and your tongue already feels so good, but I'm not gonna come down your throat tonight, so you don't have to worry about that."

That has him pulling away, which is the opposite of what I was going for, but I open my eyes to a string of spit from my cock to his lip, and it's sinful enough that I can't care about the sudden distance between us.

"Because you don't want to come like that, or because you think I don't want you to?"

"You already said I'm gonna upend your life, and I already admitted I rarely ask permission first," I point out. "If my plan for tonight was to make you swallow my load, I'd say so. But what I really want is to come all over myself while you're fucking me, so unless you've got an objection to that, you can keep fulfilling a few of your secret fantasies until you're ready to fulfill at least one of mine."

Jake's moan is perfectly timed with the bob of his head, and it takes all my self-control to keep from thrusting even further into his mouth when he actively sucks halfway down my dick. He gags for a split second, but recovers without any concern from me, and then he finds a rhythm he matches with the slick twist of his hand. My fingers are still buried in his hair, but I'm content with the pace he's set. When he slows to lick me from taint to tip, the drag of his beard intentionally wicked, I think maybe he needs no guidance at all.

"Jesus *Christ*," I hiss. "If you're trying to change my mind, you're well on your way."

He chuckles, and that turns me on, too. "No, I like what you had in mind."

"Oh? You gonna repeat that one back?"

I get my dick sucked more first, Jake still learning but quick about it. At Trailhead, he doesn't require much of my attention, and I've never felt the need to go out of my way to give it, but everything has changed tonight, if not every night since Jake's accident. I can't look away and wouldn't try anyway, and Jake isn't being quiet enough to make me think I should.

And then he finally presses his tongue to me one last time and lets me go.

"I want you to come while I fuck you."

Chapter Ten

Jake

I want to be surprised by what I've said, except that something broke when I crashed my bike, and after Darren put it back together a little bit crooked, I was happy to let it heal that way. My heart has been racing since I heard him close my garage door, but there hasn't been a moment I've thought about asking him to leave, and now we're both worked up enough for him to stay. And if he *had* wanted me to swallow for him tonight, I would've done it without regret, but this—as much as it's difficult for me to be so blunt about it—is a daydream come true.

"Come here," he says, quietly cocky with his command.

I obey easily, if that's really what we'd call it, his naked body beneath mine while both of us shake. I'm close to asking him whether he's cold, but I'm almost certain he's not, and I don't need another explanation for it when I have a few of my own. When I'm back to where we started, it feels right to kiss him again, and while I have no idea whether that's something that happens so often when he visits any of his other friends, I won't ask him that question either.

"This still feels so good," I murmur. "All of it, really. I meant it when I said I haven't been a martyr. I don't need this. But I want it. And I want it with you."

There's a temptation to clarify something so honest—to attach a disclaimer to it and make sure he understands that it's still only about the sex—but this is Darren I'm talking to, and if he stays until morning, it'll already be one of the biggest commitments he's made. I'm safe here, and I think he knows he is too, so I say nothing else about it, and open my mouth for his instead.

I feel a shift then, though I can't tell whether we speed up or slow down, unable to separate even as we're getting louder about the ache between us. Darren's already given me enough relief tonight to keep me from begging now, but as admirable as his stamina might be, his grip on my hips is nearly bruising and the noises I catch between each kiss are closer to a whimper than anything I've heard from him so far. I don't know whether he's waiting for me, but I know what's within reach, and I stretch sideways long enough to open my drawer.

"I've got approximately zero experience with lube," I say. "And not much more than that with condoms."

"Lucky guy."

"Mmmm. True then and now, I think."

Darren smiles as I set the bottle and packet on the bed next to us. "Flattery will get you everywhere."

"And where do you think I want to be?" I ask, lowering myself to him again.

"Deep, deep inside me."

Our next kiss is filthier than the rest, and I feel him bring his knees up on either side of me while the heat between us makes the slide of our bodies slicker than before. I want to lose control in a way that hasn't been true in a decade or more, but I need to pay attention to everything, maybe to do it all right, or maybe to remember it over and over again. After the scrape of my teeth against his lower lip and a quick bite to his neck, I put some room between us and sit back on my feet. The sight of Darren so physically bared to me, solid and thick and uncut, has me wrapping my hand around myself. Everything about the moment is overwhelmingly primal, but then I take a deep breath and pick up the lube while he stares, beautifully needy.

I don't think I've compared him to anyone in a while.

He says nothing when I wet my middle finger and touch him for the first time. I'm probably teasing him, but I don't think it's my goal when I'm only eager to see how his body responds, and when I push forward, relief has both of us arching into it.

"You're so tight," I say, immediately groaning. "No, wait, that sounds like a line from terrible porn."

"It's a line from a lot of porn, terrible and not," Darren chuckles. "But please don't let that stop you. Tell me everything."

I don't let anything stop me, but I'm slow enough with each back and forth to make Darren serious again. I'm mesmerized by an intrusion that should be uncomfortable, but he seems mesmerized by me, his eyes tracking whatever expression lingers on my face when I look up again. Then when I pull my hand away, he's there to catch me, predicting my hesitation before I could've.

Without a word, he glances toward the bottle on the bed, and I add more lube to the fingers of the hand he holds. I already know what will happen next, but something about it still takes me by surprise, Darren's grip steady around my wrist when he nods and guides me forward.

Steady, but not particularly gentle.

"Darren."

"Use two."

I almost say something about not wanting to hurt him, but it's stupid even as a half-formed thought, and I extend a second finger before he takes control of my hand again. I relax then, and he moves for me until I'm ready to make it an entirely mutual thing, my fingers opening him up while he mumbles a dozen promises about how good it feels to use me this way. It's vulgar, but I'm so far gone already, and I don't care when I promise things, too.

When it's all too much for me—or not nearly enough—I pull my hand back again, and Darren doesn't mind letting me go. He takes my breath away instead, saving the condom packet from my slippery fingers and opening it with an intriguing combination of arrogance and awe. Then he sits up long enough to slide the condom over me, a lubed hand stroking there before I even realize he's reached for the bottle.

"It's been so long."

I'm not sure I meant to say anything out loud, and whether I'm referring to this specific touch or using protection or having anyone in my bed at all, I really don't know. It's all true, and maybe it doesn't matter more than that. Before he lies down again, Darren uses the tip of his pinky to trace the ugly scar left behind by a wound he did his best to close, and if I had the words, I'd thank him for it one more time. But he falls away then, and when he's on his back, I'm left more speechless by how easily his legs fall open for me, his hand in a lazy up and down over his own length while he waits.

I take a deep breath.

This is another familiar moment, lowering my body to be welcomed by something that feels a little like home. I freeze when I get there, though, because home hasn't been the same for a while, and it won't be again.

Darren's hand returns to the back of my head, and he uses it to bring me into a kiss while I'm buried deep inside him. I take what's being offered, this chance to get trapped by things that weigh nothing and won't leave me hurting tomorrow, and once my tongue is moving against his, I'm able to move my hips, too. He's good enough at this to read me, and if this was supposed to be as quick and distant as our gallery escapade, I've already flipped us upside down, and Darren's already caught us there. His arms are wrapped around me—his legs too, actually—and there's no sign he has plans to stop one kiss from rolling into the next. Friend or not, I need this chance to adjust to something that's only ever meant more, and he lets me have it.

Then, when he arches to meet one of my gentle thrusts, he groans. "I haven't been slow-fucked like this in forever."

In response, my next thrust is harder or deeper or more intense, and both of us seem to tremble, my mouth falling to his sweaty neck. I start to apologize for something, even as I try to meet new demands, but he clings to me, and the pressure of his body around mine causes my rhythm to stutter when Darren goes on.

"Hey, no. That wasn't a complaint. Not even a little," he says. "Everyone else can fuck me however they want. You should fuck me like Jake."

I suck at his skin before leaving him there, and he relaxes his grasp on me because, once again, he must've known what I would do before I did. Back on my knees, I pull out and reach for him like I had before, relishing in the sound he makes when my fingers slide forward. He's still plenty wet, and I take my time with him now, practicality traded for pure pleasure while I watch. When I meet his eyes, Darren nods, and I don't think it's about anything but what I'm doing now and the hundred possibilities of what I could do next. I want to give him what he's asked for, though—whatever accidentally slow thing felt a lot like me—and I leave him empty only long enough to get some clumsy grip on his waist before I'm inside him again.

To fuck him, even if I'm not likely to say it that way.

This time, I don't move closer, not even to kiss him. Instead, I watch myself like this too, every sublime second of sex with a man—*this* man—something I never want to forget. I'm glad he and I know this isn't about romance because I left my heart behind a while ago, and I'm trying so hard not to look in that direction tonight. The way he clenches around me when I rock into him helps too, and eventually I let my eyes fall closed and my head fall back, his body's hold on me a sensation I absorb into my damn marrow.

I finally drop my head to look at Darren again, his hand up and down his shaft quickly enough for me to want to catch up, and I fall forward to brace myself over him as I stray from the languid pace he'd encouraged minutes ago. Any attempt at conversation is becoming close to ridiculous, our eager breathlessness and a dozen broken moans interrupting most of what I think I'd say.

Still, I find a few words as I drive into him again and again. "What do you need from me?"

"This," Darren says. "So much of this."

"This?"

"Anything. Everything."

It's a lot—the freedom to do whatever I want after years of wanting nothing—but I catch his wrist mid-stroke and pin it next to his head, the gorgeous groan I earn one I'll remember long after we've moved on. I grab his other wrist next and let every instinct carry me through the next several seconds of having him at my mercy, Darren left hard and dripping against his stomach when I close the short distance between us.

I could kiss him, but I'm struck by the memory of what Darren had done on the balcony and overcome by the scent of him here. He doesn't have as much body hair as I do, but I want to press my face to it anyway, this brand new desire unlocked and utterly untamed. With his arms stretched above his head and my body curled just the right way to keep myself moving, I nuzzle his armpit and moan softly and breathe and breathe and breathe until I've abused his patience long enough and lift my mouth to his ear.

"Can you come without either of us stroking you off?"

"Probably."

A shiver rolls down my spine, even when I'm sweaty and warmer than I was all summer, and I haven't stopped rocking into him. I don't know that I could even if I wanted to. The sounds made by the collision of our bodies are pulling me forward as much as anything physical, the absolute filth of the noise something I hadn't realized I'd missed. With Darren's wrists still pinned, I finally kiss him again, though that ends up being just as filthy when neither of us is still long enough to keep it under control. His legs are wrapped around me like before, and we're mostly panting against each other as I slam into him, unforgiving—and unforgivable—except for how greedily he takes everything I offer.

"Warm. Wet. Tight. Beautiful," I rasp.

I could be talking about anyone, but Darren's the only one on my mind now, and I pause on my next thrust to feel him around me. And maybe *beautiful* is all wrong here, for this thing we're doing and what he is to me, but I can't be anything but honest, and sucking on his neck again is the only thing that keeps me from saying anything more.

Darren struggles in my grip. "Let go of my wrists."

There's a moment in which I panic, worried that I've read something wrong, but our bodies remain in sync and Darren's breath is still perfectly heavy at my ear. I relax my fingers but don't make it any further than that before he's threading his between them, giving both of us a way to hold on. We're kissing loudly and pleading more quietly, and somewhere between each slide of his length between us, I feel him twitch or imagine something close.

"Please."

He understands that it's all I've got left to say, and he nods as well as he can. "Gonna come all over us while you fuck me through it. Wanna make you come, too."

It's a given, but I enjoy hearing him say it, and when Darren's hands clutch mine and he growls something vulgar and my chest becomes almost shockingly sticky, there's no chance of me doing anything else. I'm thoughtless in the most literal sense, and then I feel myself tighten and unravel, the echoes of my orgasm leaving me jerking into him until I collapse entirely. I think I try to roll to the side, but he hasn't fully let me go, and we're a tangled mess I don't mind at all.

We stay close while our breathing slows to something normal, and then Darren's reminding me about the condom, and I'm half delirious when I stumble to the bathroom, though I think he would've taken those steps for me if he could. As it is, he's not far behind me, helping himself to a washcloth right after I do, the double sinks a wasted luxury when he stands at my shoulder instead. We meet each other's eyes in the mirror, and something so unexpected hits me that I duck away from the view and return to my bedroom to grab clean boxers.

"Do you want to borrow shorts again?" I ask.

Darren comes close enough to shut my dresser drawer. "Nah, I'm good. I'm, um—I'm gonna get dressed and head home in a minute."

"You're not—you don't want to stay?"

He kisses me then, his tongue almost demanding I take my question back and apologize for getting it all wrong. Darren wants to stay, maybe. He just won't.

It's probably not how any of this works.

"Even after a late night, you're gonna wake up early and have things to do," he says. "I'll sleep half the day away, and then the longer I'm around, the more my bad habits will be impossible to hide."

"Is that part of how we get to know each other better? Hiding our bad habits?"

"Hey, no, Jake—"

I shake my head and cut him off. "I'm not mad or upset or anything like that. You can go home anytime you want. Always. I just don't want you thinking you need to leave because I might see something I don't like. You wouldn't be here at all if that were a concern of mine."

He frowns for a split second I almost miss, and then he reaches for the side of my face and holds me more gently than most people might imagine. The brush of his nose against mine is his goodbye, and it's just tender enough for me to consider begging for another few minutes of friendship before he goes.

Darren backs away then, and after I've pulled my boxers on, I watch him get dressed, something nearly as sexy about it as was true in reverse. He grabs his things, and we're both quiet when we make our way downstairs, the middle of the night suited for keeping his departure a secret. I expect one more kiss before he goes, but I get a smile instead, and it's just as good.

When I fall asleep and dream that night, I smile, too.

The following afternoon, I get a perfectly profane text and the not-so-subtle reassurance that my arrangement with Darren hasn't come to an abrupt end. But then he returns to his late nights at Trailhead, and I stay home with good food and good wine and no company to keep, far from lonely but curious about whether I might want someone around anyway. The temptation to do anything about it is shelved with the reminder that our friendship probably has boundaries I still need to learn, and anything more would require effort we haven't agreed to make.

Two days after that, I take a closer look at my work schedule to find a solution for something else. I send a text and wait for a call that comes sooner than expected. I fire off a few emails and responses to those trickle in, a reliably busy Monday slowing everyone down. I'm as patient as it takes, but things wrap up as smoothly as I could've hoped, and then I pick up my phone again and smile through another text.

Bad news...I can't beat you at trivia this week. Good news...I'm going to see Lucy and I'll bring lots of wine with me when I come back.

Darren's reply appears in seconds. **You're not running away from me are you?**

At least part of me is, and I know it. And if he's asking, he's already got a decent idea of the answer, too. Either way, I dodge the question.

I haven't told her about my accident yet. Might as well do it in person so she knows I'm fine.

Okay just gonna say one thing

Go ahead.

Being friends still matters to me more than the rest. Don't forget that while you're gone

My sigh pairs well with the shake of my head. *I'm bringing back wine and I want to drink it with you. We're still friends.*

Good

He doesn't say anything else, and I don't need him to, any invitation to see him before I leave one I would turn down just so neither of us breaks rules we don't have.

I work hard the next two and a half days, and pack somewhere in between.

And on Thursday afternoon, I make the drive toward Palm Springs.

It's mid-fall, but still plenty warm in the desert, even if most vacationers have come and gone. When I pull my bike into the parking lot of the sprawling resort, I can already tell it isn't over-whelmed with guests, and I'd hoped for as much when I'd called Lucy to see if she'd mind a visit. I mumble some small thanks to the blue sky above me as I trade my helmet for my duffel bag and walk toward a lobby that promises to be breathtaking. I've never been inside, but Michelle and I stayed at a few nearby places, and the combination of overdone air conditioning, overhead instru-mentals, and overwhelming extravagance is familiar years after our last visit.

I make my way to the reception area, where I'm greeted with a grin that might be genuine, and I smile back, giving my name to the young host pulling up my reservation. He types quickly and then looks up at me with wide eyes.

"Oh, Mr. Callahan. You're Ms. Callahan's father. She men-tioned that you'd be arriving this evening, and I'm sorry I didn't notice the resemblance."

Lucy mostly takes after Michelle, but I don't argue, grateful for the compliment. "No need to apologize. And she doesn't actually make you call her that, does she? Ms. Callahan?"

"Oh, no, not at all. She hates it. Corrected me on day one," the host giggles. "But you're a guest, and her father, and I thought some respect might be due."

I return the laughter. "Well, you can respect me just fine by calling me Jake. And do you happen to know where I could find—"

"Dad! Why didn't you text from outside?" Lucy interrupts. "It's hard to give you special treatment when you sneak in."

"You know better than to even try that. It's more than enough that you comped a room I could've paid for."

She rolls her eyes just as I sweep her into a hug, my sigh of relief spun into a kiss to her temple. Her high heels make her about even with me, so we're eye-to-eye when I drop my gaze to study her perfectly tailored pinstripe blazer and flared skirt, the chocolate brown a delight with her honey colored hair and wise, hazel stare.

"We get free dinner, too." Before I can respond, she speaks softly to the host and swipes my room key from him. It's pressed into my waiting hand, then she nods toward a small hallway and a sign for the elevators. "I've got a few things to wrap up down here. Go ahead and get settled in your room, and then I'll holler when I'm done. Probably about an hour, if that's okay?"

"More than okay."

My room is simple but stunning, and I'm high enough for my balcony to afford me one hell of a view, palm trees and swimming pools basking in the sun. I leave it behind because my ride has left me with the need for a shower. The pressure is perfect, and the steam soothing, and when I stroke myself, it's a little of both. My body has demanded attention like this more often lately, and I'm not stupid enough to pretend I don't know why, only grateful that I have the privacy to do something about it.

By the time I'm out, it feels good to escape the heat and wear nothing but a towel when I perch on the side of the bed and retrieve my phone from the nightstand. There are emails waiting for me, but I ignore them to open a message Darren sent a few minutes earlier.

Hope you and Lucy are having fun. We miss you here

The *we* is significant, and I appreciate the reminder that Darren and I are only two friends among a group of them. With the gallery opening behind them, it's possible Beau and Adrian will show up at Trailhead tonight, laughing with Noah while Darren and Riley keep the drinks coming. I'm missed because we all have fun with trivia night, and they like my company as much as I enjoy theirs. My usual appearance at the bar wouldn't have turned into more than that.

Not tonight. And maybe Darren will only ever come over after a special occasion.

I miss all of you too. Lucy and I are going to dinner soon.

His reply comes faster than it should while he's working.

Check in with me later?

It's easy to agree to that, and once I have, I drop my phone onto the bed and get dressed in something nice enough for any restaurant in the resort. My beard is already trimmed, my hair is simple to style, and I smell like hotel body wash and the deodorant I've worn since my wedding. I figure I'll have more time to kill and consider starting up a conversation with Noah or Beau, but then Lucy lets me know she's done with work and several steps beyond hungry, so I get directions to the seafood restaurant on the opposite side of the building.

She steals another hug from me—or it's the other way around—before we get ushered past several hellos and into a small booth, Lucy treated well by people who seem to like her a lot. Even fully aware of how protective I can be, the sight of it relaxes me more than I knew I needed, and I take a long, slow breath after thanking the hostess for the menu I'm given.

"I'm fine, dad. Good, even. It's good here," she says.

I don't have a chance to respond right away. A server stops by to recite the specials and offer us a wine recommendation we eagerly accept. In the quiet that follows, I find a macadamia crusted mahi-mahi entrée calling my name, and Lucy probably knew what she wanted before texting me, so we both place our orders when our bottle arrives, and then she sits back to study me.

But I cut her off with my hand in the air. "I didn't actually come here to check on you. Not like that. I've believed you every time you've told me you're doing well."

"I believe you believed me *and* I think it's already done you some good to see it for yourself, even in the short time you've been here."

"It has."

She nods with a wine glass in her hand, but doesn't take a sip. "When we talked, you also swore you weren't coming to drop some kind of life-changing news in my lap. I mean, that was a hell of a meal we had when you and mom told me about her diagnosis, but—"

"I seem to recall you treating us to a very nice dinner once upon a time," I say when she trails off. "Probably the opposite of what we did to you, but yes, I can see why you're concerned about my visit."

"So, you *do* have something to say," Lucy smiles. "You're just classifying it a few notches below 'life-changing.'"

I drink some of the wine she's ignored, and then I make the eye contact we both need. "I crashed one of my Harleys last month. I'm obviously fine now, and it wasn't even that bad at the time."

"Go ahead. Fill in the blanks."

"I was on a late-night ride, just clearing my head. On the off-ramp, an animal ran across the road. I swerved and ended up in the dirt with the bike on top of me. My phone was busted, and I didn't want to wave anyone down for help, but I was also too far from home to walk, so I went to Trailhead instead. Darren was just closing the bar and had the time to patch me up."

Lucy narrows her eyes. "He's a bartender, not a doctor."

"And I'm stubborn," I shrug. "He did what he could, and then he drove me home and stayed in the guest room just in case I needed anything. I was up early the next morning, went to work, and had a friend check me out there. All is well."

If it's possible, her eyes narrow all over again. "You let someone stay the night?"

I want to repeat the part about the guest room, but the truth feels a lot like a lie. The image of Darren on his knees—any of the times it happened the night of my accident or afterward—warms my entire body, and I trade wine for water to clear my throat.

"He threatened to get all of Trailhead involved if I didn't."

"Ah, so he's stubborn, too."

I let that slide. "Everything is fine now. I've got a scar on my leg and a busted bike, and one bothers me more than the other."

"Well, I'm glad you're here to tell me about both."

We're late to it, but Lucy holds her glass up for a toast anyway, and my smile grows at the soft sound of the contact between us. We pull away just as the food arrives, our tickets probably pushed to the front in an attempt to delight the boss. The next few minutes are centered around our food, and compliments to the chef. Then we exchange stories back and forth, settling into the unspoken relief of being able to catch up in person instead of through tired phone calls.

She tells me about the rush of guests at the resort over the past weekend, when they'd hosted some huge celebrity wedding, and the welcome drop in chaos over the past few days. I get the gossip about people who are close to becoming friends and those Lucy would rather never speak to again. There are construction projects to be coordinated and new entertainment to book for the upcoming months, and the mention of music has me filling her in about Darren's plan to hire a band to play at Trailhead.

Lucy brings up the idea of expanding the resort's retail wing—currently limited to a semi-traditional gift shop and a clothing boutique full of swimsuits and sundresses—to include a bookstore and some kind of art gallery. That reminds me to tell her more about Adrian's grand opening, beyond whatever quick story I've given her already. We talk about the pictures and Darren and Beau, and somehow we end up waxing poetic about tapas. Then the subject of tapas leads us to wine, and an intense discussion of the bottles I've already tasted at home, and the others I'm looking forward to trying soon.

Our dinner is incredible, and the company is even better, but I'm not particularly surprised when Lucy pulls out her phone while we pour the last of the wine and wait for dessert. She has an important job, even if she's officially off the clock, and I don't mind the interruption. I'm close to reaching for my phone too, but then she tilts her head and grins across the table at me.

"Darren's the one who's great at trivia, right?"

"He's very good, yeah, but I—" I pause, confused about what Darren's quiz skills have to do with my daughter's job, and then surrender to a shrug. "He's usually busy working those nights, but he's definitely the best competition I have there."

"You're missing out on trivia night tonight," she says.

"I am, but I'm sure I'll be back there next week."

"He's *extremely* attractive."

"Who's extremely attractive?" I ask, afraid I already know the answer when Lucy dangles her phone over the table. I take it, look at the picture of Darren she's pulled up, and sigh. "Well, yes, that's why he makes hundreds in tips while wearing a work uniform that leaves half his body bare. I thought you were checking work emails, though. Why are you looking at him?"

"I don't know, dad. Why have you been talking about him? In the past hour, I've heard about his favorite tapas, his take on the wine I sent you, which of Adrian's photographs he bought for himself, which of Adrian's photographs reminded him of you and me, the bad music he listens to in his car, and the nursing skills he might've picked up from his mother. So, now that your motorcycle accident is old news, is there anything *else* you'd like to tell me?"

There's so much mischief in her eyes, but I don't miss the spark of hope flickering just behind it. She's all Michelle for a moment, and it takes my breath away, but even once I've recovered, I'm not sure how to answer her. Whatever guilt I've been waiting for still doesn't arrive, but I don't think it's time for a confession either way. Or it's exactly the time for it, as long as I pretend everything is as simple as I want it to be.

"I'm still not lonely, and I'm still not looking for a special someone," I say. "But it's been damn nice getting to know my friend."

CHAPTER ELEVEN

DARREN

That first night Jake was in Palm Springs, when I'd asked him to check in with me, I think I was half expecting to get a dick pic or some suggestive text that might help one thing lead to another between his hotel room and wherever I could find a moment alone. Then I remembered it was *Jake*, and I expected nothing that explicit. I ended up at the diner after my shift, and scrolled through my phone for other people's pics within other people's texts, before moving to one of my apps for the chance to find someone new.

None of it held my interest for long, and I found myself rereading Jake's messages instead. There was a little about mahi-mahi and wine, and a lot about Lucy's discovery of the videos I'd blasted on the bar's social media accounts without thinking he'd see them. I couldn't gauge his reaction, and tried not to care. Then I wondered whether sending *him* a dick pic might help.

Sage threw an ice cube at my head—a bad habit she picked up from me a long time ago—and I spent the rest of the night with my phone face down and every app closed.

I wish I'd stayed away from it for so much longer.

Typically lazy, I was still in bed late Friday morning when I started messing around on my phone. I've always been an attention seeker, and I'm sure it's why I was eager to look at everything I'd posted the night before. There'd be likes and shares and comments, and I'd feed off it before I even had breakfast. But then my stomach turned.

The timing was weird, and pieces of the past few weeks returned to me in waves. My recent habit of checking the social media presence Adrian had helped us grow. Jake's questions at the gallery grand opening. My need to post a video my friends were unlikely to watch. Beau's big mouth calling me by name on that video, though maybe it didn't matter.

Maybe my father was always going to find me.

Hey Darren. I'm not too far from Trailhead. Would love to talk about stuff you have going on at the bar. I'll DM you soon

The comment was left by Andrew Barrett. Drew. The name enough to give me goosebumps, and the man someone I don't know. A man I've never needed to know. A man who so fucking casually made his presence known—made his *closeness* known—without giving me the choice to ignore it. He'd said he'll contact me privately if I don't stop him first, but I hate conflict more than almost anyone I know, and I haven't been able to do anything but brace myself since.

Jake's visiting his daughter. My father wants to talk to his son.

It's been two days since I read the comment, and I haven't said a word about it to anyone, but I have the night off and I'm crawling out of my skin and I need things I'm only supposed to want.

You still having fun in the desert?

He could already be on the road, I suppose. It's what I tell myself when he doesn't respond to my text within the first ten minutes. Twenty. Forty. But then, when I'm in the middle of my second beer and reality tv toxic enough to make my life feel downright boring, I catch the notification from the corner of my eye.

Yeah just finished an early dinner. Returning to real life soon.

I should leave it at that, but I rarely do. *Can you come over?*

Tonight?

Yes

To your house?

Yes

You don't invite men over.

No

He calls then, and I probably should've predicted as much, everything about Jake screaming that he'd rather talk than type. I'll give away more than I already have if I speak, but I answer because his voice will help even if he uses it to tell me no.

"Hey," I start, immediately clearing my throat. "It's fine."

"Are *you*?"

"I'm sure you're tired after your long weekend. We can catch up on Thursday night."

"Darren. What happened?"

"You have to work in the morning," I say.

"I do, yeah. So, I can't stay the night."

Fair's fair anyway. I left him the night we fucked at his place. "Okay."

"Okay," he echoes. "Send me your address. I'll be there in a couple of hours."

It's not the kind of thing anyone can promise with L.A. traffic, but he makes it pretty fucking close, and while I'm sure desperation isn't a good look on me, my brain is too busy for me to slow down and do something about it. The best I can manage is to keep myself from opening my door when I hear him pull into my driveway, waiting for him to knock instead.

"Jesus," I breathe.

It's not the best greeting, but I can't help it when I see Jake standing there, all sweat and hair and leather and *man*. I pull him inside and shove him up against the door, his size advantage be damned, and if he minds my tongue in his mouth, he doesn't say. I'm grinding against him shamelessly, and he lets me take whatever I want, this kind man who doesn't understand that I'm untethered in a way so unfamiliar to me. I'm a cocky son of a bitch, and people rarely get the upper hand when I don't care enough for it to matter. The past two days, though? I'm not doing well, and I make it Jake's problem.

He's my friend, and he'll help make it okay.

"Happy to help however I can," he tells me, and I wonder what

I'd said out loud. "But do you mind if I take a quick shower first?"

"Do you mind if I join you?"

His mouth is open against mine, and I think that means he's fine with it. My hands curl around his leather jacket and I drag him away from the door and through my small house until we reach the bathroom. We run into the sink and the wall, and then I'm fumbling to get the water turned on amid all the groping. Jake reminds me we need to get undressed too, and that chaos lasts longer than I'd like, but then we're naked and under the spray and I cling to him as pathetically there as I have everywhere else.

The shower is decently spacious—Beau had insisted, once upon a time—so when Jake finally backs away from the kiss, there's plenty of room for him to look at me.

"What happened?"

It's the same thing he'd asked on the phone, and I hadn't answered then. I'm not quite ready to answer now, and do what I can to deflect with a joke.

"What?" I scoff. "I can't be horny?"

"I've watched you be horny for years. We both know this isn't that."

I nod, closing the distance between us again as I reach for his cock and stroke it. He's been at least half hard since I got him in here, but it's a thrill to feel Jake swell in my grip. Our next kiss is slower than it should be, but he's already seen through me, and I let it happen.

When I try to talk again, I barely mumble. "Can we talk about it after?"

Jake takes my face in his hands and holds me still, studying me with caution that doesn't surprise me when I let him go. He's gorgeous just like this—warm and tired and serious—and staring back is far from a hardship. I'm waiting for an answer, but it never comes, and there's some relief when he helps himself to my soap and washcloth. He's been on the road and he wants to get clean, and there's no reason for me to be in his way more than I already am, so I take a half step back.

He catches me there. "Turn around."

I do it without thinking, and then I feel the washcloth pressed to my shoulder before Jake uses it to scrub me everywhere, slick and strong. Nobody's touched me like this in years, and while I don't remember the last time I cried, it suddenly feels like a near thing. Jake kisses the back of my neck while he continues to move his hands over me, and I don't understand why he isn't washing his own body.

I'm grateful though, because I want to do it for him.

It's a few minutes before I'm given my turn, but I make the most of it. I start with his hair—mine hadn't been a priority when I'd showered just hours ago—and massage his scalp to relieve any ache a motorcycle helmet might have left behind. He moans, and I'm greedy when I arch forward to chase contact that's not mine to enjoy yet. But then I refocus and rinse his hair and clean his body and carefully drop to my knees behind him, the spray at my back.

"Darren," he says, his voice so low the water almost drowns it out.

Jake doesn't go on from there, and maybe he isn't sure whether he was trying to turn my name into a warning or a plea. As always, I don't slow down long enough to demand an answer, my hands curved over his ass until I can open him up to me. He falls forward to brace himself against the tiled wall, and I think I'm almost smiling when I first touch my tongue to his hole. After that, I'm too busy learning new things about him to worry about the expression on my face. I'm slow and fast and gentle and firm, and without a word, I encourage him to want more—to take what I'm trying to give.

He does, stunning sounds muffled and a series of muted prayers offered up while my tongue works him over. In between a dozen other practiced moves, I back up to brush a wet fingertip over him, and watch closely as his body reacts and he hisses above me. For at least a couple of reasons, I have no plans to push Jake any more than this, but it might be fun to talk about it later. Tonight, my selfishness demands something else, and after another minute spent on knees that will hate me tomorrow, I push myself up and embrace Jake from behind.

I grind against him and wrap my hand around his dick. "I don't want to be in the shower anymore."

Jake turns when I release him, unashamed about how deeply he kisses me beneath the water. He's coordinated enough to turn off the spray too, but the kiss doesn't end for another several seconds, and even then he mostly mumbles against my lips.

"No?"

I don't answer, guiding him out of the shower instead and

handing him a towel from the rack. It's warm enough in the bathroom that I'm not all that concerned with drying off, more focused on wiping down the mirror that's been lost to the steam and tossing my towel to the floor. Jake's eyeing me, probably closer to suspicious than curious, and maybe it reaffirms something for me, my next step toward him aggressive and needy.

There's still a towel in his hands, so I take it from him and drop it on top of mine, and then my hands are on his hips, rougher than I've been with him yet.

"You've gotta fuck me."

His head tilts. His eyebrow arches. "I don't think I've *gotta* do anything. Friendship usually carries more free will than that."

"Okay," I agree. "I'm willing you to freely fuck me. How's that?"

"Are we going to talk afterward?"

"You said you can't stay the night."

Jake sighs. "That bad, huh?"

"Fuck. Me."

I make the demand—intensely unfair to a friend who's only done this once—and then turn my back on him, opening a drawer to pull out a condom and set it next to the bathroom sink. With the mirror mostly clear, a glance at our reflections is enough to show me that Jake is watching over my shoulder. I'm still looking at him when he speaks.

"What about lube?"

The same drawer opens and closes. A small bottle lands next to the condom. I growl, and maybe Jakes does, too.

"Don't need much," I tell him. "Trust me."

"I'm far less concerned that you're lying to me, and far more bothered by the idea that you might think you're telling me the truth and be so, so wrong about that."

I chuckle. "None of my other fuck buddies turn my eagerness into a study of self-deception."

"If you're expecting me to apologize for being different from the rest of them, you'll be waiting a long time," Jake says. "And don't worry, I won't expect you to apologize for breaking your rule about inviting someone over."

He's quiet after that, and I don't go looking for a fight I'm pretty sure I could pick if that were my thing. We're both naked and not as hard as we were a few minutes ago, but I still need this, and Jake's going to help because he said so.

I'm counting on him being a man of his word.

We're already so close to each other, but he presses himself to me and reaches around for my jaw, turning me until he can kiss me, a slow but utterly filthy thing. He finishes by biting my lip hard enough for the sting of it to linger, and then he pushes me to bend over the sink and pours lube onto his fingers. It's still more than I need right now, but I have less to argue about when he isn't slow about anything that follows. He presses two fingers against my hole, feels the way I relax under his touch, and slides them forward before I can find the right way to beg.

However much Jake is inexperienced—or just out of practice—he reads me well and doesn't need the mirror to do it. He opens me up just long enough to satisfy something for himself, and while I continue to ache with need, I hope he needs me, too.

It's not much longer before he crouches for one of the discarded towels, and I tear at the condom wrapper, handing it over this time because I'm not drawing this out for anyone's pleasure. We'll both come, but I didn't ask Jake to stop by for either of us to make it cute.

I'm still bent over, but somehow I'm not ready for how roughly he slams into me. The bruising grip on my hips and the ease of each perfectly crude thrust pulls questions to the tip of my tongue, but I lick my lips and leave them there. I drop my head and surrender to everything I've asked him for, Jake taking me out of my head after I've been stuck there for two days.

"So good," I pant. "Don't stop."

He doesn't stop, and he doesn't talk either. I'm barely able to think past the vulgar collision of our bodies, but I notice when Jake's hands are seemingly everywhere at once. He squeezes my shoulder and scrapes his way down my spine, and when he curls his fingers in my hair, I whimper pathetically until he does it again. I think he eventually murmurs something behind me, and his hold on me tightens as his smooth strokes stutter. The sudden clumsiness does nothing to distract me from how fucking deep he is and how little he prepped me, the delicious burn something I still want to feel tomorrow.

I grab my dick then, no more gentle about that than Jake's being with me, and I know it won't last much longer for either of us. It's a race, maybe, and I want to win tonight, but he's encouraging the same, his hand back in my hair while I fucking *whine* until I'm coming all over the cabinet door and the bathroom rug. I'm boneless and breathless, and Jake hasn't stopped driving into me, his energy renewed by a shower and a willingness to soothe something that's remained unspoken. He raises me then, strong arms wrapped around my body until I'm half standing and watching us in the mirror, and it's so perfectly obvious when he comes inside me that I shudder all over again.

Jake is slow to let me go, but I figure he doesn't trust me to stand on my own yet. It has to happen eventually, and when he pulls out to take care of the condom, I grab a towel from the floor to clean up some of my mess, then leave it on the rug to deal with later. I'm not sure what's supposed to happen next, but he's silent when he puts his jeans on without the boxers that must be uncomfortably sweaty after the ride here, and I mumble something about washing them with my stuff. Then he stands there and waits while I follow his lead, slipping back into my sweatpants under his stare.

I'm ready to say *something*—to challenge him or send him home or ask him for impossible things—but then he tugs on my hand and leads me past a bedroom that isn't his. Jake has no claim to the living room either, nor my couch, but they must feel familiar enough for him to lead me there. He sits first, his back against a couple of throw pillows and one leg extended across the cushions, and then he beckons me toward the space in front of him, the invitation frustrating me because I know what he wants.

And I'm afraid of how bitter I'll sound when I talk.

Jake hasn't known me for anything but a smile.

I nestle between his legs anyway, and lean back against his bare chest, one of his hands so gentle in my damp hair and the other pressed to my heart whether he means something by it or not. And once again, I know I have to explain myself, but he's the one to speak first.

"I didn't like that," he starts, and when I flinch in his embrace, he holds me tighter. "No, not the sex. And not the fact that it was rougher than last time. We're in this to have fun, but that doesn't always have to look a certain way. The wine and whatever else we did at my house was great, but I don't expect that every time."

"So, you're mad because I'm upset."

My statement never quite makes it into a question, so I'm not sure what I expect Jake to do with it, but the sigh isn't a surprise.

"I'm not *mad* at all, Darren. But through the fun and the friendship and whatever else you want with me, I need you to be honest about it." Jake taps his fingers against my skin, and I reach up to keep him still when he goes on. "Tonight, you said you were fine, then you joked you were horny, then you demanded that I fuck you, and you brushed off any concern about being physically ready for that. And sure, I'm not stupid. I understood you were upset. But just *tell* me that. Tell me you're upset and that you need a distraction, and let me be the friend who distracts you. Don't shuffle through a list of other excuses first, because while I'm damn good at reading between the lines, I need us to stay on the same page."

I close my eyes in his arms, falling backward until I land somewhere around the word *fuck*. Jake so rarely swears—getting him to do it in the heat of the moment was a fucking treat—and his choice to do it now makes me pay closer attention. And honestly, I haven't been with many people who cared to read between anything, so it means I'll have to try harder to get this right.

Trying isn't really my thing, but it feels like it should be.

"My father contacted me. Sort of." I take my own deep breath when I feel his against my back. "He left a comment on one of my Trailhead videos—one of the same ones Lucy found while you were at dinner. And he said he wants to talk about the bar."

"The same father you told me has never been a part of your life since he sent a birthday card 20something years ago?"

"That's the guy."

"But you haven't talked to him yet?" Jake asks.

"No, he said he'd DM me, which just—it feels shitty in some specific way, on top of the general shittiness of it all."

Jake nods, and his short beard brushes my temple. "Because now you can act nonchalant—like maybe you didn't see the comment at all—and hold on to all that tension while you wait for the other shoe to drop. Or you can DM him first, but then you take the chance that he'll see it as an eagerness to connect, and you don't want that either."

"The past two days have been awful," I say. "I spent most of last night staring at the stupid fucking barn doors, like I'd even recognize him if he came in for a drink."

"Right," Jake hums. "Because you didn't go looking for every picture you could find after you read his comment?"

He's wrong, actually, but I'm not surprised by the assumption when it's one I would've made in his shoes. I'm online plenty, and I spiral all the time, so it makes sense that I'd see my father's comment and spend hours scouring every social media profile he has. In fact, if I were Jake, I'd figure I'd already spent years tracking the man, if only to find the reason he didn't want me.

I've thought about it a lot. Poked around just a little.

But I've built a life around distances designed to keep me from feeling the empty ache I was born with. I've never met my father, but I'm just like him, careful to leave before I believe anyone can miss me. Beau's been the only person I've let close enough to break that rule, and that did enough damage to both of us. I'm too much of a coward to chase a love I've never known.

I wasn't enough for Drew Barrett once. I'm not sure I could handle that being true twice.

"I saw the tiny version of his profile pic, but didn't get any further than that. I burned a birthday card once upon a time, and I don't think I need to go looking for the ashes."

"Those ashes haven't existed for a while," Jake says.

"For me, maybe not. But that birthday card was never the same again." It's an ugly way to explain any of what I'm feeling, and as has been true most of tonight, Jake deserves better. I have nothing left though, and I do the most innocently dishonest thing I can think of, quietly shifting the topic back to him. "How old were you when Michelle had Lucy?"

"23."

"Older than my mom was, but that still seems kinda young, yeah?"

"It *felt* very young," Jake chuckles. "But we got married when we were 19, which I can't even fathom now, and as soon as we finished undergrad, our very Catholic families wanted their very Catholic kids to have kids of their own."

"Did the two of you want kids?" I ask.

He takes a few seconds to respond, and I wonder if he'd rather go home than lie on my couch and talk about the past. It's been a long weekend for him, and he's already done everything I've asked. Staying now, and basically cuddling on my fucking couch, is a choice he doesn't have to make, but he doesn't change his mind.

"In hindsight, I know we did. At the time, we didn't think about it that much—it was the next step. But the only thing we would've changed would've been figuring out the rest of school and career stuff first. Michelle took a break for a few years before going back for her master's, while I kept at it. It worked out better than I could've imagined, but nothing was perfect."

"Why—" I cut myself just as quickly as I've begun because it's none of my business, and I have self-control now and then.

Jake nudges me. "Go ahead. It's fine."

I squeeze his hand. "Why didn't you have any more kids? Not that—obviously I don't think anyone has to have any kids, and I'm sure Lucy meant the world to you from day one. Perfect or not, you had Michelle and your baby girl, but I'm sure your families had something to say."

He'd encouraged me to continue, but Jake tenses somewhere in the middle of everything I've said, and I feel him force himself to relax. I'm close to turning around and kissing him to reassure something I don't understand, but I can't decide whether it'll make anything better or worse. In the end, I lift his hand to my mouth and brush my lips against it, too soft for friendship and too quiet for the guy he's known me to be.

He hums, the noise small and comforting as it fades into his answer.

"They did, but I think having a kid helped us prioritize things. We juggled work and school and parenthood, but didn't start trying for another baby for a while. Then when we finally tried, it didn't work, and it was always the three of us—until it wasn't."

I do turn in his arms then, because that has to be better than asking about his dead wife, no matter how much he's been willing to tell me about her. He's ready for me, his mouth open, and everything is easier when I'm not using him to clear my head. And as much as I'd do this all night, it was never part of the plan.

"You've gotta go," I remind him.

"Mmmm."

"Will you be at the bar on Thursday?"

"I'm a little out of practice," Jake says with a small smile. "Think I'll do okay?"

I bump his nose with mine before I back away and scoot to the opposite side of the couch. "Being out of practice hasn't been a big problem for you so far."

Jake shakes his head with a chuckle, then stands to go in search of the rest of his clothes. He returns from the bathroom a minute or two later, mostly put back together by the time he makes his way toward the front door, bracing himself on the wall while he tugs his boots on. I haven't moved any further, and he doesn't seem to expect me to, another smile thrown toward me instead.

"So, I'll see you soon?"

"See you soon."

We don't see each other soon, though. We text throughout the week, but Jake is exhausted after the weekend in Palm Springs and his visit to me and an avalanche of work he hadn't expected to hit so hard upon his return. I bug him with some trivia questions he missed (Who wrote the Manfred Mann hit song "Blinded by the Light"? What popular soda was originally made to be a mixer for whiskey?) and he answers far too quickly (Bruce Springsteen. Mountain Dew). Other than those very intentional moments, our exchanges are briefly flirty things I might've shared with anyone.

I can't be all that upset that Jake doesn't make it into Trailhead, because neither does my father—I don't hear from him at all, actually—and I think maybe the universe is trying to balance something for me.

When I don't see either of them the following week, I wonder whether the universe is paying attention to me at all.

And I hope I haven't fucked anything up, one way or another.

It's unfair of me to expect answers or place blame. Jake got called to replace a colleague at some big conference in the Bay Area, and I'm certainly not mad that he has important things to do. I rarely see him more than once a week anyway, so going this long without seeing him is fine. I spend a few late nights with Sage. I fuck around on my go-to apps and exchange pics with some strangers. I don't make it out to any of the bars or clubs that would let me get to know a stranger any better.

If I get off thinking about Jake while he's gone, so be it. It's better than losing sleep checking for messages from my father. And maybe *soon* means something different to Drew Barrett, or maybe he was just testing me to see if I'd jump to respond. There's only one person who would have a chance of being able to answer questions like that, but I have no plans to tell my mom anything about the message, especially when I don't know what he wants from me.

She's family. He's not.

Chapter Twelve

Jake

Since the night of the gallery opening, I've had more energy than usual, even while feeling more tired. And it might go back further than that, to the aftermath of an ugly accident and a recovery that was buoyed by promises that made me crave things I never believed I'd taste. I'd physically hurt then, just like I carry a sleepy ache with me now, but I'm humming with a long dormant need I'd missed more than I'd imagined.

I want Darren close to me again—as close as we have been a few times already—and recent chaos at work hasn't allowed for that. We check in with each other when there's a good enough reason for it, and I've stayed up a little too late the nights he's teased me. He still has the advantage of experience and a filthy mouth, but I think there have been a few times I've surprised him with a risqué text or two.

I hope so.

I'm having fun, and after the night we shared a shower and I bent him over his bathroom sink, I think we've both needed the reminder of silly, sexy things. Or I have, anyway—I assume he's been busy with silly, sexy friends in the couple of weeks we've been apart—and on a Sunday morning when our text thread has been quiet for a few nights, I realize I miss him. I wait until close to noon before I poke at him to see what happens.

Are you awake yet?

Darren replies quickly. **For about 30 mins already**

Busy night at the bar?

It was. Everyone loves a saturday night

Busy night after the bar?

You really want me to tell you about the nights I get fucked after work?

I sigh. I guess it's what I was asking. *You've never kept it to yourself have you?*

Nope. Except for the night of adrian's party and your return from palm springs

He's being plenty loud without having to shout, and I can hear him just fine. I'm slow about saying anything else, even though I'd texted him for a reason, and I almost wonder whether he'll go on about his weekend. He doesn't, and I type again.

I was thinking about making dinner and spending some time in the spa later. Care to join me?

You don't have to work tomorrow morning?

I do. But I still need to eat dinner. And relax.

And have dessert?

That could be part of the relaxing.

What are you planning to eat?

That question feels like trouble, and I dodge the innuendo. *Curry spicy enough for fans of the scoville scale.*

Lol. Do you have more of lucy's wine?

Lots of it.

So you're planning to take advantage of me

Or I'm asking you to take advantage of me.

Darren starts to type too many things too many times, and the butterflies I feel make me fifteen again. In the end, what I read is probably far from where he started.

I'll be there in time to help with dinner. And the rest of it

Just like that, I'm close to taking a few steps backward when I freeze instead. I don't want his help with dinner, and for all the honesty I've demanded, I don't know how to tell him that. It's easier to adjust the plans on my end, and it's all I do for now. Darren knows about sacred things, and maybe I can admit something about them later.

With hours to kill, I head into my office to handle a few work emails and review notes for a meeting I've got first thing tomorrow. Having an early morning responsibility will keep me from asking Darren to stay long, and it's a buffer that keeps me from worrying that I've invited him here for something that feels a lot more like a date. The night at the tapas restaurant, we were just friends. The night of the gallery opening, we were a lot more than that. Combining the two into dinner and dessert leaves me staring at the ceiling for too long.

Once I've refocused, and I've settled something inside me with spreadsheets and lists, I turn on music throughout the house—classic rock over country for today—and then go upstairs to change into my swim trunks and a hoodie. I make sure the bedroom is neat, though it usually is, and I'm not sure Darren will come up here tonight anyway. With two towels in my hand, I'm ready to go back downstairs, but I pause at the last second to grab condoms and lube because I don't actually know what will happen or where, and I'm not pushing myself into those kinds of predictions.

A minute later, the towels get taken outside and placed onto lounge chairs, and I stash the rest near the built-in barbecue where they're out of sight, out of mind. I flip the switches for the lights in the pool and spa, then the one for the overhead string lights—ones so similar to Trailhead's beer garden décor, though I'm almost certain mine came first. The music plays on, and I go inside again.

When I check the nearest clock, I'm grateful that my restlessness has run out of time, and I set the table before I do anything else. Back in the kitchen, I gather everything I'll need to make dinner, this recipe memorized years ago. I work quickly, my solitary dance well-rehearsed, and I try not to think about why having someone in my bed has been easier than allowing myself a partner here. My chest is tight and I can't explain the pain away as easily as I'd like to.

Dinner's almost ready when the doorbell rings and breaks one thought into three or four. I've let Darren out through the front door twice, but it's the first time he's arrived there without following me in. I hurry to wash my hands before I answer, mad at myself for not leaving it open for him before I started on dinner.

"Hey, sorry, come in," I say, backing away from the open door with a dish towel still in my hands.

He's wearing swim trunks too, plus a long sleeve t-shirt and sneakers he toes off before he pushes them against the wall with a bare foot.

"What're you sorry for? Hot guy invites me over for dinner and some time to relax in his gorgeous backyard? I have no complaints."

"But you *do* have an appetite?"

"Almost always," he teases. "Even brought cheesecake bites for dessert, just in case we end up craving something sweet."

I lock up behind him, and he leads me to my own kitchen, putting the cheesecake into the fridge without needing direction from me. Before he can close the door, I catch it and nod to the wine I left chilling there.

"Will you grab that and pour a couple of glasses, then take everything to the dining room?"

It's then that Darren glances around the kitchen. "Jake–"

"Actually, there's a wine chiller in there, too."

"Jake."

"You can put everything on the table and—"

"*Jake.* Stop. You made dinner alone. I got it." He pulls the bottle, grabs the corkscrew I'd left with the glasses, and wields it as effortlessly as he does most things. With his hands full, he looks at me again. "Take a deep breath and finish whatever you need to finish. We can talk while we eat."

His smile is more than I deserve when I've basically kicked him out of my kitchen, and Darren leaves before I can push or pull more than I already have. Alone again, I do exactly as he'd suggested, exhaling deeply as I plate the curry, rice, and naan. When I join him in the dining room, he's not sitting yet, standing with his back to me as he studies the backyard. It's difficult to see from where I am, but he turns his head just enough to make me think he's looking at my reflection when he speaks.

"You know, being on the same page isn't just about how we fuck."

I nod because I think he can see it. "I know."

Darren turns as I take a couple of steps and set the plates on the table. In another few seconds, we're sitting within reach of each other, and he plays with the cuff of my hoodie, maybe just to keep from holding my hand.

"I told you that first night, if there's any space that doesn't get to belong to me, just say so. I've got plenty of places to go if I don't want to give a shit about someone, but this isn't that."

I nod again and don't take the thought of his *plenty of places* any further. "Thank you. For coming over."

"I like it here."

He's said as much before, and a large bite helps keep me from nodding a third time before I swallow. Contrary to my mid-invitation teasing, I'd kept the curry reasonably mild on a night that could lead anywhere, but the flavors are abundant, and now I just want more of *Darren*.

"Talk to me. Please. I don't—I've missed talking to you. I know times have changed and all that, but texting just isn't the same."

"No, it's not," he agrees. "And I've missed talking to you too, old man."

The endearment is soft, but Darren compliments me on dinner, helps himself to some naan, then becomes animated as he catches me up on more than select trivia questions. He tells me that Noah, like Beau and Adrian, has been stopping by the bar a little less often. Riley, for as much as they strike me as a homebody, has been lingering around Trailhead after their shifts, and Darren mumbles something about writing on coasters that I don't quite understand but ignore for now.

"Have you talked to V about replacing the bull with a band?"

"I got the green light, and a long lecture about figuring out how to clear out the space before I bring in anyone to fill it."

"Ah, it's almost like she knows you well."

"Almost," he winks.

"Why do I feel like you aren't going to behave?"

"It's almost like you know me, too."

I chuckle at that. "How many bands have you already contacted?"

"None yet," he says, taking a sip of wine before he goes on. "Obviously there was already some chatter about us having live music—I mean, that's how it all started. I've just kept the conversation going here and there, and may have mentioned that we'll be doing more after the holidays."

I'm impressed by his restraint and say as much. Darren eyes me carefully. His bare foot makes contact with mine and neither of us pulls away from it. For the hundredth time, I wonder what he does with his other friends, because every blurred line remains unfamiliar to me. I like it though, and I won't insult either of us by pretending otherwise.

We talk about my job briefly, and then about Lucy for a while, and we're nearly ready for dessert when I run my finger along the stem of my glass. "So, would it be correct to assume you still haven't heard from your father?"

Darren swirls his last sip and stares at it a beat too long. "Do you want more wine?"

"Yes."

The bottle isn't any closer to Darren than it is to me, but I let him have the moment he needs, and he pours for both of us while I enjoy the last of my curry and set my fork on my plate.

He takes a long drink and then shrugs. "It would be very correct, yeah. And this Riesling is really fucking good. You should tell Lucy."

"Will do."

Darren's final bite goes uneaten, and he offers me an uncertain smile before he pushes away from the table with his wine in his hand. His frustration isn't about me—other than whatever blame I'm due for mentioning his father—and I don't take any offense when he walks away entirely. He steps into the backyard, and I rise to clear the table, the mess in my kitchen a reason to give him a few minutes alone in my space.

I get the dishwasher loaded, leave a few other things to soak in the sink, and wipe down the counters. Then I go to the refrigerator for the dessert Darren brought, a welcome complement to everything I'd made. This night has been strange, reminders of both Michelle and Darren's father causing us to stumble a bit, but even our roughest edges continue to fit together smoothly. It leaves me wanting him and needing him, and when I finally step into the backyard, the small box of cheesecake bites in my hand, his visible exhale makes me think he feels the same.

He lifts the glass to his mouth, and then his arm is pressed to mine and I lean into the touch. My string lights leave us with the predictable play of brightness and shadows, and the beginning of a breeze means the spa will be a welcome relief when we make it there. For now, Darren offers me his glass and steals dessert, feeding me a bite before he looks toward the pool.

"So, I asked you about skinny dipping, but what about parties out here? There's no way you guys had a backyard like this and didn't use it."

"We had a lot of parties, yeah," I confirm after chasing cheesecake with wine. "Friends, colleagues, neighbors. It was nice, it's just—I haven't bothered."

"Not since Michelle died?"

"Technically, there was one." I take another sip and feel it all the way down. "Lucy and I hosted a reception here after the funeral. Michelle planned most of it—the menu, the playlist. Everything. It was the wrong time of year for it, but a really gorgeous day, actually. Better than I could've imagined."

Darren makes a small sound, like a beautifully broken hum. "I'm glad you had all that. All of it."

It's probably more sincere than what the average Trailhead drinker might expect, but I've known better for a while, and I only wait to see if he has other questions for me. He helps himself to cheesecake instead, and I set the wine glass down near the things I'd tucked away earlier. It's too hard to keep track of time when I'm with Darren, but I know it's getting later than I want it to be, and he knows it, too. I watch him pull his shirt over his head and toss it toward a lounge chair, his body one I've admired for years and can more openly appreciate now. For a moment, I think he might leave his swim trunks behind too, but then he takes a few steps toward the spa, and another few steps into it, lowering himself until he's only visible from the shoulders up.

His eyes fall closed and I stare for several more seconds before I speak. "The jets aren't on yet. You're missing half the experience."

Darren cracks an eye open. "Pretty sure I'm missing more than that."

I remove my hoodie and throw it on top of his shirt, and then I press the button for the jets and listen to them come to life. I'm pleasantly steady when I take the last few steps toward the spa, and then I'm sitting across from him. With wet hands, I comb my hair back from my head and feel more relaxed than I had just a minute ago.

"I love being in my backyard," I tell him, stretching my legs across the spa until my feet rest next to his hip. "That's always been true, but tonight—this is really nice."

Darren reaches for me beneath the water, a hand around one of my ankles like it's nothing. "You know I'm not gonna take away your solitude. Just want to disrupt it now and then."

"I know, and I'm glad."

"For not taking it away, or for disrupting it?"

"Both."

"Mmmm. So, what do I have to do to convince you it's time to host another party?"

It takes me a second to follow him from whatever we're doing tonight to whatever else he's planning for the future, but I get there and nod slowly.

"For everyone at Trailhead?"

"Of course," Darren says. "And Adrian could invite Mason. Maybe Mason knows someone who can finally turn Noah. Oh, maybe Mason knows someone who'd be good for Riley. Plus, there's a hot guy Mason was talking to at Adrian's thing, who I also saw at the bar one night, so maybe we could all get to know him a little better. And then Beau is basically the equivalent of three other people, so—"

"*Beau* is, huh?" I chuckle.

Still amused, and warmed by wine and water, I tip my head back to look at the stars and take some time to think about what to say next. As much as I'd love to understand more of Riley's situation, I was raised with the belief that some things are none of my business, and it might apply to them above everyone else I know. And Mason is always talking to everyone, so the hot guy Darren mentioned escapes me entirely, though I have no doubt Darren could get to know him very, very well. But there's something else on my mind when I look at Darren again, and his cheeky grin isn't enough to keep my mouth shut.

Some things are none of my business, but occasionally I'm curious.

"What happened between you and Beau?" I ask.

He's unbothered, but the corners of his mouth fall a little. "You were around for all of it. And I don't believe for a second you weren't paying attention."

"I know you cheated on him, he wanted to work things out, and you said no. Then he moved out, and you stayed in your house. Things were bitter for a while, but he never stopped hanging out at the bar, and you both suffered—probably unnecessarily—until you figured out how to be friends again."

"And that's the story," he says, his head cocked. "What do you think you're missing?"

I shrug. "You've loved him all along, but did you get to the point where you didn't want to be married anymore? Or did you not want to be married in the first place?"

The lights just barely catch something ugly in Darren's eyes, and it makes me think he's asked himself the same things often. Maybe even recently.

"I'm reckless and arrogant. I don't know how to commit to anything. I tried to convince myself I could be better than that for Beau, but it was a lie that had no chance of making me believe I could keep from screwing up. And yeah, he would've stayed and let me hurt him over and over again, but while I have a long list of faults, I sincerely hope cruelty isn't among them."

With a closer look at Darren's list, I'm sure I'd find a lot of faults that shouldn't be among them. It sounds like he's delivering a speech he's rehearsed for years, but his loyalty to Trailhead, V, and his friends is close to unmatched, and his reckless arrogance is likely a combination of confidence and a short attention span. I'm not going to argue with him now, though I wonder what I'd put on my own list if I were asked.

And whether Darren might argue with *me*.

My curiosity vanishes when he lifts his perfect body out of the spa, his trunks clinging to him when he sits on the tiled edge with his legs dangling in the bubbling water.

"Too hot for you?" I ask.

"Maybe I just felt bad that you couldn't properly objectify me while I was mostly underwater."

"And am I supposed to feel guilt or gratitude in response?"

Darren's teasing turns into something startlingly serious. "I hope you never feel guilty about this. Any of it."

There are ways I can respond to that—ways to offer reassurance most people wouldn't think he'd need—but I say nothing yet. Instead, I slowly cut through the water and let him track my every move. I kneel where he'd just sat, and bring my hands out of the water, my wet fingertips starting at his knees and dragging along the inside of his thighs from there. I'm probably shaking some, and I wonder when that will change, but Darren doesn't seem to mind, nor does he care when I finally make it to his waistband and tug.

"Take them off."

He does, with none of the cocky commentary I would've expected, wriggling under my loose grip until he's naked and breathing more heavily than necessary. He's on his way to aroused already, whether it's his default state or the result of my command, and my hands land on his thighs again, braver than either of us thinks I am.

"What now?" he asks, licking his lips. "What do you have planned?"

"I want to try again. I want to get this right."

"I don't think you got it wrong last time."

"Maybe not. But I didn't get to finish."

Darren whimpers, though I don't think it's a conscious thing, and I almost ask how many times he's gotten off to the fantasy of coming in my mouth. I say nothing though, and I'm not sure whether it's because I assume he has other people on his mind or because I'm not up for another confession of my own sins. Either way, we're relatively quiet when I take his length in my hand, slide the extra skin out of my way, and lower my mouth to his tip, the chlorine only doing so much to disguise the taste of *him*.

It's addicting, and I'm the next one to make a desperate little sound, able to take him deep when he's still shy of fully hard. That's addicting, too—feeling him grow in my mouth—and I already know I want to tell him that another day.

For now, I focus on what I'm doing, and moan when his hand moves to the back of my head, gently encouraging as I find an imperfect rhythm. The last thing I want Darren to do is treat me like I can't take whatever he gives anyone else, but I don't think this tender touch is a condescension. It's the freedom to explore with nothing expected of me before, during, or after, and I hum my thanks before I tease him with my tongue and then suck in earnest all over again.

Darren leans back some, bracing himself with one hand while the other still combs through my hair. My fingers are either splayed across his thigh or moving in tandem with my mouth, and I'm beyond turned on, only quiet about it because I'm listening to everything Darren has to say above me.

"That feels so fucking good. Right there. Christ, please. Don't stop. Love how you suck my dick. I've thought about it for so long, Jake. It's so fucking good."

The way he says my name—lets it fall broken and breathless from his tongue—has me shoving my swim trunks down so I can reach for myself and keep my own orgasm at bay. I look up at him too, eager to see what he looks like when he continues to speak, his words more obscene by the minute.

I barely pull off him, spit still between us when I do my best to beg. "Keep talking."

"Yeah? You want directions? Want to hear how much I think about this?" he asks. "Or do you just like the sound of my voice?"

"Yes. To everything."

He finally puts pressure on the back of my head, guiding me over him again, though he doesn't thrust up into me even when I have no doubt he could. I'd like to find out on some other night.

Right now, I'm content to let him have this much control, each long second lingering on the perfect side of rough while I learn what he likes.

And I'm still listening. Definitely listening.

"You're so sexy like this, Jake. Fuck." Darren moans long and low when I go as far as I can and drag my tongue along the underside of his shaft the whole way back. I moan because he said my name again. "I've made myself come so many times imagining you sucking me off. Is this why you wanted to see me tonight? You wanted to suck me off in your spa?"

His questions are mostly rhetorical, but I'm not sure how I'd answer anyway, torn between admitting how much I've wanted exactly this and arguing that I also loved all the conversation that came before. I loved dinner and wine and ending up in my backyard with him. The smiles and stories. Even the mistakes I made and his mixed-up feelings. The night has been full of all the things Darren and I have agreed to share, and our friendship matters as much as the ache in my body I won't be able to ignore forever.

"You're gonna make me come so fucking hard," he pants. "So much better than when I'm alone. Your mouth is perfect, and you're so fucking hot like this, baby."

If I thought hearing Darren say my name was arousing, it has nothing on the pet name that could've been an accident or habit. My hips thrust toward the jets that have a chance of taking care of what my hands are too busy to finish, and even dazed and needy, Darren notices.

"You like that?" He tugs on my hair then, and I want and I want and I want. "Jake, baby, look at me. Can I come in your mouth? Will you suck my cock 'til I come down your throat?"

Wide-eyed and wasted, I nod as well as I can without letting him go. Darren's hand leaves my hair long enough for him to trail it over my beard, pausing when he can drag his thumb through the saliva on my chin. I thrust toward the jets again, and he smiles.

"Get messier for me."

I don't have time to think about the specifics of a relatively vague request, though it's easy to rid myself of restraint when Darren demands it of me. I'm not sure there's a way to get this wrong, no matter how eager I am to get it right, so I suck on his sac and twist my hand around his length and bob my head and work him over with my tongue, all while letting it all get wetter. Louder. Filthier.

Messier, just like he wanted.

"Yeah, that's perfect. Fuck, baby. I'm so close. Want you to taste me. And I want you to make me taste myself on your tongue."

Oh. That does it, the last of my self-control gone when my orgasm courses through me, my body still untouched by everything but the water. The hand not stroking Darren is clutching his side, and I groan while my mouth moves over him again and again. He wasn't lying about being close, and he chants something about it now, mumbling with no apparent beginning or end. Whether it's my instinct or his grip on my head, I ease back to focus the pressure where he wants it, and then I'm right there when he jerks forward and starts to come.

It's interesting, knowing on an intellectual level what to expect and still being surprised somehow, my first experience with this one I won't forget, even as I'm still dizzy with my own pleasure. I want more of this—of *Darren*—but he's sitting forward and grabbing for me and his tongue sweeps into my mouth and I give for as long as he wants to take. There's nothing careful about the kiss, his arms around me when he guides us back into the water.

"Have you had enough of my objectifying you?" I tease.

"Not even close," he says, reaching down to where my trunks rest around the middle of my thighs, then smiling against my lips. "You came already. With my cock in your mouth."

His certainty keeps it from becoming a question, and I don't answer when he carefully tugs at the waistband and covers me up again. Steam from the spa surrounds us in the cool night air, and I don't want to leave it behind, especially while Darren has become almost reverent with his touch. I sit so he can straddle my lap, naked and soft and stunning, and I hold on to his hips because I don't know what else to do with my hands.

"*Baby,*" I murmur. "Do you—is that a regular habit of yours? Calling people baby?"

Darren doesn't look away, but his head tips sideways, and I can almost count each exhale while he decides what to say to me. He'll be honest—I'm not concerned about that—but it's not a surprise that there's no simple yes or no.

"You liked it. I know you're not asking me because it bothered you."

"No, I'm not."

"And you know who I am," he says. "You've never accused me of doing anything wrong."

"Not at all."

And he couldn't be doing anything *wrong*, anyway. That would make no sense. There's never been the slightest suggestion that our arrangement be anything but casual, and I'm not insecure enough to worry about how I compare to the men Darren is with on the nights he and I don't speak. Still, I'm not a fool. I've seen him in action for years. I don't know whether he uses the same lines with everyone—it's why I'm curious about it now—but I'm certain our friendship makes something different, and I think I'm trying to figure out where that difference lies.

"Yeah, I call a lot of people baby while we're fucking. It's sexy. It makes them feel good, which makes *me* feel good. I can't promise I'll stop, with them or with you, and I don't think you're asking me to. But what I can promise is that when I'm fucking you, I'm fucking *you*, Jake. And I wouldn't be doing that at all if I didn't want to."

"Because you're not in this for charity."

"I'll leave the good deeds to you," he says.

The insinuation that he's any less generous than I am is laughable, but the quick flicker of hurt in his eyes isn't funny. I almost ask about it, but Darren kisses me before I can, a remarkably slow thing that I never want to stop. It won't lead anywhere, and with each perfect stroke of his tongue against mine, I realize this might've been what I meant to ask before.

Is *this* a regular thing?

Does Darren kiss everyone as if sex was always going to be the second best part of the night?

Chapter Thirteen

Darren

I don't actually kiss that many people.

Well, I guess I kiss a lot of people, but I don't kiss them just to kiss them. It's a means to an end. Hello and goodbye. Please and thank you. I love to fuck. I love to come. Kissing is a fantastic addition to a hundred ways I can get off—and all the ways I can get someone else off—but I don't give it much thought on its own. I don't spin fantasies around a kiss. Or several of them.

But I can't stop thinking about how much I kissed Jake the night I went over for dinner.

At some point it became a goodbye, and I might argue that it was always thanks of some kind, but if I shut up long enough to admit the truth, I never wanted it to be about anything else. I just wanted to fucking kiss him.

Once our pet name conversation was done and the kissing had begun, I lost track of time, my body in Jake's lap and his to hold.

He did exactly that—he *held* me—while we kissed for quite a while, but when the heat and the jets and the water were all a little too much, he guided me out of the spa without a word. There was a halfhearted attempt to towel off, but neither of us wanted to be apart long enough to do it well, and Jake found it easier to drop his wet trunks to the ground instead. Then he led me into his house, laid down on his couch, and pulled me on top of him, a throw blanket pulled on top of *me* to keep us cozy while we made out.

Eventually, I was half hard again, but it didn't matter when none of our kisses led to anything but the next. Sometimes we broke apart enough to nuzzle into each other's necks or comb our fingers through each other's hair, whispers coming and going, but everything was about feeling good.

Nothing was about sex.

I almost told Sage about it the next time I saw her, but she's got an exhausting job and a house full of siblings and the ability to see right through me. Most of the people I fuck don't get that kind of view, and there was no good reason to bare myself to her. We talked about our favorite love songs instead, and none of them were about me.

Jake made it to trivia night that week, and I wanted to kiss him then too, even if I couldn't make it happen. Aside from his aversion to becoming another tally on the keg room wall, having Riley, Noah, Beau, and Adrian witness our departure would've caused quite the conversation. It's one I don't think Jake is ready to have when his privacy is a thing he treasures, and I could do without the lecture I probably deserve. I'm still going to talk him into hosting a pool party someday, but for now, I can be his dirty little secret just to save us both some trouble.

We've both kept my father a secret, and I can't tell whether it's saved me any trouble at all.

I *did* get to kiss Jake the week after that, when he stopped by my house after some kind of work thing in Burbank. There might've been time for something quick and easy before I had to leave for my shift, options plentiful even if we made it no further than my living room floor, but I pressed him against my front door instead. And then we kissed as if I had nowhere to go.

As if he might've needed me.

It certainly couldn't have been the other way around.

In between trivia rounds three and four that week, with Jake predictably ahead of everyone at Trailhead, I decided it didn't matter who needed whom, and I snuck off to the keg room—alone—to fire off a text.

Are you doing something with lucy for thanksgiving?

I realized there was a chance Jake didn't have his phone out, everyone on the honor system while questions were being asked, but his response came fast.

No. She's working. Are you doing something with your mom?

No she's working. you doing something with anyone else?

Is this an invitation? There's no trivia next week, right?

Right. But I'll be here and it'll be quiet.

So you want company?

For a moment, I considered explaining what I had in mind, but

Jake needed to answer someone else's questions, and I needed to pop caps and pour shots.

Yeah. and then I want you to follow me home

Feels like there's a joke to be made about a feast.

Stuffing too

Of course.

So is that a yes?

Yes.

By the time I stepped behind the bar again, Jake was talking to Riley as if he and I hadn't just made plans to fuck on Thanksgiving. I winked and didn't worry about whether anyone could see the way my dick strained against my jeans.

And now, after what has felt like a suspiciously long week, Jake saunters through the same barn doors that had once ushered a broken and bleeding version of him into my arms. The memory is grossly poetic, and I want to pour myself a drink just to blur it better. I don't move though, uninterested in blurring this vision of Jake, his black jeans and leather jacket typical, and his sweater another expensive one I desperately want to touch.

"You weren't kidding about it being quiet," Jake says, sliding onto a stool.

"Nah. Last night was wild, but kitchens and couches are keeping most of the crowd away tonight," I tell him, leaving a pint glass on his coaster before I nod toward the handful of drinkers across the room. I'd been bullshitting with them for a while before Jake had texted that he was on his way, and they've been here often enough to recognize him and wave a quick hello. He returns it with a smile that keeps more secrets than it's ever given away, and then I shrug and smile, too. "The loneliest among us have probably found a shittier bar—something about insult and injury, I think. The guys who showed up here are probably bored as much as anything."

"And you? Are you lonely or bored?"

"Rarely lonely, often bored, and neither one right now."

Jake takes a sip and then grins. "You're welcome."

Because kissing is still on my mind, I'm terribly tempted to taste the confidence caught in the curve of Jake's lips, but I move away to deliver two bottles to an older couple content to spend the holiday with sawdust and beer. In the short time I'm away, Jake has had another sip, and his stare is as cool and calm as I've ever seen it. If he minds being here with me tonight—straddling the line between public and private—it doesn't show.

I have plans for us to straddle something else, but I'm not ready to tease him with that yet.

And he takes the conversation in a different direction.

"Does V ever have to work a holiday?"

"Not if I can help it," I shrug. "My mom's the only reason I'll bail on this place, but she's always had a non-traditional schedule too, so we're used to celebrating things whenever."

"Except for her birthday, right?" Jake asks. "You always go to San Diego for that."

"I do."

"Okay, so V and Noah are with their family, and Beau is with Adrian. Would I be prying if I ask about Riley?"

I almost laugh at the idea of that, but he's serious. I lean forward with my arms crossed and resting against the bar, closer to him than I'd typically dare.

"You haven't pried about anything in all the years you've sat here," I say. "And I only know that they're with their brother today and tomorrow. I assume that means they're *not* with Ethan, but I didn't want to get my hopes up too high, so I didn't ask for details."

Jake's eyebrow arches. "I don't think I've ever heard Riley mention a brother."

"An identical twin, actually. And V might be the only other one who knows about him. Or maybe Beau does, I guess."

"And the Ethan situation?"

"What have you heard about that?" I ask.

Jake taps his fingers against his glass and frowns. "Only that it's not a great relationship for Riley, and everyone here would like it to end."

"It's not and we would. But Riley is smart and strong and stubborn, and at the end of the day, they'll have to make that decision without a bunch of well-meaning misfits doing it for them."

I watch as Jake lifts his beer again, and because I'm behaving, I back away to help myself to a bottle of water I have stashed beneath the bar. A minute or so later, I close out someone's tab and remind them to drive safely when they go, and then I stand in front of Jake again, my bare body facing his perfectly clothed one. The combination of cashmere and leather continues to make me dizzy, and he knows it.

"You probably won't mind if I ask more questions about you."

"I definitely won't," I confirm. "Already told you I'll answer anything."

And that's what I do. Or what we both do, really.

Jake asks me about the traditions my mom and I had when I was younger. I've got plenty to say, and he's kind enough to ignore when I push aside the father-shaped spaces I usually pretend aren't there at all. I ask him about the traditions his family had when Lucy was a kid. Leaning close to him again means I catch the split second he grieves the things he's lost, but before I can offer him a way out, he takes a deep breath and shares a couple of stories. Clever, or used to dodging the memories that hurt, he asks for another Guinness and drags me back several more years as soon as he can set aside the more recent past. I learn that Jake's the oldest of five, and I laugh hard enough to draw the attention of half my remaining customers when he tells me about their antics in church pageants, and on camping trips, and through several weddings and more than one funeral.

He mutters something about Irish families and follows it up with what sounds like a prayer, and I laugh at that, too.

I entertain him with tales of my restless childhood, unofficial hobbies and organized extracurriculars doing little to stop the constant hum that demanded I move on before I was done. Jake doesn't seem surprised that I've always been an avid reader, even after the stories of my inability to commit to anything, and I love that he understands a contradiction I never have. Then his lips remain tightly pressed together as I tell him about my cocky teenage years, when I surfed almost every day and kissed lots of girls right up until I spent seven minutes in heaven with a cute boy.

"And then you stopped kissing girls?" he teases. It's careful, though. Maybe he already knows what I'm going to say. Maybe he doesn't like it.

It won't keep me from being honest.

"I've never totally stopped kissing girls," I say. "But they generally deserve better than someone like me, and if I'm looking for an easy fuck, I'll say no to them, and yes to a hundred different men instead."

Jake chuckles. "Gay sex as sacrifice? Redemption? Self-flagellation? Do I need to drag you to Mass and teach you a thing or two?"

"That's an unexpectedly sexy threat, babe."

I'm about to respond with a deep dive into his religion and what it means for us, but there is no *us*, and I'm not sure I've got a great grasp on holiness. I back away then, and I work as much as I need to, the already low demand getting lower as the time ticks closer to closing. My drinkers say goodnight one or two at a time, and when the last cowboy tips his hat, I've got another half hour before I can lock the barn doors. There are things I can get away with on an occasion like this, though. I swap Jake's empty glass for a smaller one with Jameson and pour one of my own, then hold it up for an unnecessary toast.

"To gratitude."

"And friendship," Jake adds.

I nod, and we savor the whiskey. When I leave him behind again, I clean the tables, restock the little that's been used over the past several hours, and start to run the receipts for the night. Jake is patient, and I'm beginning to wonder whether inviting him here was a good idea. He could've met me at home, or I could've gone to his again, but I've brought him here to tell him something, curious about whether he's up for anything else tonight.

Once we're finally locked in, I'm slow to approach him, but his eyes never leave mine, and I know it's time to talk.

"So, I found someone who wants to buy the mechanical bull from us, and we've scheduled a company that'll transfer all the parts from here to there."

Jake barely blinks. "When is it happening?"

"The week before Christmas," I say. "The new place wants it by the end of the year, and we don't need it, so I was able to make a decent deal."

"And then you'll have someone clean up that space and build a small stage?"

"That's the plan."

"Then you'll be able to audition bands, and Trailhead will have another draw, on top of karaoke and trivia."

"The challenge is that we actually have to *pay* the band, so it needs to be worth it," I note with a bit of a sigh. "But there's a lot of potential if I can get this right. And I really, really want to get it right."

Jake hums to himself and takes a long look around the room. "Did you ask me to come here because of the bull or the music?"

"You don't miss much," I smile.

"No, I don't," he agrees. "And while I have no objection to conversation as foreplay, you probably have an entire list of alternatives for that. So, either there are some songs you want me to hear, or you think I'm about to ride that bull, and I'll admit one of those seems more likely than the other."

I glance over my shoulder and back again. "Have you ever been on one?"

"I ride my Harley."

"Great. Maybe on another night, I'll get a turn on that."

There are only a few seconds of silence, but it feels long enough for me to consider pouring another round of whiskey. I don't reach for the bottle—the two of us will drive away soon—and the way Jake clears his throat might've been enough to stop me anyway.

"Have you ridden it much?"

"Not as often as you'd think."

"Of course," he teases. "Why straddle that when you can climb on someone less eager to buck you off?"

"And toys are great, but I don't need one that could crush me."

"Mmmm, looks kind of fun, though. Might be a shame to miss out on a thrilling new experience like this before it's gone."

"Oh, yeah. You definitely haven't had any thrilling new experiences lately. Nothing different about your life these days. Nothing you've let a friend talk you into trying."

Jake rolls his eyes. "My impromptu trip to the desert was a little unexpected, but not entirely new. And I've shown up for plenty of trivia nights in plenty of bars, Darren."

I laugh often, but this one takes me by surprise, and I'm grateful I didn't have a mouthful of liquor. Jake's expression hasn't shifted much, but the small curve in the corner of his mouth suggests he knows exactly how much he's amused me.

Wiping the tears from my eyes, I wave toward the bull. "Okay, point made. You're ready for a thrill, and I was hoping for exactly that. Let's do this."

Eager or not, Jake barely waits for the words to leave my mouth before he's sliding off his stool and shrugging out of his leather jacket. I try and fail to keep from staring when he makes his way around the far side of the bar to where the bull awaits, and it's unsurprising how easily he hoists his strong body over the back of it. He makes himself as comfortable as anyone can while sitting on a cheaply upholstered animal, and I allow myself a deep breath as I finally move closer. I take a second to unlock the control panel and grin when I know Jake can feel the hum of the bull beneath him.

"We're not going too wild with this," I warn. "Just put your hands up for a second."

"Okay, hands are up," Jake says, but then his eyes narrow. "Wait, we?"

The bull rumbles a little more, then it kicks into a slow roll, enough to make him reach down to steady himself before he raises his hand again. I rub my palms on the front of my jeans and then leave the controls behind so I can jump on, sitting so I'm facing Jake, my legs draped over his thighs.

"Yeah, we," I answer, pulling on his arms until his hands land at my waist. "This okay?"

"It's, well—yes. This is very okay. What about the cameras?"

Of course he knows we can be seen here, but I've been prepared for that question, and my reputation can only help us.

"It's fine. You're not gonna fuck me while we ride this thing. We won't even kiss each other," I promise. "V knows I'm a flirt and you're hot, so this is just me being typically horny and using you for a good time. She'll probably remind me that there are plenty of men who don't lust after me, and that I should leave those men alone, especially when they're as well-respected and off-limits as—"

"Don't make me kiss you just to shut you up," Jake interrupts.

It would be too easy to test him, so instead, I stop talking. The mechanical bull continues to roll, and when Jake's hands tighten at my hips, I respond to his grip by reaching for the sweater I've admired for hours. I flatten my palm against his heart, the beat of it better than the music I could've turned off a while ago, but I don't stay there for long. The fabric is stunning, but I'm drawn to more than that, the contrast of his skin calling for me to touch that, too. I lift a fingertip to trace just inside the collar, dragging from one shoulder to the other and back again, tempted to press against his heartbeat one more time just to see whether the rhythm has changed.

I don't do it, stopped by the darkness bleeding into the familiar light of Jake's eyes, a small smile there and gone before I can fuck up the moment by commenting on it.

Then Jake's mouth falls open, but I never hear whatever request he might have made, maybe because he doesn't want to fuck this up either.

We remain silent while the bull bucks us gently, and my touch moves higher. I slide my hand into Jake's hair, even if I shouldn't when V might see, and I pull his head back to expose his neck. I won't break our rules, but I bury my face in the warmth I find, impossibly hungry and denying myself every taste. A second later, I shiver when I feel his fingers against my lower back, half my body still bare and my goosebumps there to tell him anything he needs to know.

My eyes are closed—I don't know or care when that happened—and I can feel everything at once. His thighs are solid underneath mine, the heat the sum of so many sparks between us. His hair is soft, and the skin still teasing my lips is less so, but it's my need to grab his sweater again that reminds me the cotton bandana around my neck should be on the floor with the rest of our clothes. Jake's fingertips travel all the way up my spine and almost tickle me on the way back down, and when I moan more than I giggle, his hold on me tightens and at least one of us arches toward friction we can't catch yet.

The bull rolls on.

I open my eyes as I pry myself away from his neck, gone only so I can grab Jake's arms again and drape them over my shoulders, our embrace almost unbearably intimate as we continue to rock together.

We still don't talk.

But that doesn't mean we don't make a dozen other noises, every gasp and groan and hum and sigh so quietly loud, and just enough to be heard over some sad country song.

We still don't kiss either.

But our hands never stop searching for more, clawing and stroking and clinging and scratching like there's something left to learn about how much we might want this.

And there's a routine unfolding here, though neither of us would dare to take it to the wood dance floor favored by my ex. The bull carries us through a slow up and down, and each round is wholly predictable until one particular wave catches Jake when he's already leaning. He lets it carry him all the way down, and with his back against the bull, he's as relaxed as I've ever seen him, the beautiful lines on his face faded now. I think I'd fuck him right here if I could, but with my legs still on top of his, I only slip my hands under his sweater and pretend I've pinned him, like both of us aren't fully aware he could throw me to the ground if he wanted to.

I think I'd fuck him there, too.

Jake doesn't stay down for long though, the distance between us more than either of us wants in a place where proximity is all we can have. We're wrapped up in each other again within seconds, our foreheads pressed together and my dick almost painfully hard. This close to each other, it's clear that we're both breathless with no reasonable excuse for it, and I smile where he could trace it with his tongue.

He sighs. "I really, really don't care about cameras right now."

"Don't kiss me, Jake."

"Why not?"

If it's possible, we pull each other even closer, my answer touching the corner of his mouth. "Because you don't have to give up anything for me. You deserve better than this."

"And because we'll be at your house within the next 30 minutes and I can kiss you before we've even made it to the front door?"

"That, too."

We let the bull move us for another few seconds, but my shitty self-control is about to give up on me altogether, so I peel my needy body away from his and shut it all down. Jake's perfectly capable of putting himself back together, so I mumble something about lights and music, and I take care of those before I swoop behind the bar just long enough to gather everything I need. It doesn't take me long to finish up in V's office—receipts filed, deposit secured—and when I return to the bar with my hoodie on and my keys and phone in hand, I'm met with a stare that suggests we hurry home.

Jake has the advantage of riding his motorcycle, the late November air helping to keep him cool, sexy leather jacket or no. I roll down a window and press the heel of my hand to my cock when it twitches again, determined to make it so much further before I come. This late at night, especially on a holiday, there's little traffic, and we don't get separated until a stoplight a few blocks from my place. It means Jake beats me there, and when I get out of my car, his helmet and bike have been left in my driveway, and he's leaning against my house like he knows he's the hottest goddamn 50something in all of California.

He could be anywhere tonight. I love that he's here with me.

"What's a guy like you doing at a place like this?" I ask.

Jake grabs me by the bottom of my sweatshirt and pulls me into him for a long, deep kiss. I moan into his mouth but don't rush anything because it's the last sweet moment we'll share for a while. When I grind against him, I realize he's as hard as I am—again or still—and every slutty part of me screams that I need more of that, and less of a kiss that might never end. I stay where I am though, mostly because he tastes like a lot of things I've never had, and it's only when Jake whimpers that I think maybe I taste like a lot of things he misses.

I bite his lip and back away and fumble with the lock so I can get us inside.

My thoughts aren't nearly as clear after that.

Jake and I slam into the door and a couple of walls, and our shoes and jacket and hoodie and sweater make a messy trail on the floor in case one of us needs to find our way back. The hallway isn't long, but we stop there to palm each other through our jeans and pant into each other's mouths. Someone's zipper is loud. Someone's moan is louder. We move again, and kissing mostly leads to needy laughter when we can't do much more than lick and nip at any bare skin we can reach. More clothes litter our path, and I don't care.

When we stumble into my room, Jake breathes against my ear. "I haven't been in here before."

"This is the bed," I say, pushing him onto it. "You can look at everything else later."

We're both naked, or close enough to it, and together we kick and pull at my comforter and pillows and anything else in our way. I've never seen Jake like this before, and without the desperation driving me now, I think I'd stop to admire whatever I've done to him. Instead, I rut against his leg, and he ruts against mine, and we're kissing again because I don't need air unless it's coming directly from him.

When that's not enough—when I need Jake inside me—I crawl onto my hands and knees and arch my back and assume he'll figure out the rest. He's been the smartest guy at Trailhead for years, and as he fumbles with my nightstand drawer, I'm glad he's the smartest man in my room, too.

Seconds later, I hate him.

Everything Jake found in the drawer gets set down somewhere behind me and left there, his hands warm and steady and too fucking gentle when he uses them to bare me to him. His tongue opens me next, and I hiss when he's just as gentle there. I would've begged for this on any other night—have fantasized about it plenty—but my patience got dropped somewhere near the front door, and I want so much more now.

"Come on," I whine. "You can't tease me like this."

Jake chuckles, though he sounds nearly as choked by his arousal as I am by mine. "After that stunt you pulled with the bull, I'm pretty sure you deserve to be teased exactly like this."

He has nothing else to say, but a lot he wants to do, and whatever experience he has with something just like this comes in handy as he starts to take me apart. Jake's confidence is devastating for my restraint, his mouth open and wet and eager to make me weep. I can't help but reach for my cock, stroking it madly until he gives me a reason to slow down.

"No," he whispers. "Be good. Wait for me."

As if his breath against me wasn't enough to make me cry out, the quiet command would've done it. I hurry to say something, just so he can't call me on it.

"I didn't expect this from you."

"There are so many things I didn't expect from you," he says. backing up to run a finger over my hole. "So many things."

The very idea of that is laughable when I'm the same guy he's watched fuck strangers for years, but I can't do anything but drop to one forearm and chase any of the pressure that will leave me feeling less empty, unabashed in my impatience. I'm teased by another few seconds with Jake's tongue, but then I feel him growl against me when his control falters too, and I let go of my dick just to reach back and finger myself.

All's fair in sex and war, or however the saying goes.

Jake knocks my hand away and slides two lubed fingers deep inside me before I can wonder when he opened the bottle. I'm not hurt and confused like I was the night I bent myself over the bathroom sink for him, and he's not being careful about the way he's prepping me with a touch that isn't out of practice anymore.

He trusts me, and he trusts himself, and he'll take what he wants while I get everything. I give a lot of people a lot of freedom to fuck me their way—my instincts are good and it's rare for me to be disappointed in anyone I've dragged into a dark corner—but Jake is about to fuck me *our* way, and I don't even know what that means.

My hand returns to my cock, my grip looser this time because I want to be good, and my head is still lowered to the mattress. I'm a live wire of anticipation while wholly relaxed, and when he slips his fingers free, I know he's not going to drag this out any longer, even if we're both aware he could. Jake proves me right a moment later, a condom wrapper thrown off the bed just before he grabs my hip with one hand and, presumably, guides himself into me with the other.

"God, I've missed this," I say. "Why does it feel like it's been forever?"

Jake rocks into me, eases backward, then bottoms out again, his perfectly manicured fingernails likely leaving marks up and down my spine. "It's been a month or so for us, not counting the fun we had in my spa. Not sure what else you've been up to, but I'm glad I'm back."

I don't have any interest in thinking about anyone but Jake right now, and I'm grateful when he picks up the pace, each quick thrust barely leaving me time to miss him before he's deep inside me again. I can't see him, and he doesn't make much noise at all, but everything about his hold on me—a hand pulling my hair now and another ridiculously steady somewhere just below my ribcage—makes it impossible for me to keep from chanting his name like a fucking mantra.

I guess Jake would call it a prayer.

I'm fine with that if it means he'll make me see God.

Chapter Fourteen

Jake

It's easy to say that Darren and I haven't had this particular kind of sex when I've only been inside him twice before, but tonight feels like *us* in a way that's too difficult to define beyond that. We laughed and teased and tripped our way here, I took a minute to taste him in a way I hadn't before, and now it's all heat and speed and the hunger I'm happy to feed until my appetite changes.

With my heart pounding and enough sweat to make me shiver, I watch Darren's body welcome mine over and over again. He's saying my name, profanity filling the spaces in between, and I don't know how to offer what he needs in return when I'm still not used to using my voice in a moment like this. I'll get there soon, but I feel him clench around me and I stay buried inside him for an extra beat or two, frustrated that I can't kiss him while we're connected so perfectly.

It's when I decide perfect isn't enough.

I'm working from memories I won't dwell on for long, careful when I separate myself from Darren too, the reasons for it practical and not.

"Jake." It's so soft. It's all it needs to be now that our bodies are still and the room is quiet. When I don't answer right away, Darren rises onto both hands and looks over his shoulder at me. "Hey, talk to me. You don't—we can stop. We can lie down and stop everything else."

The raw need bleeding into Darren's words suggests it's not what he wants, but I don't doubt the sincerity of his offer, and I shake my head because it's not what I want either. My next move is probably clumsy, and I can't explain myself as well as I'd like to, but I use what leverage I can to encourage him to move forward, away from me and closer to the wall we face.

"Hold on to the headboard. Let me hold on to you."

Darren does as I've demanded, his hands curled around the top edge of the wood and his body on display for me take just as roughly as I had minutes ago. It's not unlike the night I'd watched him in his bathroom mirror, but nothing is the same either, and I move until I'm pressed against his back and can reach around to stroke him while I kiss his shoulder. I'm still so aroused and can't keep us apart much longer, but I give myself another few seconds to do nothing but tease his opening with my tip. He's patient with me in a way he must despise, but I think I reward him just fine when I finally thrust into him again, no warning provided to give my intention away.

His long moan rattles something I thought was left hollow. I bite into his skin to keep from saying so.

I don't return to the same unforgiving pace right away, and my slight size advantage means I can curl around Darren once I've put us back together. His grip on the bed suggests he's not going anywhere, but I like having my arms around him, and when he turns his head to catch me for a messy kiss, I figure he has no plans to break free. I'm moving plenty—our embrace means the rhythm is easy to keep—but his mouth is a stunning distraction for as long as it's open against mine.

"Thank you," he murmurs. "For coming back."

Whether he means tonight or just seconds ago, I don't know.

It's hotter now, our bodies slicker with each slow slide. Darren breaks away from the kiss and drops his head between his arms, time punctuated by the pretty sounds he makes all because of me. One of my hands rests over his heart, certainly accidental and a reason for me to hurry after a beat I can't ignore, and he trembles enough for me to discard the fear that something is wrong and decide instead that everything is very, very right.

"Thank you for letting me fuck you like this."

The expletive slips free before I can remember swearing isn't a bad habit of mine. Darren goes in search of another one when he opens my mouth with his tongue again, rough and pleading, and I'm so close to indulging him further.

I slow my hips but he speaks first. "You can fuck me any way. All ways. Always."

It's the last thing either of us says—that either of us *can* say—for a while.

I'm holding him like he's my tether to a world I'm just discovering, and I suppose that's exactly right. It's all gratitude more than desperation, and I assume that's part of why I've been given carte blanche in a bedroom that doesn't see guests. The tension coiling in me is driving me forward, more selfish by the second even if I'll be encouraged long before I'm damned, and I give into it now, reckless with the way I'm using him. For a moment, I tell myself it's fine because Darren will take care of himself, before or after I'm done, but then I'm letting his body go just to cover his hands with mine, our knuckles white around the headboard. He's left without the ability to do anything but come untouched again, and maybe we'll break his bed before it happens, but I'm not sure that matters more than anything else I've forgiven myself for.

What's left of my control stutters then, and my release rockets through me before I can try to memorize the moment. *Moments,* actually. Many of them. I can't quite catch my breath and I'm not at all bothered by the loss, sucking somewhere near Darren's spine when I finally stop thinking about myself. My hands fall away from his, and I'm weirdly relieved when I look over his shoulder and find that he's not done yet, understanding with abrupt certainty how to make him come apart in my arms.

I don't know how we fall to the mattress—only that we do—and while I should've removed the condom right away, it's destined to be a disaster now. I'm on my back, sated and spent with my head at the foot of the bed, and Darren lands mostly on top of me, facing heaven as though it's something he believes in. My mouth is close to his ear, and when he wraps his hand around his length, I could talk to him forever.

And because I clocked his reaction when I first told him to wait, I have the right words now. He doesn't need anyone to praise him for his bartending skills or his enviable abs or his ability to make a stranger unravel while upright and hurried. But this subtly sensitive man needs to believe, if only for a moment, that he was something more.

Something harder to let go.

"You were so good for me. So, so good," I whisper. Darren arches into his own grip and drops back onto my chest again, his whimper a sound with an echo of its own. "You're so beautiful, sweetheart. So undone. And now you can fall apart while I hold you. Please. Fall apart while I watch."

He does almost immediately, arching and whimpering all over again. I'm mesmerized, maybe more so because I'm still dazed by my orgasm and the things I've spoken out loud, and I don't think much before I drag a finger through the mess he's left on his stomach.

If Darren minds, I can't tell.

And I'm certainly not going to ask him to move.

Eventually, he does anyway, but only so he can face me, so wonderfully careless when we kiss like we have all night. I'm not ready to tell him we don't, his tongue welcome against mine.

"Sweetheart?" he asks somewhere before and after it all.

"Turnabout is fair play?"

Darren smiles where I can feel it. "Ah, because of the 'baby' thing."

I comb a sticky hand through his hair and hold him steady when we kiss again, something we've done far more over the past few weeks than I would've guessed the night he knelt in front of my broken body and asked to be my first. It feels good, and it's the best way to keep me exactly where I am, Darren's mouth so damn gentle when years of innuendo at Trailhead might've made me suspect the opposite. He doesn't have to keep me here, and I won't stay forever, but neither one of us wants to crawl away from this bed we've made.

At some point, the condom is gone. Soft sheets do what they can to wipe us clean. When they fail, Darren wordlessly drags me into the bathroom and kisses me until the shower runs hot enough to soothe or scald. Under the water, I nuzzle his jaw and my lips skate over the goosebumps on his neck.

"It just came out. *Sweetheart.* I wasn't thinking."

"Okay."

I back up and raise an eyebrow. "Is it?"

"Stop worrying about the reasons it wouldn't be."

There are a lot, and Darren knows it, but he doesn't elaborate and I don't ask him to—he only plays dumb for tips, and I've never made a habit of it in the first place. He cradles my face and kisses me instead, and I want nothing more than for that to be okay, too.

When the moment has passed, we both wash and rinse and dry, and still naked, Darren moves to strip his bed and throw the dirty pile to the floor. I go in search of my clothes, strewn from there to here, and I've only just picked up my boxers when he catches my wrist and I close my eyes.

"You know you can sleep naked, right? I'm just gonna grab clean sheets and then we can crash."

"I know. And if I were going to stay, I'd sleep naked with you."

"If," he echoes.

I nod and start to get dressed. "We haven't spent the night together yet."

"And you're superstitious about sex?"

"That sounds like more of a Beau thing," I tease, my smile small and sleepy. "I just figured everything has been going well between us, and there's no reason for me to sneak out silently in the morning when I can say a proper goodbye right now."

It's Darren's turn to nod, but he's quiet long enough that I find my jeans before he speaks. "If I ask you something, will you answer it honestly?"

"I haven't lied to you before."

"Are you leaving because of anything that happened tonight?"

"No," I say, and it's as simply honest as I can be. "I'm leaving so I can sleep in my bed while you sleep in yours. That's all."

I turn away from him then, moving through his small house to finish what I've started, and Darren gives me space, making his bed without bothering to find something to wear. It's late, but he's used to this, and I don't know how much longer he might stay up once I'm gone. Of course, I'm in no rush to rid myself of the image of him sprawled naked across his bed while he watches some terrible tv show or scrolls through a dozen apps on his phone.

I'll be asleep within minutes of walking through my front door, but I might as well have pleasant dreams.

Eventually, Darren meets me for the goodbye I've promised, his hands all over me and my sweater. "Text me when you get home."

"I will."

"And thank you for riding the bull with me."

I shrug and reach for his jaw, leaning close enough to brush my lips over his. "Had to do it before we ran out of time."

"A lot of things are like that, aren't they?"

Nothing I can say will answer that rhetorical well, so I kiss him instead, deeply enough for both of us to forget I'm leaving. For two people I'd never describe as being clingy, we almost hold on too long, friendship passed from tongue to tongue until one of us pushes away and the other sighs with anything but relief.

"Goodnight, Darren."

"'Night, Jake."

The holiday season is an interesting time for those in palliative and hospice care. Family members who have been around, suddenly aren't because their lives become too busy. Family members who haven't been around, suddenly are because there's nothing quite like guilt trips and good deeds. Even among an incredible staff, there are vacation requests and winter illnesses, and I have a list of others who want to work overtime just so they don't have to go home.

Joy is high. Depression is high. Plenty of people are hit with both, patients and caregivers alike.

I get a break from medical conferences and training seminars, but I spend more days at the hospital than usual, virtual meetings traded for handshakes and chaos that require my presence. It's nothing new to me. I'm happy to meet the demands of the job, and I made peace with my own feelings about this time of year long ago.

The holiday season is an interesting time for Lucy and me.

It's when Michelle died.

Of course, Lucy's always been nearby before, and we've found ways to celebrate a little of everything. We'll do that from a distance this year, and I've been prepared for that for months. I'm restless though, and I want to be mad that it has so little to do with my daughter, and so much to do with the man I miss more than I should.

It's been nice to have someone to talk to. It's been nice to have someone to touch. It's been nice to rediscover pleasure in a way I thought I'd buried years ago, only to have a friend wink and place it in my lap.

To be fair, Darren and I have still talked and touched, and I've welcomed his continued interest in my lap, but it's been a series of fits and starts, and probably more my fault than his. I haven't made it to Trailhead, which means trivia banter has been traded for text messages and voice notes. My schedule has been less flexible than usual, so planning for a movie or dinner or a night in my spa feels out of reach. And the touching has happened during fleeting moments of pleasure, initiated by whichever one of us is a little more awake and usually beginning and ending against somebody's front door or bent over a couch, the hellos and goodbyes implied on either side.

It's fun the Sunday afternoon Darren stops by on his way—and slightly out of his way—to work. I've been keeping my mind off the rest of the world by narrowing mine to the Harley I wrecked a few months ago, and when he texts to say he has a few minutes to spare, I warn him I might be too filthy to entertain him properly.

He sends an *lol* in response, and I'm nothing but sweat and grease when he pulls into my driveway.

"I tried to warn you," I say as I push myself up from the garage floor, the black smudges covering my hands and arms keeping me from reaching for him. "I'm a mess. Been stuck inside my head all afternoon."

Darren grins, brimming with mischief when he steps closer and brushes a knuckle up and down the zipper of my jeans. "Bet I can make you messier."

His own jeans hide nothing about what's on his mind, and a bulge I've admired for years has me licking my lips now. I'm not exactly sure how this will unfold when none of my nearby rags will get me clean enough to help, but Darren isn't concerned, and

I'm all too happy to let him back me into the closest wall. I land somewhere between my workbench and a row of gardening tools organized on perfectly placed hooks, and my groan carries further than usual when he unfastens my button without looking.

"I'll get you dirty if I touch you," I continue unnecessarily. I've made my point a couple of times, and Darren hasn't given up on me yet. "Is this like the gallery opening, when you got me off and didn't let me return the favor?"

"Nope. I can't work an entire shift with my dick like this."

"The keg room will be right there."

His tongue is in my mouth right around the same time his hand is in my pants, pulling me free from my boxers and kissing me until I stop picturing him with anyone else. I kiss him back, giving as well as I get, and regardless of what happens over the next several hours, I'd like to think he'll have trouble forgetting this. While I wasn't fully aroused when Darren's fingers first curled around me, I'm getting there fast. Whether my open garage door has something to do with that is anybody's guess.

I don't have time to think about our audience either way, his clean hands working quickly to undo his jeans and push his clothes out of the way. Mine, too. Then Darren has both of us in his grip, the spit he adds causing me to make some unholy noise, and I can't tell one detail from another after that. We're kissing, panting, biting, and growling while he braces himself with one hand next to my head, careful to keep from smelling like gear oil when he arrives at Trailhead. I can't help but stare down at where he's stroking us together, and though this should take longer than it will, I'm not sorry that I start to shake. I glance across the street, then I forget about the neighborhood again when I'm compelled to watch myself spill all over Darren's hand.

"Yes, baby. Give me everything."

I do—anything else is a physical impossibility—and he uses the mess he promised to finish himself off, tipping forward just enough to make sure my old t-shirt gets painted with everything he can't wear to work.

When Darren leaves, I wear it longer than I should.

We talk a handful of times in the days after that. We touch briefly when I stop by his house on the way to a hospital fundraiser. But everything is less fun on the Tuesday afternoon he mentions coming over again. He has the night off, and I'm already home, keeping my mind off the rest of the world by narrowing mine to the woman I lost ten years ago. When Darren texts to say he has no plans for the next several hours, I warn him I might be too distracted to entertain him properly.

It's the anniversary of the day Michelle died.

There's no *lol* from him. He calls me instead. Even as I answer, I'm not sure what else to say, but I know Darren can handle it—I'm counting on it, actually—and I bite my tongue hard just before I let it go.

"Too blunt?" I ask.

"Not even close. And now I just need to know whether it would be better for me to come over or leave you alone."

"Better for whom?"

"You," he says. "Only you."

"I haven't eaten in a while."

"Okay. Is anything off limits?"

I'm not sure whether he's asking about my stomach or a decade of memories, but clarification won't change anything. "No."

Our goodbye is quiet and quick, and I push myself off the couch where I've been thumbing through one of Michelle's old architecture books. Lucy and I had talked for about an hour earlier, and I'd gone for a longer ride up the coast afterward, stopping in Santa Barbara for coffee and a croissant at a place I've missed, then turning around to come home. A shower felt good. So did a nap. I would've been fine either way, but taking care of myself was the smart thing to do.

The jury is still out about visits from friends.

It's a while before I hear the knock at my door, and I let Darren in without the fanfare that would feel out of place today. One of his arms is wrapped around a full paper bag, and his free hand holds a six-pack of mediocre beer. For all I know, he doesn't intend to share them.

"Carne asada tacos, chicken fajita burritos, a cheese quesadilla, chips, salsa, guacamole."

I shake my head as I lead him into the kitchen. "Did you invite half the bar to join us?"

"I *will* get you to throw that pool party when it's warm again."

"And in the meantime?"

"In the meantime, I bought enough food for you to have options."

He doesn't make a bigger deal of it than that, and I turn to look at him in his gray sweatpants and the Trailhead hoodie that should bore me by now. Darren's smiling while he studies me, maybe tired of the same comfortable clothes I always wear at home, and I close the distance between us long enough to bump his forehead with mine.

I step back and decide we don't need to make something formal out of this. "Backyard?"

"Sure."

He's still carrying everything when we get outside, and I set up the firepit, the December night not meant for outdoor dining any other way. I've got blankets nearby too, and nothing as simple as that should remind me of my wife. We both get settled on the patio sofa, and I think I take him by surprise when he notices the joint I'd left behind, but then he tears into the paper bag, a pile of foil-wrapped food the biggest temptation between us. He waits for me to make the first pick, twists a bottle cap, and takes a long drink.

"Is this day always hard for you?" Darren asks, scoffing at himself a moment later. "Sorry, that was stupid. Obviously it's not a great one."

"It's actually—" I stop and help myself to a bottle. "It's not hard. It's not even bad. It's a chance to wallow if I want it, but I can't remember the last time that happened."

"Okay, so what is it?"

"I tried to warn you," I wink.

He chuckles. "You're not all that messy now."

"No, just stuck in my head again."

"Does this have anything to do with me?"

I'm about to take a bite, but my head jerks up at that. "You're not a replacement for her."

"Can't imagine I'd ever be stupid enough to try."

He doesn't say more, and we eat in silence because we've known each other long enough to be okay with it. One beer becomes two. We finish an absurd amount of food and share the chips and guac. I realize I never turned on the string lights, but the flickering flames from the firepit suit the evening well, so I don't move now. I could make it through the rest of the night without speaking another word, and Darren probably expects exactly that, but when anyone else might make an excuse and leave me to it, he gathers what's left of our dinner and opens the last two beers.

I take a sip of mine. He does, too. Then he grabs one of the blankets and lies back on the sofa, making room for me between his legs like I'd once done in his living room. That night he'd summoned me from the desert to exorcise a demon he's never known.

I'm desperate to believe we're not doing the same thing tonight.

I make myself comfortable in his arms anyway and let him hold me, the blanket covering us both. "This is the first year Lucy hasn't been here. And I knew that—I was prepared for that. But I'm used to talking about Michelle all day, and being alone today made it feel like everything inside me had nowhere to go."

"What do you usually say about her?"

"Just stories. Memories. Silly stuff. Things that make me smile." I sigh and know he feels it. "I don't cry about her. Haven't for a very long time."

"Will you tell me? The things that make you smile about Michelle?"

And for the next couple of hours, with one of Darren's hands in my hair and the other clasped in mine, I do.

Christmas is a couple of days later. I go to Mass in the morning and talk to Lucy when I get back, and she and I open gifts over the phone. I call each of my siblings, all four of them scattered around the country with families of their own, and I hear about the ways they're celebrating. Somewhere between one brother and another, I put *White Christmas* on. Then I wonder whether it's too early to check in with Darren after last night's Christmas Eve shift.

I'm wondering a lot of things.

I don't have experience with this friends with benefits arrangement Darren and I have enjoyed the past couple of months, but I think our time together makes sense when we're being friends and reaping benefits. Conversations across the bar, and texts with trivia questions, and dinner, whether I cook or Darren brings us takeout. Orgasms we achieve in minutes or more than an hour, or sometimes not at all, all the kissing and grinding occasionally enough for us to claim the pleasure we've sought from the other's body.

But what happened between us in my backyard the other night was far more intimate than the rest of our friendship, and without a single kiss, it felt short of everything else. Darren held me and listened to me, his warm breath in my hair and his thumb in a soothing back and forth against my hand, and I shared stories that shouldn't matter to him. They did matter though, and if none of my other friends would carefully caress me through that welcome ache, and if my sometimes lover wasn't going to caress me any further than that, I wondered what those hours meant for us.

Neither of us has the heart for more, but Darren's embrace had felt a lot like sunshine passing through a stained glass window, and I've never been able to stray far from church.

For his sake, it might be time for me to walk away from *something*.

Regardless, I decide I won't think too much about it today, and that works well until I'm staring at a Christmas tree I decorated out of habit. My phone startles me with a call, a ridiculous picture of Darren's charming bartender grin on display when I look down.

"Merry Christmas," I murmur, excited to hear from him, and weighed down by the reasons I shouldn't be.

He doesn't say anything back—not for a while—and the silence drags on just long enough for me to worry, my head perfectly clear when I'm about to go in search of his voice by calling his name. Before I can, Darren clears his throat, and I wait for an explanation, as patient as I've been about anything.

"Hey, I—sorry, this is—it's Christmas, and I shouldn't—"

He stops there and coughs, too many words caught in his chest while he's concerned about apologies and holidays, and I take the deep breath he can't find.

"Darren, it's fine. Just tell me."

I reach for an ornament Lucy made me in kindergarten. The past is a hell of a thing, and I step away from it now, but Darren doesn't have it so easy.

"I met my dad last night."

CHAPTER FIFTEEN

DARREN

There are about the same number of people in Trailhead tonight as there had been on Thanksgiving—some faces are the same, too—and when the barn doors open again, I'm eager for the relief they'll usher in. I keep myself busy behind the bar while Jake makes his way to the stool he favors any time it's free, and there's a Guinness in front of him before he can ask for it. His smile is careful, and I want to deserve it.

"Merry Christmas, Jake. And thank you for coming."

"Merry Christmas, Darren. And you're welcome."

We hadn't talked on the phone for long before I'd given up and asked if he'd mind hanging out for a bit. His answer was immediate, and he only wanted to stop by the hospital first to check on everyone there. I don't think he has anywhere else to be after this, but I'm not needy enough to push him to stay with me tonight.

Or maybe I don't want to hear him say no.

"Guess you probably want to know about last night."

Jake shrugs. "I want to know whatever you want to tell me."

"It feels like a lot," I admit.

"I'm sure it does. He got to you."

"What do you mean?"

He takes a sip and shrugs again. "You've always referred to him as your father before. When you called me today, you said *dad* instead."

I flinch at that and take a swig from my water bottle before I leave him there to pour a couple of drinks. To be honest, I don't remember what I said on the phone, but I don't think Jake is a liar. He's unbothered when I return, and I fuck around with a stack of coasters.

"We weren't busy. Even quieter than tonight, actually. And when he came in, he walked right up to me and held out his hand and said, 'Hi, Darren. I'm Drew Barrett, and it's an honor to finally meet you.'"

"An honor?"

"A motherfucking honor. Like he couldn't have been honored over and over again my entire fucking life." I throw the coasters into one of the sinks and hate that I'll have to clean up my mess later. "I wish I could've denied it—that he's my father—but I look exactly like him. So much for not recognizing him, huh? He's a stranger, and I look exactly fucking like him."

We're quiet for a minute because I need to calm down, and Jake is rarely in a rush. Eventually, he taps the side of his pint glass.

"Did he tell you what else he wanted? His original comment was something about Trailhead, right? Back in October?"

"Yeah, it's about the band."

"The band? As in the one that was barely more than a hypothetical back then?"

He glances over my shoulder, to where an empty space awaits a small stage we'll need built sooner than later. I just sigh.

"I guess he's got a connection to one," I say. "And before you ask, no, he said he wasn't stalking the bar. Told me someone else mentioned the live music thing to him, so then he saw me in one of the videos talking about it—"

"And not only do you look like him, you've got your mother's last name and none of your personal social media accounts are private, so he probably did stalk those."

"Yeah, he admitted that much. Anyway, he wanted to talk to me back in October, but then there was some personal thing happening behind the scenes, so he was dealing with that, and when he finally had time to look us up again, he saw that we're gonna make it official and want to talk to people in January, so he was getting a jump on that like being my dad will help his friends get this gig."

In all my babbling, I've accidentally made Drew Barrett my dad again, and while I doubt Jake missed it, he doesn't call me out. "But you'll meet the band?"

"Sure. I don't really think there's a good way around that if I want to do what's best for the bar."

"I agree."

"Gee, thanks," I mutter, biting my tongue before I say anything about being fair to a band that might be full of really great parents.

Jake shakes off my shitty attitude. "You took this project on, and it comes with a lot of pressure, even without your father being part of the equation. I'm happy to tell you when I think you're doing something right."

"More praise, huh?"

"It seems to help," he smirks. "So, other than being honored to meet you, and wanting this band to replace your mechanical bull, did he have much to say?"

"You mean, did he explain why he bailed on my mom and only looked back long enough to send one birthday card?"

"Something like that."

I roll my eyes and probably look like a child. I sort of feel like one. "Nope. He asked if we could meet for lunch sometime. Catch up on an entire lifetime over burgers and fries."

"And you said yes."

He knows the answer already, and I can't respond before the barn doors open again. It's unexpected on this chilly Christmas night, but I'm warmed by the familiar laugh of my ex-husband—he's not quite Santa, but it's close—and the sight of his pretty boyfriend. They're dressed for plans bigger than a queer country bar, and hotter than they have any right to be. I glance at Jake, but he looks as surprised by their arrival as I am, so I turn back to Beau and Adrian with a lime wedge in my hand and throw it at a target big enough for me to hit.

"What the fuck are you doing here?"

"Merry fuckin' Christmas to you, too," Beau replies, laughing all over again as he makes his way to Jake's side. I think it's the first time I've seen him in the bar without his hat, and it amuses me on a day I need it. "Adrian's sister and her wife are in town, and the swanky rooftop restaurant at their hotel is open tonight. We sat around and watched movies all day, but figured as long as we were gettin' dressed to go out with them, we'd stop by to keep your sorry ass company. Didn't realize Jake had already taken the charity shift for us."

He wraps an arm around Jake and kisses his cheek while I blow one to Adrian. "Since Lucy's busy with work, I thought Jake and I might as well be alone together."

"Didn't you say you were here for Thanksgiving, too?"

My head is down while I fetch two coasters from the sink and grab Beau's beer, so my reaction to his question goes unnoticed. I hadn't realized that Jake had told Beau about that visit, but I have no idea how often they talk outside of here, and it's probably none of my business.

Well, it's sort of my business, but I pull a ginger ale from the cooler, pour Adrian's drink, and don't worry about anyone's secrets now.

"I guess it's Darren doing the charity this year," Jake says.

I'm absolutely the sinner to Jake's saint, so it's easy for everyone to chuckle and move on from a quip like that. When I lean across the bar, we all catch up on what we've missed over the past couple of weeks. I ask Adrian whether he's had an uptick in sales with people wanting to buy his pictures as gifts. Beau asks Jake about work and how Lucy's doing. Adrian asks about my mom and when I'll head down to San Diego again. Jake throws a soft look my way while he waits to see whether I'll mention my father.

I don't. He disappeared for two months after he first contacted me. He disappeared for decades before that. Expecting him to make it to lunch feels frighteningly foolish, so really, there's nothing to tell.

A few people leave from a table in the corner, and I grab a towel to wipe it down and collect the empty glasses they've left behind. From there, I check on the handful of others in the room, then I return to the bar and pour Jake another Guinness. It's nice having the four of us here like this—nearly an impromptu double date if two of us were actually dating and another two weren't so intent on disliking each other—but it doesn't last, and I can't complain.

The barn doors open again, and Riley walks in.

They're dressed at least as nicely as Beau and Adrian. And they're at least as hot.

I wave from behind the bar and watch as they remove their earbuds, their eyes darting to take in everything at once. I'm not sure why they're here, except that they must have wanted to see me and couldn't have predicted our little Christmas crowd. Riley's not spooked exactly, but they need time to adjust to the presence of three other people they'll have to talk to now, and I offer them an out I don't think they'll take.

"Merry Christmas. You wanna go out back?"

Riley smiles and moves closer, grateful but prepared to kick my ass if I'm too fucking nice. "No, but you can get me a beer. Same as Beau's."

"Sure, why the fuck not? This holiday is full of surprises," I say, already popping the cap on their bottle. "Are we celebrating something? You look like you're about to crash Beau and Adrian's fancy dinner."

They're quiet at first, but Jake moves to an empty stool so Riley can sit next to Beau, and once I've handed over the beer and poured myself a shot, everyone holds up their drinks to toast the unknown. I have to swallow quickly and leave them there when someone at the opposite side of the bar is ready to close out, but Riley's eyes are on me when I return, and I don't think I've missed anything.

"Ethan."

I nod. Beau raises an eyebrow. The other two just wait for Riley to go on.

"I broke up with him today."

It would be rude to cheer, or even congratulate them, no matter how well intended it might be, so I watch as one of Beau's big hands covers Riley's. The move isn't one the rest of us could make, but Riley's entire body relaxes, and I feel the same sort of relief.

"Guess we didn't need that whiteboard after all," I say. Then I remember they'd come in here to see me, and I return to being a bartender as much as a friend. "Do you want to talk about it, or am I on a mission to make you forget?"

"No mission. And there's not much to talk about. He was with his family all day. We had reservations for dinner. He was late. Everything had been so quiet. And I—" Riley reaches for the bottle but doesn't take a drink. "I didn't want to go. I didn't want to go late, but I realized I didn't want to go at all. Not with him. Not ever."

"What did he say when you told him that?" Jake asks.

Riley shrugs. "He sort of laughed. Said it was a shitty thing to do on Christmas, but at least I had an opinion for once. I stood in the middle of my living room, and he went to gather the few things he'd left around. Then he came back and said he didn't have time to worry about the rest when he'd already found someone else to meet him for dinner."

"Jesus," Adrian breathes.

I look from him to Beau to Jake and back again, unsure which one of them is most likely to spit fire. I'd do just about anything for Riley if I thought they needed my help, but the other three are more likely to interrupt Ethan's brand new date and bloody his dessert.

"There's not much happening tonight, but when we get more people in here again, you're welcome to show off the keg room to anyone you meet. I've got you."

Adrian chokes on whiskey. Beau glares at me.

"Darren."

"What? You give your brilliant advice, and I'll give mine."

"I haven't seen *you* show off the keg room in a while," Riley says. "Should I worry that you're trying to pass the baton?"

"Careful," Jake warns, a small smile barely hidden. It surprises all of us, I think. "You're dangerously close to euphemism territory, and I can't imagine you're interested in Darren's baton."

That sets off a round of laughter among people who deserve it, and I glance at Jake, suddenly aware that the joke was an attempt to distract everyone—himself included, perhaps—from the question of why I haven't been fucking around on my shifts. When I meet Beau's eyes next, I'm not sure it was a success.

And I don't want to explain myself to either of them.

"Well, as much as I would love to stay and chat about my ex-husband's sexcapades, Adrian's sister is expecting us." Beau empties his bottle while Adrian throws a twenty on the bar, and I scowl at the bad example I know Jake and Riley will follow, my tips just fucking fine without their help. Maybe Beau thinks my expression is about something else, because he slides off his stool and winks. "We can talk about his sudden aversion to workplace hookups another time."

The two of them say their goodbyes to Jake and Riley, and leave without giving me any more shit about things they don't understand. No refills are needed where I stand, so I do a quick sweep of the bar, and the few people left are doing just fine. When I return, there's a quiet conversation happening in front of me, and I'm happy to leave them to it, but Riley looks up at me, blue eyes so goddamn wise and still unsure.

"You guys are happy, aren't you? About the breakup?"

"I don't think *happy* is the right word for it," I say. "And not to pick on the guy who already lost big tonight, but he's an idiot to think you lack opinions, and it's why I don't believe for a second you ended things with Ethan to please *us*."

Jake taps the back of his finger against Riley's beer bottle. "We're happy for *you* more than we're happy about what you did."

"And you're eager to help me find someone new."

Riley directs that one to me, so I shake my head. "Only if you want me to. There's no way you actually *need* anyone's help with that. You're stunning."

"So, how long until you fuck a musician or two as part of the audition process?" Riley asks, nodding toward where the bull used to be.

It's an obvious deflection, but I don't have a habit of making them uncomfortable, perfectly content to let it be the other way around. And I'm about to deflect, too. Still, before I say anything, I look at Jake and wait for him to nod.

He does. I speak.

"V's gonna want you to hear these auditions too, so I'm sure you'll be around to see plenty, but I—I'm already in touch with someone who wants to bring a band in here."

"In touch? Is this a 'friend' of yours?"

Their use of air quotes makes me smile despite everything else. "Just about the furthest thing from it. He's my father."

I'm proud of myself for getting the word right this time, and I catch Jake when he washes down a comment about it with his Guinness. Riley's confused though, and they lift their beer to buy time. It's unnecessary when they can just ask—and I already know they will—but I walk to the end of the bar and back just to make everything easier.

"I don't remember you ever mentioning your father before," Riley says when I return. "I usually remember things."

"Yeah, no, this is on me, not you. He left my mom when she was pregnant with me. He's never been worth a conversation. I didn't even meet him until last night."

"But he knew we're looking for a band?"

"Saw it online, yeah," I confirm. I leave out the details of the message in October because it only reminds me I exist most often as a memory, and my father's comment then changes nothing about lunch plans now. "Came by last night to talk—about the band and about getting to know me, I guess."

"He doesn't deserve that," Jake mutters.

I frown. "I thought you said you agreed with me."

"I agreed you should give the band a fair chance. I don't think you owe *him* a damn thing."

"It's just lunch."

Jake shakes his head. "It's not *just* anything. He walked out almost 40 years ago, and he walked back in when you could do something for him. You called him a stranger, and that's exactly right. Some people shouldn't be parents, Darren. And just because he showed up now doesn't make him one."

"Maybe he never wanted to be one," Riley says. "If the pregnancy took them by surprise—"

"Plenty of pregnancies take people by surprise," Jake interrupts. "Plenty of kids are born long before people have any idea how to be good parents, and they still stick around."

"And plenty of those kids would've been better off if their parents *hadn't* stuck around."

"It's selfish to run instead of trying to learn. If they put in the effort, they could learn to love raising a kid they weren't ready to have."

"It's arrogant to think everyone has something to learn," Riley spits back. "Some of them can love the kid better by not raising them at all."

"Making that commitment can be so worth it, though."

"Making that commitment can hurt everyone."

"Sorry, but I think more parents should stay."

"And I think a lot of them should go."

"Speaking from personal experience?"

"Not at all," Riley tells Jake. "Are you?"

I want to be turned on by watching two of the calmest, most beautiful people in my life get heated like this, except that it's about me without being about me, and I don't want either of them to take this too far.

"Hey," I say, trying to make eye contact with them as evenly as possible. "You know I love you both, and if you want to kiss and make up, I'm here for it. But please let this fuck me up, not you. I'll have lunch, we'll audition the band, and then we'll go from there."

"Maybe they'll suck," Riley muses.

"And maybe nothing else has to change," Jake adds.

Riley takes a deep breath, then kisses Jake on the cheek. It's not what I'd meant, but I'll take it.

"Things change all the time," Riley sighs.

The rest of my strange Christmas night passes quietly, Riley and Jake leaving within minutes of each other, though neither of them bothers kissing *me* goodbye. Trailhead stays as slow as I expect after years of experience, and when Zach finally quits a few days later, I can say I expected that, too. We'll have to find a new bartender, obviously, but business will be slow for at least the next month or so, so it's something we can handle while we're looking for a band.

Just before the new year, I meet with V to give her a run-down of my plans to audition bands on upcoming weekends. A handful have already expressed interest, giving me options that have nothing to do with long-lost family. In between, I'll hire someone to build a simple stage—we don't need anything fancy, just something that looks worth a small cover charge—and talk to Adrian about helping with some basic promo. He'd set us up before we launched karaoke and trivia night, and even with the gallery keeping him busy, I think he'll lend a hand if I beg right.

In another week, I've got four bands calendared. I've also got my father wanting to set up a time for lunch, but as clever as I am, I haven't decided whether it's better to meet with him before or after I've heard his friends play.

I'd ask Jake for advice, but we've barely talked, and I'm not interested in starting a fight he's already had with someone much nicer than I am.

I end up in a booth with Sage instead.

"Listen to the band first," she says. "You're as close to neutral as possible right now, so if you're gonna give them a real shot, do it before you've spent an hour with a man who could sway things in either direction."

"You really think he could make me like the band *more*?"

"You really think he couldn't? You're a softie, Darren."

I shove a french fry in my mouth and watch her steal five from my plate. "And I think you've had too many years with a good dad to know what it's like when one isn't around."

Sage snorts. "I know plenty about him not being around."

"Okay, but there's a difference between someone being gone because he's working two jobs to support his family, and someone not staying long enough to meet his kid in the first place."

"Yeah, I guess there is."

The next day, I pull up the last DM from my father and respond with a few excuses about why I'm busy for a while. He doesn't argue—maybe he doesn't like to fight either—and we make plans for a couple of days after Supine plays for V, Riley, me, and any wayward country rock fans who might be drinking that night.

Supine. Lying on one's back. Or passive in a way that suggests moral weakness—a failure to act, maybe. Submission. I'm well-versed in enough of those concepts to appreciate the band's name, whether it has a deep meaning for them or was picked when one of them threw a dart at a dictionary. If Drew Barrett and I run out of things to talk about at lunch, I suppose I could ask.

Either way, I have a lot going on at the bar, but I miss Jake, too. He makes it to trivia night, and when the host asks who sang backup on Carly Simon's "You're So Vain," something about the question leaves him staring at me before I stick out my tongue and answer—correctly—Mick Jagger. Still, everyone else is around us, and I can't kiss the expression off his face. His good-night is no different from the ones that came before the past few months, and I pretend I don't notice.

I go in search of something better, though. After the first couple of bands audition, both of them entertaining enough for everyone to have a good time, V offers to close, and I wind up in WeHo, drunk in a club I rarely dance in. When grinding against strangers in the middle of a crowded floor leaves me sweaty and close enough to high, I come down on a walk that leads me past Mason's studio and Adrian's gallery. I wonder whether Jake ever went back to buy a picture, and hate that I haven't been in his bedroom recently enough to check for one there.

I go home to sleep alone.

And I keep chasing things I can't name.

Jake and I text. Beau and I text. I see Riley at work. Noah is the only one who stops by for a drink during trivia night that week. I visit Sage twice, and she doesn't ask why. My apps bore me, so I go for a drive to nowhere and back, and I try so hard to avoid thinking about the man who doesn't think about me.

Drew Barrett had texted to let me know he'll be at the upcoming audition, but I can't imagine I kept his attention long after that.

I hate that I don't know how to forget about him first, and I pace behind the bar the night Supine will play. Riley grabs a pen and a coaster, advice going in the opposite direction tonight.

Sometimes the keg room can be a good place to hide in the dark. It's quieter there, too. You don't have to bring anyone with you if you just want a break.

"Before or after I see my father?"

"Whenever you need it," Riley says. "You're not the only one who can cover for a friend."

I smile, tucking the coaster into my back pocket. "Sometimes it feels like *friend* isn't the right word for whatever all of us are."

"All of us?"

"I don't know—you, me, Beau, Adrian, Jake, Noah."

"Beau's your ex-husband. Is that a better word?"

"No."

"Darren! Great to see you again!"

Riley and I both turn at the sound of a too-friendly greeting, though I can't tell whether it's been made fake by dishonesty or nerves. My father is approaching the bar, and most people around don't seem to care, but V steps closer to me, and it's only now that I realize I should've given her a heads up. The back of Riley's hand brushes against mine, and it means everything.

"Welcome back," I say. Then I lean to look past him at the group of four loaded with instruments and other gear. "I guess that's Supine?"

Drew nods. "Maxwell Kerr, Banjo Kaminski, Layla Martello, and Sebastian Sadler."

Thick glasses and freckles for days. A long-ass beard and tight-ass jeans. A leather bustier and a purple braid to rival V's gray one. A mess of soft caramel curls and striking green eyes.

My father still looks too much like me.

When I forget to say anything else, V speaks to the band, guarded on my behalf. "You can pile any extra stuff in the corner for now. Get everything set up and start playing whenever you're ready. You've got an hour for your set—less than that if you cause everyone to leave."

"What if they cause people to stay?" Drew asks.

"Darren and Riley already do that," V answers. "And you are?"

She must've figured it out already, but the question pulls the cockiness from my father's smile, and he holds out his hand. "Drew Barrett. Darren's dad, and a friend of the band. Really just here for moral support, so I'll stay out of everyone's way."

I want to question his familiarity with the words *moral* and *support*, but say nothing when V delivers a more professional response.

"It's a bar. You can have a drink or two while you enjoy the show," she says. "Other than that, being out of everyone's way would be great."

"Nah, I'm good on the drinks, but thanks. Darren, we'll catch up during the week, right?"

"Right."

To my surprise, and maybe Riley's too, he wanders off. Riley grabs beers for a barely legal couple who look nervous to be here, and V grabs my elbow to lead me to the far side of the bar.

"Sounds like you and I should catch up, too."

So, while we serve our Saturday night crowd and listen to Supine play, I tell her about a pregnant nursing student and a burned birthday card and a comment left on a video and a lunch planned for this week. She listens like the mother she is. I ache like a child missing something they never had. Trailhead pulses around me, alive with the music and everyone's enjoyment of it. For once, it's all too loud for me, and I blame the fun being had more than the sounds themselves.

The sounds are perfect.

Supine is smart. Their set is mostly country rock covers—songs popular enough to hold the attention of anyone sitting down to listen, while encouraging others to fill the dance floor and move to a beat they know well. When they introduce a couple of original songs, the transitions are smooth and the choruses easy to learn, but they never stray from the familiar for long. To top it all off, the lead singer's voice is the right kind of rough, and as attractive as he is, he knows being in a band only makes him hotter. It makes *all* of them hotter.

A few of my usually quiet regulars—guys named Brett, Rhett, and Jet who have spent several of my shifts shooting pool—whistle for the band amid the applause and shouts from the rest of the crowd. Riley, V, and I pour round after round, and I try to forget how much the absence of anything, or anyone, can hurt.

Time passes either way, and Supine wraps up. They pack their things and disappear through the barn doors. My father follows. I leave much later, and drive to the diner.

Sage does her best to help, but a chocolate milkshake isn't enough, and I apologize for being trouble she gets paid for regardless of whether I smile. Bars everywhere are closed, but I turn my car around and drive toward WeHo anyway, a bad habit I haven't quite kicked. I could pick up my phone when I get there—there's no shortage of fun to be had—but I stay on the road and keep driving 'til I almost hit sand. For what it's worth, the beach is closed too, but I park and close my eyes and take as much of a nap as someone like me ever gets.

When I wake up, it's still dark, but I do pick up my phone then.

You awake

It takes a while to get a response, and my eyes are closed again when my phone vibrates with Jake's text.

Barely. Shouldn't you be asleep?

Yeah

What's keeping you awake?

Typing out an answer could take until dawn, and I don't bother with it now. *Can I come over?*

Is your bed that uncomfortable?

Haven't made it home yet. I'm in Santa Monica

Alone?

I hate that he had to ask. If anyone else did, I think I'd be proud. *Yeah I'm alone*

Jake is quiet again, and I brace myself for anything—a lecture, a refusal, or a hundred more questions. None of it comes, and maybe he just needed to rub the sleep from his eyes.

Drive safe. See you soon.

Even in a metro area known for its traffic, it doesn't take more than half an hour to get to Jake's home in the hills at this time of day. I pull into his driveway and look down at the extra message he'd sent about ten minutes ago.

Door's unlocked.

I haven't decided how I feel about that, but I'm also not going home, so I let myself in, leave my shoes at the door, and peek into the living room and kitchen before I figure he must be up-stairs. When I reach the top of the stairs, I will my heartbeat to slow for something I've done too many times for me to dissect the details now. Nothing is better when I get the answer to my question about Jake's return to Adrian's, a framed photograph of a carousel and a little girl in pigtails displayed almost proudly on his hallway wall. My eyes only fall closed for a second, and my socked feet don't make a sound against Jake's carpet, but he obviously knows I'm here, his gaze ready to meet mine when I step through his bedroom door.

He's still in bed, propped up on a couple of pillows with a book in his hand and glasses low on his nose.

Jesus. Fucking. Christ.

"I've never seen you wear those before."

"I don't bring them to the bar, and we haven't spent much time reading when you've been here," Jake says, setting the book aside. He keeps the glasses on for another few seconds, but then they end up on top of the book, and he beckons me closer. "What happens if I ask you how you're doing and why you're here?"

I shrug out of my jacket, pull my shirt over my head, and unfasten my jeans, which probably answers the latter half of his question just fine. But as I move toward him, my fingers trailing over his bare arm, I attempt the rest.

"I've always told you the truth, right? Even after you got back from Palm Springs, I—it just took me some time."

"I don't want this to be like it was then. I want to know what happened."

Jake pushes at my jeans until I take over and finish undressing, leaving a pile on his floor. By the time I'm done, he's added his own t-shirt to it, but I'm the one to tug the comforter away and reach for his pajama pants. Any morning wood has come and gone, and what I can feel growing thicker beneath my touch is all mine, but I'm impatient this morning and I want his dick inside me. I just need to give him what he wants first.

He lifts his hips so I can get him naked, and I smile as well as I can with too many things on my mind. "My father's friends played the bar tonight, and he was with them. They were good. Great, actually."

"You're busy on Saturday nights," Jake says, finally pulling me into bed with him. I straddle his lap without it being more than that, our cocks getting harder against each other while we wait. "Did he get in your way? Talk to you all night?"

"No. I think V scared him. He only said hello and left to sit near the stage."

I kiss him then, slow and long and deep because the sun is just starting to rise, and Jake's house is silent except for each shared breath we take. I've never seen him like this, still undone by the vulnerability that comes with sleep, and not yet put together again. The closest I came was the night of his accident, but that was a different undone, and it wasn't the kind of thing I could enjoy except for the moments he and I fantasized about something like this.

His arms are wrapped around me now, so when I break away, I can't go far.

"He didn't bother you. And the music didn't bother you," he says, words warm against my neck. "So, what went wrong, what have you been up to the past few hours, and how do I get rid of that look in your eyes?" I won't ask what he sees—either I already know, or I don't want to—but I bring a hand to his jaw and give him as much honesty as I can.

"I don't think anything is *wrong*. But I feel like I'm scrambling to keep up with myself, and then keep falling further behind. I went to visit a friend for a while, and usually I go home after that, but I drove around instead, and then I—I wanted to see you."

Jake's teeth drag over my shoulder. "Because one friend wasn't enough?"

I kiss him again because he has the wrong idea, and I don't know how to correct it without getting into a couple of years of something I can't explain. My friendship with a cute 20-year-old diner waitress makes little sense to anyone not in the booth with us. Maybe it's true of whatever I have with Jake too—someone like him doesn't need someone like me—but I cling to him while I can.

"Condom and lube."

They're within my reach too, but he's the one who won't fuck me until he's heard enough. Apparently he has, though, or the constant tease of my dick moving against his has made him as impatient as I always am. Once he's rolled the condom over his cock, I stroke him with the lube and wipe my hand on my thigh and rise on my knees just long enough to lower myself again.

When he's buried inside me, it feels a lot like home.

But I don't live here.

CHAPTER SIXTEEN

JAKE

My hold on Darren tightens because I need to remember who he is.

And who he's not.

This early in the morning, with the sunlight just peeking in, thoughts of Michelle cut through my bedroom, and wishing away the warmth they offer will be a sin I'll carry to church a few hours from now. I'm plenty warm here, with him, and I haven't figured out whether the pull at my heart is a wound reopening or one being stitched back together. Either way, I try to get closer to Darren's heartbeat just so I don't have to feel my own.

When it doesn't settle right away, I remind myself that this is just sex, something that was never true with Michelle, even when we fumbled our way through a series of teenage firsts. It's physical pleasure, and I know I'm allowed as much. Any distance I've tried to keep over these past several weeks has been from a dozen less carnal moments—drying dishes, making curry, and the very idea of hosting a pool party—the sacred things Darren's acknowledged from the first night I had him in my bed.

I'm allowed those, too. Michelle had made that explicitly clear before she said goodbye. But I'm a stubborn old fool, and the wrong one of us was left behind.

"God, you feel so fucking good. *Christ*," Darren hisses, so painfully slow when he rises and falls that the blasphemy makes itself at home between us, and I don't look away. It's just more forgiveness to seek. "I needed this. I needed you."

The idea of that hits harder than it should when I'm the second person he's been with since he left Trailhead, and I can't figure out how honest he's being with himself while he's in my lap. I lift my hand to his lips, and I think I mean to tell him to be quiet if he feels the need to lie. Instead, I slip two fingers into his mouth, another chance for me to think about that first night, when he'd done the same to me.

I've changed since then, but it turns me on just the same. "I needed this, too."

Darren sucks my fingers while he rides me, and my other arm remains wrapped around his back to feel the play of his muscles as his body moves up and down, still lazier about it than I would've imagined. Staring into his eyes is intense, morning sex a different experience, the intimacy of it usually reserved for those who have spent an entire night together. This isn't that, for at least a couple of reasons, but we're lost in each other anyway, and I'm finding it harder and harder to care.

Eventually, I pull my fingers free and let them drop to where Darren's dripping for me, the pad of my thumb teasing him until my hand finds its perfect fit around his length, each stroke matching the pace he's set. His hands angle my head upward for a kiss that makes me feel more naked than I already am, the way he reads me almost painfully undeniable. I try to read him back, and begin to meet each slow slide of his body with a careful thrust of my own. The guttural noise he makes suggests I've done something right, and I take my time when I do it again, his mouth open against my cheek and his breath warm while I moan.

"Mmmm, you were so good, telling me why you're here. So good, sweetheart."

He clenches around me as he chokes on a sob my words have pulled from his chest. I chase another kiss and catch his lower lip between my teeth before I let him go.

"Nothing else—nobody else—" he starts.

"No, shhhhh," I say, moving with him in a way that belies whatever out I try to give him. "I'm here. I'm coming undone, and you don't have to make promises. Just be you. Be honest and be *you*."

Darren's the one to bite his lip this time, maybe as afraid as I am of all the other things he could say. There's an expiration date to an arrangement like this, but I don't want him to think he has to put on a show before we reach it. And endless trivia questions will keep us close as long as we play this part right. It's why my slow strokes stop altogether, and I release him there just to keep him closer everywhere else, both arms around him when we get rough.

He uses me—maybe it's what I told him to do—and we find a new rhythm together, sweating and panting while we leave at least a couple of marks on each other's skin. It can't be painless for him, but it's not the same as when he'd needed to get out of his head weeks ago. The confession of his restlessness is on my mind, but it's not heavy enough for me to want less than this, my physical strength outlasting anything else Darren takes from me.

"Jake, Jake, Jake," he chants. Whines, really. He's breathless about it, and it's real. "Just you. Jake. Needed you."

I kiss him wherever I can, all of it fleeting when I can't fight anymore. "You can have me. For as long as you want."

Darren kisses me back, or tries to, but when I feel him tighten around me again, some practiced talent wielded against me, I growl or swear or pray for a way to keep going.

He mewls. I become feral.

I flip him over, a long-buried instinct surprising us both. We're sideways across the bed, I think—diagonal, maybe—and I brace myself above him while his knees are bent to his shoulders, his hips raised so I can rock into him relentlessly. He's not reciting vows now, and his blue-gray eyes grow so damn dark in the morning light when he uses my name again, his hands fisting the sheets.

"Jake, please."

"Please, what?"

"Jerk me off. Make me come while you fuck me like this. That's not—it's honest. It's me. I want to make a mess."

It's honest, but it's not new. We're back to that first night one more time, but I liked the mess then, and I'm more than ready to like it all over again. Shifting my weight as smoothly as I can without pulling out entirely, I reach for him and care little about being gentle. And Darren definitely doesn't care, torn between chasing each of my thrusts and arching into my grip, every whimpered plea more obscene than the last.

I find myself wishing I could take off the condom, and just barely stop myself from saying so.

I can't stop anything else. "I'm so close. I'm—"

My warning gets lost when Darren comes, convulsing beneath me when he spills all over his stomach and chest—and all over my hand. I look down at where it covers my skin, and that's all it takes for my control to snap, my body falling against his as I thrust those last few times and wish I could've made a mess of my own.

We come down together, and I stay inside him as long as I can, even less interested in separating us when he's the one to drag a couple of fingertips over his chest this time. He feeds them to me, an offer more than a challenge, and I suck from them without hesitation, my tongue in his mouth a moment after that. It's fierce, that kiss, and I feel Darren moan before I hear him.

"We have to stop, or I'm gonna keep you here 'til your dick's hard enough for round two," he mumbles against me. "And I might fall asleep under you in the meantime."

"You say that as if I'd mind."

Darren smiles, and I feel that, too. "You might. What if I

snore?"

"Do you?"

"No."

"Good to know," I say, smiling back as I ease away from him. "Shower, though?"

It's an imperative—I'm going to church soon and doubt Darren is eager for a sticky car ride home—and something of a habit that satisfies us both. Those minutes in the water provide a buffer between worlds that are close together and far apart, and sharing that space under the pretense of something wholly practical means we don't have to decide whether leaving each other afterward requires a tiptoe or a leap.

We're quiet through it all, but once we've dried off and Darren goes in search of his clothes, I lean against the bathroom doorframe and bring him back to the night before.

"So, the band was really that good?"

"They were, yeah. Exactly the vibe I'd hoped for—more rock than trendy pop." Darren zips his jeans and looks up at me, rolling his eyes before I can point out the obvious. "Yes, I know it's not what I *listen* to, but it's what's good for the *bar*. And as busy as we were, Riley seemed captivated by the set and whatever charm Supine brought to the bar afterward, so I figured that was a good sign. Riley loves music and despises bullshit, so if I'm going to trust anyone's gut response to people we're bringing in, it's theirs."

It's on the tip of my tongue to argue something about Ethan, but I don't know enough about how all that started for me to think it's a good idea. And I actually think Darren is exactly right about Riley. That admission stings, even while I'll keep that to myself too, mostly because it's one of the reasons I think I've been too hard on Adrian for the past year. Beau had been distracted by his bittersweet attraction, and Darren is rarely guarded about welcoming a new regular, but Riley and Adrian had quickly slipped into quiet conversations that suited them well. My history with grief made it easy to judge Adrian's mishandling of his own, but Riley's opinions felt clouded by almost nothing but an intuition I admired.

Smart money was on Riley being correct about Adrian then, and maybe just as right about Supine now.

"How many more bands are you auditioning?"

"Two more on Friday, and then I think I'm gonna invite our favorites back to play Saturday night," Darren says. "I've already told all of them to keep the night free just in case."

I nod, finally grabbing some boxers from my drawer while Darren pulls his jacket on. "Do you want me there?"

"I always want you there."

"I'd only be drinking beer and listening to the bands while you work."

"My answer stands," he shrugs. "And I'll tell Noah, Beau, and Adrian to come too, just so you don't feel so lonely while I work."

"Ah, yes, because loneliness is something I've complained about often."

It's supposed to be a lighthearted thing—not quite a joke, but certainly something we should be able to chuckle about on Darren's way out the door—but it falls onto the carpet between us, silent when it lands. My denial is a reminder of why I didn't need to do this thing with him, everything about my life fine before I bled in his arms and let him look too closely at the past ten years. He knows it too, but he's smart and kind and probably too tired to excavate anything I buried long ago.

"Complaints or not, I'm happy to help where I can."

"Mmmm, but it's not charity," I murmur. "Inviting the rest of the group to hang out with me, I mean."

Darren's eyes flicker with something wise and wounded. "No, it's never been that."

He's quiet when he says it—still part of the smart and kind and tired, I assume—but I step forward so we can leave this conversation behind when I walk him out. A goodbye kiss would've been a given when we first left the shower, but I don't even try now.

Neither does he.

"I'm gonna get some sleep, but we'll talk before Saturday?" he asks.

"I'm sure we will. And I'll see you then."

I'm unusually late getting to Trailhead on Saturday night, and I'd be stuck standing against a wall somewhere if it weren't for the friends who have saved me a seat at the bar. Beau's the first to spot me, and the first to greet me when I reach our little group, wrapping me up in a hug I needed more than I knew.

"Glad you made it."

I don't think he means anything in particular by it—certainly not that he's privy to the awkward way Darren and I had left things a week ago—but I can't do much more than nod and kiss him on the cheek the way he usually kisses me.

"I'm glad I made it, too," I say, sliding onto my stool. I greet Adrian and Noah, and accept the beer Darren leaves for me with his usual wink and smile, watching as he goes to pour drinks for someone else a moment later. "How much did I miss?"

V walks by just as I ask, and she offers a grin I return before she's gone again, maybe to help Riley at the far end of the bar. Adrian and Noah are turned to face each other, back to whatever chat I might've interrupted, so it's Beau who takes a long pull from his bottle and answers.

"Overpour started the night, and—"

"Overpour?" I interrupt.

"Quite the name for a bar band, huh?" he chuckles. "They've played already—basic country pop sung by a guy who looked like he'd cover Johnny Cash—but everyone here seemed to have a good time, and the band's shootin' pool now."

"Is that Supine?" I ask, nodding toward the stage.

"Nope, that's Happily Never After. Bit of an edge to them, and allegedly the bass player used to be married to the drummer and the keyboardist—one at a time, not a whole threesome thing—but they just started playin', so we'll see how it goes."

"There's a bit of an edge to their name, too," I say. "I guess after two divorces they're not big on fairy tales."

"Some people aren't meant to live one, right?" Darren asks, his return to us expected, though the timing throws me.

Noah snorts as he turns toward us, too. "I can't even get past the first chapter."

"And plenty of stories are over before they should be," Adrian adds. "Maybe those endings would've been happier with a little more time."

I'm sure he's referring to himself as much as anyone, all of us aware of how Adrian's long-term relationship ended before he and Beau found their way together. Still, no amount of Guinness is helping me wash down anything I could say about Michelle—or Darren, if I let myself imagine impossible, unwanted things—and I turn my focus to a band I suddenly dislike for no logical reason. At least I can be grateful for the distraction it provides.

It works right up until I notice a man sitting within arm's reach of Riley, a cocky grin on his face and familiar dimples visible from this far away. He's at least a few years older than I am, but his gray-blond hair looks good on him, even while his tired eyes give other secrets away. There are a few people crowded nearby, and one jumble of mischief and curls laughing loudly next to him, but I hide a frown behind my glass when I take a sip. I dislike this man more than I'd disliked Happily Never After, but I think it's perfectly logical this time, and I can't help but shift my gaze to the beautiful son he'd abandoned without ever attempting to be a father.

"Are you okay?" I ask.

"I was just wondering the same thing about you," Darren says as softly as he can in a loud bar, both of us confirming that the other three are busy talking before he goes on. "Running late, getting upset by what Adrian said, glaring at my father—maybe you should've stayed home."

"You're rescinding my invitation?"

"Absolutely not. To answer your question, I've been better ever since you walked in."

I glance to my side and back again. "Do they know about him yet?"

"Nope. I asked Riley to lure Drew and Supine to their side so I could have some time to figure my shit out," Darren explains.

"You're already one band into the night, and Beau's finished a couple of beers. Is time really the problem?"

Darren stares at me for a few seconds, his expression as neutral as I've ever seen it, but then a couple at the end of the bar waves him over for another round, and I pretend I care about the music again. Someone on stage is singing about lost love, and across the bar, Riley is busy pouring a drink. I'm content to watch them move, everything about them a reliably graceful break from chaos, but it's not long before I realize I'm not the only one seeking something calm. A head of curls turns to track each easy move, and I wonder whether whatever had captivated Riley last week might have been a mutual thing.

"You."

I startle more than I should, and I blink up at Darren. "Me?"

"I was waiting for you before I told them. I wanted you here."

"Me?" I say again.

He rolls his eyes. "You're smarter *and* wiser than I am. Don't fuck with me now."

"Never," I promise, looking past him to the back of Riley's head and a smiling stranger with curls and the empty spot where Darren's father had been. I assume he's gone to the restroom, or maybe to fetch something for the band, but we're dealing with a ticking clock one way or another, so I reach for Beau's shoulder and pat him there until he turns. "Sorry to interrupt, but Darren has something to tell you—all three of you."

V returns then, several empty bottles and glasses in her hands after a sweep of the room. "Unclench, boys. He's fine. He just needs his friends."

"Yeah, no, I—" Darren pauses for a deep breath, and then checks for thirsty customers like they'll give him a way out.

"Nope," V says. "You talk, I'll serve."

I'd squeeze Darren's hand if I could, but he's picked up a stack of coasters to shuffle while he tells Beau, Adrian, and Noah about his father's existence, sudden appearance, and ties to Supine's audition at Trailhead. Beau's heard pieces of the story for years, and none of it is all that unusual, especially for men who spend so much time listening to much taller bar tales, but Noah and Adrian aren't used to seeing Darren's natural brightness dim like this, his confidence a magnet that's drawn people to his side for as long as they've each known him.

Beau knows Darren better—far more so than I do—and his warm brown eyes narrow to something carefully chilled. "He's here tonight, then?"

I reach for Beau's shoulder again, some kind of respect for his elders the only reason I don't get knocked aside, and I put enough pressure there that he has to look at me when I lower my voice to speak.

"Don't cause a scene. Darren doesn't need two of us being dicks about this, and I've already had plenty to say."

"And not for the first time," Adrian mutters.

Noah takes a quick swig of his drink. And whether it's the fact that I haven't let him go or his desire to avoid a fight between Adrian and me, Beau finally relaxes.

"Okay, fine, but—"

Anything else Beau wanted to say gets lost to loud laughter from the opposite end of the bar, an impressive level of noise given the speakers filling the room with Happily Never After and no small amount of longing. We all look over at a woman with purple hair, her hands gesturing madly as she tells a story that leaves a few people doubled over and one wiping away tears. I can't see Riley's face from here, but they've found no reason to step away, and their willingness to forgive the sins of someone else's father is something I'll let slide tonight.

Enough other emotions are running high.

"I guess we don't even have to ask," Adrian says.

"Drew fucking Barrett," Beau growls. "Why's he gotta have your dimples?"

"Pretty sure I have his," Darren answers.

"So, you said he wants to have lunch with you, but you've been blowing him off?" Noah asks.

"I haven't blown him off—just told him I've been busy with all the band stuff and we could do it when things settle back down."

Adrian plays with his glass and then tilts his head. "You think he'll disappear again if you don't hire his friends? Are you *hoping* for that?"

"I have no idea what I'm hoping for," Darren sighs. "And I'm not convinced he'll stick around even *if* we hire his friends. He doesn't have a great track record of staying close to people who are supposed to matter. Then again, maybe the band—"

He shrugs, and I bite my tongue—still or again—and soothe the sting with my beer. Darren doesn't look at me.

Someone changes the subject, and everything goes back to being a rowdy Saturday night.

With Darren busy, I talk to the other three, any latent animosity between Adrian and me easy to ignore when Beau and Noah make every story funnier than it has any right to be. I limit the number of times I look across the bar, maybe for my own good as much as anyone's, and I go back and forth with myself about whether I want to spend a few minutes in the beer garden just to feel the late January chill. In the end, I start on my second Guinness just as Happily Never After wraps up their set, and I think I'm too far in already when Supine is ready to take the stage, my blood warm and humming along with music they haven't played.

V is the one to introduce the band, and it makes plenty of sense when she owns the bar, but I'm almost certain Darren would've done the honor if it hadn't required eye contact with the past.

Beau presses his huge hand to my thigh, and it's only then that I realize my leg was bouncing, a tell that doesn't belong to me at all.

"Hey, handsome, if that fucker needs the shit beat out of him later, you know I'll be right by your side—or in front, if you'd let me," Beau says. "But Darren looks okay tonight, unless there's something you think I'm missin'?"

I find some skepticism and aim it at him. "Right. When did you stop knowing Darren better than the rest of us?"

"Oh, I don't know," he shrugs. Supine's first song starts with the curly-haired one taking the mic, and Beau goes on. "I fell in love with someone new, stopped starin' at my ex-husband three or four nights a week, wasn't in the loop about his father, didn't spend Thanksgiving with him—"

"You were there on Christmas."

"That I was. Any chance you're goin' to San Diego in a few weeks?"

I open my mouth to answer, then take a sip instead. Beau's question is loaded, and we both know it, his challenge barely hidden when Darren's trip for his mother's birthday is a long-established fact. The two of them made the drive together for years, but as Beau said, he's moved on to other things—another relationship—and he wants to know whether Darren has done the same.

Of course, I won't be going to San Diego. I can't imagine Darren would want to introduce me as the friend whose bed he crawls into when he doesn't want to be alone. Too many other friends could be introduced to her the same way, and an affinity for trivia only gets me so far.

"No, Darren is not taking me to meet his mom," I say, my beer still in my hand when I turn toward the music again. "He was right about Supine, though. I like them already."

While I'm not in the habit of lying, I'm honestly not sure whether I mean it or whether I'm that eager to change the subject. Beau taps his bottle against the rim of my glass and bails on me to kiss his boyfriend, and it's an easy thing I envy more than is fair. I had that for so long. Hell, I think I'd found it before Beau and Adrian were born.

And I think I need to walk away from it now.

I drink the last of my beer, and I'm not opposed to having a third I can enjoy more, but the restroom calls, and I slip away. When I'm finished, I don't even make it a full step past the door before there's a hand at my hip to push me against the nearest wall, light eyes serious in the dark.

"Are you okay?" Darren asks.

"Didn't we discuss this already?"

"Barely."

I cover his hand with mine and look over his shoulder to where we're being very generously ignored. "Beau knows something is going on between us."

"And you're mad."

"Mad?" I shake my head and search for words I might not have. "No, I'm not *mad*. There's just not much to say about it, right? 'Yeah, Beau, remember when we were down in WeHo and Darren got horny and wanted me to stay with him after the rest of you went home? Well, he got off with some other old man, and I wondered what that must've been like, so when I crashed my Harley, and he offered to be my first—'"

I trail off because I'm explaining myself about as terribly as expected, and Darren's thumb has found its way under my shirt, as usual, arcing over the bare skin there.

"Was that the first time you wondered what it would've been like? That night in WeHo?"

"No."

It's not a surprise, or it shouldn't be by now, and Darren doesn't react or take it any further. Instead, he gets curious about something else, and if anyone else needs him, he doesn't seem to care.

"Why did you come here in the first place? You'd been married to a woman. I'm guessing you hadn't frequented gay bars together." He tilts his head and sighs. "You could've gone anywhere."

"It won't make sense."

"Try me."

Having this conversation here and now is all wrong, but Darren is as sincere as I've ever seen him, and I can't say no. Maybe he doesn't understand how serious this is. And maybe I can lie to myself about that another day. Far away from where we stand, Supine starts in on a cover of a Bill Withers song that's made me ache for years, and I clear my throat.

"I went to other places first. Michelle had made me promise I wouldn't stay at home every night. She didn't expect me to date right away, but she made me swear I'd at least go out and be around people, so I did." I frown for a split second and zero in on the feeling of his thumb, still so gentle against me. "But going out with friends was awful. They either tried to make me forget or help me remember, and all of it was suffocating. So then I went out alone, and I was okay for a little while."

"And then?"

"And then a woman approached me, and she was beautiful and funny, but I—I couldn't talk to her. She just kept *trying*. Flirting. Touching me. I thought my entire body was about to turn inside out, and if I could have literally run from her, I would've. And when I finally got out of there, still buzzing with the sensation of her hand on mine, I knew I couldn't do that again, so I decided to go to a gay bar instead."

Darren smiles softly. "You've had a hundred men try here, too. They've always flirted with you, even at the beginning."

"Sure. But none of them made me think of her," I say. "And if I wasn't going to take any of them home, my criteria for company didn't have to be any more complicated than that."

"You took me home."

"You invited yourself there."

"I want to invite you to my house," he murmurs.

"When?" I ask. "Tonight?"

"Mmmm."

"You don't have anywhere else to be?"

He smirks, and I'm close to kissing it off him. "I'm not big on obligations, actually."

There are things I could say about that, but Darren steps back and pivots toward the bar. My stool is waiting for me, and I'm still open to the idea of another round, but I don't follow him back, setting my sights further away when I spot another open seat. I ignore Beau's unasked question on my way—Darren's already busy with several drinks—and don't stop until I'm next to Drew Barrett. He's turned his back to Riley so he can see the band, and I do the same as soon as I've been able to say a silent hello, taking the stool Supine's lead singer had occupied the last time I was paying any attention.

"I was wondering how long it would take one of you to come over here."

"One of us?"

Drew glances my way, and then over to where Beau, Adrian, and Noah still sit. "You're Darren's friends, right? Or three friends and an ex-husband?"

Since he already has his answers, I ignore him and nod toward the stage. "What's his name?"

"Sebastian. You think he's good?"

I almost ignore that question too, but the truth is that Sebastian is very good—the whole band is—and whatever frustration I feel has nothing to do with him. Besides, it was my decision to sit here, and I don't think it was my intention to bite my tongue for the rest of the night.

"He is," I agree. "His voice is great, the energy is right for a place like this, and it's obvious that his charisma is off the charts. The two of you are close?"

"Incredibly close, but not in whatever way you're imagining."

"Don't tell me he's like the son you never had."

Drew's laugh is derisive at best. "Wasn't planning on telling you anything."

"How much have you shared with Riley?" I ask.

"About Sebastian? I'm almost positive anything those two want to know about each other doesn't require my presence at all."

So, he's noticed their mutual interest, too. Of course, *I* know Riley's only a month out of a bad relationship, and that Sebastian is good friends with a man with a knack for walking away without a proper goodbye, so any enthusiasm I might have had remains dulled for now. I look at the nearly empty glass in Drew's hand and wonder whether he wants another, then give up my concern to listen to Supine for a blessedly peaceful few minutes. I'm biased, probably, because they play the sort of acoustic country-rock-blues I love, but it creates quite a conflict for me when I open my mouth again.

"If they get hired, are you going to be here every week?"

"I doubt it, but some of that will depend on Darren. Any idea how long he'll keep me on the opposite side of the bar?"

"I've heard good parents tend to know when their kids want them around."

"Ah, good parents," Drew nods. "Like you, of course. You have a son, too?"

I flinch at the quick assumption. "No, a daughter. And she doesn't work this hard to avoid lunch with me."

"Darren only postponed lunch until after the auditions. We're going out on Thursday." I flinch again, and he clocks it. "Oh, did he not tell you that? I wonder whether that's because he realized you're less interested in protecting him and more concerned with how I've ruined the reputation of parents everywhere."

I'm trying to figure out whether Darren lied to me or simply elided the details well, but all of it makes my stomach turn, and I take a few moments to breathe through it before I sigh.

"Where have you been? How were you able to stay away?"

Drew sighs too, his weariness unfair. "Okay, look, how about we agree you don't owe me a damn thing about Darren, and I don't owe you a damn thing about me?"

"Fine."

"Great."

I stand and look at Riley for a long time.

I turn my head and watch Supine for another few seconds.

I don't spare a glance for Drew Barrett, and return to my side of the bar instead.

Three of them stop their conversation to look at me from their stools, but I have something I need to say before I do anything else. Darren pushes a full pint glass my way, and I wrap my fingers around it when I meet his cautious stare and open my mouth.

"Now you've got an obligation."

Chapter Seventeen

Darren

Noah, Adrian, and Beau all swing their focus from Jake to me and back again, trying to decipher a coded sentence that made perfect sense to me. I don't explain anything to them, nor do I look behind me to figure out what caused that look in Jake's eyes. I know he was talking to my father, but there's nothing I can do to make him feel better right now—other than providing the Guinness he's got in his hand—and I think all of us are better off enjoying the rest of Supine's set.

A while ago, Riley had come over to make sure *I* was okay, and I promised them I would be.

It's more true with Jake in front of me again.

I cling to that comfort, but once the band is done playing, the late-night crowd begins to thin. All four of my friends leave within minutes of each other, Jake going home to shower before he meets me at my house later. And because we'd made it clear that an announcement wouldn't be made tonight, Overpour, Happily Never After, and Supine follow soon after—Drew in tow.

The downshift in energy is palpable, but I don't mind it, even if it makes V's quiet stare feel loud. Stalling for reasons she understands, I wipe down my half of the bar and give Riley more time than necessary to pour shots of Jack for a couple of frat boys on the opposite end. When they stare too, I toss the towel aside and take a long sip of water before I finally sit on one of the coolers. If Riley were anyone else, I think they'd be on my lap already, pinning me down for the conversation the three of us need to have. It says plenty when they rest a hand on my bare shoulder instead.

And when their fingertips press into my skin, I wonder whether the contact isn't only for my benefit.

"You did a great job putting this together," V says, still watching me closely. "I honestly don't think we'd go wrong with any of them."

"But—" I start, trailing off because she'll finish the rest of her thought without my help.

"But I think we all know Supine has an edge in almost every category," she shrugs. "Raw talent. Stage presence. Their sound. The songs they chose to cover. Early on, we'll need to put in some work to spread the word about anyone playing here. But once people hear Sebastian sing, they're gonna talk and they're gonna come back."

Riley's hand tightens again. "Will you be okay if that means your father comes back, too?"

V nods. "You matter more than the music. I need you to make this call."

My next sip becomes a necessity, and if I had enough words, I'd explain that I'm not choked up about my father. It's this—*them*—the family I have right here in our little gay bar. *They* matter more than a man who might want me, but hasn't yet.

"Hire Supine."

She doesn't push me any further than that. Doesn't ask whether I'm sure or need more time to think about it. V won't coddle me any more than I've coddled Jake in the months since I bandaged him up and drove him home, and I stand to give her a hug without saying more about it. By the time I've backed away again, Riley is saying goodnight to the frat boys, and I have a ridiculous moment of worry that I've made Jake wait too long. V has no idea, of course, but she waves me away and says she'll handle closing. I only protest for a few seconds before Riley promises to stay a while longer in my place, and then I focus on any small ways I can help them until I'm officially done for the night.

When I reach the parking lot, I send Jake a quick text, then head home so I can shower, too. And as soon as I'm out, my head mostly clear and nothing but a towel around my waist, there's a knock at the door and my dick twitches in response.

I let Jake in, and the sex is incredible.

I'd understood at Trailhead that he was the one who ached for this connection tonight, even before he'd walked into a conversation that seemed to hurt him more than it helped. Still, something about his need catches in my chest, and setting it free feels so fucking good. Jake's still mostly dressed when he shoves me onto my couch and sucks my soul through my cock. He returns it to me a moment later with a kiss that might've made me come again if I weren't creeping closer to 40. When I can finally look at him again, I admire his swollen lips and wet eyes, and then I drag him to my bedroom.

With my towel already left behind, I strip him between his polite growls and my vulgar whispers, and when he slams me against a wall hard enough to rattle one of Adrian's framed photographs, I wonder if he'll fuck me right there. He doesn't, probably only because there's not a condom within reach, but he lifts me until my legs wrap around his waist, and he holds me long enough for us to appreciate how well the position could work.

Next time, maybe.

Jake lets me down after another merciless kiss, and I push him backward until he hits the bed and I can climb on top of him, the comforter beneath us because we don't care to get anything out of our way tonight. Every position is perfect and not quite right, so we move from one to another, his frustration taken out on me in a way I'd stop if I were a better man. I should make him talk about it, or at least do some talking of my own, but I let him turn me onto my stomach and fuck me. When his fingers end up in my mouth again, I almost smile around them before I start to whimper and drool a little, each of Jake's thrusts angled just right.

I come. He comes. The comforter gets pushed to the floor. He cleans up. I grab a blanket.

He crawls back into bed with me, and I don't think I'm as surprised as I should be. I love him like this, so sleepy and sated at my side. Still warm, his hands lazy as they move over my body, our legs tangled together. The tension is gone, and only a steady heartbeat remains in its place.

I love him like this. And maybe I just love him.

I close my eyes. He closes his. It's a very long time before I'm awake enough to notice that anything has changed, but by late morning, the other half of my bed is empty, and I'm a lot more surprised than I should be.

I'm pretty sure I doze off again, restless about it but uninterested in getting up to face the day, my blanket wrapped around me like a cocoon that will allow me the time to become something else. When I decide I can't stay there forever, I roll out of bed and tug on the briefs I pull from my drawer on my way to the bathroom. I need a haircut and a lot of coffee, but I splash some water on my face and tell myself Jake only left because he doesn't like to miss church, even when he's sleeping with temptation.

The note he left on my nightstand was too vague for me to know for sure.

I brush my teeth to keep myself from trying to call him now, and pace in front of the sink to stay an extra couple of steps away from being able to text. My mouth is still full when I hear a knock at the door, and it's embarrassing how quickly my body reacts to the sound. I hurry to finish what I'm doing when I realize it's late enough for Mass to have been over for a while. And I want Jake to know that he can let himself in just as easily as he let himself out, but I think I lack the words to make that clear to a friend like him.

In my small house, it doesn't take long to make it to my front door, and my mind is still racing past my heart. I could be sexy or funny or as silent as the man Jake left hours ago. Or I could be wrong about everything, and stunned when I open the door to greet someone else.

"Well, I have to say it's more than I thought you'd be wearin'," Beau snorts. "Lucky me."

I glance down at my bare torso and the dick that still wants to get hard, even in the face of disappointment. "You know I'm not an early riser."

"Yeah, sure," Beau chuckles, following my gaze before he holds up a familiar paper bag. "It's been a while. Thought we could have my favorite breakfast burritos, unless you're expectin' someone else?"

"I'm not."

I step back to let him into a house that used to be his, and he stops before making himself at home because *used to be* matters to him. After I've closed the front door, I swipe the food from his hand and march toward the kitchen with a certainty I don't feel, and Beau is right behind me, understanding everything when he takes the bag back.

"Was he here last night?"

Anyone else might've accepted a lie from me just to be polite, but I don't even try it with him. I don't answer him either, pulling two mugs for the coffee that brewed about an hour ago. Then I realize I don't have enough for him if I want my usual three cups.

"It's fine," Beau says, beating me to whatever excuse I could've offered. "I had some closer to sunrise."

I nod and pour mine, and he sits at our small kitchen table to tear into breakfast. He's wearing sweatpants and a flannel over a t-shirt he's had forever, and I consider leaving him long enough to find pants of my own, but he's seen everything already and couldn't care less. I drop into a chair across from him and pull a burrito toward me.

"You know, I brought these to Adrian the mornin' after he dropped his ID at Trailhead."

"You mean the morning after you fucked him?" I ask.

Beau smiles. "After *he* fucked *me*, but yeah."

"You still owe me for sending you on that errand, don't you?"

"Maybe that's why I'm here."

He's probably right, and we're about to end up in the same place no matter what I say next. We look at each other, years of love and dishonesty between us, and then I take a bite and watch him do the same. Beau's good at being patient and sitting still, while I've always been awful at both. I do it now because the breakfast burrito is fucking delicious, and my ex-husband almost certainly has the upper hand in whatever game he wants to play.

He distracts me with some small talk about Adrian's gallery, and I mention a pool party without saying a word about who would host it. The coffee goes down easy, and being close to Beau is rarely anything but, so once my food is gone, I crumple the foil wrapper into a ball and confess.

"He left before I woke up. When I heard the knock at the door, I thought maybe—" I shake my head and wave off his concern. "It's not a big deal. We usually bail on each other right after we're done, so I haven't fallen asleep with anyone since you, and—I don't know. I think my body was thrown off."

"Ah, yeah, your *body* was thrown off for sure."

I toss the foil at him. "It's not like that. We've been getting to know each other better, and it's been fun to fuck around with him, too."

"I'll admit that the bulge you brought to the door supports your point, but the look in your eyes makes me think it got more complicated than that. It's not what I expected to see, actually."

"My bulge?"

"I haven't been surprised by that since the first time I got my hand on it," Beau grins. "But the struggle of someone who might've fallen harder and faster than they'd planned? Yeah, no, I thought I was comin' over to see how you were doing with the whole daddy dearest situation and give you shit about landin' Trailhead's most wanted. Definitely didn't expect to break your heart by not being him."

"How much do you know about Jake and his wife?"

Beau shrugs. "The basics, I guess. They married young, had a kid, she got sick and died, he's been hangin' out at Trailhead ever since."

"Yeah, so, he's already loved and lost. He's not gonna do it again."

Beau laughs at me. Fully fucking *laughs*. "You can't possibly be lookin' at me and believe that for a second."

I push away from the table and pour myself another cup, my back turned to him while I look out the window at the small yard and a quiet morning—or daytime, I suppose. He's obviously right that people can fall in love again. He and Adrian are proof of that, and I'm not interested in starting a fight they've already won. But it doesn't change my more specific point about Jake.

Everyone knows I've broken vows before, and I have no intention of doing it again.

"I promised him I understood."

The scrape of Beau's chair against the floor is louder than I expect it to be, probably because nothing else makes a sound. He's standing behind me a second later—crowds me there, really—but now that we're divorced, I'll melt into the safety of his embrace long before I'll run from the threat, and I don't mind him throwing his size around just because he can.

"Understood what?" he asks, his question practically pressed to the top of my head.

"That the friendship comes first. He and I had been attracted to each other for years, but I don't think either of us would've ever done something about it." I pause and choke on something too honest. "Well, I know he wouldn't have."

"So, what changed?"

"Trivia night and a motorcycle wreck."

Beau hums thoughtfully. "So trivia's the gettin' to know each other better that you mentioned a minute ago, and then what—the night you thought he might be concussed, you slept with him?"

I finally turn at that, though he doesn't give me much room for it, and I don't expect him to. It's familiar, his presence here, and for a moment, I let myself miss what we could've had if I'd been cut out for commitment. I let myself envy what he's found so completely with somebody else. It's been close to a year since Beau and Adrian got together, and I haven't taken the time to care that it means this kind of closeness doesn't belong to us anymore, but I do now. I hold on to his flannel and I look up at him and I fucking *care*.

He lifts his huge hand to my cheek, and I lean into the tenderness he offers because he cares, too. His thumb sweeps over my lips, and I stare at his before I remind myself to find his big brown eyes. I'm on my tiptoes before I really think about it, just trying to get closer or crawl inside the safety of his presence entirely. Then I drop back down because I'm exactly the kind of man who'd ruin everything with a single kiss, but Beau's not.

The fact that he hasn't let go makes me wonder whether he has a different kind of faith in me.

"I promised him we'd be friends."

"So you said," Beau murmurs, only moving to comb his strong fingers through my messy hair. "Don't suppose you also promised to stop bangin' random bargoers, hmmm? We all heard what Riley said about the keg room."

My eyes fall shut. Whether it's Beau's touch or his words making me hide, I don't know, but I'm slow to open them again. "I haven't said anything to him about that."

"What about WeHo hookups? Old friends in your phone?"

"Haven't said anything to him about that, either."

"But when did you stop fuckin' 'em?"

My head drops to his chest and I silently beg Beau to wrap his arms around me. He does, of course, Riley probably the only person he doesn't regularly overwhelm with physical affection. His hand is still in my hair, and I let his heartbeat fill the time between his question and the answer I utterly fail to deliver.

"Jesus Christ, Darren," he whispers. "You stopped a long time ago."

"It doesn't matter, babe."

"You've gotta tell Jake. You've gotta tell him you're in love with him."

I look up again to stare into the endless warmth in Beau's eyes. "It. Doesn't. Matter. That's not how friends with benefits *works*. The sex is amazing. Spending time with him without sex is amazing. None of that needs to get fucked up just because I got stupid."

"So, you're just gonna stay where you are and deal with the pain?"

"It's better than breaking a promise to the man I love, isn't it?"

The only other man I've loved flinches—I can feel it from head to toe—and then he grabs my chin and presses his thumb to my lips one more time, like maybe he can stop me from saying another stupid thing. It remains too intimate for what we are now, but for better or worse, I think it's what's left of everything we've been. My chest rises with the awareness of the mistakes I still have time to make, then falls with the certainty that I won't make them, my mostly bare body meaning nothing to him when he has someone else at home.

"You pushed me away," he says after another few seconds.

"Yeah."

"You're rarely close enough to anyone else to have to do that much. You make sure you can just leave."

"And I do."

Beau nods. Takes a deep breath. Smiles. "Jake's gonna figure it out, even if you keep your dumb mouth shut. But here's the funniest fuckin' thing about it—I think he's gonna stay where he is, too."

When I hear from Jake later that afternoon, his texts have nothing to do with our friendship or anything else we've been up to. Instead, he apologizes for any trouble he might have caused with my father and asks me whether V, Riley, and I made a decision about which band to hire.

I suppose I could've told him about it if we'd stopped to talk while he was here, but there's even more to say now. V had sent an update somewhere around the time I was eating a breakfast burrito or almost kissing my ex-husband, and Supine will officially start playing at Trailhead in mid-February.

Just like karaoke and trivia night, live music will be a weekly thing, but there will be a small cover charge for anyone arriving after a certain time. The hope is that some people will start drinking earlier and stay for the band, and others will pay the money and offset the bar's costs. Adrian has already agreed to help me with the social media hype and general marketing, and I'm guessing he'll take pictures of Supine for us, even if we don't ask.

V seems hopeful about everything. Riley seems—actually, I can't quite tell how Riley feels. They were worried about me when they shouldn't have been, but I remember the pressure of their hand on my shoulder, and I'll have to remember to worry about them, too.

Later, though.

For now, Jake's tone is muted in our back and forth, and I blame the inherent weirdness of texts. At least until he gives up and calls me instead.

"Were you ever going to tell me you're having lunch with your father this week?"

"Yeah, I—Jake—" I stop, sigh, and start over. "It's not a secret, but you don't think I should spend time with him, and I didn't want to frustrate you by bringing it up."

"And I don't want you to keep things to yourself because you think I'll get upset."

"Okay."

"Okay?"

I sigh again. "Yeah. Now you know I'm having lunch with him, and I'll tell you all about it afterward. And we're both fully aware that the likelihood of him sticking around the bar would be impossible to predict, but I won't hide whatever is happening there either."

"Don't hide anything, Darren. We're friends, remember?"

My mind runs wild between one sentence and the next, any chance of me spilling everything to Jake immediately hampered by his reminder that we're friends. Beau's suggestion that I tell Jake how I feel was great, and I'm sure someone without a history of fucking up would've done something about it. Unfortunately, that's not me, and I don't want to go back on a word I gave on my knees when Jake could barely stand.

"Yeah, I remember."

We let each other go then, but I bring him dinner on Tuesday night. We listen to one of his favorite playlists while we watch our breaths disappear into the backyard on a surprisingly cold night. The sex waits until we're back inside and warm again, and the music remains the loudest thing we hear for hours.

Thursday, I meet Drew Barrett for lunch at a local sandwich place, arriving before he does as though that might give me any sort of jump. He pays for my food, and takes my advantage away, and we sit across from each other, two versions of the same man born twenty years apart. I take a bite because I don't know where to begin, too many questions clamoring to be first, and I consider starting with something about the bar or the band or maybe the fucking weather. Before I can swallow though, my father looks in about four other directions, finds me in front of him again, and takes a deep breath.

"I fucked up."

I come close to choking and take a quick swig from my water bottle. "Wow. Diving in dick first, no lube, huh? Not my first time, but you might want to slow down a little."

My father rolls his eyes, a move I mastered as a teen when he wasn't around to see. "I don't know if I'll get a second chance to sit down with you like this, so I figured I wouldn't waste time."

"You've already wasted 38 years."

"More than that, if I'm being honest."

I wait for him to go on, but it's his turn to stall with a bite, so I try to set up the story. "She's never said much about you. My mom. I know you guys met through friends of friends when she was in college. You loved hard, you partied hard. And then when she got pregnant with me, you left."

"I don't think it changes anything, but for whatever it's worth, I left before I knew she was pregnant. I didn't find out until a month or so before you were born."

My mom's voice replays in my head, but I can't remember enough of the words to tell whether she skirted the truth or outright lied. He's right, though. It doesn't change anything at all.

"You could've come back then," I say. "But you stayed away

instead."

"I did. She'd obviously decided she wanted to go through with it whether I was there or—"

"Go *through*? With *it*?" I interrupt, my forearm hitting the table hard enough to rattle everything on it. "Hi, I'm your son, and you're talking about me like I was the consequence of a *dare*."

He sighs and sits back in his chair. "Yeah, look, I've had a lot of tough conversations over the years, but I'm not sure I've ever been good at them, and it feels like this one matters more than most."

"I guess we'll find out."

"The point I was trying to make is that she'd already decided to keep you, and your grandparents were still alive back then to help, plus she had friends and a good life ahead of her."

"And you didn't think you could be part of a good life?" I ask. "Hers or mine?"

"I *knew* I couldn't be," he answers.

I think back to the argument between Jake and Riley—the back and forth about whether some kids are better off when a parent walks away, or whether parents should stay and learn how to raise those kids—but I couldn't figure out who was right that night, and I still haven't come to a conclusion now. My father picked a side, obviously, and I do what I can to simplify it for both our sakes.

"You knew you wouldn't be good for us because you weren't ready to be a father."

"I knew I wouldn't be good for you because I was an addict. *Am* an addict, really."

He leans forward to pick up his sandwich again, and I'd think he didn't have a care in the fucking world except for the careful way he's waiting for me to say something about his revelation.

What I blurt out is just plain stupid.

"But at Trailhead—it's a bar."

"Ah, Riley hasn't told you? I've only had club soda and lime."

"Riley minds their own business."

My father nods and swallows another bite before I do the same. "It wasn't just alcohol, though. Way back then. That group of friends—most of us were in college, at least half of us came from money, and all of us were spoiled—we could get our hands on anything. There was a lot of booze, a lot of weed, a lot of coke. Whatever we wanted, as often as we wanted."

"My mom, too?"

"I'll sit here and tell you anything you want to know about me, but I'm gonna follow Riley's lead for the rest of it."

"Fine," I say. "You partied a lot. Go on."

And he does. While we eat, I get the story of how my father started to slip further away from routines and responsibility, chasing highs his friends could limit to weekend parties. His grades suffered, he withdrew from his family, and he found it easier to lie. His relationship with my mom suffered, but they loved each other enough for the passion to reignite quickly. Then that Thanksgiving weekend, with time off from school, one friend got them an invite to a party up in Malibu. It went on for three days, and when it was time to drive back down to San Diego on Sunday night, most of them did exactly that—including my mom.

Drew Barrett and a friend didn't want to be done, and headed up the coast in search of more.

"You dropped out of school?"

"I did, yeah," he says. "Said some bullshit to my parents they never really believed. Found parties and places to crash. Made a few bucks by picking up odd jobs and a proclivity for petty theft. And we just kept roaming, getting high whenever and wherever we could."

I shake my head and smile without a trace of levity. "Meanwhile, my mom was pregnant with me."

"And like I said, I didn't find out for a while."

"You were still together, weren't you? Why didn't she tell you sooner?"

"Well, *she* didn't tell me at all. My friend got the news when he was checking on things at home." He stops and levels me with a stare. "As for why she didn't tell me? Darren, I was a *disaster*. Who cares that we hadn't officially broken up? I left my entire life behind to find more drugs and didn't think twice about it. Why would she want me around?"

"So, that's it? You found out your girlfriend was pregnant, realized you would be a bad dad because you were coked out of your mind too often, and stayed gone?"

"Fuck, no," my father snorts. "I found out my girlfriend was pregnant, realized going home to be a dad might take me away from being coked out of my mind, and stayed gone. The clarity of what that meant—that you and Tash were better off without me—came much, much later."

I startle at his use of her nickname, but he doesn't notice or care when he goes on about years of alcohol and drug abuse, and a couple of stints in prison. Rounds of rehab fell in between, and all but the last one failed. He found out what he could about me in the moments he was focused enough to care—and saw me as a baby the one time I already knew about—but my mom made it clear that we were doing just fine without him in our lives, and I think she must have been right. The birthday card I burned wasn't the only thing he ever sent, just the only one I ever saw.

My father tells me he's been clean and sober for seven years now, but settled in the L.A. area more recently. He's already admitted he'd had an eye on my social media accounts, and that he knew about my job at Trailhead, so I don't think I have any questions about that—

Until one thing confuses me.

"If you wanted to have lunch with me, you could've shown up at the bar anytime. Why'd you wait and use a band gig as an excuse?"

He shrugs. "You still don't need me in your life, and I'd always figured I'd continue to leave you alone. I wasn't using anything as an excuse to meet you."

Something about that hurts. I appreciate the honesty, but however much I didn't matter to a Drew Barrett who was looking to score more cocaine, I also don't matter to a Drew Barrett who's put his life back together. Or really, I only matter in whatever way

I can help his friends and their little band.

"You're just using me to help Supine?"

"Using you? God, no. I feel so much better knowing you're there, but that's not—I don't believe in the universe or anything, but—" My father trails off and frowns, and as much as he's been willing to answer my questions, he seems frustrated by this one. "I'm really not using you, but I won't be at Trailhead every week, and I—I'm glad you will be. Riley, too. Not for Supine, but for Sebastian."

"For Sebastian?" I ask. "Why are you glad we'll be there for Sebastian?"

My father pauses again, careful when he finally stops minding his own business.

"Because he's an addict, too."

CHAPTER EIGHTEEN

JAKE

*H*ey old man. We're going to weho tonight. You in?

I've barely read Darren's text in the group chat—and definitely haven't responded to it—when I get one from Beau.

Miss you. Love you. Promise not to give you shit about anything if you come out with us tonight

I smile before and after I see a text from Riley.

I'll be there too

Their message says a lot without saying anything, a reassurance that I'm wanted by more than just the loudest in our little group. I look at the time and try to figure out whether the three of them are together already, but both Darren and Riley will be off tonight while V works with a bartender she hired a week ago, and Beau is probably between afternoon appointments.

I'm busy working at home, but I'll have it wrapped up in an hour or so.

Sure. What's the occasion?

Darren, unsurprisingly, responds first. ***Impromptu promo for Supine. Adrian made stuff***

That last bit could've come from Beau, but he surprises me with a different follow-up entirely.

The lead singer will meet us there to help with hype

Sebastian Sadler. A recovering addict who will promote his new bar gig by traipsing through a city with no shortage of vice fulfillment. It all feels like a bad idea wrapped in a slightly worse one, but I suppose Riley and I—and probably Adrian, though I'm loath to admit it—will offer the calm, steady presence the others can rely upon. And as far as I know, Darren and I are the only ones aware of Sebastian's history.

I don't think I'm supposed to be, but a week and a half ago, when Darren had showed up at my door after lunch with his father, I'm pretty sure I became privy to every thought he'd had throughout their meal and every second since. He was angry—or as angry as Darren ever gets, I suppose—but I watched the gray overtake the blue in his eyes when too many of his father's failures aggravated scars of his own. We didn't have much time together before he had to go home and change, especially because he'd driven completely out of his way to see me, but I took care of him however I could and whispered a quiet goodnight. We haven't seen each other since, but I've checked on him as much as any friend would, and I hope it's helped his eyes return to blue.

When I walk away from my computer, I head upstairs, shower, and change into a pair of dark wash jeans and a black button-up I leave open enough to show off my chest hair and a decent amount of ink. I've never been afraid of how I look, but I think I own it differently now, and the confidence I'm bringing to West Hollywood tonight has changed, even from the night of the gallery opening.

The last time we promoted Trailhead like this, Darren enjoyed the company of a stranger while I sat at a bar without dreaming of doing the same. If he and I stay out late tonight, I'm curious to find out whether I'm ready to be the one who steps away from *him*.

Part of me thinks I should try, just to make sure I can.

I hop on my bike and stop trying to plan a night that hasn't really begun. It's also worth remembering that it's an unremarkable weeknight, and maybe not the best time for any of what we hope to accomplish, together or separately. That takes any pressure back off me, and by the time I'm parked and walking toward Darren, Riley, and Sebastian, I'm ready for anything.

Darren eyes me up and down, a secret kept from the other two. "That's a new look. I like it."

He knows he'll have at least as many admirers as I do, drawing everyone's attention with a long sleeve mesh shirt in the deep purple I favor and black pants I want to touch. I smile a thank you and take in Riley's sinfully soft sweater and Sebastian's combination of leather and plaid. We're missing two others, and I'm not ashamed to admit I'm eager to be reminded of how attractive they are, too.

"Do I even want to know why Beau and Adrian are running

late?" I ask.

"Beau's not shy," Darren says. "If you liked Adrian a little more, he'd probably invite you to watch."

It's a joke, and Riley nearly chokes on their laugh, but I do them the courtesy of saying nothing about it when I step forward and hold out my hand to Sebastian.

"Hi, I'm Jake. Nice to officially meet you."

He takes it, and his green eyes hold me still. "Sebastian. Nice to meet you, too. Darren says you've been a Trailhead regular forever."

"Forever feels like a pretty accurate description sometimes, but they haven't thrown me out yet."

"You're one of my favorite people," Riley says. "Nobody's allowed to throw you anywhere."

"Hey, wait, I thought I was your favorite."

We all turn at the sound of Beau's voice and watch as he whispers something in Riley's ear that's probably both filthy and endearing. Riley ducks their head in response, Beau cutting right through any potential embarrassment with a quick kiss to their temple and an exaggerated wave for the rest of us. For his part, Adrian offers more mellow hellos, and then we make a quick plan to hand out gorgeous postcard-sized invitations to Supine's debut. We're all sticking together, strength in our numbers on a quieter WeHo night, and it's easy to lose track of time as we roll from one conversation to another. Sebastian is a hit with everyone, his charm as undeniable here as it is on stage, and Beau and Darren have always made the world fall in love with them.

Along the way, all three of them get slipped personal info and the suggestion that they reach out anytime. So do I.

Mason greets us when we approach his studio, Adrian having already given him a heads up that we'd be around, and in typical Mason fashion, he makes quite the scene, whether it's intentional or not. I'm not sure where the overlap lies between collectors of erotic paintings and fans of acoustic country rock, but we work to find them and get a few promises in return. We're still riding those small highs when we step back onto the sidewalk, reorienting ourselves to something calmer just as Darren turns and nudges us back toward Mason's window display.

"Hey, how about you go ahead and hit the next place without me? Or see if Mason has any other ideas about where we should go tonight? Or just go—anywhere? I'll catch up with you in a minute."

He hurries off, and Beau chuckles when he looks around at us. "How about we definitely do *not* do any of that?"

"Is he okay?" Sebastian asks. "Everything seemed fine a second ago."

I'm nodding already, fairly sure Darren's fine, though the young woman he's with now is a little less so. They're about a block away from us and across the street, so there's a limit to the detective work any of us can do from where we stand, even with a streetlight keeping them from the shadows. She'd been leaning against the stucco façade of an urgent care clinic until Darren wrapped her in his arms for a hug I shouldn't envy, and because it lasts a while, I'd guess they're talking, too. When he finally pulls away, he wipes tears from her face and kisses the space left behind, making her smile in a way that's probably cuter than it is pretty.

"Well, they're close," Adrian says, an unnecessary observation that settles nothing. "Do any of you know her?"

Riley shakes their head. "I've never seen her before."

I shrug. Beau mumbles something. And Sebastian has another question. "Any chance it's a girlfriend he hasn't told you about?"

"No," Beau and Adrian answer in unison, glancing at each other before Beau raises an eyebrow at me.

For what it's worth, I think they're right regardless of Darren's willingness to hook up with a woman from time to time, but I'm not sure I'm the reason for it, and I raise my eyebrow right back. Any argument I could make aloud gets swallowed down, a private thing I don't need to leave in a West Hollywood gutter.

Besides, Adrian cuts me off. "Maybe she's the result of something that happened 20 years ago."

"A daughter?" Riley huffs. "Anything's possible, but I doubt it."

She's laughing now, evidence of Darren's successful effort to bring her back from whatever had upset her. A second later, she's looking over his shoulder at us, saying something from too far away for me to read her lips. I've got no hope of knowing what Darren is telling her either, but the conversation ends before I can think too hard about it, a young man stepping out of the clinic to join them.

Darren seems to know him too, though they nod a hello and stop short of the easy affection we'd witnessed a few minutes earlier.

"No, I don't think that's his son," Riley murmurs.

I turn away from all of it before I can catch their goodbyes, Beau snagging my arm and pulling me close. There's nothing he needs to say to me, and I think he knows that, simply holding me at his side when Darren returns.

"Let me guess," he sighs. "Beau told you not to listen to a word I said."

"Not sure any of us needed Beau to tell us what to do," Adrian says.

Beau flips him off and stays next to me when he grins at Darren. "Who is she? We've got all sorts of guesses over here. Lover? Love child?"

"Her name is Sage."

Darren starts walking again, waving for us to follow, and though all of us do, Beau isn't ready to shut up about the mystery woman yet. Neither is Adrian, which isn't much of a surprise to me, nor am I shocked by Riley's silence. Sebastian is either taking cues from Riley, or he feels out of place enough to opt for the safest way past this, and I respect his decision either way.

As for me, I'm on Darren's side. I also really want to know more about Sage.

The subject changes eventually, Darren giving up nothing about something that clearly matters to him, and everyone caught up in more of the flirting and fun that comes with new conversations we start. There's near constant touching among most of us and the strangers we meet, the casual closeness of community spilled onto these sidewalks for anyone open to it. Riley has taken my place next to Beau as an easy way to avoid most of what the rest of us are ready to embrace, but there's an unspoken question in their eyes because I'm not usually this eager to attract the attention of men I don't know.

Tonight, I think I want the attention of everyone, and I couldn't say why.

"You okay?"

I startle at Darren's question, and then again when his hands are at my waist, pushing my larger body backward until I hit a wall and inadvertently moan. A quick look around tells me we're outside a record store, our friends probably inside while Darren steals a quick and dirty kiss from me here.

"Yeah, my mind was just wandering a little," I tell him.

"Your hands, too. You're having fun tonight."

It's not an accusation, especially when I could say the same about him, so I cover his grip with mine and tilt my head. "Do I get to know anything else about Sage?"

"Did you put your money on lover or love child?"

"Neither."

"Good," Darren says. "She's a friend of mine. Works at a diner I go to a lot. And the kid who came out right before I said goodbye? That was her younger brother, River."

"They were at urgent care. Is everything all right?"

"Mmmm, their mom sprained her ankle pretty badly, and they—" He frowns and shrugs. "Money's tight in their family, so Sage was panicking about her mom's job, and her own, and how to help with her younger siblings, and I—I don't know, I just tried to calm her down. It'll be hard on them for a while."

I nod. "Whatever you said worked, at least for a moment."

"I hope so. She won't ask for more, so I'll have to get clever about that later."

"She looked over at us. Dare I ask what she knows?"

Darren laughs. "I might've told her I was hanging out with a musician, a coworker, my ex-husband, his new man, and the friend I'm fucking now."

"That almost sounds like the start of a joke."

It's supposed to make him laugh again, and I'm almost positive I'm trying to smile, but his hands slowly drop from beneath mine and his fingertips drag against the front of my jeans before he takes a step back. I can hear everyone else coming, and I do the best I can to breathe normally while Darren stares at me like he and I are the only ones in West Hollywood tonight.

"Doesn't feel like a joke at all."

Nobody ends up in a bathroom with a stranger that night.

All of us are at Trailhead for Supine's very successful debut.

When Darren goes to San Diego for his mom's birthday, I go to Phoenix for another work thing, a conference that would've kept me from joining him even if I'd been asked.

We've talked a lot about how much he planned to tell—or

ask—his mom about Drew, but as far as I know, he hasn't decided. While we're both busy, none of our conversations last long enough for me to bring it up again, our texts limited to friendly flirting and pictures he might've sent anyone. I'm of the opinion that she should know what's going on, but maybe I'm a biased parent intent on keeping my own secrets while wanting Lucy to be comfortable enough to share all of hers.

Of course, I'm ignoring that even welcome secrets can have sharp edges, the small cuts from them unnoticed until something otherwise benign makes them sting. I also don't dwell on the very different versions of single parenthood at play. Darren's mom and I may have plenty in common now, but I didn't raise my child alone.

I'm home from my trip a couple of hours before trivia night, and I miss being at Trailhead. I really, really do. But if I'm honest with myself, I'm also tired and grouchy and bad company for anyone, even and especially my friends.

I send Darren an apology.

He hasn't told me anything about San Diego, and I haven't asked.

I think about his friend, Sage, and whether she knows more than I do.

Darren says he hopes to see me next week, and I miss him too much to tell him so.

When trivia night rolls around again, I have a Guinness in my hand just as the host asks the first question.

"What song, whose title appears within the lyrics of 'Bohemian Rhapsody,' knocked Queen's hit from the number one place on the UK singles chart?"

After a brief pause, I leave my beer on the coaster and scribble my response. Around me, I can see people quickly singing to themselves, a task complicated by the low hum of music and energetic chatter, but a few seem to figure it out. When I meet Darren's eyes, I know he has.

Noah elbows me expectantly, so I sing just enough ABBA for him to get it. For a moment, I worry Darren is making plans to get me to karaoke night when he licks his lips and stares a little too long, but he slips away to grab a bottle for someone else, and I'm not sure I would've come up with a good excuse to avoid it anyway.

The host interrupts me before I think too hard about that.

"Who was the first woman to host *Saturday Night Live*?"

"Oh, I actually know this one!" Noah squeaks, clutching my arm just as Darren returns. "It's Candice Bergen. My mom loves her."

I smile at how easily he gives away the answer, though it's one I could've handled just fine on my own. I jot down my response, and even knowing it might make me miss the next question, I use the opportunity to finally ask mine.

"Speaking of moms, did yours have a nice birthday?"

It's such an innocent thing to ask, and I hope Darren understands I've done my best to time it well. He's busy with work, and Noah is inches away from me, so if he waves me off with a word or two, it's fine. The only potential complication would've come in the form of a flannel-clad ex-husband who'd flip him off and call him out, demanding to know it all.

But Beau isn't here.

"She did, yeah," Darren says, bottle caps and coasters becoming his playthings. "Good food, good drinks, an emotional kick neither of us deserved, and then more good drinks."

Trivia comes and goes, and I remain quiet when Noah slowly nods. "You told her your father has been in here."

"I think I had to. She knows my bullshit better than anyone, and I'm probably lucky she didn't make me spill it over the phone weeks ago." He stops then and laughs at Noah. "Like you don't fucking know how that works. There's no way you can keep anything from V."

"It's been a long, long time since I've bothered to try."

We all chuckle, and then Darren looks at me, silently asking me to wait, as though I had plans to run off while he serves a group of four that just walked up to the bar. From where I stay, I watch Riley, their rhythm steady, and a wider glance helps me find and forget a bartender whose name I haven't learned. Noah and I have missed another question or two, and I don't care when I've never accepted a prize before and wouldn't have started tonight. When Noah bumps my knee with his, I tune back into the host long enough to answer something I think most people probably get correct, and raise an eyebrow when Darren comes back as casually as ever.

"Are you good at seeing through Lucy's shit?" he asks.

"I have to be now. I think I owe it to her to be good at it

now," I amend, shaking my head. "Michelle was always better with Lucy, and I hate that I didn't pay closer attention to things when I should've. I wasn't absent by any means, but I told myself Michelle could handle everything, and that wasn't fair to any of us. Then when Michelle got sick—I don't know. Lucy's never let many people get close to her, so for a while, it had to be me. And over the past year, with her moving away, and her priority being her new job and not new friends—"

I shrug and tap my fingers against my glass, falling silent as I remember unfair periods of mourning and ignorance that wasn't bliss. Lucy and I really only have each other, but maybe I'm trying to see through her before she sees through me.

A loud whoop from a table in the far corner distracts me from any other wayward regrets, and I smile as the host comes around to collect other players' scoresheets. Noah makes small talk I don't mind, Darren serves a dozen guests, Riley doesn't miss a step, and the new guy does fine without V being here to look over his shoulder.

The next round of trivia is as typical as anything around here ever has been. I get nine out of the ten correct—one of them a lucky guess—and finish my second beer.

What happens after that isn't exactly unusual, but while I'd been prepared for it in WeHo, something about it throws me here. Noah leaves to use the restroom, but I'm only alone for as long as it takes a stranger to step into the same space, an unfamiliar hand on my thigh.

"He comin' or goin' with you tonight?" the man asks, nodding in Noah's general direction.

His drawl is out of place in Southern California, even in a country bar, though it reminds me of Beau. I take a moment to look him up and down, probably in search of other similarities, but only his cowboy hat and boots keep the comparison going. I shake those off easily, finally staring at the attractiveness I tried to ignore at a glance, his lighter hair and smaller build making me wonder for the first time whether I might have a type.

"Neither. He's a friend," I say, stopping before I can tell him that the same is true of a few others at Trailhead.

"Can I buy you a drink?"

I've barely opened my mouth to answer when a full pint glass lands within reach, beer spilling over the side when the delivery isn't gentle. The new guy laughs, and I don't need to turn my head to know Darren doesn't, a silent claim made in a way I find surprisingly endearing. Possessiveness has never been my thing, nor do I think it's Darren's, but maybe we're both unclear about where erasable lines should have been drawn.

I'm close to asking for a marker, just to settle it right here. The palm pressed to my inseam feels really damn good, but I'd ask him to take the touch back if I knew I belonged somewhere else.

My hand covers the one I don't know intimately, and that feels good, too. "I'm okay for now, but thank you."

Noah is back, hovering nearby while he studies the situation. He's spent enough of his adult years here to be well-versed in ridiculous gay bar mating rituals, even if this isn't quite that, so I'm not surprised when there's a small smile on his face as his gaze drifts from me to the stranger to Darren and back again. He stays quiet, though. Darren mumbles something. This handsome man nods, a knowing grin tugging at the corners of his mouth.

"If you change your mind, I'll be over by the pool tables. With *my* friends."

I squeeze his hand, slower to let him go than I should be when I've already turned him down, and he winks before he goes, Darren mumbling all over again.

"I think that's the most I've ever seen you touch someone back," Noah says, handing me a blank answer page. The trivia host must have passed them out when I wasn't paying attention, and I'm sure we've already missed a question or two of the current round. I don't care, still distracted a couple of times over when Noah slides onto his stool and goes on. "Do you think you'll go talk to him later?"

"No."

That single syllable carries enough weight to keep Noah from pushing for the explanation he might've wanted a few seconds ago, but it doesn't stop Darren.

"Jake touches us back all the time," he argues.

"Okay, yes, he touches *us*, but we're not trying to get into his pants." Noah takes a quick sip, nearly choking when he has something else to say. "Oh shit, I've gotta tell Beau and Adrian."

"Tell them what?" I ask.

"That you were practically holding someone's hand and undressing him with your eyes."

"I was not un—"

"You don't need to tell Beau and Adrian anything," Darren sighs.

Ignoring more of the trivia I'd come here for, I think back to the night Beau had done everything but ask me outright if I was sleeping with his ex-husband. I'd told Darren then that Beau knew something was going on, but I don't know how much they've talked about it since, and I won't bring it up now. And Noah is too easygoing to worry about his excitement being dismissed, so he and I drink our beers and refocus on the quiz while Darren remembers how to tease and flirt and have some fun.

It's all a little easier when we're asked the next question.

"The Café Parisien and the Verandah Café permanently closed on the same day due to what historical event?"

I'm thinking it might have something to do with a war, but I honestly don't know.

One look at Darren's dimples tells me he does.

"Was there a battle?" I ask. "An invasion or attack of some kind?"

"Nope."

"Were they in Europe?"

"Nope."

"Were they near each other? Not in entirely separate states or countries?"

"Yep," he smiles. "Very near each other."

I'm out of time, and wouldn't cheat with Darren's answer anyway, that line left empty on my paper when I write the response to the question that follows. But I'm stubborn and curious, so I stare him down once he's done pouring shots of whiskey for a couple who might've ridden in on a bike like mine.

"What century?"

He smiles again. "Twentieth."

"Will the year give it away?"

"Weren't you alive for most of the 1900s, old man?"

"Shut up," I growl. I get another answer correct, and stay frustrated by the one I don't know. "Fine, just put me out of my misery."

Darren leans forward, his arms crossed on the bar and his face too close to mine when Noah is still right there. "The restaurants didn't *close* so much as they sank to the bottom of the ocean."

Jesus.

"Wait, they were on the *Titanic*?" Noah asks.

"They were on the *Titanic*," Darren says.

He's gone without gloating, though he deserves the opportunity and might take it later. Noah and I wrap up the round, and I'm careful not to look toward the pool tables because I'm not that thirsty and I could have another hand on my thigh if I bother to ask for it. Not tonight, though. I'm already getting tired, and Noah is checking the time on his phone before he pushes his empty bottle toward Darren, along with the kind of tip we'd leave for anyone.

Noah waves goodbye to Riley and rests his hand on my shoulder. "I've got an early meeting, so I'm gonna take off. I know it'll be tough, but I'm sure you can handle the final round just fine on your own."

An adorable grin follows, and then Noah nods at Darren one more time before walking away. I do what I can with the last of trivia night, even when my mind still wanders, and Darren's involvement is limited while he's closing out tabs and charming as many people as he can until they're on the other side of the barn doors. My beer is mostly gone by the time the host announces the winners, and I need to work in the morning too, but I get another silent plea to stay where I am, and I find it difficult to move.

I do it eventually, only because I want to use the restroom before I go. When I'm done there, I get stopped by Riley's smile and the chance to ask a question that surprises me even as I open my mouth.

"If I were to host a pool party, would you come?"

They tilt their head. "It would be at your house?"

"Yes."

"And you'd invite me?"

"I absolutely would," I say.

There's an expected pause then, and while I could reassure them they wouldn't have to come to the party, my silence matters more. I can feel Darren watching us, his interest in our brief conversation predictable, but I still have my eye on Riley when they nod.

"Yeah, I think I'd come. I'm guessing you have lots of quiet corners for anyone who needs to hide."

They're not wrong, but I raise my eyebrow. "I live alone. Aren't all the corners quiet?"

"You love motorcycles and music, so I doubt it. Actually, I'm not sure you like silence much at all. But you're gentle, and you make space for important things, so tell me when to be there and don't worry when I disappear into the dark."

It's easy to promise them everything, and I say goodnight as long as I'm there, both of us returning to our sides of the bar a moment later. Darren doesn't ask about anything he thinks he's missed, welcoming me back with the magnetism that drew me to him long before either of us would say so.

The magnetism that drew everyone else to him when they were ready to be loud.

"So," he starts. "Speaking of boats and restaurants."

It's the same way I'd spun a trivia question into something more personal earlier in the night, and I just shake my head. "Nice segue. Is this your way of inviting me over to watch Leonardo DiCaprio and Kate Winslet fail to share a floating door?"

"It is not. But I was thinking—"

"Dangerous."

"Always," Darren admits, looking around as though he needs privacy. And maybe he does. "A guy I know works on one of the Catalina ferries. And a friend of mine runs a kickass restaurant on the island."

A guy I know. A friend of mine. Magnetism. Loud.

"You're going to Catalina?"

"*We're* going to Catalina," he says. "Or we could, if you want to. We haven't really gone out since we had tapas. And the gallery opening, I guess. Everything has been here while I'm working or at our houses when we're fucking around, and I—maybe it would be nice to eat and drink and not be anything else."

"All friends. No benefits."

Darren blinks. I do, too. Then he shrugs. "Have dinner with me."

Chapter Nineteen

Darren

It's a couple of weeks before the Catalina dinner happens, our ever-conflicting schedules—well, conflicting.

I make the arrangements and text Jake a couple of options for dates and times. They're casual, my questions, because I'm not wining and dining him. Like he'd said so succinctly at Trailhead, we're friends, and for this trip, it stops there. I don't know what had made me ask him out in the first place, and I've tried to stop thinking about it just as often as I've started. Jealousy is so unfamiliar to me that I can't imagine it had anything to do with it, but seeing Jake talk to someone else—seeing someone else's hand on Jake's thigh—had reminded me that our friendship is all we've promised each other.

And I want more time with my friend.

When the day arrives, or when I wake up several hours into it, it's gorgeous, the mid-March sun peeking out from behind scattered clouds. I shower and tug on a tight pair of chinos, and a deep blue button-up, my sleeves rolled. The music I've got playing in my car on the way to pick up Jake is more his style than mine, but making him happy is a decent reason to push my pop princesses aside.

I'd told him I was on my way, so he steps outside as soon as I pull into his driveway, this stunning man who doesn't have a habit of climbing into anyone's car. The pale green of his sweater does something to his eyes, but I'd get lost there if I tried to figure it out, so I drive us away from the huge house in the hills and toward the ferry that will take us to Catalina for the next several hours. Jake hasn't been into the bar since I asked him out, nor have I chased him down, our texts mostly limited to chatter about Supine and the offhand observation that I haven't heard from my father.

So, Jake and I haven't seen each other at all, and I assume both of us knew spending this time together didn't require constant contact in the days leading up to it.

Or someone was worried the afternoon would get called off altogether.

"I asked Riley if they'd come to a pool party at my house."

We're about halfway to the port, and silence has kept us company more often than not, but I so rarely feel out of sync with Jake, and I haven't been bothered for a moment of the ride. Still, his voice fills spaces inside me I forgot were empty, and I take a slow breath when I glance at him before focusing on the road again.

"Does this mean you've decided you'll do it? You'll throw a party?"

"Mmmm," Jake hums. "We need warmer weather first."

I chuckle. "Spring is only days away. Pretty sure it'll work out for you."

"For me?"

"No?"

"This wasn't *my* idea," he points out.

"Ah, you're saying you need my help."

"I need very little of anything, actually."

It's hot—that touch of arrogance. Sexy as fuck, and somehow sweet when it's barely a rumble. And I smile when I ignore it. "Riley must've said yes."

"They did."

"Good."

"It is."

Jake must like whatever song starts then, because he turns up the volume and relaxes further into the passenger seat. I let myself wonder what a road trip with him would be like—or whether he'd even want to travel that far if he's not on his Harley—because sitting still for long periods of time has never been my thing, but I think he might be the one person to convince me otherwise.

Maybe he already has.

When we reach the port, I can't possibly take Jake's hand, so I tell him to stay where he is while I go in search of a guy I've known for years and sucked off once or twice. I get everything situated quickly, and we're aboard the ferry not long after that, the wind on the water forcing us inside. All my attention is on him now, and his on me, but Jake talks about the only time he's ever been to Catalina, and I tell him all about the high school friend of mine he'll meet tonight. Back and forth, we share stories and laugh so hard we have to wipe tears from our eyes, and I'm curious what we look like to anyone else. We've got drinks in our hands, and we're curled toward each other because nothing else makes sense, but we haven't touched in a while, and I don't know when we will again.

We arrive in Avalon hours before our dinner reservation, but if Jake is concerned about how we'll spend the afternoon, he doesn't say. I don't know my way around, but I've done some research, and I find it easy to lead us from one place to another. We visit a museum, a botanical garden, and a ridiculous number of cute stores, conversation coming and going. Every now and then I step back to watch the way he interacts with everyone because that's still mostly new to me, this version of Jake who isn't just a Trailhead regular.

It has me saying something before I've thought it through. "You should invite Lucy to the party."

"I should *what*?" he asks, a book about the history of Catalina Island in his hand when he looks over his shoulder at me, incredulous at best.

"Is it—I mean, I know she's busy with work, but—" I sigh. "Sorry, maybe I shouldn't have said anything, but now that I have, is your reaction because you're worried that *she'd* be uncomfortable or that *you* would be? You know none of us would embarrass you, right? You know *I* wouldn't embarrass you?"

Jake turns away and takes his time returning the book to the shelf he'd pulled it from, and I don't miss the slow rise and fall of his shoulders. On instinct alone, I take a step closer to him, but I stop before I reach out a hand, matching my next breath to his.

"Will you give me some time? I'll answer you later, but please give me some time."

I'll give him anything, but I don't say that, shrugging even while he can't see me. "Of course. Yeah. Are we okay in the meantime, or did I fuck up the rest of our night?"

"You didn't."

"Jake."

He spins slowly, his eyes narrowed. "Yes?"

"I didn't what, Jake?" I smirk as much as I think I can, and he shakes his head as he closes the distance between us, his fingertips just barely grazing the front of my shirt. This is the teasing friends do—just like the night we stood by his car and I asked him to tell me he'd made himself come in his shower—but there was a spark there then and it's back now. I don't care whether it burns me before I put it out, just as long as he isn't left with another scar, so I hold his hand for a beat or two before I push it away. "Please. You know it's one of my favorite words. Let me hear you say it."

"Fuck—" He pauses there, the crispness of the *k* slowly crumbling between us when he smiles. "You didn't fuck up the rest of our night."

The view from the restaurant is gorgeous. It's romantic for any-one looking for that sort of thing, and relaxing for the rest of us.

My high school friend had greeted me with an enthusiastic hug when we'd arrived, and later, after appreciating the flare of envy in Jake's stare, I'd explained that Steven was terribly straight and very monogamously married. Otherwise quiet, we'd been led to a deck overlooking the water and treated to a bottle of wine, a glass already in my hand when I'd flirted with danger.

"It's not quite as good as the stuff Lucy could bring us," I'd said.

"Subtle," he'd responded.

We're much further into our meal now, the table crowded by half-empty plates of delicious food we share as often as not. The low hum of the restaurant is steady and full of promise, and I feel it inside me, too. Warm. Comfortable. I lean into the sensation, trusting that I won't fall from such a sturdy chair.

"Tell me something," I say. "Anything."

Jake swallows the bite in his mouth and thinks about my re-quest for a moment, but it doesn't take him long. I'm sure he has a million stories.

"I played baseball when I was a kid. And once, when I was about fourteen, I was sitting next to a teammate in the dugout after practice. Our moms were always the last two to pick us up, so it wasn't unusual for us to be together like that, but most of the time we'd be playing catch or racing each other or something. That day was too hot, though. We waited in the shade instead."

Aside from my experience with surfing, I know very little about sports. I *do* know that baseball players are cute as fuck, and I'm invested in whatever young Jake was up to that day, still a few years before I was born.

"He and I talked about school and the team and our friends, and then he reached over and curled his pinky around mine, and he tugged until our hands rested on the bench between us." Jake frowns for a split second as he pushes a roasted potato around his plate. "My face got warm, and my heart was pounding—it was *so* hot that day. I looked straight ahead, toward the parking lot, even when he whispered my name. And then I saw my mom's car, and I pulled my hand away from his, and I didn't look back."

"And nothing else happened after that?" I ask.

"Nope," he says, finally setting his fork down. "But I saw him years later at a reunion. He was married to another man. We didn't talk for more than a few minutes, but I was unsettled for a long, long time afterward."

"Because he was gay?"

Jake shakes his head, but stills when he's brave enough to meet my curious eyes. "We missed out on something we both might've wanted because I didn't realize that what I was feeling was more than just heat."

My throat is dry, I think. It's the reason I go for my water and ignore that Jake's hand is on the table now, close enough for me to touch my pinky to his if I thought it was a good idea. It's not, and I'm tempted to walk away so I can call Beau and beg him to remind me of all the reasons I can't do this—why I can't love a man who deserves better than anything I've ever been.

Of course, Beau would try to tell me I can love just fine.

I nod to acknowledge too many honest things and change the subject instead. "We're gonna need lots of food, lots of drinks, and lots of pool noodles."

"Does that mean it's my turn to ask whether I messed up the rest of our night?"

"No."

"No, it's not my turn?" Jake asks. "Or no, I didn't mess up?"

"Both. Neither. Nothing's messed up. I'm just excited about the pool party."

"We don't need pool noodles. Lucy isn't twelve."

I perk up at that. "You'll invite her?"

"I will."

"Do I still get an answer to the other things I asked? Or is that it?"

"Do you want that to be it?"

"I want pool noodles."

Jake tries so hard to avoid laughing—to avoid encouraging my nonsense—but he can't help it, and I switch back from water to wine now that I feel better about everything. After we've taken a few more bites of dinner, the server clears our plates and sells us on a dessert we'll share. Between quick hits of chocolate, caramel, and ice cream, we play around with menu ideas for the pool party, and I remind him he doesn't have to make a bunch of stuff from scratch.

And that if he really wants to, I'm happy to help.

He's been resistant to that so far, and my offer is careful because I assured him months ago that I wouldn't step into spaces he needed to keep full of untouched memories.

"So, what exactly do you think you need pool noodles for?" he asks before pressing his tongue to his spoon long enough to make my dick jealous.

"So I can fight with Beau," I reply easily, something else occurring to me a second later. "And maybe you should fight with Adrian. Nobody can hold a grudge after a pool noodle fight. Or—"

"Yes?"

"We could chicken fight."

"Chicken fight?"

"Yeah, so two people are in the pool and then—"

"I know what chicken fighting is," Jake interrupts, a perfect little grin pulling at the corners of his mouth. "Are you planning to chicken fight *with* pool noodles, or did your brain go sideways again?"

I shrug. "Sideways, I think."

Our server brings our check then—I notice our dessert has been comped on top of the wine he'd already gifted us—and once I've paid, we stop to thank Steven again on our way out the door. Jake's hand rests on my lower back when we step back onto the street, and I'm not sure how much of it's for show, but I let myself enjoy it while I can.

All friends. No benefits.

We have a ferry to catch, but we've got some time to walk off dinner first. We end up on the back side of several shops because the wind is better blocked that way, and body heat only gets us so far when I hadn't thought to bring something warm.

"Hey, come here," Jake murmurs, backing into a nondescript stucco wall.

He's got my wrist in his hand already, but as soft as his command was, his hold on me is gentler than that. Jake pulls me toward him, then lets go to reach for my sleeve, unrolling it slowly and smoothing it over my forearm. It conceals my goosebumps, but I shiver when he does the same thing with my other sleeve, and I can't remember the last time a man touched me like this. Covered me up. Put a layer between his fingers and my bare skin.

And the way he's looking at me. I think I could cry or come, and I really don't know which should embarrass me more.

I don't have time to worry about it when he wraps his arms around me and holds me against his chest, his mouth pressed close to my head as he starts to talk.

"I don't know whether she'll be able to make it to the party, but Lucy wouldn't be uncomfortable at all. She's heard about all of you for years, and I know she'd love to meet you guys."

"But you," I mumble into him. "You're uncomfortable letting her see you with us?"

"Not uncomfortable. Overwhelmed." Jake sighs, and while I feel the obvious hesitation, I don't get in the way of anything else he has to say. We stay there, silent, until he takes another deep breath and goes on. "I got my goodbye with Michelle. I've grieved and I've celebrated and I've made friends and I've—I found you. I've had this time with you. But we'll all be there, in my backyard, and it's been so long. It's my fault, but it's been so long, so if Lucy is there, too—it's everything, all at once. That grief and celebration and her and you and—I don't know. I'm just not sure what to do with all of that."

"Do you have to do anything?"

"What do you mean?"

"It's a pool party, not a wedding reception," I say softly. "The sun will be out, and some idiots you know will whack each other with pool noodles, and I'll be co-hosting simply because I'm the asshole who pressured you to do any of this in the first place. That's it. If there's something you still need to celebrate or grieve, do it. But don't make it about Lucy. And definitely don't make it about me. Just enjoy the fucking party."

He nuzzles me for a moment so brief that I might have imagined his beard against my hair. I only know it's real when I feel him kiss me a second later, his mouth warm at my temple. Without thinking, I turn toward more of it—toward more of *him*—and whimper when his lips part so easily for me, my tongue sweeping past them for a taste. Jake makes a sound too, and I want to hear another and another, already desperate for the intimacy I've missed for weeks. We're moving slowly enough that everything in me aches, but our kiss is the kind that matters more than the way my cock is straining against my zipper. Jake's arms are fully around me now, and I hold his face between my hands like the precious thing it is, only backing away to whisper two words.

"The ferry."

"We can get a hotel," he says, chasing the offer with another devastating kiss.

It's impossible to stop right away, or maybe I don't want to try. Before I consider making any genuine effort, Jake breaks the kiss and spins us effortlessly, his mouth back on mine when I land against the wall. He's so impossibly good at this, one muscular thigh between my legs so I can practically ride it while I attempt to argue with him.

"Can't. We're friends. I promised," I pant. "Tonight was dinner. Just us."

Jake moves both hands to my hips to help me rut against him, his voice unfairly steady. "Dinner was great. And the hotel can be just us, too."

"Friends."

"We're still friends, sweetheart."

"Neither of us wants to fall in love."

"No," he agrees. "So, let me get us a hotel room. Let me get you off."

He swallows my yes before it's fully out of my mouth, and I have no hope of telling him I'd also be fine with him getting me off right where we stand. That wouldn't be enough, though. I need to make him come too—at least once—before I remind myself of all the reasons I need to stop thinking with my dick.

And my heart.

We get the hotel room, and we break in entirely different ways while Jake praises me for too many things. We share the jetted tub and a bottle of champagne someone at the front desk must have thought we'd earned. We fall asleep naked and reaching for each other in the dark.

I wake up alone—again—and find a note on the bathroom sink.

Went to get coffee and make some work calls. Might try calling Lucy. Let me know when you're up and ready to go and we can catch the ferry back. And thanks for letting me talk you into staying...it was a really fun night.

He'd signed it with a beautiful *J*, and I trace it with my fingertip now.

Friends. We're friends. Because neither of us wanted to fall in love.

It just sucks that one of us already did.

Jake comes to see Supine perform that Friday night. Coincidentally, it's the first time my father has returned to Trailhead since our lunch, but the two older men in my life have nothing to say to each other. I need to talk to at least one of them, though I'm just nervous enough to reconsider the idea. It's the right thing to do and the wrong thing to do, and I wait until Jake has had half his beer before I bring it up, easing into my real questions even then.

"Have you heard anything else from Lucy?"

"Just confirmation of what we'd already assumed," he says. "The best chance for her to get away for a night would be sometime mid-week. And we know that works for almost everyone else, too. Noah and I are the only two with traditional jobs, and I've got flexibility with mine."

I nod. V can help cover for Riley and me the night of the party. Beau's first appointments won't be until later the following morning, and both Adrian and Mason have help for their places on either end of the day, so working around their schedules isn't a problem. And because the resort is busiest on the weekends, Lucy's off days line up well for our plans. Now we're just waiting for springtime, and the sunshine that will make everyone eager to play in the pool.

And maybe the more, the merrier?

"How would you feel about inviting a few others?" I ask.

Jake raises an eyebrow. "Do I even want to know what you're thinking?"

I turn to look at the stage and say nothing else right away, certain it won't take Jake more than a heartbeat to figure it out on his own. Riley is watching Supine too, though they've been less eager to serve the band before or after each set. I keep thinking they'll ask me to trade sides with them—at least for one night a week—but maybe that would call attention to things they'd prefer not to admit aloud. With the smallest shake of my head, I return my attention to Jake.

"Might be fun to get to know them better," I shrug.

"Is a backyard pool party with unimaginable amounts of alcohol the best place to get to know Sebastian?"

"This is a *bar*."

Jake rolls his eyes. "Sure, but there's a difference between the nights they're working here and a night we're all relaxing for hours on end."

"So, a bad idea?"

"I'm not going to say no to you, Darren."

"It's your house."

"It's *our* party," he fires back. "And you know there's someone else you can ask. Someone who knows Sebastian a lot better than you and I do."

"Riley?"

Playing dumb doesn't work, and Jake doesn't even bother to roll his eyes this time. "Go ask Drew."

"You're encouraging a conversation now?"

"Let's not get carried away. You barely need complete sentences for this."

Someone flags me down for another round of whiskey, and it saves me from having another argument about my father when I don't know what side I'm on. My own, I guess. Either way, I finish pouring and wipe my hands and don't look at Jake before I slip from behind the bar. I know he's watching me, and that's fine, but I'm a surprise when I reach my father's side, and he blinks quickly as though I might disappear even though I've been here all night long.

"Darren."

"Sometime soon, whenever it's hot enough for it, there's gonna be a party at Jake's. Riley and I will be there. A few friends from here." I take a deep breath and look at Supine again before I return to the curious tilt of Drew's head. "I was thinking we could invite the band, but it's a party. With a fuckton of booze. And I—you might have some insight into whether a party would be a bad place for Sebastian to be."

"You realize this is a bar?"

"But there's a difference between him playing here and relaxing there," I argue. On behalf of Jake. Or something. "I don't want to act like he's not a grown-ass adult who can take care of himself, but I also don't want to set him up for failure when you've already asked me to keep an eye on him."

He huffs. "I'm not sure that's *exactly* what I did."

"Close enough. So—yes to the party or no to the party?"

Drew Barrett flashes those fucking dimples at me—the same ones I use to get *my* way—and I wonder whether there's any chance I'll be able to refuse whatever request is about to be made. I glance over my shoulder at Jake like he can save me from myself, but turn back to my father for the question I know he's going to ask before he asks it.

"Can I come, too?"

"Fine."

"That's it?"

"I have to get back to work. You want me to say it's not fine?" I ask.

"Just thought there would be conditions with the invitation."

"You invited yourself," I remind him. "But okay—don't drink, make sure Sebastian doesn't drink, stay away from Jake, and enjoy the water."

I don't tell my father to stay away from me when it feels like a given, and I leave him before he remembers that he's better at that than I'll ever be. There are a few beer bottles to clear on my way back to the bar, and Jake is busy talking to V with his Guinness in his hand, but as soon as I return, she pinches my waist and leaves us alone. Jake takes a sip and hides a smile.

"Well?" he asks.

"Plus five."

"Ah, of course."

"You're not surprised," I mutter. "But you know he might not show up."

Jake's smile fades then, but what remains is important. "I'll be there either way."

"The party's at your house."

"The party could be anywhere. My point stands."

I run the pad of my thumb over the rough edge of a bottle cap and don't look away. "You mean that, don't you?"

"Every word."

"I definitely need pool noodles now," I sigh.

Jake sets his glass aside and wipes away another grin. "So, now we've got me, you, Beau, Adrian, Riley, Noah, Mason, Lucy, Maxwell, Banjo, Layla, Sebastian, and Drew?"

"Yes, plus anyone Mason brings. There's always someone."

A second or two pass, and I grab my bottle of water while Jake does whatever math I'm not privy to. "Do I get to make a guest list suggestion, too?"

"It's *our* party," I tease.

"Have you considered inviting Sage?"

I nearly choke. It's not that it's a bad idea, but I definitely wasn't expecting Jake to drop her name, and I wonder how long she's been on his mind.

"Why Sage?"

"Because she's a friend of yours," Jake says. "But there's a reason you don't talk about her with the rest of us, even though I'm guessing she knows us pretty well, so if you don't think we'd all get along—"

"No, no," I interrupt, waving my hand. "She'd fit in really well, which is why I—no, it's—yeah."

"*Which is why, no, yeah?*" Jake snorts. "For a short sentence, you managed to take that in several directions at once."

"Yes, I will invite her. And she just turned 21, so I won't have to act surprised by her familiarity with adult beverages."

Jake chuckles, but doesn't quite let me off the hook. "Are you going to finish whatever other thought you abandoned back there? About her fitting in?"

"Nah, it's barely a thing." I stop there, but my brain doesn't quiet, skipping from one thought to another in a way that I'm used to, but is probably unfair to the man sitting in front of me. *Sage. My father. Beau.* Jake's watching me like he knows I have more to say, even if I've dismissed his question. And because I've already stopped myself from one unformed thought, I don't bite my tongue in time to keep myself from going on about something else. *Sebastian. Riley. Lucy.* "Would Michelle have liked me?"

The multicolored lights around the bar are pretty when they strike the tears Jake won't let fall. And I think I'd take back what I've said, but I know he doesn't want me to. Not when he smiles at me with awe I don't deserve.

"I was thinking about that the night I wrecked my bike, actually," he admits, and *that's* not what I was expecting. "I'd been lying in the dirt and missing her like crazy, and I wondered what it would've been like if I could've somehow brought her here. And yeah, she would've loved you."

I take a deep breath and look from a half-drunk Guinness to the place where a ring should've been and then up to eyes that shine with something else now.

And then I nod. "I would've loved her, too."

JAKE

I 'm exhausted and sweaty and dirty. Filthy, actually. I need to shower, but I also don't want to move from where I am. I could stay here all day, in fact. The warmth. The quiet. The simple fragility, or the fragile simplicity, or a dozen other pretentious descriptions of a moment I don't want to leave behind.

And I don't have to go anywhere yet.

I don't have to say goodbye. Yet.

Wiping my brow with the back of my arm probably leaves a streak of soil behind, but I don't grab the rag I gave up on hours ago. Instead, I refocus on the last of the weeds in a garden that only sort of belongs to me. The beds of flowers on the opposite side of the backyard have always been mine, but I inherited the vegetable garden I'm kneeling in front of now, and I ache from the inside out, the pain a fact of life twice over.

I'm getting too old to do this as often as I'd like, and I desperately miss my wife.

Ask Darren to come over and help.

The voice inside my head isn't wrong, but it isn't right either, and I do what I can to keep it silent for now. Crashing my bike on an L.A. off-ramp had left me obviously bloody and bruised, but I'd also been fractured—almost intimately so—and I'd healed with Darren caught between more cracks than I can count. Doing anything about that now would require new attention to old wounds, and most of them became welcome scars a very long time ago.

I tug one of the gardening gloves from my hand and reach for the dirt because having anything in my way feels unbearable now. A deep breath follows, and then I sit and rest and let the voice return.

You didn't resist his offer to be your first.

No, I didn't. I'd spent years imagining what it would be like to be one of many. I still think I would've let him take anything my broken body could've given him the night I crashed, when he'd held me close and then put me to bed. The sex was never going to be the breaking point, though. Sex wasn't the most important part of my *marriage*, and saying yes to Darren didn't tread on hallowed ground.

He'd known it, too. Way back then, he'd mentioned movies and lounge chairs because he'd understood that being naked with him wasn't what made me feel bare.

I kept him out of my kitchen instead.

And by then it was too late to matter.

I'd realized a long time ago that trivia night was the irrevocable shift between us. It was something Michelle and I would've loved doing together. We *had* loved it together, here and there, her intelligence arousing enough to make me beg for more. Now she's gone, and someone else turns me on. He takes me to dinner and plays my music and asks me for silly toys and tells me about things that hurt.

I've avoided Trailhead the past few weeks because Darren and I are about to host a pool party in the house I shared with Michelle, and I want his hands in this dirt and his help the next time I cook. We're friends, but he's made some of my fractured pieces whole, and it feels important to keep him close enough that I don't break again.

None of that comes from a voice in my head, and if I weren't so busy pushing myself off the ground and tossing another glove aside and wiping dirt on the front of my jeans, I'd pause to feel it in the beat of my heart.

Still too busy after that, I give in to temptation and undress completely, my phone left on the discarded pile of clothes before I dive into the pool. After a lap or two, I pull myself back out and retrieve my phone, then drop into a lounge chair to dry while I text Darren.

There's a heat wave all next week.

He responds quickly. He usually does. **Yeah? You ready?**

No pool noodles.

Believe it or not I can have fun without them

I believe it just fine. *V is still okay with it?*

My phone rings with Darren's call, and I glance down at my naked body as though it matters. He's seen it before, and will again. Probably. It's only been a week or so since the last time he stopped by before his shift and we made a mess of each other in my living room, and I want him back again.

"This isn't bad news, is it?" I ask.

"Nope," he says. "V's still good with it, and she told me to take the night before too, in case you need help with anything. So, I'll just swap both shifts unless—have you talked to Lucy yet?"

"I called her this morning. She said she'll drive up the day of the party and crash here that night. I'll need to go into work for a few hours before everyone gets here, but—"

"You don't have plans the night before," Darren finishes.

"None. And I don't think there's much to prep, really. Not that far in advance."

"Okay, so I can keep that shift or—"

"Come over for dinner."

"I was really hoping you'd say that," Darren laughs, low and just a bit rough. "Do you want me to grab takeout?"

With the phone pressed to my ear and the spring sunlight on my face, I close my eyes. It's not always easy to remember 28 years of marriage so clearly, but very little escapes me now. The laughter and the tears and the noise and the silence and his and her gardens and sex by the pool and a long goodbye and the chance to let someone else all the way in. I'm overwhelmed, but comforted by the weight of so many good things, gratitude thick in my throat until I clear it away and do my best with words that betray nobody.

"No," I tell him. "I want you to cook with me."

"You know the routine. Pick a bottle, open it up, and pour."

Barefoot in my kitchen, and wearing nothing but a thin t-shirt and cotton shorts, Darren bends to study the selection of wine I've left on the island. I don't have much on either—just a tank top and sweatpants—but once he's made a decision, he locks his mischievous eyes with mine instead of leering.

"How many people would think we've been fucking because you're an older man who tells me what to do?"

"Ah, well, how many people tracked your daddy issues from a mile away?"

"Ha, yeah, that's fair," he chuckles. With a bottle in one hand, he snatches the corkscrew with the other, and doesn't look at me again until I push two glasses his way. "Were you concerned about that? *Are* you concerned about that?"

"No to both."

"Why not?"

Something quivers between those two words—a detail so subtle Darren could deny it without blinking—and I move swiftly, skirting the island to pull everything out of his hands before I kiss him. With my fingertips trailing over his jaw, I'm tender about it, but I open his mouth enough to make sure I know how the next sound tastes, and then I pull away so I can see his face when I answer.

"I would never have met those needs for you, and it wouldn't have occurred to me to try. Everyone else can praise you however they want. I'll praise you like Jake."

"Jesus—"

"Now be good and pour," I say, letting him go with a wink. "It's time to make dinner."

"What are we making?"

"I figured we could make the same pasta I had the night of my accident."

"Mmmm, I remember those dirty dishes," Darren murmurs. "So, is tonight an attempt to change bad memories into good ones?"

"Oh, I don't know. I'm pretty fond of what happened back then."

"Ugly scar and all?"

"Ugly scar and all," I say, working my way around the kitchen to gather everything we'll need.

I'm not concerned about Darren keeping up, a scribbled recipe on the counter for him to decipher if he wants. He wants, of course, and as soon as we both have our glasses of wine, he picks up the page, his hands never still for long. When he speaks, I expect a question about the food, but he hasn't left the past behind, and I know a little about what that's like.

"Do you think we would've ended up here if you hadn't shown up at Trailhead that night?"

"Yes," I answer easily. And maybe I just want that to be true, but I shrug either way. "Trivia night was starting to feel like—I don't know. The flirting. The teasing. It turned serious. There was an edge to it, like we both knew if we pushed a little harder—if we said one more thing—we could get answers to anything we wanted to know."

"I wanted to know everything," Darren says. "Still do."

We both take a sip, and then I turn to fill a pot with water. "I should take some of that back."

"Oh?"

"I'm not sure we would've ended up *here*. I think we would've slept together, but I'm not sure it would've been more than something quick and casual."

Darren frowns. "I never had plans to drag you into the keg room like everyone else."

There's a sheet pan in my hands now, and I drop it in front of him and nod toward the recipe before I preheat the oven. He's quick to grab the next few things he'll need, but I flatten my hands on the island until he's looking at me again.

"It wasn't until you knelt between my bloody legs and found out no man had been there before that I became a real challenge."

"Jake, you've been a real challenge since the day we met. Knowing I'd be your first only stopped me from sucking your dick before sunrise."

"Glad we got past that."

"So am I."

He pops a cherry tomato into his mouth then. Swallows it and steals another. Of all the things I've imagined him doing, this isn't one of them, and I think I must have been naive not to have seen it coming. His smile is unapologetic, and the only reason I don't kiss it off his face is because I'm too busy clinging to a moment I've missed for the past ten years.

Darren must know because he doesn't ask.

And he returns to the recipe because he's here to cook with me.

We're both on our second glass of wine by the time we sit down to eat, and we're far enough apart to have plenty of room to breathe. It won't last, this space between us, but I appreciate it for as long as either of us needs to pretend this is a meal shared by friends who will go their separate ways again and again. After every few bites, we talk about the rest of the groceries we'll need to pick up tomorrow, and the ice we'll grab for coolers we've borrowed, and the side gate we'll unlock to let everyone in without having to lead them through my house.

We finish the wine.

The playlists are ready. The décor is going to be minimal.

The last of the pasta is gone.

My daughter will get to meet the people I love dearly. And they'll get to meet her.

"Your face just did a thing," Darren says. "Michelle?"

"Lucy."

"You're protective."

"She doesn't need me to be. Not now."

"And not around us," Darren points out. "But I'm nervous, so I get it."

I smile, dazed by that. "You're nervous about meeting my kid?"

"Of course I am."

He doesn't explain, and I don't need him to. His feelings make sense on more than one level, and examining them too closely feels unfair when I'm holding on to a few of my own. They're all better unnamed tonight, and I lift my empty wine glass to help distract myself under the gaze of a man who might have other things to say. Darren nods and gathers our plates, then wanders toward the kitchen as he promises to take care of the dishes tomorrow. I'm not surprised when he reappears a couple of minutes later with a second bottle of wine and dimples for days.

"Thank you," I say as he pours for both of us.

"Of course."

With the bottle left on the table and his glass in his hand, he leans back against the dining room wall, as attractive as I've ever seen him, maybe because he's not trying to be attractive at all. We both drink, and we could stay here and keep talking about grilling supplies and inflatable rafts, but he might want to go somewhere else, and I know I do. Eventually, I push out of my chair and make my way to him, effectively pinning him where he stands without making contact at all.

"Take your glass and the bottle into the living room. I'll be right there."

His grin goes nowhere, and whatever he thinks I'm up to, he's almost certainly wrong, or at least wrong for now. We're months into this thing we've been doing, so it's not difficult to predict that our night will end with us deliciously spent on the couch or upstairs in my bed or anywhere in between. But tomorrow there will be a limit to how much Darren and I can touch and play and tease, and I want to revel in it tonight.

When I join him in the living room, I bring a pint of ice cream—rich and dark and perfect with the new bottle we've started—and a single spoon. There's not much wine left in my glass considering I haven't had it all that long, but I set it and our dessert on the coffee table next to the bottle that's already there. Then I crouch in front of the fireplace, the warm day giving way to a cool night that makes this reasonable. I breathe easily at the first flicker of flames, and chuckle when I hear his low whistle behind me.

"Hot," he whispers.

I think it's an understatement when I turn and really look at him, so comfortable in my home when he relaxes against the sofa cushions, takes another sip, and waits for me. It feels like I can't possibly screw this up, and he might be the one person who'd be gentle with me even if I prove myself wrong. A couple of steps bring me to his side, and I lower myself to the couch, careful not to jostle the glass of wine in his hand when I top both of us off. It's far too late for a toast, but we drink together until I glance at the ice cream, and he licks his lips.

"Want some?" I ask unnecessarily.

Darren moans a little. "I want it all."

The ice cream is soft enough for me to get a decent spoonful when I stretch toward the table, and I bring it so close to Darren's open mouth before I change direction and feed myself, sucking on the spoon for good measure.

"Mmmm, this is great," I say, my mouth still full.

"That was so fucking mean," Darren whines, and he wants so badly to come after me, but we both have wine in our hands and there are better ways to ruin my couch than to spill everything now. I watch as he unceremoniously empties his glass down his throat instead and sets it aside, his eyes wide and needy when he turns to me again. "Chugging that was the least sexy thing I've done in a while, and I'll bet every sommelier I've ever been with just shuddered without knowing why."

I push ice cream past his lips before the words are fully out of his mouth. "Well, my apologies to that entire subsection of suffering suitors."

Darren kisses me then, his tongue still cold when it finds mine. I take eagerly for as long as he's willing to give, and when he finally pulls away, I hurry to finish my wine, too. We make a classy pair, but when we both get the giggles about it, I can't possibly care. I'm still laughing and trying to put my glass down and wipe my eyes and fumble my way back to anything resembling control, but it's too late to do anything about Darren and how easily he takes the spoon from me after swiping the ice cream from the table. He digs into the carton and taunts me with a messy bite, climbing onto my lap until he can straddle me and hold the spoon just far enough away.

"Say please, baby."

"Please, baby."

He snorts and feeds it to me, his gaze more unfocused and his smile a mile wide. "Okay, so who do you think's gonna fuck at the party?"

"Why does anyone have to fuck at the party?" I ask.

"Have you seen our guest list? Hell, Beau and Adrian are right there."

"Oh, come on," I argue after another bite. "Beau will not fuck at my house."

Darren snorts again, amused by wine, ice cream, and how smoothly his favorite word keeps slipping off my tongue. "Beau will fuck anywhere. And given how they started, I'm gonna guess Adrian isn't all that shy."

"Fine. They can do whatever they want. Drew absolutely cannot."

"I love that you're shutting down *my* father before *your* daughter."

"Whoa, no. Nope. Uh-uh," I sputter. "Lucy does *not* need to be part of this conversation."

I steal the spoon from Darren and shove ice cream into his mouth before taking more for myself. I'm tempted to have another glass of wine too, especially if we're going to be on this subject for long, but I have a beautiful man on top of me, and moving away from him is unfathomable.

"Hey, if she wants to entertain herself tomorrow night, she could do a lot worse than Noah," he says. "Although *I've* never been able to figure Noah out, so—oh, what about someone from Supine?"

"Maxwell and Banjo both wear wedding bands."

Darren tilts his head, charmed somehow. "Someone's been paying close attention, hmmm? And I guess that leaves Layla and Sebastian."

"For Lucy?" I ask. "I don't think Layla's her type, and I'm pretty sure Sebastian is off limits."

"Because of Riley?"

"Because of Riley."

"Not sure I've figured out what's going on there, either. Those two seemed to hit it off really, really well at first, but Riley barely looks at him now."

"Maybe whatever might've happened between them already did," I suggest. "And the ice cream is melting."

"You're the one holding the spoon."

I shut him up by keeping his mouth full, then silence myself the same way, the two of us going back and forth until most of the pint is gone. When I shake my head and leave the spoon in the carton, Darren leans backward to slide it onto the table and returns to press a cold hand to my beard. My eyes flutter closed for a moment, but I don't want to miss a thing, and I find myself staring at him again.

"What about us? At the party?"

Darren brushes his thumb over my lips and shrugs from my lap. "Kinda figured we'd get the fucking out of our system tonight."

"We've been doing this since the gallery opening, and it's not out of our system yet."

"No, it's not."

"And I'm not sure when it will be."

"Neither am I," he says.

He hasn't let go of me, and I haven't looked away from him, and when he rocks forward, it's so subtle that it's only my body's immediate response that makes me sure it happened at all. I put my hands on his waist and wordlessly ask him to do it again, and Darren barely nods. Everything is hushed, a bottle and a half of wine reducing our world to this, and when he presses his forehead to mine, we just breathe.

By the time we kiss, our mouths are open for it, nothing starting tentatively when we've been here so many times before. It's all so gentle, though—every touch and plea and slow drag of his tongue against mine—and I feel each sound before I hear a damn thing. He scrapes a hand through my hair and holds on, and I wrap my arms around him while he continues to grind against me, our arousal undeniable. But even the roll of his hips is unhurried, the heavy hum of alcohol in our blood keeping a rhythm I sort of love.

I'm not sure how to say that exactly, but I break the kiss and drop my lips to his neck. "I don't want to get you out of my system."

"Does that mean we shouldn't fuck?" he asks. "Would you rather keep me right here?"

"We could come like this."

"We could."

When I'm quiet too long, Darren tugs on my hair and makes

me groan. But I lift my head and fall back into another seemingly endless kiss. I ache, and I need to say so, but it won't take much. Nudging him backward, I tip my head toward the downstairs bathroom.

"Go."

He nips the underside of my jaw and peels himself away, and while his shorts do nothing to hide how eager he is to get there and back again, a couple of quick strokes over the material give him the relief they can. I don't know why I hadn't thought to have a condom and lube within reach already, but we've kept some relatively close for weeks now, and I don't worry about whether Beau will borrow anything tomorrow. When Darren returns, he adds to the pile of vices on the coffee table and crawls back onto my lap, cradling my face with both hands now.

"Hello."

"You're not drunk, are you?" I ask.

Darren rubs his nose against mine. "All I said was hello."

Any other point I might've made is forgotten when he opens my mouth with his own, still perfectly languid while his body seeks the friction it had loved a minute ago. My hands slip beneath the back of his shirt, smooth skin everywhere I can reach, and his fall between us, Darren's nimble fingers pulling both of us free. I expect him to do more then, but he only drags his thumb over my wet tip and sucks it clean and kisses me deeply. There's no way for me to know what he had planned next, but I'm not patient enough for it, and I tighten my hold on him. As soon as I stand, he instinctively locks his legs behind my back, and I think

I could carry him anywhere.

I don't actually go very far.

It's a little clumsy, and probably hilarious if we were any less turned on and tipsy, but I lower him to the thick carpet and feel him arch up into me immediately. We're clear of the coffee table and not close enough to the fireplace to be bothered by the heat. And with our waistbands still low enough to leave us bare to each other, I slide my length against his and say his name with the reverence I assume few men have shown.

His entire body is so pliant beneath me, his legs loose around mine now, and his hands light against me like they're simply there to reassure him I won't leave. And I don't want to, but at some point I chuckle into our kiss and have to push at the sweatpants in my way, Darren on the verge of laughing, too. The clumsiness returns—or maybe it never fully left—but then we're wearing nothing but our shirts, and I can press my smile to his again.

Everything is still syrupy, the wine causing me to move as slowly as I would've liked to anyway. With minimal preparation, I could bury myself in Darren from here and kiss him while he whimpers for more, but it feels so good to rub against each other like this, and I go in search of another minute of that instead. Finally more coordinated, I shift until my legs are on the other side of his and I can straddle him, lining us up and taking both of us in my hand. He reaches up for the lube and grins as he drizzles it over our tips, and whether he thinks I've gone back on my word about what I want tonight, I'm not sure. Dropping the bottle, he sits up to chase another kiss while I stroke us together, and nothing else matters.

"You're so fucking hot," Darren groans, one hand in my hair and the other barely wrapped around my wrist as it continues up and down. "I love the way your cock feels against mine. I love how wet you make me every time."

It's true, and the biggest reason we probably could've done this part without any help. I watch as his fingertip glides through a few drops of it now, but lose sight of his hand when it moves behind me. And then I feel him against my hole, slick and ready for anything I might want.

"Yes," I breathe, my mouth at his temple.

"Yeah?"

Darren's never really been inside me before. The closest he came was the night he dropped to his knees in his shower and teased me with his tongue more than his finger. His mouth has made me writhe several more times in the months since, but he hasn't attempted more than that, maybe because I haven't asked for it, or just because we've discovered so many other ways to touch each other.

Tonight, though. I don't think I'll have to ask for much, and I can't imagine a single reason I'd say no to him—not about anything, even and especially if there's a way he wants to use my body. I invited him into my bedroom, and then into my kitchen, and I'm not interested in telling him to leave anywhere else now.

"Please," I try instead.

I feel him nod, and though my rhythm has been thrown, my

hand still glides up and down where I've been stroking us for a while. I embrace the familiar sensation while I'm introduced to something new, Darren careful but confident as he opens me up with a single fingertip. He's gone and there and gone again, murmuring reminders of a hundred things, and after another few seconds, he pulls his hand away and taps my thigh.

"Let go and lie down."

If I hesitate, it's only because everything in me aches for *something*, and Darren is offering to take most of my pain away. He waits me out, and then I'm moving until my back rests on the carpet and I feel him push my legs up and apart. I suppose he could do anything from there, but he kisses the back of my thigh and says something I don't hear, and I open my eyes without having realized they were closed.

I press a hand to the back of his head. "Show me."

He starts with his mouth, of course, but it's never been quite like this before. The focus on something that isn't one of several fun stops on the way to somewhere else is different, and I press my lips together to avoid begging him to be casual about an act that was always going to fall far short of a goal like that. He devours me as tenderly as anyone could, and however vulnerable I am, I know I'm safe, too.

By the time he's sliding a lubed finger forward, I'm trembling, and he can feel it when he continues to reassure me at every turn. He doesn't coddle me—that promise was made in my bedroom a long time ago—but he sucks my sac and licks just below it and gives me time to adjust to the pressure of a single finger long before he adds one more. I arch off the floor, but he's still got me, sucking and licking and working me over with skill that would make me jealous if I were that kind of man.

Instead, I reach down to where I've gone mostly soft, soothing myself with a touch I've known my whole life, and Darren hums against my skin.

"You okay, baby?"

"I'm relaxed. And the complete opposite of that," I pant, coherency long gone. "It's so good. You're so good."

After another round of forever, his fingers curl, and when I arch again, it's so much better and so much worse. The most intense kind of pleasure is right there, and still out of reach, and more slowly than I would've thought possible, Darren's tongue trails over my sac and along the underside of my shaft until he can suckle nothing but the tip, his eyes on me the entire time.

"Hello again."

"You're not drunk," I whisper.

"No, I'm not," he agrees, easing his fingers from me until I'm clenching around a loss I feel everywhere. His mouth is there for another moment or two, his tongue still so wet and eager as he drags it over my hole a few more times. "I'm a lot of things, but I'm not drunk."

"Me, too. A lot of things."

Darren hums and nods and kisses along the inside of my thigh as he lowers each leg to the ground, and I let myself go just to reach for him again. It doesn't stop, really—his kissing or my touching—and he spends several seconds over the worst of my off-ramp wounds before he crawls up my body and lets his mouth map ground he knows well, pushing my tank top out of his way as he goes. After he finally discards it completely, I claw at his shirt too, and he's completely naked when he resumes his beautifully torturous trek.

He pauses when he reaches my heart, and my breath catches the moment he nuzzles me there.

I pray for sin as his tongue traces the rosary I made part of me a very long time ago, the ink alone some kind of sacrilege. His attention to it is the silent scream of a confession that would bring me to my knees, but it's impossible to fall from where I lie, and I'm not convinced I'd be afraid of the landing.

"Does this hurt you?" Darren asks.

"The tattoo?"

"Any of the reasons behind it."

"It's no secret that God and I have gone a few rounds, but we're good now," I answer. "Nothing hurts tonight."

Something wild flashes in Darren's eyes, and it reminds me of the fire still burning behind us. He's perfectly hard against my leg, and we're sticky everywhere, and as much as I could stare at him like this until morning, I'm relieved when he shifts to cover my mouth with his. The kiss is built from the same contradictions that have followed us for months, and I don't care about parsing any of it now. Instead, I hold him close and pour his name down his throat when his hand slips between us, his fingers wet again without me knowing how. It's as overwhelming as the first time—or maybe more so—because our kiss never ends and my body has become greedy, the two of us chasing the pleasure of it together.

But then Darren's lips are at my neck and everything is warm and good when I hear him speak, his fingers still deep inside me.

"Tell me you'll let me fuck you."

Chapter Twenty-One

Darren

Tell me you'll let me fuck you.

It comes out like a demand, which is both the opposite of what I intended and exactly what most people would expect. I'm spoiled and selfish, but my charm means I get laid easily and often, even when I'm bossy about it. I've given a hundred men the lines I want them to say, and they repeat them back like eager little understudies in a show I've directed for years. And then I flash my dimples and bend beneath their hands, and by the time I leave them behind, they'd swear it was all their idea.

It comes out like a demand because I'm used to getting my way. It won't be taken as one because Jake is nobody's understudy, and he sees through me better than anyone but Beau.

I only wish he loved me half as much.

"I will."

His voice startles me, and I rise from where my face has been buried in his neck, my fingers slipping free so I can hold on to his hip. "What?"

"I want you to."

In every other scenario, I'd tease the fuck out of him—literally—pouting or begging or flirting through an entire charade of "You want me to *what?*" until he'd utter the word in that perfectly low growl of his. Tonight, I don't even try. Jake's said plenty already, and I think fucking is so far from what's about to happen between us that it's probably safer to keep from describing it at all.

I kiss him again, fully aware of how close we are already. I'll only need to nudge his legs further apart. Get my cock wet. Press a hand to the back of his thigh. Ease my dick past his body's predictably quick objection to it. Continue to kiss him and kiss him and kiss him until we both sigh with relief.

We don't need a condom tonight, but I brought one from the bathroom just in case. Maybe he'll want me to wear it. Maybe he won't understand what I'm really saying when I tell him why I can fuck him bare.

Fuck, it's been so long since I've done this.

We're still grinding against each other. Sort of. Barely. Jake's hard again, and I haven't stopped dripping everywhere, but the wine has made us so unhurried. I think I only start talking again because the wine has made me softly honest, too.

"We've been careful all this time because I—you know about the keg room and bathrooms and backseats and—"

"I know I'm not the only one, sweetheart," Jake interrupts. "It's never stopped me from wanting you. I still want you now."

"You are, though. The only one. You have been."

My courage falters, and I push my tongue into his open mouth, stealing whatever uncensored response might've made at least one of us bleed. I don't know whether I want him to understand right away, or whether his incredulity would be better, but for another several seconds, I don't have to worry about it. Jake's tongue becomes the aggressor, and I submit without question, his hand curled into my hair. It's the roughest he's been tonight, but I know it won't last, and I'm ready to let it go.

When his touch turns gentle, he murmurs against my lips. "For how long?"

"Tapas."

"Darren."

"I know."

"That was *October*. That was before we—"

"Can I fuck you without the condom?"

I'm already pulling away from him when I ask, and he's staring at me as I kneel between his legs. The click of the cap is too quiet to make either of us look at the bottle in my hand, and Jake's busy nodding anyway, his blue-gray eyes darkened by want and fear.

I know both feelings well. My heart has kept their beats for a while.

His legs have mostly fallen open for me, and his hand's on his cock when I stroke mine with more lube than we'd need the other way around. I use my dry hand to bend his leg and drag the head of my dick over his slick hole a few times, turned on that much more when I see how it flutters in response. He gasps when I first rock forward, so I make eye contact again and tell him I've got him and wipe my hand on the first shirt I grab and slide deeper and deeper. Jake's instincts have him seeking and escaping in equal measure, and just as I wonder whether I should give him more time, he shakes his head and covers the hand on his thigh with his own.

"Don't you dare."

It's my turn to nod, and as long as Jake is still so focused on me, I take the opportunity he's offered. I'm overwhelmed as soon as I think about what I'm doing, and I must be shaking, but I don't stop moving until I'm as connected to him as I've been to anyone.

Well, one other person. Ever.

Since the night I'd looked up at him from V's office floor, I'd known that Michelle had been it for him, but there'd been no need for him to ask the same thing about me. And I hadn't spoken up because there was only one good reason for it to matter, then or now. But I don't top very often as it is, and for all the times I've been careless enough to bottom without protection, Jake is just the second person I've fucked like this.

There's no chance I'll marry Jake, and after I've taken a moment to mourn whatever secrets I have to keep, I roll my hips and lower myself to him.

"So many things."

We're far removed from when he'd acknowledged that I'm not drunk—just minutes earlier but so, so long ago—and I'm not sure he has any idea what I'm talking about. I don't ask either, more concerned with finding a rhythm that works for him, searching for the truth in his eyes while hoping he isn't busy doing the same. Then he stretches toward me for a kiss, both hands cradling my face, and I meet him there without hesitation.

I continue to rock back and forth, and he wraps himself around me when each new breath comes easier than the one before. He's brave and strong, but neither of those qualities is important tonight, and I think it's his stubbornness that serves him well when he's eager to pull me deeper, and his body is slow to catch up. One of his hands ends up on my ass, and I'm not even sure he knows what he wants when he mostly moans and mumbles and melts underneath me.

"More."

It could mean anything, and if I were doing any better myself, I'd encourage him to talk to me and ask me for things and make me take care of him the way he deserves. But I'm a mess and I can't do more than show him why, so I force an arm beneath his body and change the angle enough to make him cry out on my next thrust. We're barely coordinated, but there's nobody I'd rather do this with, the two of us trying so hard to kiss each other through it when we need to keep *moving*.

At some point, I register that Jake's got his hand on his dick, and I clumsily reach for his face, sweaty and so fucking in love and unable to do anything but chant *baby, baby, baby*.

He arches his back and looks at me like he *knows*.

A better man would've broken eye contact because it's unkind to lie so boldly, but if I'm going to lose him eventually, I need to remember this one chance I had. Jake lets me stare—maybe he's even staring back—and for as much as I once wanted him to tell me about the time he came while thinking about me, I don't need to look between us now. This might be a first for us, but his staccato whimpers mean he's close, and I already know he'll drag me with him.

"Please," Jake says, because he's so goddamn polite.

"Come for me," I command, because I'm really not.

Still wrapped around each other as much as possible, I drive into him again and again, and I memorize the split second before this stunning man seizes and nearly screams in my arms. I feel his cum hit my chest, and I know it must be covering his, but I'm close to blacking out as I break above him. Something hopeless and feral trips down my spine when I surrender to the insistence that his body be allowed to milk mine, and when it's over, I want to believe I've gained more than I've given up.

It's probably impossible, but I won't do the math until I can be trusted not to cheat.

"Darren."

I lift my head from where it's fallen onto Jake's shoulder. "Hmmm?"

"Stay."

I'm already beginning to soften where I'm buried inside him, but I attempt a couple of careful thrusts because it feels really fucking good to flirt with overstimulation, and I'm suddenly afraid of leaving. I close my eyes and slide back and forth, and it's so much wetter now, and I can feel it and I can hear it and I can hear *him*. But then Jake shivers, and while the fire does what it can to keep us warm, we're coming down from one hell of a high and won't be able to relax here forever.

I open my eyes, kiss him, and speak. "As much as I'd love to pull a blanket from the couch and cuddle with you until I'm hard enough for round two, we're filthy and I promise you don't actually want me to be *this* close to you for much longer."

"No, that's not—we should shower."

"Yeah," I agree. "That's sort of where I was going with the whole 'filthy' thing."

Jake shakes his head, and I worry about the frown I catch before I rub my thumb over the crease between his brows. My touch doesn't fix everything as quickly as I think it should, so I frown too, and wait him out.

"We should shower and then you should stay with me," he says. "For the rest of the night."

"I haven't stayed here before."

"No. And I've always left you early in the morning."

At my house, and then again at the hotel. I remember both, and it doesn't matter that he's the one bringing it up now—I'm already wondering how he'll sneak out of his own fucking home.

"Okay," I answer, because I'm just dumb enough to want to find out.

I have to pull out then, and I use my t-shirt to help clean what I can before we leave the rest behind, wine and ice cream and dirty laundry becoming tomorrow's problem. Neither of us is all that steady when we stand, and if we talk at all while Jake puts out the fire, it's about nothing that matters. We stay so close to each other, though—maybe unreasonably so—and he takes my hand when we head upstairs.

He doesn't let go until we step under water hot enough to give both of us goosebumps, and he pushes me against the cold tile to give me more. "Did you know you wanted to do that?"

"That I wanted to fuck you?" He nods, and I shrug. "It's one of a million fantasies I've had about us, but I didn't have some secret plan to surprise you with it tonight. It just felt right, so I asked."

Jake ignores the fact that I *didn't* actually ask. "Good."

"What about you? Did you know you wanted me to stay?"

"I didn't have some secret plan to surprise you with it, but it felt right, so I asked."

He didn't ask either, but I return the favor and ignore that detail, too. Jake kisses my forehead and backs up to wash his body, and I take the same opportunity to wash mine, the two of us dancing around each other like we've done this a thousand times. We don't move fast, the sex likely making us more sluggish than the wine now. And we have little to say, but I'm as comfortable as I've always been with him nearby, and maybe I didn't give as much of myself away downstairs as I'd thought.

I'm the one to shut the water off when we're done, and he grabs towels I've used more than anyone but him, then we hurry to dry off, his bed practically calling to us. The living room floor, while far better cushioned than any I've fucked on, is still a floor, and both of us crawl under the sheet and sigh with relief.

"So," Jake starts, tugging me closer until my head is on his chest and he can comb his fingers through my damp hair. "We're having a pool party tomorrow."

"We're having a pool party tomorrow. And you have to go into work?"

"For a little while."

"I sleep late," I say. "You might be gone before I wake up."

"You're not going to wake up alone, Darren. Not tomorrow."

I hate how easily he reads me, but I don't know how to let myself be left behind when a lifetime without a father—and a few years with a husband who never would've said goodbye—taught me I should always be the one to go. Jake kisses the top of my head and pulls the sheet up to my bare shoulders, but he makes no attempt to roll away from me. I trail my fingers up and down his ribcage as our breathing syncs, and I know we're both so close to falling asleep, but my mouth opens one more time.

"I'm sorry she won't be there."

Jake's quiet for a minute, and I think maybe I didn't catch him in time, but then he presses another kiss to my head. "So am I, sweetheart. So am I."

He's snoring softly before I swallow around the lump in my throat, but it's impossible to do anything but relax when I'm being held like this, so I close my eyes and let myself rest. If I'd been worried that I'd have any bad dreams, that proves impossible too, my brain falling as deeply as the rest of me already has.

We move some, and while I'm mostly asleep, I barely register that I've pushed the sheet toward my waist. I wonder how long it'll be before Jake complains that I sleep hot. Then again, I'm not sure he'd complain about anything like it, and I'm not sure whether that has anything to do with me.

After a while, I end up on my side with Jake curled around my back, his hand splayed over my hip. When I force my eyes open, I'm surprised that we've been sleeping for less than an hour. I'm careful not to wake him when I cover his hand with my own, but then I feel his mouth warm at my neck.

And his dick hard against my ass.

"You awake, little spoon?" he asks, his voice gravelly. Sinfully so.

"Probably," I smile, letting him hear it in the dark. "But shouldn't *you* be asleep, old man?"

"Do you want me to go back to sleep?"

"No."

Jake kisses my shoulder and takes a deep, deep breath. "I'm tired, but I think I want this too much."

"Want what?"

"To be bare inside you, too."

He doesn't wait for an answer, and I'm grateful because most of what I'd have to say aren't things he needs to hear. I push the rest of the sheet away and listen as he retrieves the lube and covers his cock with it, feeling him only when his wet fingers smear some of it over my hole. Jake doesn't prep me any more than that, and I love that my body's been his long enough for him to know how to treat it right, more than ready when he fills me with one perfect thrust.

His hand is dry now, and when it returns to my hip, I grab it and pull until his arm is around me and his palm is flat against my chest. I have nothing holy inked there, but maybe something about my heartbeat will bring him peace. Jake fucks me slowly, and I would've expected nothing else from him—not tonight—and I twist until I can kiss him for it, our tongues lazily needy. When I turn away again, he keeps his lips against my skin and rocks into me almost silently.

Almost endlessly.

As much as whatever happened between us downstairs felt I was being cracked open, this seems like we both are. Each new second spills secrets we can't see, and even when Jake's hand slides down my body to stroke my cock and massage my balls and stroke my cock again, it's the tender kind of torture that might make both of us talk. I'm close to rolling onto my stomach and begging him to fuck me harder and faster than he ever has, but I want *this*, and I'm beginning to think there's a reason he wants it too, even if it makes his voice break.

"October."

A kiss to my temple fills some of the emptiness left behind by a word that means too much. I reach back for him—clinging to him—as if it's not painfully easy to believe he won't give up on me now. Then he makes a desperate little sound, and I don't know if it's the right time to keep this conversation going, but I respond to him anyway.

"Yes."

"Damn you," he whispers. "God*damn* you."

"I know," I choke. "I'm sorry."

I'm so heavy and hard, and I would swear he's fucking me like nobody has, confusion and anger and grief and love buried inside me again and again. He's leaving more of himself behind each minute he keeps going, and I'm grateful for anything that can become mine.

"We promised," Jake says.

You know I'm not looking for the love of my life.

None of the men who fuck me are.

"We did."

He lets go of my dick and finds my hand, but then we're jerking me off together, and his rhythm is faltering. There's so little left to say if neither of us is ready to call this what it is, and I think my voice would fail me either way. A teardrop trips sideways over the bridge of my nose and my chest is tight and my throat is closing around everything, but I'm sure I can keep all of that to myself too, right up until I realize I'm not alone.

I feel Jake's tears on my neck and my ear, and then finally on my own face when I turn toward him. The sob I can't swallow is mostly caught by his open mouth, but an actual kiss never quite happens when we're busy loving each other without a single fucking word. However far gone he and I are, our bodies don't slow—maybe we're even moving faster now—this primal connection refusing to be overthrown by the emotion that wants so badly to take control. The grip we have on my cock is relentless, but it's Jake who comes first, everything about it both loud and fragile. It's probably the knowledge of what he's done that pushes me over the edge just seconds later, and our fingers are covered in the mess I've made long before either of us stops stroking.

That we can keep moving through it is soothing in a way I won't attempt to explain.

"Darren."

I crack an eye open and close it again when the sunshine strikes.

"Darren, wake up."

It's morning. Jake's sitting up in bed next to me. My heart soars because he's still here. My hand pulls a pillow over my head because I want to keep sleeping.

"Beau keeps calling you. Judging from the texts he sent *me*, there's a bit of a kid on Christmas morning thing happening, but I don't think it would be a great idea for me to answer *your* phone to calm him down."

"He already knows everything," I mumble.

"Everything?"

I push the pillow toward the headboard and open both eyes this time, and it's only the view that makes it worth the effort. Jake is wide awake, his glasses perched on his nose as he does a crossword puzzle like the handsome nerd he is. He taps his pen against the page a few times and sorta kinda tries to glare at me, even if it's mostly probably not working all that well. But then I hear his question again and think he must want to know if everything means *everything*, except that every memory of *everything* rushes back and makes me dizzy, and I really should go back to sleep, morning wood and all.

Jake stayed, though. He damned me, and we cried, but he stayed.

"Okay, you're right," I sigh. "There's no need for him to know I'm with you at whatever ungodly hour this is."

"It's 9:30."

"Exactly." He sets my phone down in the space between us, and it's the first I realize he must've gone downstairs to fetch it at some point. I spot his coffee mug next, and then I push enough of the covers away to see the waistband of boxers he probably put on hours ago. I'm certainly not upset that he didn't literally stay in bed all morning, but I don't miss his choice to keep from getting any closer, and my blurry eyes lock with his perfectly clear ones. "You're about to get up and get ready for work, aren't you?"

"You're awake and have a phone call to make. I figure going to the hospital sooner means I'll also get home sooner, and just in case Lucy arrives a little early—"

"Right. Definitely wouldn't want her to catch your friend here without you."

Jake's nostrils flare. "It's not like that, and you know it."

"Do I?"

"Call Beau. Spend some time with him today if it'll help either of you," he says, setting the crossword aside and climbing out of bed. He puts his hands on his hips and looks down at me, a smile and a frown at war. "I'm going to handle everything at the hospital and grab any last-minute party stuff on the way home, so text me if you think of something. And then we'll talk later?"

I nod. I'm not sure what else I can do.

He closes the door to the bathroom while he showers, either to mute the sound of the water or because he needs that barrier. I call Beau and give him shit for bothering me so early, but his enthusiasm has always been contagious, and I'd missed it in the months before he met Adrian. Now that he's in love *and* in party mode? I can't possibly stay annoyed for long.

While I go downstairs for my own cup of coffee, I listen to Beau ramble about things Jake and I covered last night and find the kitchen and living room clean. When I return to Jake's bedroom and hear Beau's song suggestions, I tell him to send me a list just as I realize my shorts have been up here all along. As Jake emerges from the bathroom, naked and in search of something to wear to work, Beau tells me about a pool volleyball set he saw at the store, and I give him the green light to buy it. And because Beau loves food as much as Jake and I do, he wants to expand on our simple grill menu, and I don't have the heart—or the stomach—to turn him down.

I must've left my coffee somewhere because it's not in my hand when I open the balcony door and step outside to look over the backyard. Beau says something about s'mores. Jake joins me in the fresh air and kisses the back of my neck. When I turn around, he wraps his arms around me for longer than I could've hoped, and my next breath is the deepest one I've taken all morning.

"You okay?" Beau asks me.

Jake raises an eyebrow, and I nod as though Beau can see it. "Yeah, I'm good, babe."

Once Jake's slipped away, I tell Beau to fuck Adrian thoroughly this morning so they don't defile our generous host's home later, and he's still laughing when I hang up. I need a shower before I do anything else, so I wander into the last wisps of steam and borrow something clean from Jake's drawers—too big, but so incredibly comfortable—after I'm done. Raiding the kitchen for breakfast is quick and easy, and I don't have any excuse to stay longer than that, so I double-check that I haven't left signs of myself everywhere, and I head home.

I find a terrible reality dating show and pass out on my couch for a couple of hours.

I wake up and eat pizza that's been in my fridge too long.

I change into swim trunks and a tank top and bring a hoodie for when it cools down tonight.

Standing in front of my bathroom mirror, I admire how fucking good I look, and I know I'm going to laugh with almost everyone at the party. I'll be causing chaos in the pool, and making sure everyone is fed, and dancing whenever one of Beau's favorite songs plays. I'll go in search of pool noodles we never bought and play volleyball in the water with people more competitive than I am. I'll stay just on the right side of drunk, and I'll do what I can to keep everyone else on the right side of it, too.

After so much time keeping her my little secret, it'll be fun to introduce Sage to my friends, and them to her, especially if what I think might happen in a few weeks actually does. I have no plans to get to know my father more than I have, unless he's decided he wants to get to know me, because holding my breath already hurts. I would love to talk to the members of Supine, especially if there's a chance I can figure out what spooked Riley. Well, *Sebastian* spooked Riley, but I want to know why.

And speaking of spooking—any nervousness I'd had about meeting Lucy has only gotten worse since last night. It was gonna be one thing to shrug and do the whole *yeah I adore your dad he's definitely a great friend of mine and I love hanging out with him* routine, but now that Jake knows it's bullshit, I don't know how well I can lie to his daughter. And I hate how much I don't want to.

I'm home now.

I read Jake's text and glance in the mirror again, steadier there than I would've guessed when reading between the lines is easy. Everything I helped supply for the party is already there, but I leave the bathroom to grab the bag I've packed—so I have dry clothes, not because I'll be spending the night again—and throw my phone and wallet on top of a pair of briefs. I probably should've let him know I'm on my way, but my flip-flops are on and I'm out the door before I think maybe I forgot to reply.

The heat through my sunroof. The pop music blasting on the radio. The cars crowding the streets. The beat of my heart as it begs me for answers about what Jake and I are doing, and where we could go from here. I lift my fingers from where I've been drumming along with something that will be stuck in my head all night, and I press my hand to my chest to quiet everything there.

I'm in the hills after what feels like forever and only a few minutes, turning onto Jake's street like I've done so many times before. Pulling into his driveway is second nature too, but I jerk to a stop when I remember I can't lazily drift into the middle of it and park however I please.

Well, no. *Remember* is the wrong word, actually.

I'm *reminded* that I'll have to park on one side because there's already someone else parked on the other. A small SUV. California plates I don't recognize. The engine probably still warm from a drive through the desert because I definitely would've been warned about this if it had been here long.

I drive those last twenty feet or so and turn off the car, scrambling for my phone just to find a second text from Jake, sent about 30 seconds after the first one.

Come over whenever you're ready. Lucy is already here and she's excited to meet you.

So much for that talk, I guess.

Chapter Twenty-Two

Jake

They're getting along exactly as well as I've always known they would.

From the moment I opened my front door to Darren and silently apologized for the conversation we had to postpone, Lucy has kept him smiling with the dry wit she got from me and the fearless warmth Michelle had in spades. He's older than she is, and he knows his way around my home just fine, but they both understand that she has the upper hand, and she's wielded it gently. As she's led him from place to place, they've compared notes about bars and resorts, and they've taken inventory of the food and decided to make a boozy fruit punch, and they've laughed in between everything.

I had to walk away from them a while ago.

On any other day, I think I would've ended up filthy on the floor of my garage, working on whichever bike needed me most, but this afternoon I would've been reprimanded twice over for the trouble. Resigned, I made my way to the backyard under the pretense of cleaning an already clean grill or arranging chairs that required no such thing, but Darren and Lucy tumbled into the same space eventually, and I let them have it.

I'm in my bedroom now, and with the door to the balcony still open from when Darren had wandered out there this morning, I can hear the hum of the activity below. There will be so much more noise later, and a dozen more voices, but I'm already undone.

"I'm in love with him."

It's the first time I've said it out loud. There's nobody around to hear it, and I think it's better that way. If I practice a few times, maybe it won't sound like an apology anymore.

There's nothing to be sorry for, and I understand it on every logical level. Michelle would be happy for me. Even in the shadow of half-truths, Lucy already is. I'm aware now that Darren has been a couple of steps ahead of me, and I assume he's only been worried that I'd never catch up. I have though, and I think I mostly want to apologize to myself for thinking I shouldn't or couldn't or wouldn't.

I'm in love with him, and every beat of my heart reminds me of the things I stand to lose. Louder than that is the reminder of everything I have to gain, and instead of covering my ears to block out the sound, I shuffle to my dresser to roll a joint. I'm just about finished when I get a text.

We're on our way. Get dressed or get ready for a couple of not

so secret admirers

I roll my eyes at Beau—and the idea that Adrian would bother admiring anything of mine—before I respond.

I'm dressed. Darren and Lucy are here. See you soon.

Nobody else is expected for at least another hour, but after Beau blew up Darren's phone earlier, I'm not surprised he's eager to come over. Music pulses through the house, and I consider smoking as much as the next few minutes will allow, just to help dull the questions it carries with it. *Does he want anyone else to know about us? Do I? Does he want to continue under the pretense of something more casual than it is? Do I? Does he want us to live togeth-er? Or get married someday? Do I?* Sighing, I leave the joint unlit for now and clean up my mess before I head back downstairs, grabbing an extra stack of towels on my way.

Darren is just about to step inside when I step out, and his smile is uncertain enough to make me think he's been hearing the same questions. There's no time for answers, and we both keep walking, but I'm stopped by my daughter the second my arms are empty.

"Did you get the break you needed?" she asks, and I don't quite play dumb, but my hesitation gives her time to go on. "Your worlds collided today. Sure, you knew it was about to happen, and maybe you still don't want to admit that he's one of your worlds, but there's something between you two, and it was al-ways going to be hard for you to let me see it."

"What about you? Is it hard for you?"

Lucy scrunches her nose—a habit she's had her whole

life—and glances around the backyard. "Before I pulled in here, I parked on the street about four houses down—where the Hansons used to live. It didn't matter that I've been home a hundred times since mom died. Today was gonna be different. It's why I almost didn't come, and why I knew I had to."

"You didn't have—"

"I did. For you. For me. For her," she argues. "So, I parked, and I reminded myself how much I want to meet Beau and Riley, and I rolled my eyes when I remembered how many times you've called Darren your friend, and I took a break until I stopped shaking about all of it."

I struggle to swallow, then nod. "I'm not shaking."

"Then I guess your break worked, too."

There's some commotion then, and we both look toward the house. Darren has let Beau and Adrian in, and it's just the beginning of the fun that will last the next several hours, even Adrian loud enough to be heard from where Lucy and I stand. She's delighted by the scene already, and there's no reason for us to avoid joining in, so I pull her close while it's still just the two of us and give her a quick kiss on the side of her head.

"He is," I tell her.

"He is what?"

I pull away because I need space for the last few seconds I can have it, but I turn just as I reach for the back door. "One of my worlds."

"I think this is the closest they've been so far," Beau says, looking over the grill at the pool.

He doesn't need to elaborate. I simply follow his gaze to where Darren and Drew are facing each other, only a volleyball net between them while they play a game with very few rules. Drew appears to be right-handed, and Darren's a lefty, so the mirror effect is stunning, and Beau places a spicy sausage atop my bun as I shrug.

"Darren probably warned him to keep his distance, right?"

"Oh, I don't know about that. Darren has wanted this for a very, very long time."

I frown. "He told you that?"

"Fuck, no. I doubt he's even aware of it. There's a lot of safety in wantin' the man who walked away to stay away."

"Because if the man can come back once, it means he can come back again and again."

"And if at some point he doesn't—" Beau continues.

"Then it's worse than if he hadn't come back at all," I finish, shaking my head. "So Darren does his best to ignore that he wants someone to stick around. It just becomes obvious when he stops sleeping with half of Los Angeles County."

The pivot is abrupt, but easy for Beau to follow. "You know about that."

"So do you, apparently." I watch him add two shrimp and

steak skewers to my plate—more so than the sausage, they're expectedly over-the-top—and then pivot back. "What are you and I gonna do about Drew? Do we ask him to stay or go?"

"We don't do anything about Drew. We just love the fuck out of his son."

"We can do that."

Beau gives me a kiss on the cheek and a little shove. "Still can't believe you've been keepin' this place a secret from us all these years."

"Oh, please. I told you about my garden a long time ago."

He's still laughing when I walk away with my food.

I sit down at my patio table with Lucy, Riley, Mason, Maxwell, and Banjo. It's a motley crew, but everyone is relaxed and smiling, no doubt helped along by beer or boozy punch or any of the eight kinds of flavored vodka Mason brought with him. As we eat, the others peel themselves away from the pool and form a small crowd around Beau, who might be in heaven. I look at Darren, Noah, Adrian, Sage, Layla, Sebastian, Drew, and the tall, quiet friend Mason brought—Dominic, if I remember correctly—and I try not to miss anyone who isn't here.

Everyone around me keeps moving enough that it isn't as difficult as I would've thought. It's a party, and even delicious food doesn't keep anyone still for long. The music continues to play. Several people end up in the pool again, another few splashing in the spa with the jets turned on. Beau's dancing like a fool. Lucy is content to sit on the edge of the pool and dangle her feet in the water. Darren's fingertips tease the waistband of my swim trunks when nobody's looking, but then he's gone again, and the ache in his eyes suggests he might be for a while.

We have to talk, and I don't know how to say everything he needs to hear. He deserves better than the few words I'd spoken to an empty room.

For now, I throw back his very fruity punch and turn away from where Mason and Dominic are on the verge of indecent against the wall of my house. Sage is laughing with Beau, Adrian, and Noah. Supine has more or less sequestered themselves in the deep end with Drew—apropos of nothing, I'm sure—and I watch as Sebastian gets the giggles about something, fueled by nothing more than lemonade.

The sight is enough of a reason to look for Riley, and I find them sprawled sideways on one of the chairs arranged around the firepit, a t-shirt in their hands. There's no fire burning yet, but the sun is beginning to set, and eventually the night will cool down. After admiring everyone else's fun for another few seconds, I make my way to them.

"Mind if I get this started?"

Riley removes their earbuds, shakes their head, and smiles carefully. "Do you think a fire will bring everyone over here?"

"Not for a while. Most of them are still hyped up," I say. "Once it's dark, a few more people will crowd the spa, and others will end up close to the fire."

"For the warmth, either way."

"Yes." I'm far too old to take up whatever position Riley's in, but once I have the fire going, I settle into a chair next to them.

The crackle of the burning logs reminds me of the night before, and I blink away the memories, trading them for the chance to follow Riley's lazy stare. Across my spacious backyard, Sebastian remains amused by something, his curly hair wet from the pool and still a beautiful mess. "You know, if you'd like the fire to bring *him* over here, I'm sure I could make that happen."

"No."

"No, you don't want him here? Or no, you don't want me to make it happen?"

"He should stay with his friends," Riley responds.

That doesn't answer my question very well, and while I've had a longstanding habit of not prying into Riley's personal life, I feel like I've been given an extra glimpse or two over the past several months. That and too much punch have me pushing a little now.

"When the band first came around, you and Sebastian seemed to hit it off. And once they got hired, you pulled back. Is it better for you this way?"

"Are you going to make me a pros and cons list?"

I raise an eyebrow. "A pros and cons list?"

"It's a Darren thing," Riley explains. "To help me sort out my head."

"Ah. So, he's more organized with your head than with his own."

"Maybe so. But what about you? Do you need a list?"

We're both watching Darren now, in the spa with Beau, Adrian, Noah, and Banjo. And he's staring at me until Beau gives him a wet willy, and Darren climbs into Beau's lap to fight back. I catch Riley looking at me again, and I wonder how tapas turned into this. It's absurd how badly I want to march over there just to kiss him in front of our little world, but I scrub a hand over my face instead.

"No," I sigh. "I already know the answer."

I leave Riley then, offering anything and everything I can before I go. I'm inside before I think much about where I'm headed, and a voice stops me just as I reach the bottom of the staircase.

"Running away from your own party?"

I turn and bite my tongue at least once before I answer Adrian. "It's only half my party, and everyone seems plenty entertained. A brief escape doesn't feel unreasonable."

"Does it bother you?" he asks. "The way they are with each other?"

It takes me a moment to remember the spa scene from just seconds ago. "Darren and Beau? Not in the slightest. Does it bother *you*?"

"I don't think it should."

I nod and leave the unsaid things—unsaid. "Do you have an aversion to weed?"

"No, I—it's—what?" Adrian sputters.

"Come with me."

He's barefoot and wearing a towel around his waist, but he's got me beat, my swim trunks still damp from when I was in the pool a while ago. I can grab a towel from my bathroom if I want one, but as I lead him upstairs, I don't actually care that much. I won't be sitting on anything that can't get wet.

We step into my bedroom, and Adrian laughs awkwardly. "Is this your way of getting back at them?"

"I already told you I'm not bothered by anything they're up to. I just want to relax away from the crowd."

"Like Riley?"

"They're correct about things more often than not," I say, picking up the joint I'd left on my dresser earlier. There's a lighter outside already. "Come on."

Adrian follows me onto the balcony, and I nod to one of the chairs and let myself feel the quick catch of my breath that gets me every time I remember I have two of them out here now. Again. The feeling passes, and he's comfortable and watching me closely by the time I slowly exhale.

"Huh."

I take another hit, then hand it over. "What?"

"I would've thought a weed habit would help knock someone off their high horse. Remove the stick from their ass. Keep them from holding ridiculous grudges."

"I've never been high at Trailhead."

"That explains everything," Adrian says, undeniably pretty when smoke flows past his lips. "And gives me hope for the next several minutes."

We smoke and enjoy a perfect view of the spa, the noise from the party a comforting constant. I know Darren has already noticed us, but I don't think anyone else has, and I prefer it that way. We each take another hit or two, but this conversation has been a long time coming.

"You can't possibly believe Beau would cheat on you."

"And you're not high enough if you're still set on judging me."

"I'm not—"

"It's your entire *thing*," Adrian interrupts, choking on his next inhale and waving me off until he can argue more. "I did grief wrong. I fell in love with Beau wrong. And to be fair, you don't only pull that shit with me. Beau forgave me wrong. Darren forgave Drew wrong. Drew did parenthood wrong—"

"Drew was never a—"

"Oh, of course. Here we go. Drew was never a parent. But *you* are, and you do it the correct way. You've loved correctly and grieved correctly. Do you even hear how self-righteous you are? You're a sanctimonious dick. Stop acting like you're perfect, Jake."

That knocks the wind out of me, and I scan the backyard again, the joint back in my hand. "I'm not perfect."

Adrian snorts. "Yeah, *I* know that. Try telling Beau and Darren and Noah and everyone else craning their necks to get a good view of you on that pedestal."

"I don't want to be on a pedestal."

The way he looks at me is almost painfully disarming. "Then climb the fuck down."

"Okay, yeah," I sigh, done with smoking for now and dropping my head back to stare at the stars for a while. "I think they'll always touch each other like that, right? It's who they are. But it doesn't have to mean anything."

"What did Darren tell you about the morning Beau brought

him breakfast?"

There's a giant splash in the pool, followed by laughter. I blink stupidly at the night. Maybe it's the weed, but I don't think so. "I didn't know Beau brought him breakfast. Was it recently?"

"Nah, at least a couple of months ago."

"Okay. What did I miss?"

"Well, I can't spoil *all* the fun," Adrian says. I'm still looking at the stars, but he must want more of my attention because I feel his foot against my thigh, and it doesn't bother me nearly as much as I want it to. When I drop my head and meet his eyes, he continues. "They were talking about you—or you and Darren, I guess. Whatever. Obviously you guys haven't gone public with it yet."

"Now you're telling a story wrong," I quip, as dry as I've ever been.

Adrian's foot applies more pressure to my leg. "Anyway, Darren was dodging feelings or something, and Beau cornered him in the kitchen, and Darren was clinging to him, and Beau was touching him back, and they had a whole fucking moment about it."

"How far did they go?"

"They almost kissed, but that was it."

"And since you weren't there, I assume Beau told you this."

"Yeah, when I got home that night," Adrian says.

"You've very pointedly accused me of thinking I'm correct about everything, and this is the worst possible way to refute that, but I really don't think you need to worry about them," I murmur, wrapping my hand around his bare ankle. "You and I both remember what it's like to say goodbye too soon, but they—they've still got each other, and I won't begrudge them a few moments that I'll never have again."

Adrian sighs and slides his hand over mine. "You know he loves you, right?"

"I do and I don't," I admit. Until I talk to Darren, it's the best I can do. "But you know Beau loves you."

"It's not always enough, though. Loving someone."

"No, it's not. So, I suppose you'll just have to trust that this sanctimonious dick *is* actually correct once in a while."

"God forbid," he groans.

There's a knock at my bedroom door then, and I turn to find Darren leaning against the frame. The distance he's kept suggests he doesn't want to intrude, but I think Adrian and I have said as much as we plan to tonight, and we pull away from each other and stand without needing to confirm it. We both return to my bedroom, but I stop a few feet away from Darren and just barely catch Adrian's wrist before he can leave.

"I'll start climbing down, okay?"

Adrian smiles and slips free just to squeeze my hand. "I'll buy you a drink when you reach the ground."

"What the fuck was that about?" Darren asks as soon as Adrian is gone. "Did you get him high?"

"I got both of us high. How else were we gonna take the edge off while he was being very Adrian and I was being very Jake?"

"Okay, yeah, I don't think I actually need to know any more

than that. I was a little worried when I saw you up here, but—"

He doesn't finish, and I don't ask him to. There's still something too cautious about the way he takes a step toward me, and I'm sure it's my fault for running out on him this morning. I stay where I am now, my hands in the pockets of my trunks so I don't reach for him and forget to talk.

"Will you still answer anything?"

"I always have," Darren says. "And I don't really want to stop now."

I knew that already, but the same could be said about the other things I'm going to ask. It's unfair, maybe to both of us, to do anything but sweep him off his feet and kiss him until we're too wrapped up in each other to return to the party we're hosting. My only compromise is to pull one hand free and watch as my fingertips draw shaky lines from Darren's collarbone to his side so I can hold him there.

"Do you love me?" I ask, my voice strong but soft.

"Yes."

"Are you *in* love with me?"

The distinction matters, but it changes nothing. "Yes."

"And you knew that before last night?"

"Yes." Darren pauses then. Tips his head sideways. "Did *you* know before last night?"

"That you're in love with me?"

"That *you're* in love with *me*."

A surprised little laugh escapes me before I can stop it. "You sound incredibly confident about that."

"I don't think I was *confident* about it until about twelve seconds ago," he says. "But when you cried last night, I—it was just a matter of figuring out whether they were good tears or bad."

"They were confused tears, I think. I knew we weren't just playing around anymore—I knew I was crossing lines in my head—but I hadn't put a word to it yet. I didn't think I could."

Darren reaches for me, his fingers moving over my hair and my beard and my lips like he needs to memorize the way this feels, apart from the riotous beat of his heart. Or maybe that's only my heart. Either way, I let him take what he needs, my other arm finally curled around his waist when his lips brush over mine.

"Have you put a word to it now?"

I kiss him, a deep and delicate thing that spreads like a salve over wounds mostly healed years ago. His tongue tastes like early morning laughter and late night promises and a thousand adventures in between. The life he breathes into me is as real as any I've lost, and I'm okay with how my chest cracks open again if that's the best way to let Darren all the way in.

"I don't know how it happened," I mumble against mouth, another small kiss too tempting to ignore. "But somehow I'm the lucky bastard who's fallen astoundingly, voraciously, irrevocably in love one more time."

We kiss again, for longer this time, and then Darren's head falls to my bare chest, heavy with relief. "Are we keeping this to ourselves for now?"

"Well, I think at least four people down there already know."

He slowly raises his head at that, but I only catch the corner of his frown before he looks over his shoulder at the framed photograph hanging in my hallway—the one Adrian had taken of a little girl on a carousel—then back to me again.

"Speaking of keeping things to ourselves, why didn't you tell me about Lucy? She was surprised you hadn't."

"I don't know why she'd be surprised. She knows I don't have a habit of talking about her personal life," I say. "But I'm sorry if it feels like I lied to you that night."

I nod toward the same photograph now, and remember when Darren had asked me whether I have pictures like that from when Lucy was little. I'd answered him as well as I could when we *did* ride carousels and I *do* have pictures and it's true that I haven't looked at them in years. But it's tricky when I'm not good at admitting she wasn't Lucy back then—that we didn't know she was *she* back then.

I've never known how to share those details with other people, even if Lucy gave Michelle and me permission long ago. Part of me wants to drag Adrian back up here just so I can tell him there's definitely one thing I've always done wrong, but then Darren is wrapped around me again.

"Hey, no," he murmurs. "It's okay if it's complicated for you, but according to her, you've always been the fucking best. And that's a quote, by the way—'the fucking best'—because your daughter swears almost as often as I do."

"Not around me, she doesn't," I huff.

Darren just laughs. "Maybe she doesn't want to get grounded."

I laugh too, and then I have to wipe a few different kinds of tears out of my eyes before we hear cheers and whistles and applause from the backyard. Darren and I look at each other, amused and at least a little nervous about whatever is happening. And whatever is about to happen.

"We could just rejoin the party," I suggest, already stepping through the bedroom door, Darren only half a step behind me. "See what they're up to. Announce nothing and hide nothing."

"Soft-launching our relationship in your own backyard. I like your style."

"Our relationship. We'll have to figure out what that looks like, I guess."

Darren nudges me toward the stairs. "It'll look like anything we want."

He says it so plainly that it settles something in me, and we make our way to the backyard without getting more into than that. I can tell the chaos has quieted before we reach the patio doors, but it's when I hear someone strumming a guitar that I realize how much changed while I was gone. I thread my fingers through Darren's and take a long look around, smiling at a scenario I hadn't expected, and probably should have.

Supine is crowded on the patio sofa, but three of them are taking the night off, the guitar in Sebastian's hands while he's the only one who sings. Stripped down more than at Trailhead, his voice is stunning, and nearly everyone else has gathered to drink, watch, and listen. Now that most of the party has moved to the firepit, Riley has relocated, content to lie on a lounge chair closer to the pool, and Drew has taken over their chair. Lucy, Dominic, and Mason are nearby, passing a bottle of vodka back and forth, and Sage is lying on the cement so blissfully that I almost miss being 21.

We walk past the firepit, and Darren squeezes my hand just as we find Noah, Beau, and Adrian getting out of the spa and toweling off. Only one of them is surprised that Darren's mouth is pressed to my bare shoulder.

"Wait," Noah gasps. "You two are—"

"They are," Riley answers, gesturing toward the open chair to their left. "Now, lie down and listen to the music."

I chuckle at the command, and while it wasn't directed at me, I stretch out on the other side of Riley, dragging Darren with me until he's relaxing between my legs and resting his head on my chest. Noah does as he's told, which means Beau and Adrian claim the chair on my right, pushing it up against mine so they can curl around us somehow.

Protective. Affectionate.

Overwhelming. Perfect.

One of Darren's hands is on my leg now, the other clasped in Beau's, so my breath catches when I feel someone else's fingers wrap around mine. After a few seconds, I chance a glance at Riley, but they're too focused on Sebastian to acknowledge what their touch means to me tonight.

And really, I'm not sure I'm ready to acknowledge it either.

I just want to hold on.

EPILOGUE

DARREN

"When you said you wanted to keep me up late tonight, I definitely wasn't imagining we'd end up here after your shift."

Jake's just parked his Harley outside the diner—his first time here, and maybe my last—and I'm slow to pull my arms from where they're wrapped around his waist. I hadn't been on his bike until tonight, almost certainly one more holy moment he'd needed to approach at his own pace. Holy for him, at least. It's been kind of horny for me, the speed and the vibrations and the sheer power between our legs making me grateful Jake doesn't mind my needy dick pressed against him. But the rumble of the engine has quieted now, and we're about to walk into a sacred space of my own. I'm nervous for no reason, and I tease my way out of it when I finally remove my helmet and hand it over.

"If you've got a list, we can absolutely work through whatever was on your mind. In fact, I'd like very much to hear about all the ways I could keep you up. Every filthy detail. Talk slowly."

"Nope. Now I'm hungry. And not for that." I pout dramatically until he laughs. "Okay, not *only* that. But I assume we're here so we can hang out with Sage on her turf, so let's go grab something to eat before I fall asleep right here."

Jake's rarely out at this hour, only staying at Trailhead past closing tonight—or really early this morning—so we could come here as soon as I was done. No matter what time we finally fall asleep when we get back to my place, he'll be up too early and I'll sleep too late, but I don't think either of us minds these days. Whichever house we're at, he continues to do his thing, and I continue to do mine, but he won't leave without saying goodbye, and I never demand that he stay much longer than that.

He usually does, though. It's fun to have lazy sex in the middle of the day.

Now, he follows me into the diner, the bell above the door as silent as ever, and I lead him to the booth that might as well be named after me at this point. We're a mismatched pair, this stoic badass in his boots and jacket, and my pretty dimples on display alongside anything else I can show off to the adoring public. I don't know how many heads we've turned, though. There are even simpler things on my mind.

"Make yourself comfortable," I say. "The vinyl's cracked, but clean. Menus are at the end of the table. Sage already knows what I want, but she'll slow down for you, old man."

He flips me off and doesn't need more than a minute to figure out what he wants. Sage waves hello as she approaches. "Jake, sorry it's the middle of the night, but thank you for letting Darren drag you in here. What can I get for you?"

"A stack of blueberry pancakes, a side of bacon, and a cup of decaf. Please."

She leaves, and I tear off a piece of my napkin, roll it into a ball, and flick it at him. "Since when do you drink decaf?"

"Since I realized I need to balance a 2:30am diner experience with my desire to sleep as soon as I get home."

"To *my* home," I smile.

"To *your* home, yes," he agrees. "Where I'll get my payback by waking you up for something indecent long before noon."

"Oh, no. How terrible for me. Please don't wake me up with your mouth around my dick."

Jake rolls his eyes, and I love it. I love *him*. And so much of this thing between us has been easy, especially once we decided to play by our own rules. There's no marriage in our future, but more than that, we have no plans to move in with each other, either. We have different work schedules, different sleep patterns, and different habits while we're wide awake. I think we both know we *could* live together and compromise in all the small ways so many other couples do, but neither of us *wants* to.

If I often end up at Jake's for days at a time anyway, so be it.

We're mostly quiet until our food comes, probably because he's too busy yawning to carry on much of a conversation. I kick his boot just because I can. He sips his coffee while I play with the straw in my shake. And as reliably as ever, Sage returns after a brief wait, plates stacked on her arms and an adorable smile on her face.

I'd seen her without it the night we'd all gathered in WeHo, when I'd hugged her outside the urgent care clinic and wiped away her tears. I hope I've helped with at least some of the worry in the few months since, her family so full of love and chaos, but never enough time and money.

"So, how's your mom doing? Did she get back to work okay?" I ask her as she pushes the plate of fries toward me and steals a handful.

"She did, yeah," Sage says. "And she'd still love to know the identity of the angel who sent us a basket full of gift cards for groceries, gas—"

"Oh, sorry, angels are big into the secrecy of it all, and I'd never spoil that for them," I laugh. "But hey, River's graduating soon, yeah?"

"He is. And I'm sure he'd like me to thank you—*again*—for getting him a better job. He's looking forward to picking up more hours this summer. He'll work hard and learn a lot."

I nod and try to dodge brain freeze. The gift cards were probably terribly typical of me—a way to be generous without too many people knowing I can think with something other than my dick—but doing something for River was a bit of a surprise. In a strange turn of events involving the friend of a friend of a friend, I found out about an opening at the same tapas restaurant Jake and I first tried last fall. But really, River did most of the work on his own.

"I didn't get him the job—I just got him an interview. But I do think he's about to learn a lot. And I guess that makes two of you."

Sage takes a deep breath and a few more fries. "It's fine that I'm nervous, right?"

"It's absolutely fine, and you'll be great."

Jake's watching us, his mouth full of pancakes, but I can't reassure Sage any further when another table waves her over for their check. Once she's gone, Jake swallows.

"What big thing does she have coming up?"

"Mmmm, nope. I've kept my mouth shut about this for so long. Let me hold out for five more minutes."

He narrows his eyes, but moves on. "Is their father in the picture? Sage and River's?"

I pause just before I take a huge bite. "Yeah, why?"

"I wasn't sure if maybe that's why you've been helping them," Jake says. "Like a surrogate sort of thing."

"No, I—" I shove the food in my mouth and buy myself a few seconds to come up with the best possible explanation. "Their dad is basically the anti-Drew. Married to their mom forever. Has seven kids. Loves them all so fucking much and works his ass off to provide for them, except that it means he's hardly around."

"So, he's the anti-Drew, with the unfortunate side effect of barely seeing his kids more than a guy who bailed entirely."

"Exactly. It's why I try to give the whole family a break here and there."

Jake finishes his coffee and sets it aside. "And speaking of Drew, he wasn't there to watch Supine tonight."

"Nope. Haven't seen him since the party."

Three weeks ago. And this is probably something Jake and I could've talked about during that time, but I guess we found a hundred better things to do.

"Any DMs?"

I snort. "Not since we had lunch, actually."

He's silent for a minute while I eat, but then he reaches for my free hand. "If you ever want me around while you burn another birthday card, you know I'll be right there. But if you decide to start keeping those cards, or maybe send one of your own, I'll be there for that, too."

Sage reappears then, and I'm so fucking grateful because I don't think I could speak any other way. She starts clearing the table. I tap her arm, then gesture to the rest of the diner.

"Where are all the banners and balloons and confetti and cake?"

She blushes, just a little. "There *are* actually a couple of balloons in the back. And I'm definitely stealing a slice of apple pie because—apple pie. But there's not, like, a going-away party or anything."

"Where are you going?" Jake asks her. The five minutes I asked for expired a while ago.

"Darren didn't tell you? Tonight's my last night because I got a new job at—"

"Hold on a second," I interrupt. "I didn't bring balloons or confetti, but I have a small gift for you. Or—not really a gift, exactly. I don't know. I thought it was cute, but it's totally up to you. We can always—whatever, I also have a trivia question for Jake."

Sage giggles, and I get a side-eye from Jake. "I should've been asleep hours ago. I hope you remember that if I get this wrong."

"You won't." I promise, clearing my throat dramatically. "The scientific name of this plant is derived from a Latin word meaning 'to save' or 'to heal,' and its common name is shared by the newest bartender at Trailhead."

Jake's head whips up to look at Sage, his smile exhausted but beautiful. "Oh, congratulations. Or I'm sorry, depending on how often you're stuck with this guy."

I stick my tongue out at him and pull a small gift from my hoodie pocket, Sage already tearing into it before I can explain that I'm really not objectifying her. She deserves far more than someone like me causing her problems, even if I know a whole group of friends who will have her back. She must know it too, or just not care right now, because she seems thrilled.

"Oh my god. It's so fucking *cute*," Sage squeals, unfolding a cropped tank top with the Trailhead logo printed across the front of it.

"If you'd rather wear a regular t-shirt like V does, we can make that happen. But I thought it might be fun to play around with something different."

"Oh, you mean I can't be shirtless like the rest of you?" she says. "No, seriously, this is perfect. And V already gave me my rainbow bandana, so I'm gonna look so good. Hey, maybe I should get my belly pierced."

"Hot. Everyone loves Riley's piercings."

Sage gets called away again and sets our check on the table just before she goes. "If I don't see you guys before you leave, I'll definitely catch up with you soon. And Darren? Thank you for everything."

Jake nods his goodbye and looks at me. "She'll make a lot more at the bar than she does here, huh?"

"And the hours will be better for her."

"Time with her family?"

"Time to herself, too," I say.

"Is she the first woman to work there, other than V?"

"Mmmm, yeah. I mean, now Layla's there once a week, too. And we've always served plenty of women, but as we've gotten busier with karaoke and trivia and the band, I think the crowd is becoming more queer in every direction. Seemed like a good time for a change."

I tuck some cash under my glass, and Jake and I scoot out of the booth in time for him to nudge me with his shoulder. "And because she'll be more reliable than every other recent hire, you might be able to take some time off soon."

"I might," I agree. "You're still up for a little road trip?"

"As long as I'm in charge of the music, yeah," he says. "I've got a conference in Seattle next week, but then my schedule is clear for a while. We can drive down to visit your mom for a bit—"

"Then up to see Lucy—"

"So you can finally get that fancy resort vacation you're using me for."

"And then a slutty side trip to Vegas, which I assume you're using *me* for," I tease, stopping when we reach the Harley. "You gonna send Adrian a postcard from the road?"

"I don't know. Are you planning to send one to Beau?"

With my hand on his chest, I back Jake up until he sits on the bike. "What about Riley and Sebastian?"

"You want to send them postcards, too?" Jake asks.

"Nope. Just wanna know what's going on there."

"Sebastian really likes Riley. Riley doesn't really like Sebastian."

I kiss him, sloppy about it because we're in the middle of a diner parking lot a few hours before sunrise. "Nah, don't think that's it."

"Mmmm, okay," Jake mumbles, his beard against my cheek until he pulls away to grab his helmet. "Do you think we can discuss this in the morning?"

"It is the morning."

"Later in the morning. After I've had sleep and coffee."

"And sex?"

"Always a good start to a conversation, yes."

I smile as I back up and give him room to straddle the bike, a helmet in my hand, too. "Then let's go home. To *my* home. And tonight after work, I'm going to your home and your bottles of wine and your spa and your bed and your picture of my ex-husband's bulge and—"

"You bought the picture. Pretty sure that means it belongs to you."

"It looks so much better in your room, though."

He chuckles, though the sound of it gets lost when he starts the motorcycle. "And it can continue to hang there until we commission Adrian for a picture of *your* bulge."

"Mine?"

"If you're really good, maybe we'll ask him to take one of both of us."

"Jake—" I choke.

"Get on, sweetheart," Jake says, revving the Harley a couple of times.

"But—"

"I can't hear you, sweetheart."

I climb on behind him and mutter about ten increasingly profane insults, but he can't hear those either, and by the time I'm wrapped around his laughter, I don't care. We're going to my house to spend the night together. He'll wake up and make coffee. I'll wake up and drink it. He'll do a crossword and I'll watch bad tv. We'll fuck before or during or after that.

And then I'll be making an appointment with West Hollywood's hottest photographer.

MORE TO READ

Coming in 2026:

Nothing to Know

Available Now:

Margins

Take It Outside (Trailhead Book One)

ACKNOWLEDGEMENTS

I'm sure she'll roll her eyes after a few more of these, but my first paragraph remains dedicated to my wife, Natalie. Public displays of affection aren't really my thing, but I'm so sincerely grateful for her relentless love and support. I continue to write from our bedroom closet (yes, really), and she only interrupts to ask me what we're having for dinner (every. single. night.). She indulges me as I tell her about books that haven't made it past a very ambitious spreadsheet. She stays mostly still while I show her pictures of characters in lingerie and quotes far too explicit for someone who prefers sexy sapphics in her romances. She even encouraged me to read the first four chapters of this book out loud on our way to Silver Falls State Park and back. I'm pretty sure I got away with it because she loved Darren and Jake long before she knew their entire story, and I'm so glad she can finally hold a copy of this book in her hands. Maybe it's time to warn her how much sex is in it.

The next round of thanks—now and always—goes to my kids. As they get older, they understand more about why they can't read these books yet. I'm sure there's some embarrassment incoming, especially as they embark upon this journey known as middle school, but my son loves to tell me when he reads about a character who reminds him of one of mine. And just the other night at dinner, as I described some upcoming plots and characters, my daughter got excited trying to predict which of my books will be the one everyone loves the most. I'm fortunate to have them on my side, and I look forward to all the ways they'll make their own dreams come true.

My betas continue to help me shape these love stories into something worth sharing with you, *and* they give me the confidence to share them at all. I cannot overstate how fortunate I am to have Zahli, Ryan, Brittany, and Dhara on my side, especially when they were all so gentle, kind, and honest about my words—when I got them right and, more importantly, when I got them wrong. They took care of Darren and Jake, and they took care of me, and there are only so many ways I can say thank you, but I mean it always. And Zahli. Well, I talk to her every day, and brainstorm with her about as often. She'll share a silly post, and I'll spin a story around it. She'll make a comment about a potential character name, and I'll spin a story around it. I think she's read all my books more often than I have, and she's encouraged the aforementioned spreadsheet that suggests another several (ten? twelve?) are on their way. Plus, she flew to the USA to attend Queers and Quills with me? Amazing. <333

As long as I'm on the topic of Queers and Quills, hello to everyone I met there! It was such an incredible weekend with some of my very favorite authors and so much safe, honest, queer love. See you in 2027?

Thank you again (and again and again) to my extended family for continuing to love me through this adventure. My gratitude to Kandi, Kari, Donna, Emily, Mark, and Nancy comes with the knowledge that so many people don't have the same support in their lives. It's my sincere hope that everyone finds family somewhere, and in the meantime, my mom will hug all of you. Anytime. Anywhere.

Estee, Angelina, LJ, Janice, Lisa, Kri, K, Teenie, Lo, Grace, Jon, and Jack have affected me in endless ways. I struggle more often than I let show, but their encouragement buoys me. All the DMs and smiles and I love yous have meant so much, and my general aversion to human emotion probably keeps me from thanking them as often as I should. Here's my love and gratitude, etched in stone. Or typed on a page, I guess. Or maybe they're just words on a screen, but I mean them all the same!

To Grey, for tattooing the *Margins* ISBN on my wrist. I look forward to the fun we can have with Trailhead designs, too.

Again and always, thanks to my mutuals. Mwah!!

Again and always (part two), thanks to everyone I've totally forgotten to mention. I'm going to blame it on the fact that it's cruel to make an author come up with more words after so many of them got us here. But a lot of people love me, and I love a lot of them right back. The end.

ABOUT THE AUTHOR

After decades of dreaming of being an author, Landry Brennan published her debut novel, *Margins*, in 2024. Early in 2025, she introduced readers to her Trailhead series with *Take It Outside*, and she's excited to welcome everyone back to the bar in *Second Nature*. Always happily brainstorming, Landry has many more love stories to tell, both within the Trailhead universe and not, and all of them celebrate the beautifully complicated flaws and dreams so many of us recognize in ourselves.

When she's not writing, Landry loves oversharing with online friends, watching hockey, drinking coffee, planning road trips, and spending time with her family.

Landry lives in the beautiful Pacific Northwest with her wife, Natalie; their twins, Amelia and Oliver; and the family's black lab mix, Charlie.